VAULT
OF THE
MAGI

Book Five
Stonehaven League

CARRIE SUMMERS

VAULT OF THE MAGI

First Edition: December 2019

Cover art : Jackson Tjota
Editing : Celestian Rince

10 9 8 7 6 5 4 3 2 1

Chapter One

"ARE YOU SURE you're okay?"

Cynthia stood in the doorway of the apartment she now shared with her fiancé, Owen, and twisted the engagement ring on her finger. It had been just a week since he proposed, and the band still felt unfamiliar, the square-cut emerald catching on things when she wasn't careful. But she didn't regret saying 'yes.' Not for a moment.

But things were also...difficult right now. Even though he'd come back to her, rescued from a virtual hellscape where his consciousness had been trapped, she still worried so much about him—things weren't quite right in Owen's head, and she wasn't sure what to fix, or how. Somehow, the engagement made it worse, like she'd become more responsible for his safety and happiness. Less than two weeks ago, she'd helped save his life.

And now, it seemed her mission was to save his spirit.

Owen looked up from his seat at the simple kitchen table, his fingers tracing the scratches in the wood made by the table's previous owners. Like most of the things in their apartment, they'd recently picked the table up at a second-hand store. For Cynthia, it was still a step up from the battered furniture she'd grown up with. For Owen, son of a wealthy politician, it must have felt like living in a third-world country. But he hadn't complained. According to him, the apartment was perfect.

"Owen?"

A second passed before he seemed to register her words, and then he blinked, flashed a faint smile, and nodded. "Sorry. Yeah, I'm great, Cyn. Just waking up." He waved his hand as if to dismiss her concern and shoo her out the door. "Have a good day at work."

He claimed to be just waking up, but they'd been out of bed for an hour at least. They'd had breakfast and sat together, watching the winter sun through the window. Neither of them was a coffee drinker—she preferred herbal tea, and Owen had a thing for tomato juice. She used to tease him about it, claiming that the disgusting stuff was the one thing that gave her pause about their relationship. They used to joke with each other all the time, poking fun at the little eccentricities and habits that, when collected together, made up a person.

But now their life together felt too serious for that kind of thing. Like each moment was just another chance for things to fall apart.

Or to be precise about it, Cynthia felt like Owen was one step short of falling. He was teetering on a high wire, blind to the drop on either side. And she didn't know how to bring him safely down.

She swallowed and smiled back, then darted back across the kitchen to peck his cheek. "It's going to be a nice day. Meet me for a picnic lunch?"

Again, he seemed to require an unnaturally long pause to surface from his thoughts and acknowledge her question. He scratched his neck and looked up at her. "Sure, hon. You don't mind if we hit up a food truck though, right? I don't think you want me to prepare a picnic."

Cynthia forced out a little laugh. "You're right, I don't. Not until you make it through cooking for kindergartners at least. Noon at the usual spot?" He'd proposed on a stone bench in a little park near their apartment, a spot they often went to get out of the house.

"You got it." He reached out an arm and gave her a quick squeeze. It almost felt normal, except that his gaze was already distant. Lost somewhere she couldn't follow. Somewhere she might never be able to follow.

Owen had recently spent weeks in the hospital, comatose while the evil game AI, Zaa, had used his mind to pilot a demonic character. He'd returned, thanks to help from Cynthia and his guildmate, Devon. But he wasn't fully the man he'd been. Much like this morning, he was often quiet, speaking only when prompted. The responses he gave were appropriate, but...detached. Where his mind went in the quiet moments, she couldn't say.

Either way, she hated to leave him, but she had a career to maintain. The gaming company, E-Squared, had said they would pay Owen's pro-gamer salary indefinitely regardless of whether he logged in. They had also taken care of the hospital bills and compensated her for the time she'd taken away from work to rescue him. She and Owen could survive on money the company put into his account every two weeks, but Cynthia had worked too hard to establish herself. She wouldn't become dependent on anyone, not even Owen.

She kissed the top of his head and reluctantly stepped to the door. "I'll see you at noon."

Or rather, she'd see the parts of him that showed up. She just hoped that someday, the remainder of her soon-to-be husband would find its way back.

Chapter Two

DEVON TOOK A deep breath of savanna air, the light breeze smelling of grass and sunshine with just a hint of woodsmoke from Stonehaven's campfires. It was morning in the game, a few days after her return from the demonic plane, and she'd climbed halfway up the path that zigzagged across the cliff face behind the settlement. Now stopped, her feet planted on the uneven stone surface of the trail, she faced outward with her back against the cliff, just enjoying the view.

It was hard to believe how many people now lived here. Everywhere she looked in the bustling little hamlet, NPC villagers were hard at work hauling water, spreading mortar atop of stone blocks, and plucking weeds from the neatly planted rows in the farm plots. The sun warmed the grassy areas that were increasingly crisscrossed by footpaths, and roosting on top of the wide, umbrella-like canopies of five massive acacia trees, flocks of little brown birds chattered and basked in the light.

It was almost as if the peaceful little hamlet didn't lie smack in the path of a coming demon invasion.

Devon sighed as she looked down on everything she'd built, all the villagers that depended on her. She couldn't be *certain* that the evil AI, Zaa, would rebound after she'd rescued his prized general from the underworld, but yeah, she was pretty darn sure. When she'd retrieved Owen, she'd enabled Entwined to patch the vulnerability in their implants, shutting off Zaa from the players' unconscious minds, and probably gutting his entire leadership. It might slow down the invasion, but it wouldn't stop the demon horde massing across the Noble Sea. Soon enough, Zaa would train up new commanders, and the evil army would launch for the Noble Coast, intent on beaching their ships and marching for Ishildar.

Stonehaven stood straight in that path.

She scanned the line of the main palisade where it stretched from one end of the sheltering cliff to another. As she'd ordered, sentries occupied each of the simple guard towers along the wall's length. From Devon's vantage, she couldn't see the top of the curtain wall—it lay beyond the main palisade, separated from the taller wall by about twenty paces. There would be guards atop it as well, but not as many. In the case of an attack, all fighters would pull back to within the main encampment. Most would hurry to points atop the palisade where they could operate the trebuchets, light flames under the pots of pine pitch to heat the contents to boiling, or grab bows and shelter where arrow slits offered safe positions to fire on an enemy.

The defenses were sound, *Fortification - Advanced*, according to the game's progression system. But they had more to do to get ready.

And that didn't even begin to address the work that needed to be done on the settlement itself. Especially if Stonehaven were to endure a demon siege, they'd need accommodations for the current inhabitants—some of whom were still sleeping in tents—plus space for any NPCs or players who would seek shelter within the walls. The tradespeople needed adequate supplies to craft and repair weapons and armor, the farm plots needed to be expanded to increase food production, and they needed to start stockpiling simple resources like firewood.

Of course, there was also Devon's need to find the final relic of Ishildar, an object that would theoretically allow her to take possession of the city. Something about Ishildar was critical in the coming battle against the horde, though no one seemed to know exactly what that was. Typical for fantasy and games, all she was going on was a vague prophecy. But it was probably a true one.

Put together, it meant Devon had to figure out how to split her time between preparing Stonehaven for the onslaught and questing for the relic. Oh, and getting a mountain bike pieced together for Tamara, who would be logging in sometime in the next month or so. She shook her head. How the hell was she going to make good on *that* problem?

Anyway, there was too much work to do to stand around looking at the view. Her feet crunching on the grit that strewed the stone path, she headed back down the trail and into Stonehaven, turning for the center of the hamlet when she hit flat ground.

"Pardon me, Your Gloriousness. I...well...can I speak with you?"

Devon turned to see Tom, Stonehaven's head cook, standing on the path behind her. He'd taken off the wide-brimmed hat he wore to protect from sunburn—not that it helped much—and now held it clutched in his fists.

"Of course," she said. "How's the chef's life? Is our food supply still good?"

Tom shrugged, lower eyelid twitching. Incredibly, the man was still nervous around her despite having joined the settlement in the very first batch of followers from the tribe of Uruquat. Sometimes it made Devon laugh to herself to think about the marriage between him and Bayle, one of Devon's boldest NPC fighters. The relationship seemed to work, though.

"As you can see, we've been covering our needs."

A pop-up appeared.

Rations:

Daily food requirement: 492 basic units/day

Food production: 505 basic units/day.

Devon gave a low whistle. It didn't seem that long ago when her settlement—it was just a camp at the time—had needed just fifteen or twenty units a day to keep everyone fed.

"It looks okay, but we aren't running that much of a surplus."

He looked at the ground in front of his feet. Or maybe he was staring at her knees. Either way, he seemed too nervous to make eye contact. "We are close to capacity, both in supply and in our ability to make use of the ingredients..."

Devon nodded as she paged through the settlement construction interface to the Tier 2 buildings, comparing it to the pane where the requirements for settlement advancement were listed.

Tier 2 Buildings:

- Crafting workshop:

A utilitarian building usable by many crafting professions.

Bonus to: Weaving, Woodworking, Leatherworking, Tailoring, Stone Carving (small).

- Forge (basic):

A forge capable of working basic metals.
Required for: Blacksmithing

- Smokehouse:
Preserves raw meat, fruits, and vegetables at many times the rate of a standard campfire. Does not require a specialized worker to operate.
Can process: 40 units of meat, fruit, vegetables, or medicinal herbs per day. Capacity scales with cooking skill, up to 200 units/day.

- Barracks
Sleeping quarters for fighters. Increases squad cooperation. Sleeps 6.

- Kitchen
Every campfire chef's dream.
Bonus to: Recipe discovery (x3), Tier 2+ recipe output (x2)

-Warehouse
Basic storage of perishable goods such as leather, preserved food, grain, and cloth.
Capacity: 20 bushels

<u>Requirements for expansion to Township:</u>
- Advanced NPC: 7/25
- Buildings (Tier 2): 10/27
1 x Medicine Woman's Cabin (upgraded)
1 x Crafting Workshop

1 x Basic Forge
1 x Kitchen
4 x Barracks
2 x Warehouse
- Buildings (Tier 3): 5/15
1 x Shrine to Veia
1 x Chicken Coop
1 x Inner Keep
1 x Leatherworking Shop
1 x Woodworking Shop
- Buildings (Tier 4): 0/2
- Population: 485/500

Devon nodded again. "I'll talk to Prester and get him to task some of his carpenters with getting another Kitchen and a pair of Smokehouses built." She didn't want to mention it out loud, but the threat of a demon siege was in the front of her mind. They definitely needed to get some rations stockpiled, plus whatever materials the weapon and armorsmiths needed.

Tom shifted, eyes still downcast. "Thank you kindly, Your Glor—Mayor Devon. That should help once we have an increase in supply."

Which was the other problem. It would do no good to increase food production capacity if there were no ingredients. Next, she pulled open the settlement resources tab and scanned down to the breakdown of food influx.

<u>Food supply:</u>
Hunting: 245 units/day

Farm plots (2): 197 units/day (click to expand crop profile)
Chicken coop: 16 units/day
Orchard: 47 units/day

Okay, so that was something else she could work on. The chicken coop was probably near capacity, but she wouldn't know until she talked to Greel. If necessary, they could build another even though it was a Tier 3 construction. A source of protein would be important if a siege happened.

For now, though, she could definitely improve the farm output without having to run all over town to track down the responsible NPC. Bayle, Tom's wife, had been the settlement's first expert in cultivation, and she now managed the plots, drawing help from one of the new citizens.

"How do you think Bayle would feel about recruiting a few more farmers from our booming population. Say...4? I figure if we break ground on two more plots, we can expect to double our crop output in a couple of weeks." Fortunately, Relic Online didn't force the settlement to wait a full growing season as would happen in real life. Between the added fertilizer provided by Blackbeard the Parrot and the natural accelerated growth, it only took a few days for plots to yield.

Tom raised his eyebrows and grinned. "She'll be happier than a chef with a new sauté pan. But Mayor, there's something else. A different problem with supply."

"Oh?" Her mind started running through potential problems that might not be reflected in the UI. Lots of games tried to shake things up with periodic blights or cold snaps. "If it's something with the crops, I'll set aside time today to work with Bayle on it."

"The crops are fine. It's the hunters, actually."

Ahh, crud. This again? When the area's jungle had retreated, and savanna grasslands had taken its place, the jungle wildlife had migrated away. But she'd thought that the fauna of the savanna biome had now appeared in enough numbers to take their place—provided Stonehaven's hunters and the nearby players weren't too greedy. The area needed a breeding population to keep supplying meat. If the area was getting over-hunted, she might need to divert resources to a third new farm plot.

"Are they bringing in too much?" she asked.

"It's not how much. It's what. For the last tenday, it seems all I've had for the stew pot is rat meat and snake steaks. Needless to say, after being spoiled by a *Spiced Antelope Jerky* and *Anteater Surprise*, the townsfolk aren't too happy with *Rat 'n Snake Glop.*"

Devon furrowed her brow. "That's weird. Does it mean we have some kind of vermin problem? I don't understand why the hunters would chase after rats."

She hesitated for a moment, expecting a quest pop-up. That was usually how Veia delivered missions, by sending an NPC to explain a problem and then offer a quest with specific objectives needed to solve it.

After a long and awkward pause, the pop-up hadn't appeared.

"Well, okay then. I'll talk to the hunters." She'd been meaning to pay Heldi and Dorden a visit anyway—mostly to see how Bravlon was getting on. As far as she knew, the boy had suffered no ill effects from being kidnapped by a massive capybara who'd decided the child was her adopted son. She glanced toward the pen near the rear of the settlement where that same capybara squatted, munching from a massive heap of hay brought in by townspeople. Devon still hadn't decided whether she could—literally—stomach the notion of having the giant rodent milked to make cheese, but if nothing else, the animal's gentle presence seemed to please her followers.

"Thank you, Your Gloriousness," Tom said, ducking his head. "I'll be off then."

He hesitated for a moment as if unsure whether to wait for dismissal. When Devon smiled and waved, he whirled and trotted away.

She walked on, thinking about how to proceed. Maybe Jarleck had information on the rat situation. After all, his position as fortifications master meant he was almost always near the front gate and able to keep track of comings and goings. And she needed to talk to him about the defenses anyway.

***

"I hear Gerrald has finished your new gear," Jarleck said as she walked up.

"Oh?" She raised her eyebrows. Her previous equipment had been reduced to shreds, Hulk-style, when she'd transformed into a demon. For the past few days, she'd been wearing a plain cloth tunic and trousers while waiting for the settlement's leatherworker, Gerrald, to make her a new set.

"Wait..." she said when the man turned away in a poor attempt to hide the amusement on his face. "What's wrong with it?" At the very least, the new armor wouldn't have demon skin sewn in, but that didn't mean she'd be happy with it.

"I'm sworn to secrecy," the big man said, raising a finger to his lips.

She sighed. “I guess I’ll go see what I’m in for after this.”

Jarleck laughed. “So how have you been?” He seemed genuinely interested, but Jarleck wasn’t typically big on small talk. She suspected another motive for the question. Were the townsfolk concerned she might turn into a demon again?

Almost as much to reassure herself as anything, she pulled up her character sheet.

Character: Devon (click to set a different character name)
Level: 23
Base Class: Sorcerer
Specialization: Unassigned
Unique Class: Deceiver
Health: 361/361
Mana: 570/570
Fatigue: 16%

<u>Attributes:</u>
Constitution: 22
Strength: 17
Agility: 17
Charisma: 42
Intelligence: 29
Focus: 16
Endurance: 26
Unspent Attribute Points: 4

<u>Special Attributes:</u>
Bravery: 7

Cunning: 7
Dignity: -1

She brushed the sheet away, relieved. Her *Shadowed* stat, a manifestation of Zaa's presence in her mind, was totally gone, as was the abilities page tab holding her demonic capabilities.

Ezraxis was really dead this time.

"I'm feeling better than I have in weeks. None of you need to worry about my alter-ego." Of course, her attributes were much lower than she was accustomed to since she'd lost all her armor, so until she put on whatever butt-ugly or otherwise-embarrassing armor Gerrald had crafted, they *did* have reason to be concerned about her competence.

Jarleck grinned. "Good to hear. I didn't want to ask directly, but when it's my job to build defenses that keep demons out, it was always a little concerning that one might appear *inside* the settlement."

"You definitely have nothing to fear for me, and as far as any chance of planar rifts opening in Stonehaven, the *Blackbone Effigy* gives the Shrine to Veia enough power to prevent them."

Recovered from the Fortress of Shadows, the effigy was the second relic of Ishildar that Devon had captured. The little statuette granted extra power to any temple or shrine dedicated to the creator goddess.

Jarleck nodded. "In any case, did you come to survey our defenses?"

"I wouldn't mind checking them out...looking forward to that upgrade to *Castle - Basic*. I have a question for you, first, though."

"Fire away," Jarleck said.

Devon smirked. *Fire away,* huh? The village NPCs rarely used real-world idioms. But Jarleck was the settlement's only quest giver, which meant he had more interaction with the nearby players than anyone. He seemed to be picking up some of their speech patterns.

"Any idea why the hunters are bringing in rats?"

The big man sighed, shoulders slumping. "If I have to eat another bite of *Rat 'n Snake Glop,* I might just take up foraging myself. But yeah, I get it. There have just been so *many* of the vermin near the settlement. Rats, grass snakes, and some unpleasant-looking beetles the size of house cats. I heard Grey and Heldi talking last time they came through the gate after hunting. The wilderness is getting increasingly dangerous due to attacks by awakened creatures. So when the infestation got bad over the last few days, they say it just makes sense to bring in vermin meat instead of high-risk game. I suppose it's for the best. If it weren't for them thinning the numbers, we'd have a real problem on our hands."

Devon waited. Again no quest pop-up appeared. What the heck?

"Can you show me?"

"Sure," he said with a shrug. "I mean, I think you'll see you don't need a guide to spot the problem. But I'm keen for the chance to show you the new drawbridge anyway."

Right. The drawbridge was finished, and she hadn't yet seen it. Between her quest to cleanse the Drowned Burrow and the subsequent journey into the underworld, Devon had been away from Stonehaven for quite a few days. When Emerson had pulled her and her guildmates out of the demonic plane, he'd teleported them directly to the Shrine to Veia. Since then, she'd been catching up with people inside the walls and hadn't checked out Jarleck's progress.

Jarleck nodded and gestured for her to lead the way out of town.

As usual, the settlement's main gates were closed and barred, leaving travelers to enter and exit through the wicket gate, a small door set into the wall. She laid a hand on the wall as she passed through. The first defense she'd ordered constructed, the fortification had come a long way. The original timber palisade was now replaced by a twenty-foot-high wall of solid stone.

Outside the main wall, she and Jarleck stepped into the section of bare ground that stood between the main palisade and the curtain wall. This outer wall was now around a meter thick with a rimmed walkway on top. The gates in the two walls were offset, forcing any would-be attackers to travel a long and unprotected distance through the so-called killing field if attempting to breach the defenses through the gates. She hurried across the open area, not wanting to think about how vulnerable she was.

Unlike the main palisade, the curtain wall had no side entrance, but its gate stood open. Devon grinned to see that the new mine they'd taken from an orc horde was already productive. Instead of the timber gate she remembered, two massive iron slabs hung from hinges in the curtain wall. Though they were both wide open, sentries posted on either side of the gates would be able to close them in just a few seconds.

"Wow," she said as she stepped around one of the slabs and looked through the gate opening. Laid over the dry moat she had helped dig—earning her a score of 7 in the *Manual Labor* skill—the drawbridge looked straight out of a medieval fairytale. Massive timbers were fastened with heavy iron bolts, and chains with links the size of Jarleck's huge hands extended to the far side from ratchet and pulley systems atop the curtain wall. On the far end of the drawbridge, wooden posts were topped with carvings of mythical creatures: a chimera on the right, and what looked like a phoenix on the left.

Devon stared at the chimera. "Who came up with the idea for the carvings?"

"Uh, well..." Jarleck shuffled his feet. "Greel said you had a connection with the chimera, and one of the new arrivals from Eltera City is a woodcarver."

Devon rolled her eyes. If by *connection*, the lawyer had meant that she'd been embarrassingly trounced by one of the beasts...

"And the phoenix?"

"Well, after Hezbek thumped Greel on the back of the head with her walking stick, she suggested a second carving. To balance things out, she claimed." Jarleck shrugged. "I just work here."

Devon sighed. Regardless, the drawbridge was gorgeous.

"So all we need for the upgrade is to finish the dungeon?"

Jarleck crossed his arms over his chest. "That's it. Deld tells me the walls are solid. We'll be ready to put on the roof soon."

"Make sure you let me know before they install the final section. I want to be here to see us rank up to *Castle*."

Jarleck grinned, then sobered as he stepped onto the drawbridge. He indicated the field on either side of the nearby cobblestone roads. "As for the vermin, you see the problem."

"Holy sh—wow," Devon said. "It wasn't that I didn't believe you..."

The surrounding area was absolutely crawling with mobs. She used *Combat Assessment* and shook her head. It wasn't even like the game was *trying* to present a challenge. Everything in the vicinity was under level 5.

"I don't get it. It looks like a...like a newbie yard."

"A what?"

Devon started to say something then stopped as a terrible feeling settled into her chest.

"An adventuring area for inexperienced players."

"I see. But It makes little sense to me why such a thing would occur here," Jarleck said.

Devon clenched her jaw, thinking about how the nearest player starting location, Eltera City, had recently been devastated by a demon attack.

"Yeah," she said slowly and very loudly in case the game was more likely to listen to words spoken at high volume. "Me neither. The last thing we need is a bunch of newbies tripping over their swords when we're expecting a demon invasion."

Of course, maybe she was worrying unnecessarily. There could be plenty of reasons the game had sent a plague of rats and grass snakes into her area without offering any quest for getting rid of them.

"Well," she said after a moment. "Thanks, Jarleck. I'd better be on my—wait, who are they?"

She pointed at a strange group of humans approaching. They looked almost comically like the archetypes of an adventuring party, including someone in wizard's robes, a tank marching in heavy platemail, a leather-clad rogue, and a healer in white vestments.

"No idea, Mayor," Jarleck said.

The tank raised a hand in greeting as they neared the drawbridge. "Is this Stonehaven?" he asked.

Devon used *Combat Assessment.*

Aravon the Valiant - Level 20
Tier 1 Defensive Fighter Guildmaster

"It is," Jarleck said as Devon just stared.

"Hail and well met, then," Aravon said. "We've come a long way, sent to take up station as your class trainers for new starborn adventurers."

Damnit.

Chapter Three

DEV.

Devon blinked, nearly tripping over her own feet, then cursed herself. She'd been a little jumpy after returning from the underworld, partially because Zaa's domain had been so disturbing, partly because she couldn't stop thinking about an incoming demon horde.

She pulled open Tamara's message and subvocalized a response. "Yeah? How's it going, Tam?"

Pretty good except that it's something like zero degrees on your balcony.

Oh, crap. Devon had totally forgotten. She was supposed to go with Tamara and her parents to some Christmas Eve thing downtown. She hadn't really wanted to accept the invitation but had agreed to come because she couldn't concoct a believable excuse. Growing up, Christmas had really sucked. The memories always got her down, so for the last few years, she'd refused to acknowledge the holiday. Often that meant catching up on solo quest lines or grinding out reputation with an in-game faction—things that she tended to put off when the rest of her guild was online and ready to take on more exciting objectives.

Of course, in the games she'd played before Relic Online, the developers always shoved in some holiday-themed content. Annoying, but easy to avoid if she stayed out of the major cities.

Regardless, the thought of actually going down and participating in some strange ritual with a herd of ordinary people made her feel ill at ease at best. What if they tried to get her to sing or something? Smiling at overly cheerful strangers sounded terrifying enough.

Anyway, she owed it to Tamara and her parents, especially after they'd been so welcoming.

"Crap. I'm an idiot. Just a second."

Devon dropped to a cross-legged seat in the grass and focused on the logout button. Moments later, she surfaced into the stale air of her apartment. Devon grimaced. Along with her usual grocery order, the delivery company had sent her a gift basket full of potpourri that smelled like 20-year-old orange peels and cinnamon chewing gum. It hadn't been too bad at first, but now, even two days after she'd carried it down to the dumpster, her apartment smelled like a bath and body store that had been hit by a candy truck and left to rot.

Devon sprang to her feet, then grabbed the back of the couch when the inevitable headrush struck. She looked down at her gaming uniform, a pair of flannel pants and faded sweatshirt with tattered cuffs, and shrugged. Hopefully Tamara wouldn't care.

Her friend stood on the balcony in some kind of marshmallow-man coat that looked suited for Arctic exploration. The straps of the backpack she wore to carry her oxygen bottle dug deep channels into the puff. As Tamara cast her a grateful look and stepped through the door into Devon's kitchen, Devon felt a flash of guilt for dreading this so much. At least she wouldn't struggle to walk on the flat pavement in the downtown walking mall, her healthy lungs taking in as much oxygen as she needed. Tamara 's permanent lung damage from a mountain bike crash a couple of months ago made even a simple outing into a difficult journey.

Devon shrugged apologetically. "Really sorry. I just lost track of the day. Won't take me more than 10 minutes to get ready."

"No problem," Tamara said, unzipping her coat as she took a seat at Devon's table. She slipped off a pair of gloves and stacked them on the table top.

"Any news on the surgery date?" Devon called over her shoulder as she stepped into her bedroom and surveyed the unfortunate results of having put off folding her laundry while she'd been dealing with the whole demon-AI-invading-people's-brains thing. One overflowing basket held her dirty clothes and another had a stack of relatively clean stuff that looked ready to topple. It was hard to say which way some of the items between the baskets should be categorized.

"Yeah, actually. I'll give you an update when we're in the cab. Mom and Dad are meeting us down there."

Devon picked up a knit sweater from near the clean-ish basket and smelled one of the armpits. She shrugged. Seemed okay. When she pulled a basic black T-shirt from the teetering pile, the mass toppled. But at least the catastrophic pile failure exposed a pair of wool socks that actually matched. She pulled them on, then switched to a pair of jeans and hurried back out to the kitchen.

"Okay, ready. Sorry about that."

Tamara stared at her.

"What?"

Her friend chewed the corner of her lip. “We’re actually not in that huge of a rush...”

Devon scanned the room, searching for her purse and the winter coat she almost never had to use. There were a few reasons to live in St. George where summer temperatures regularly went over 100, and they included not having to deal with temperatures that could cause frostbite. Only lunatics like Tamara would actually go outside at night in the dark of winter when the temperature had dropped below freezing.

“Your hair, Devon,” Tamara said, glancing at the top of Devon’s head.

Devon blinked, then realized the problem. She’d pretty much gone straight from bed to gaming after scarfing down a few toaster pastries. If the hollow ache in the pit of her stomach wasn’t enough to remind her that she’d played straight through the day, Tamara’s raised eyebrow made it clear. Devon patted the back of her head and felt the massive tangle.

Despite knowing Tamara well by now and trusting her not to abandon their friendship because Devon apparently lacked personal hygiene, Devon still felt the blush in her cheeks.

“Right. Just a minute. Do you...uh...” She gestured toward the cabinets, following a vague notion of what she remembered was the etiquette for hosting guests. “Help yourself to food if you’re hungry.”

A faint look of horror widened Tamara’s eyes, likely produced by her memories of Devon’s usual diet. “No thanks. I’m good. The doctors have me on a pretty tight eating regimen to get ready for the surgery.”

Devon stopped in her tracks on the way to the small bathroom. "Wait. I thought you were still a ways out."

Tamara grinned. "I got the health go-ahead, and apparently there aren't a backlog of people signing up for surgery between Christmas and New Year's. I go in on the 27th."

"What? Holy crap! That's awesome."

Three days until the surgery plus between one and two weeks for recovery and general orientation to the implants. Tamara would be online before the end of January at the very latest. Devon needed to get on with finding crafters to piece together a bike. She wanted to be able to get her friend riding right away.

Of course, hopefully Tamara's first bike rides would be for fun, not to flee a horde of bloodthirsty demons.

***

At least a third of the people on the walking mall downtown were wearing augmented-reality goggles, most craning their necks to look at images rendered over reality, the particular sights invisible to anyone not connected to the same AR stream. Some were probably experiencing downtown St. George as a Triassic swamp, others as an alien planet. Or maybe with Christmas in a few hours, many were viewing reenactments of Bible stories or tours through Santa's workshop.

Religious streams aside, most AR experiences had some sort of game mechanic involved. But despite so many years spent gaming, AR-type titles had never appealed to Devon. The goggles did nothing to—for example—change the fact that it was colder than the underside of an iceberg outside. Why modify only your visual input when you could get in a VR pod or install a set of Entwined implants and enter a whole new reality?

"Remind you of Fort Kolob?" Tamara asked, nudging Devon with her elbow. They'd met while working together at the cheesy Wild West tourist trap. The Fort had used a mix of augmented reality and actors to deliver its hokey experience.

"I'd be totally fine if *nothing* reminded me of Fort Kolob again."

Tamara laughed. "With you there."

A few paces ahead, Tamara's parents walked arm in arm. Without goggles, they gazed at the thousands of twinkling lights that had been installed on the buildings and desert palms. Overhead, tiny glittering drones danced and flitted like fireflies, sometimes flocking together, sometimes swirling in streams down the mall. It *was* pretty. But still not worth freezing her toes off for.

Devon pulled her coat tighter.

"I know," Tamara muttered, seeming to notice the movement. "Colder than usual this year. The worst was probably fifteen years ago, though. We had wet slush falling out of the sky and a nasty wind. I think me and Mom and Dad were almost the only people down here."

Devon grimaced. "Why come then?"

Tamara gave an ironic-sounding laugh. "Tradition, I guess. I suppose it helped that I still believed in Santa Claus, and he was supposed to be sitting near the roundabout."

Devon ran the math in her head. Fifteen years ago, Tamara would have been seven or so. Still believing that a jolly fat man somehow came down her chimney and left presents. Meanwhile, Devon had already learned to hate Christmas because it usually meant that her mother gave herself an extra-large bottle of vodka or a handful of pills to celebrate. If there was a time she'd believed in Santa, Devon no longer remembered it.

She pushed the bad memories away. "So was he there?"

Tamara's mom looked over her shoulder. "He was a no-show. Can you believe it? I thought we'd never get Tamara to sleep that night because she was convinced Santa was dead and there'd be no presents. The city council heard an earful from me after that."

Tamara smirked. "I don't remember that part. Anyway...so, yeah. I guess compared to that Christmas Eve, this is pleasant."

Devon glanced at her friend, trying not to see the oxygen tube. Other than a belief in Santa, what other things had that seven-year-old girl dreamed about? Had she hoped to be a sponsored mountain biker someday? The crash that had damaged Tamara's lungs—and nearly killed her when her body had a severe reaction to the nanosurgeons introduced to repair her lungs and spleen—had stolen far more from her than the no-show Santa had. Devon hoped that Relic Online would bring back some of the adventure that Tamara could no longer experience. But seeing her friend's face, cheeks pink from the chill air, Devon felt a wave of paranoia. Had she over-promised? What if Tamara didn't enjoy the immersion? The surgery couldn't be entirely without risks, especially given Tamara's weakened state.

She swallowed, torn over whether she should say anything. When Tamara nudged her with an elbow and pointed to a stand selling chocolate truffles, Devon forced the worry away. Tamara would be okay. And she would do whatever was necessary to make her friend's experience in Relic Online amazing.

After indulging in way too many treats and wandering through countless pools of music from carolers and harpists—as far as Devon was concerned, anyone who could play an instrument bare-fingered in this cold was some sort of mutant—they finally finished the circuit of the mall. Devon parted ways from Tamara's family, grabbing her own autocab home.

On the way, she thought of her guildmates. It was hard to imagine what Owen had been going through over the last few days. Immediately after she and Chen had pulled their friend from Zaa's clutches, freeing his mind from the demonic AI's influence and his avatar's body from the underworld, Owen had logged out. Devon assumed that E-Squared had remained in touch with him and his girlfriend, Cynthia, but she hadn't heard any specifics. Right now, she figured that Owen needed time to process—it wasn't just that his brain had been co-opted. His own father had tried to use him as a political pawn. Whether Governor Calhoun really understood the danger he'd put Owen in was up for debate. But the fact that his motivation had been more for his campaign than his son's safety must have devastated Owen.

Having been through her own demonic possession, Devon thought that, someday, she and Owen might be able to help each other. She didn't really know what that would look like—Devon's "Talks about Feelings" skill was lower than her abysmal in-game *Stealth* score. But after what he had been through, she would try, if it would help him.

But that was in the future. For now, she had to hope that he was having a good Christmas Eve.

As for her other in-game friends, it wasn't entirely true that Devon had always spent her Christmases alone in game. More often than not, Hailey had been online doing the same thing as Devon. Solo quests, character maintenance, that kind of stuff. By unspoken agreement, they'd generally avoided one another, perhaps because neither wanted to have a guildmate witness to their loneliness. But thinking about it now, Devon couldn't help but want to reach out. She and Hailey had grown closer after the conflict over Hailey's secret livestream of their last raid in Avatharn Online. Maybe it was time to take that extra step and make sure Hailey didn't feel too alone this Christmas. The woman hadn't been responding to Devon's attempts to contact her via messenger outside the game, but Devon didn't want to let her own insecurity over being ignored get in the way of reaching out.

She opened her messenger and subvocalized a note.

"Hey Hailey. Merry Christmas and all that. Want to break tradition and group up tomorrow? Let me know!"

Chapter Four

HAILEY JERKED AS a knock came at her door, both shocked and embarrassed that she was lying in bed with a dinner tray over her lap. It wasn't like she let the robot bring her meals to her bedside *every day.* But today was Christmas Eve. The decision to stay in bed was an early present to herself, a temporary respite from having to walk to her table with what felt like knives in her joints and a tourniquet squeezing her rib cage when she tried to breathe.

Well, okay. It wasn't just today. She'd taken two other meals in bed last week claiming to herself that it was a reward for helping rescue the little dwarf kid from his adopted capybara mother. And the week before, there'd been another excuse. The truth was, it was getting so damn hard to force herself to move.

The knock came again, proving it wasn't some weird figment of her imagination. Swallowing, she smoothed the covers and pulled fingers to her tangled hair. Why did someone have to show up *now?*

"You can come in," she said, then grimaced. Had that sounded rude? Aside from her weekly meetings with the doctor assigned to the care facility, she hardly ever saw people. Robots cleaned her room, and even though she was supposed to have human contact to keep her spirits up—that was what the law said even though most of her needs could be met by the bots—she suspected the nurses skirted the requirement by checking in while Hailey was sleeping.

Slumbering patients didn't need to be talked to or reassured. Made it easier for a small staff to cover the resident population.

Or maybe Hailey had agreed to reduced visits, waiving her legal rights when they'd wanted to pull her out of the game at an inconvenient time. Her memory was a little fuzzy these days with all the medications. Plus she made an active effort not to think about her life outside of the game whenever she entered Relic Online. Acts of willful forgetfulness.

Hailey set down her fork when the door opened, and her doctor stepped into the room.

She cocked her head. "Were we...Did I miss our appointment?" They usually met outside her room in a different sterilized chamber where the doctor had access to more equipment and screens.

The man shook his head. "I sent you a message. I mean, my assistant did. Are you having troubles with your connectivity?"

Hailey swallowed. Yeah, so not getting a message would be her fault. For the last six or eight weeks, she'd been constantly harassed at her public messenger contact by members of the griefer guild from Relic Online. Recently, none of her attempts to block them had worked because if they were good at nothing else, they were the experts at harassment. She'd gotten fed up with deleting their nasty-grams and had decided to take a few days off. At the very least, the one-avatar-per-player rule that still held in Relic Online meant that they couldn't create new characters just to hassle her, and so she'd been able to block them there. The interaction with her friends inside the game was all she needed anyway, or so she told herself to make the situation tolerable.

"There's no problem with my connection. I just haven't been online."

An indecipherable expression crossed the doctor's face. "Well, I sent you some materials to look at before we met. I...I figured you would have had a chance to look through them and process the information."

"Process?"

"I imagine you haven't been feeling well, lately."

Hailey snorted. The last time she'd felt well was before she could legally drink alcohol.

The doctor had the grace to look ashamed. "Worse than usual, I mean."

"I guess. That or my willpower's been a little weaker."

"You shouldn't blame yourself when you need to rest. I wish we could've done more for you over the years." He clasped his hands before him, his expression genuine if nothing else.

"Wait a minute. Could have?"

"The numbers don't look good, Hailey. Your liver especially. Your disease...it..."

"I know. My body attacks my own organs like they're some kind of crazy invaders."

"I'm afraid it's ramped up its efforts lately."

"Okay...?"

"I put in another request to Cornell University. They have a new experimental treatment going into trials this month."

Hailey sighed. She appreciated the effort, but she wasn't an idiot. Maybe if she had a governor for a father like Owen, or maybe if she had some spectator-friendly super-talent for something other than livestreaming her video game exploits. Lacking any publicity or political leverage, she was pretty much a dead fish as far as applications for experimental therapies went.

“We should hear back within the week,” the doctor said. “But if it’s another ‘No’…Hailey, we need to start looking at end-of-life options.”

Chapter Five

"I CANNOT TOLERATE this," Greel said without preamble. "The incompetence around here is already pervasive. And apparently, it will only get worse. I know what happens with starborn first experiencing this realm. They can scarcely find their way out of the tavern without running into walls."

Devon was sitting on a simple bench outside the head leatherworker, Gerrald's, specialty workshop. When she'd knocked on the door, he'd cracked it open, then gone wide-eyed with apparent panic at seeing her. Apparently he was putting the finishing touches on her new armor.

"So you heard we're expecting a bunch of noobs soon," Devon said with a sigh.

The lawyer curled his lip and started pacing. "It can hardly be missed with that...*woman* lurking near the base of the cliff."

"Uh...what woman?"

"She *calls* herself a fighter trainer. Says she can instruct in the martial arts, rogue training, even ranged combat styles. But I saw her working through a training exercise. She was stiff as a scarecrow, and the sapling she targeted scarcely trembled with her blows." Greel scoffed, shaking his head in disgust. "Frankly, if we allow these people to instruct newcomers, we might as well line them up outside the walls as human shields for all the good they'll do when your demon army comes."

Devon sighed. "Who told you about the demon army?"

The man sneered. "Truly, do you think I have no powers of observation? It's been written all over your face since you returned from the hell plane. Hezbek simply confirmed my suspicion when I questioned her. You could have considered confiding your fears in me as well. If you wished Stonehaven to survive the coming trials, that is."

"Okay, so you don't like the offensive fighting trainer. Maybe you could lend a hand in getting these newcomers in combat shape, then."

Devon tried not to laugh at the look of abject horror on Greel's face. She was still holding out hope that Veia would reconsider the plan to drop a bunch of level-one players in her lap, but the torment the impending arrivals appeared to be causing the lawyer almost made the situation worth it.

"It should be obvious why I'll choose not to dignify that suggest with a response. I will, however, inquire as to whether or not you've put forth an agreement to the new trainers as to exactly which roles they shall be allowed to fill in the settlement. I assume they've gone through the same naturalization process as our other citizens."

"Uh...naturalization? Sounds like a druid thing."

The man's upper lip trembled. "Tell me you've requested their allegiance to Stonehaven in the same way you've asked the refugees to swear fealty."

"Do you mean where Jarleck or someone he delegates invites them to join the settlement? I hadn't really thought of that as *swearing fealty.*"

Greel scoffed. "Spin it how you like, Miss Overlord. When a prospective citizen accepts the invitation to join Stonehaven, they are entering into a legally binding agreement. They cannot act against our interests without suffering a tremendous reputation hit—though a codified rule set to react to such events is something I've wished to propose. We need a formal system of laws to guide our responses to acts of harm against township interests."

"Can you speak in plain English please?" Devon said. She had the gist of what he was getting at but didn't trust him not to weasel her into an unpleasant agreement with too many verbal convolutions.

Greel rolled his eyes and gave an exaggerated sigh. "We need rules, Devon."

"Oh? What kind? It seems to me that the settlement is doing fine."

"But what happens if a merchant steals from the vendor next door? Or how about if one of these bumbling fools you're so keen to accept runs over and tries to attack a Stonehaven guard immediately after entering our realm. I hear the stories the starborn tell. There are worlds where such a naive action would be penalized with death. Do we really wish to force our citizens to witness the slaughter of newly arrived humans, even if they *are* idiots?"

Devon blinked. Okay, he had a point. In tons of games, attacking city guards—or any members of a settlement—was a sure way to get marked as *Kill on Sight* by the city's faction. She'd seen plenty of noobs spawn and make that mistake. Actually *attacking* a city and taking control was a high-level objective for some guilds, so the guards could usually flatten a level-one player in a single hit.

Yeah, so getting labeled as *Kill on Sight* for kicking a guard in the shin didn't seem like the right philosophy for Stonehaven. Even if she could figure out a way to prevent the new player invasion, what if someone else from the settlement had a little too much dwarven ale and mistook a guard for an attacking antelope? What if a player from the nearby camp accidentally walked out of a shop without paying for a *Spool of Cotton Thread?* In some games, getting caught thieving could bring the whole guard force down on a character.

Or what if a player stole an item on purpose? What should the penalty be? Did they need to start recruiting security for businesses and homes *inside* the walls now too? It often felt like they scarcely had enough fighters to stand sentry against actual attacks.

Devon hadn't considered any of this stuff. There wasn't an interface in the settlement management screens to configure rules for Stonehaven citizens. She'd just assumed that the game had mechanics built in for handling the NPCs' responses to aggressive actions. But that wouldn't really make sense when each of the citizens was self-aware. Any sane person would freak out if they saw a newbie player murdered in the streets for accidentally body-checking a gate guard.

"When were you proposing to draft these laws?"

"Well, I *was* going to finish the resource accounting in consideration of the new flow of iron and gold from the mines. Plus a broader treatment of census data with the goal of determining how truly mediocre a skill set our population represents. And of course my history of the founding and early struggles of Stonehaven—I feel that account will inspire many who find themselves subject to questionable leadership. They should know there is always hope."

Devon rolled her eyes. "Yes, I can only imagine how you must have despaired when I freed you from an ogre whose greatest skill was growing moldy toe cheese. How terrible it must have been to be led to a place where we could build an actual town."

"Hamlet."

"Huh?"

"At last count, I believe Stonehaven still required dozens of buildings to qualify as a township. We're still a hamlet."

"Have you always been this pedantic?"

"Have you always been so imprecise?"

She fixed him with a flat stare. "So let's assume you put the writing of Stonehaven's history on hold, despite the two or three people who might read it someday... How long would it take you to come up with some rules? I mean, just the basic stuff. Ten or fewer rules and the consequences for breaking them. If it's longer than a page, I won't approve it."

Again, Greel's face contorted with horror. "You understand that there's a reason legal documents need so much space for so little substance. The risk of misinterpretation, it's..." He shook his head. "It simply won't work. If I am to amend the town charter—"

"Hamlet."

He gritted his teeth, cheek twitching. "If I am to amend the *settlement* charter to provide structure as we advance in time and population count, it's critical that the language be unassailable."

"One page. And I want it in twelve-point font."

"Twelve-point *what*?"

"No asking a wizard to change the size of your handwriting to fit more on the paper."

He clenched and unclenched his fist, his hunched back hunching further. "I find it very difficult to work with you."

"Yet you're still here, aren't you? Because secretly you like Stonehaven. I think you might even like me as a leader."

"I like being near to Ishildar and the chance to someday scour the city's ancient libraries and wondrous vaults—*if* you ever manage to banish the Curse of Fecundity. Besides, when the city is restored, surely there will be a need for new charters and records and grants of ownership...so much *glorious* documentation. Real record keeping, I might add. Not some ridiculous one-page scribble."

Was the man really serious? That was his end-game? Devon raised an eyebrow, but he didn't seem to be joking.

She shrugged. "Well, since it's so much shorter than the sort of document you're used to creating, I suppose I can expect a draft of the rules tomorrow?"

He growled. "Perhaps. But only if you stop delaying me with idle chatting."

Devon gestured at the path that led toward the section of housing where Greel's cabin had been built. "Don't let me keep you."

The man stood there for a moment, index finger rubbing over the knuckle at the base of his thumb. "Fine," he said before turning and stomping stiffly toward home.

"Oh, and Greel?"

His shoulders crept toward his ears. "Yes?"

"It's possible that not all the new starborn will be as incompetent as you fear. If your concerns about the new martial-arts trainer are so serious, perhaps you should keep an eye out for a prodigy or two.

Cull a couple of standouts from the mediocre herd. I'm sure they'd appreciate the chance to train with such a master as yourself."

She couldn't see his face, but she could imagine it by the way his twisted back seemed to relax somehow. His fists uncurled, and as he nodded and set out, there was a faint spring in his step.

> You have gained a skill point: +1 Leadership.
> Predictable, isn't he?

***

Devon jumped when the door to the leatherworkers' workshop finally opened with a squeak. Gerrald stepped forth, ill-concealed excitement on his face. Devon didn't want to get her hopes up—the gear he'd made her so far was...inconsistent in how humiliating it was to wear in public—but she couldn't help wiggling her toes in anticipation anyway. New stuff was always fun.

The smile fell from her face when Gerrald slowly brought his arms out from behind his back. She blinked, hoping to disguise her horror as shock. She'd seen this type of container-thing out on the walking mall in downtown St. George. Purses she understood. Women had to be able to carry things while leaving their hands free. Backpacks made sense too. They were even more practical since they weren't prone to sliding off shoulders. Whenever she had something like a water bottle or old-fashioned paperback book, she usually tossed it into a pack for the day. Back when she used to go out places during the day, anyway.

But eensy-weensy backpacks covered with sequins that sat between someone's shoulder blades like some glittering growth? No.

The atrocity Gerrald held before her was smaller than a standard purse, and the contortions needed to get out of the straps totally undid the convenience of carrying items in a small container.

To say she didn't get the allure would be an understatement.

Doing her best to hide her horror, Devon swallowed and accepted the item.

> **You have received:** Tiny Sparklebomb Backpack of Sub-par Holding
> **Container:** 10 Extra-Large Slots | 20 Large Slots | 30 Medium Slots | Unlimited Tiny Slots
> -1 Stealth
> *Aww isn't it precious?*

Devon's mouth opened, but no words came out. She remained sitting on the small bench, staring at the container. How would she ever be able to make fun of Torald's *Manpurse of Holding* with this on her back?

Gerrald grinned, clearly mistaking the reason for her shock.

"I heard some people went back into that Drowned Burrow to try to recover your backpack, but apparently the muskrats had shredded it for use as bedding for their nests. At first, I figured there wasn't much I could do with those *Tiny Scintillating Dragon Scales.* I could feel the magic in them, but they were just so tiny. It turns out, I just had to close my eyes and let inspiration guide me."

As if reliving the memory, he slid his eyes shut and swayed for a moment. Devon glanced down at the eyesore in her hands. Maybe if she found some mud to roll it in...

"Anyways, I know a backpack won't be enough to get you back out adventuring. Look inside," he said, gesturing with his chin.

Devon was afraid to unhook the sequin-plastered strap. When she finally worked up the courage, the leather slid smoothly through the buckle despite its adornments. A massive inventory screen opened, showing a vast field of slots, most of them empty.

Item: Stonehaven Jerkin
A one-of-a-kind piece of chest armor, the boiled leather of this jerkin has been blessed by Shavari, one of Veia's chosen Five. The item may only be worn by a worthy leader.
+6 Constitution | +3 Bravery | 107 Armor | 120/120 Durability
Requires: 22 Leadership, 15 Strength

Item: Big Girl Pants
For adventurers who have actually proved themselves kinda capable, these leather pants have patches of hardened hide to provide above-average armor while not restricting movement. Plus they'll look pretty snazzy on you.
+4 Charisma | +1 Endurance | 94 Armor |115/115 Durability
Requires: 22 Leadership, 16 Agility

Item: Gloves of Deceit
Crafted from the most supple of doeskin, these gloves fit as if they were sewn from moonsilk. But they weren't. They're crafted from the most supple of doeskin.
+4 Agility | +1 Focus | 24 Armor | 50/50 Durability

Item: Bracers of the Phoenix

The boiled leather of these armguards grants a hefty AC bonus against mobs that target their attacks at your forearms. Which probably aren't all that common, but the good news is that the phoenix feathers affixed to the leather provide added benefits.
+10% Fire Resistance | +10% Fire Damage | +15 Armor | 89/89 Durability

Item: Boots of the March
Durable. Good arch support. Waterproof coating. Everything the dedicated adventurer could want in footwear.
+10% Speed | -5% Fatigue Gain

Item: Night's Fang
A wondrous weapon, the blade has been painstakingly carved from an ivory fang collected from a sabertooth. The hilt is shaped from mountain mahogany, and moss agates have been set into the guard.
15-18 piercing damage | 245/245 Durability

On hit: 20% chance to inflict *Necrosis* on the target, dealing 2-3 necrotic damage/tick. Will remain on the target until the disease is cured.
On hit: 10% chance to cast *Leafcutter*, inflicting an extra 10% nature damage to the target.

Item: Spiced Antelope Jerky x 4
Delicious, if a little gamey.
Grants +2 Constitution for eight hours after eating.

Devon pulled out the jerkin and slipped it over the top of the simple cloth tunic she'd been wearing. Immediately, her maximum hitpoints increased, and her health bar pulsed as the first natural healing tick began to fill it. She pulled the bracers on next, followed by the gloves and boots. Those last were particularly nondescript, but the *Speed* bonus was amazing. She hadn't had any increase in that statistic since way back when she'd had *Tribal Sandals.* The *Big Girl Pants* looked way too tight to fit over the trousers she was already wearing, so she stuffed them back in the bag to change into later.

Gerrald shuffled bashfully. "You know I don't have direct control over the benefits granted by your equipment. Some master-level leatherworkers might, but I have no way to know. I've already surpassed the level of leatherworking my mentor back in Eltera City was capable of, and I can only guess what continued practice will grant me. But am I to judge by your reaction that the detail work and engravings on the equipment convey useful benefits?"

"The gear is fantastic, Gerrald," Devon said, running her hands over the jerkin. The gloves were so supple, she felt almost as if her hands were bare, and as for the chest armor, the leather was much harder than any she'd worn before. The chest piece felt as if it could turn aside some fairly strong blows. It was also heavier, seeming to have multiple layers of leather in many areas. At the collar and cuffs, symbols had been hammered from what looked like gold and inset into the leather. The ornaments seemed to be a representation of Stonehaven with its inner keep and the cliff behind the hamlet. The metal must have been some of the first true gold pulled from their mines in the Argenthal Mountains. It was quite an honor to be first to have an item incorporating it. And better, aside from the embossing and engravings Devon recognized as the runework that gave Gerrald's creations their magical bonuses, the garment wasn't too flashy for once. It was a good fit for her proportions and seemed to move with her as she fastened the buckles along her rib cage.

"I couldn't help but notice"—Gerrald dry-washed his hands—"and don't get me wrong. Strength is attractive on the leader, and you don't look like an ogre or anything... Anyway, I couldn't help but notice that you gained some muscle tone in the underworld. I figured the boiled leather wouldn't be too fatiguing for you anymore."

She suppressed a laugh. Right. Those extra *Strength* points she'd been forced to spend to pass Zaa's trials in the underworld must have made her look buffer. She didn't like to remember how she'd basically wasted a full level's worth of attribute points, so she'd been ignoring the effects. At least her ability to wear the heavier materials in the *Stonehaven Jerkin* was a small consolation. Depending on what happened in the days ahead, the extra armor from the hardened leather might come in useful.

Of course, Jeremy, her troubadour friend, would surely notice her armor upgrade. She grimaced, remembering how he'd gloated over her apparent decision to favor balanced attributes over specialization. He *had* advised her in that direction, which if anything was a good reason to focus even more heavily on her caster stats. But Zaa had forced her character build to head in another direction, and now Jeremy had even made up a song about how much it looked like she could bench press now.

Devon sighed. It really was too bad that the swim into the Drowned Burrow hadn't permanently waterlogged that obnoxious accordion of his.

The jerkin secured, she pulled out the dagger, *Night's Fang*, and held it carefully in her palm. "Where did you get it?" Of course, it was clear that the material from the blade came from the mysterious fang she'd looted from one of her first kills. She shook her head in amazement at the recollection. That fight seemed so very long ago now.

Getting a better understanding of the fang's properties had been a task in the back of her mind ever since, and now that Shavari had joined the settlement, citizens of Stonehaven no longer had to wonder about their unidentified items. But who had taken the fang to Shavari for identification? And who had crafted the weapon's blade from it?

She read the stats again. A 20% chance to inflict a damage-over-time debuff that could only be canceled by a cure disease spell. Devon shuddered. She had a bad history with necrotic damage. Just the thought of being cursed in such a way turned her stomach. Sure, at this point, her out-of-combat health regeneration could probably keep pace with the damage caused by the *Necrosis*. But that wasn't the point. It was a nemesis sort of thing.

Fortunately, unless she fumbled, she wouldn't have to worry about suffering the weapon's effects. And since using the blade didn't require a particular skill level in *One-handed Piercing*—unlike the unfinished fang which had required something obscene like 55 points—a fumble seemed unlikely. But maybe she should practice, though, just to be safe.

"It was Hezbek's idea, of course," Gerrald said. "She took the fang to Shavari and then approached the head crafters about fashioning a weapon. Of course, none of the smiths knew a thing about fashioning a blade from ivory. We talked to the woodcarvers—

no luck—and the stone carvers were no help either. As best we could figure, we needed some sort of shaman experienced in altering bones to shape the blade."

Gerrald stopped speaking, and a faint wrinkle of concern formed between his brows.

"Okay...?"

"We didn't think we'd be able to find anyone."

"But it turns out we have some sort of shaman crafter in town who hadn't come forward yet?"

Gerrald grimaced. "To tell the truth, Your Gloriousness," he said, his use of her old title betraying his discomfort. "We left the fang in the smithy overnight—it was tucked inside one of the supply trunks. When Dorden came back the next morning, the blade had already been carved. Of course, he's no stranger to attaching blades to hilts, so that wasn't a problem once the ivory had been shaped."

"Wait, so you don't know who made it?"

Gerrald shrugged and shook his head. "As I assume you can sense, there seems to be no curse attached. The description can't be wrong."

Devon cocked her head, wondering if that meant NPCs saw item descriptions and attributes in the same way she did, but decided not to ask. Gerrald was right, though. She'd never played a game where the item descriptions were inaccurate unless a game designer had fat-fingered something. Lacking fingers, Veia wasn't likely to make those sorts of errors. Regardless of who carved the blade, she didn't think it could be any kind of trick or trap. Just a mystery.

She absently patted her hip, feeling for the sheath where her *Wicked Bone Dagger* used to hang.

"Oh," Gerrald said. "I haven't had time yet. The finished blade was a surprise, you see. I'll work on a new belt and sheath next if it pleases you. I am still putting the finishing touches on a headband as well."

Devon tucked the dagger back into the *Sparklebomb Atrocity* and swung the backpack over her shoulder. "I won't be heading out very far for at least another day or two. Take your time."

Touching his brow, Gerrald ducked inside. With a sigh, and feeling as if everyone in Stonehaven was staring at her new bag, Devon set off for the farm plots to check out the planting progress. Between the trellises and scarecrows and sheds for tools, there was actually enough cover down there that she might be able to skill up her *Stealth* to make up for the backpack's debuff. Without needing to combat crawl, no less.

Chapter Six

"I'M UP," EMERSON mumbled, opening the eye that wasn't buried in his down pillow.

The miserable blatting coming from his smart-home speakers continued.

"Veia! I'm up." He sat and rubbed his eyes, then clamped his hands over his ears. "I know you heard me!"

"But I also know, after eighty-three days of observation, that if you remain prone while the waking alarm is deactivated, you have a sixty-four percent chance of falling back asleep." Mini-Veia's voice sounded far too self-satisfied for what appeared to be a statement of fact. Emerson was inclined to think the AI instance, a stripped-down version of Relic Online's creator AI running on his smart-home hardware, was lying about her motives. Or at the very least, bending the truth. Yeah, it would have been *nice* to create a general intelligence that was incapable of falsifying information, but when asking it to create an entire pretend world, that just wasn't feasible.

"And in case you were wondering," the speakers said, "I have independent recordings collected from your security cameras to prove it. I have saved timestamped files of your waking moments to a cloud repository. We could review them together while you enjoy your breakfast."

Emerson shook his head and ran his hand through his hair. "Ugh. No. And didn't you think that might be an invasion of privacy? I didn't give you permission to put videos of me anywhere. Especially not when I'm waking up."

"I'm not sure I understand your concern here. Is there a difference between recordings of a fresh return to consciousness and a video clip from midday? Because I have those, too."

He groaned and shook his head in exasperation, swinging his legs out from under the sheets. The hardwood floor was cool against the bare soles of his feet. The air in his condo smelled a little stale though, late December being a time when he typically didn't run the AC or open windows at night.

"Why exactly have you been storing videos of me, Veia?" he asked as he shuffled to the bathroom. Veia turned on the tap for him as he stepped in front of the sink, and the AI actually remembered to set the temperature to lukewarm this time. Of course, the functionality to adjust preferred water temperature at any faucet was hard-coded into the software that had shipped with the smart-home system. But Mini-Veia had *learned* to do it after observation.

Observation of multiple streams of cursing when he'd scalded the bejeezus out of his skin, that was.

"Wait," the AI said, "I believe I have a reasonable theory about the difference between the video clips. Is it the presence of liquid on your cheek and/or chin when you wake? I've never seen that in the midday hours."

"*Everyone* drools in their sleep," he said. "It's not a big deal."

"Huh. Well, I don't have any evidence with which to refute that claim. So perhaps there's another difference. I will continue processing the data in search of discrepancies."

"You didn't answer my question."

"Which question?"

"Why are you videoing me?"

"I am not videoing you. I am merely collecting footage from the security cameras which you have installed around your home."

Emerson took a deep breath as he rinsed his hands, then splashed water over his face. "Wait...I didn't tell you to wake me up today, anyway. So please prune whichever of your adaptive networks decided it was a good idea."

"Oh. It wasn't my decision," Mini-Veia said. "A message arrived for you. Seeing as it came from Bradley Williams, CEO, I thought it would be best to rouse you."

Emerson grimaced, looked in the mirror at his puffy face dented by red lines from his pillowcase, and grimaced harder. He focused on his Entwined implants' interface and re-enabled notifications. There was indeed a waiting message from the E-Squared CEO, but it was flagged as unimportant.

"Did you miss the part where the message is missing the urgent flag?" he asked.

"Do you really think that I would examine only a portion of the data? Of course I saw the priority. But I also know that Bradley Williams believes everything coming out of his mouth is of utmost significance. I believe his choice to forgo applying that flag is a test to see how important *you* find him."

Okay, so that was a semi-interesting insight for an AI who couldn't be trusted with the air-conditioning setting. Sometimes he wondered whether Mini-Veia's relative incompetence at smart-home adaptation was a clever disguise for the AI's secret hobby of tormenting him.

He had to wave his hand in front of the sensor to turn off the water—evidence of yet another failed adaptation. Despite finally learning his preferred temperature, Mini-Veia still hadn't caught onto the morning pattern of "wash hands, splash face, leave bathroom."

He pulled up the message from Bradley, superimposing it over his vision.

Emerson. You coming into the office today? Wanted to chat when you have a chance.

Wait, today? Was Bradley serious? Emerson glanced at the clock in the corner of his vision, bringing up the calendar to be sure. Yes, it was definitely Christmas Day, which was the reason he'd asked Veia to deactivate his alarm clock in the first place.

Of course, it wasn't like Emerson had anything special planned—the afternoon video call to his parents wouldn't take long, especially once they started asking if he had a girlfriend yet, and he found an immediate excuse to disconnect. He'd kind of been planning to finally create a Relic Online character, figuring that most people with lives would be offline and hanging out with their families or something. Not that the other players would know that the incompetent first-level character getting trounced by a field mouse was actually the programmer of the creator AI. But still, better to get the worst of the mistakes out of the way without an audience.

Especially since that audience might include Devon.

He stared at Bradley's message for a while, trying to figure out what to say. The CEO's decision to leave the Zaa AI active really bothered Emerson. Sure, the implant patch had been rolled out, freeing players from Zaa's influence. But the AI was so *evil.*

According to Bradley, that was a good thing. It gave the players purpose in the world—an ultimate enemy to defeat.

But Emerson couldn't get Devon's description of the Trial of Ruthlessness out of his head. She'd passed the test by trickery, using her abilities to make Zaa think she was torturing—physically and psychologically—a pair of low-level players. As far as Emerson was concerned, the AI's desire for such things didn't belong in any game. It was too close to what real-world monsters yearned for.

Heading into the office might mean an extra chance of success in convincing the CEO of the lunacy of the decision...if Bradley were sane when it came to Penelope's AI. But seriously, on Christmas? And anyway, what had made Bradley think Emerson would be unoccupied today? Emerson's lack of a social life wasn't *that* obvious, was it?

Still, he was tempted to respond that he'd be there. But maybe this was a chance to correct any perception that he was a nerd with no social life.

"Pretty much booked for the rest of the day," he said aloud. As his implants picked up the speech, the text appeared in the messenger prompt. "Holiday stuff, you know. Raincheck?"

Feeling rather pleased with himself, Emerson sent the message and shuffled to the kitchen to dig up a meal replacement bar before logging in.

***

Okay.

Go time.

Emerson pulled the lever to shift his chair into full recline mode. Settling into the upholstery's faux-leather embrace, he took a deep breath. As he hovered his awareness over the Relic Online icon, his pulse started to race. He rubbed his fingertips against the palms of his hands, a stupid nervous gesture. It wasn't like he hadn't experienced the game world before. No reason to be so anxious.

Except that he'd borrowed a game master's avatar to log in last time. With the ridiculous arch-wizard's robes and the superpowers granted by the GM interface, it had been easy to hide his ineptitude. When he didn't know something, all he'd had to do was wave his hands around in the air and impress people with the sparkling trails his fingers left behind. Literal hand-waving to cover his incompetence.

He already knew what his real in-game character was going to look like, having gone through the character creation process. Which, he had to admit, was pretty snazzy. His star players hadn't been given the option to customize their avatars—apparently Veia had wanted to throw them directly into the deep end—but Emerson had been able to direct the system to create him as a tall and—if he were honest—fairly handsome guy. Muscular without too much bulk. He hadn't been able to see beneath the simple cloth garb, but he was fairly certain that tunic concealed an impressive six-pack.

But yeah, no amount of flashy-fingers was going to make up for his new character's cloth garb, insignificant powers, and general bewilderment.

Regardless, he wasn't going to grow past the "n00b" phase—he was proud to have picked up *that* little term on the forums—by sitting in his chair and staring at the ceiling. He needed to get in there and play. Everyone had to learn sometime, right? And it wasn't like he would spawn anywhere near Devon or the other players he'd recruited for the game—they were far away from the areas the game had designated as newbie zones. The only way he'd wind up anywhere near Devon would be by asking the game masters to teleport him. Which he didn't plan to do until he could fight without falling on his own sword.

Okay.

Go time.

For real this time.

Emerson swallowed and activated Relic Online. His condo vanished into blackness.

His senses woke to the new world one at a time. First, the trilling of birds filled his ears. Next, he felt the sun on his skin, grass beneath his palms. Emerson opened his eyes.

He squawked at the sight of four humans bent over him.

"At last," said a man in white robes.

"Our first." This from a guy that looked like he'd just walked out of a battle with a misbehaving semi-truck.

"But whose, Aravon?" a woman said with a faint curl of her lip. "Who will take him on? To be honest, I'm not sure he has the making of an offensive fighter. Even at this level of experience, I'd expect at least *some* sort of reflexive reaction to his surroundings. He's just lying there."

The fourth person, a woman in a scarlet tunic with silver thread, raised an eyebrow. "Hmm. Given the need for *Intelligence* or *Charisma* as a foundational attribute, I'm not sure he's cut out for casting either."

Emerson blinked and sat up. Of all the undignified entries into the game, why had Veia decided to spawn him flat on his back? And who were these jerks? He half-expected the greeting committee to laugh as he planted a hand in response to the head rush from his sudden movement.

But all thoughts of the rude greeters vanished when he caught sight of the scene behind them.

The all-too-familiar scene.

Scrambling to his feet, Emerson searched the nearby surroundings for some sort of cover. What had happened to the whole "player starting city" thing? The only person who had spawned in Stonehaven before today was Devon. And that wasn't even true! She had actually spawned in the middle of the ruined city to the north.

So what the hell was the big idea with dropping him into the world right beside the Shrine to Veia that Devon's people had constructed? Was Veia trying to embarrass him? It wasn't like he could pretend not to know the people who lived here—not if he ever wanted to admit his true identity. For the time being, he'd set his character name to "Valious," thinking that it was similar enough to the word *valiant* to describe his intents for his character, but with a unique fantasy flair. Especially if he could manage to earn a title like "the Brave." He'd heard those were things.

He'd kind of hoped that Devon would be impressed with his creativity once they finally met up. But a level 1 character named Valious? Didn't quite have the same feel. And he was fairly sure he'd be doing more fleeing than valiantly standing his ground. Yeah, the more he thought about it, the more it seemed like the name was trying too hard.

He pulled open his messenger app and grabbed the contact for Darren, one of the game masters. New at the company, he probably wouldn't object to Emerson's request for special treatment.

"Can he not see us?" the heavily armored NPC asked. "Hello?"

The woman in dark leather waved her hand in front of Emerson's face, breaking his concentration on the messenger prompt as he was trying to figure out the best way to word his request. If it seemed too suspicious—especially if it sounded like Emerson was trying to pull rank—the GM might decide to ask a manager. And then it might get around the customer service department. The last thing he needed was a bunch of people hearing about the request. Better to just live with the name.

Emerson dispelled the messenger interface and clambered to his feet. "Yes, I can see you. Who are you?" He tried to look past the group to see if any of the villagers he'd met while using the GM avatar were nearby.

The woman in the scarlet tunic glanced at her peers—he noticed what looked like pointy ears sticking from her hair—and then took a small step forward. "I'm Lira the Incandescent, Master of the Casting Arts. These are my fellow trainers. We're here to help guide your development as an adventurer in this realm. Are you ready to begin your training?"

Emerson grimaced and shook his head. "Aren't I supposed to...I dunno...seek you out or something? I seriously just logged in. Just trying to get my bearings here."

The trainers shared a glance, and then the man in the white vestments shrugged. "You guys heard the chime, right? Isn't that supposed to be our summons?"

The others nodded.

"Valious," the man in heavy armor, Aravon, said. "The realm needs every sword it can gather."

When Emerson focused hard on him, a popup appeared.

> Aravon the Valiant - Level 20
> *Tier 1 Defensive Fighter Guildmaster*

> **You have gained a skill point:** +1 Combat Assessment
> *When used on allies and creatures that view you with a friendly disposition, you can perceive far more information than you would when examining an enemy.*

Flicking his awareness to banish the popup, Emerson blinked. "Okay. But I just want to walk around for a while. Get a feel for the place."

Aravon blinked, but then his face seemed to brighten as if he'd remembered something. "Well, in that case, perhaps you could start equipping yourself."

> **Aravon is offering you a quest:** Gear Up Part 1
> *Before taking on the plague of vermin besetting Stonehaven (yes, there's a plague, and yes, you'll need to help deal with it), find yourself a weapon.*
> **Objective:** Visit Dorden in the forge and see if he can spare you a sword or mace.
> **Reward:** 500 experience
> **Accept?** Y/N

"Uh, okay sure." Emerson focused on accepting the quest, and the popup vanished.

Aravon bowed. "Then be at your task. Perhaps we shall speak again soon."

Nodding, Emerson sidestepped around the group then headed for the path leading from the shrine to the center of the settlement. As his feet—damn...why was he barefoot?—hit the cobblestones, he heard one of the women mutter, "Do you think we're being overzealous? It's my first time at this, but after what happened at Eltera City, I can't help but feel we need to put forth the utmost effort."

Emerson sighed, hunched his shoulders, and hurried down the footpath.

Chapter Seven

CHRISTMAS. AS SOON as she'd left Gerrald's workshop, intent on grinding out some skill points and stuck with only her thoughts for company, the recollection of the date had forced its way back into her skull. Right now, kids were opening presents and families were heading to church, and people were...what...mainlining hot chocolate and singing carols? And meanwhile, her body was lying in a dingy apartment. Alone.

Curling her toes in frustration, she shook her head. Time to focus. Take advantage of the alone time. Today was the best day of the year for character maintenance. Solo quests. Skill grinding. Best to maximize the time.

Of course, it would have been nice to hear back from Hailey, but the woman's messenger contact had remained stubbornly inactive. Glancing again at the grayed-out icon, she shrugged. It was probably for the best. The whole "misery loves company thing" had never really made a lot of sense to her. And anyway it wasn't like she *had* to spend the holiday alone. Tamara's family had church or chapel or whatever they called it through most of the morning, but they had invited her to dinner. Devon had thanked them and declined. Soon, she would have plenty of time with Tamara in the game. Too soon, actually. She really needed to get ready for her friend's arrival. And anyway, the last few months had been difficult for the family, and she figured Tamara's parents would want some time alone with their daughter.

Anyway...grinding. If she maximized her time today, she could gain a few skill points and still have time to start sorting out Tamara's in-game mountain bike.

With that in mind, she opened her character sheet.

Character: Devon (click to set a different character name)
Level: 23
Base Class: Sorcerer
Specialization: Unassigned
Unique Class: Deceiver
Health: 403/403
Mana: 606/606
Fatigue: 6%

<u>Attributes:</u>
Constitution: 28 (+6 Stonehaven Jerkin)
Strength: 17
Agility: 21 (+4 Gloves of Deceit)
Charisma: 46 (+4 Big Girl Pants)
Intelligence: 29
Focus: 17 (+1 Gloves of Deceit)
Endurance: 27 (+1 Big Girl Pants)
Unspent Attribute Points: 4

Special Attributes:
Bravery: 10 (+3 Stonehaven Jerkin)
Cunning: 7

Dignity: -1

Devon smiled at the sight of her attributes. Finally, the game had added an option to show where the bonuses were coming from.

As for the unspent attribute points, she could spend them at any time, so she decided to wait until she learned more about the coming challenges. The real work today would be on her skills and maybe on her ability mastery. She opened the skills tab and focused on the list of stats that were still at tier 1.

<u>Tier 1</u>
Tracking: 9
Stealth: 2 (-1 Tiny Sparklebomb Backpack of Sub-par Holding)
Sprint: 8
Bartering: 6
Unarmed Combat: 3
Manual Labor: 7
Foraging: 1
Animal Taming: 1
Foreign Language Learning: 2
Felsen Language: 1
Orcish Language: 8
Climbing: 8

Okay, so maybe seeing the source of the bonuses—or in the case of *Stealth*, the debuffs—wasn't quite so pleasant after all. Devon shook her head at the reduced score. Maybe she should just give up on being sneaky. Embrace her mastery of the Orcish tongue and *Manual Labor.*

Of course, the ability to dig ditches wouldn't help when the demons came. It wouldn't even help if she *someday* got the chance to play the game like a normal person, delving dungeons in search of loot, questing for glory and reputation, building a settlement so she had somewhere to store all her treasure...

Yeah, that would be nice.

Anyway, *Stealth.* Banishing the character screen, she stepped close to the nearest scarecrow and tried to get all of her body into its shadow.

"Nice pose," Shavari said as she appeared from behind a garden shed.

Devon looked at her outstretched hand. She'd been trying to get her arm fully into the shade of the scarecrow's outstretched limb to meld with the shadows. Apparently, it hadn't worked very well.

"Just stretching out some stiffness," Devon said, rolling her shoulder.

Shavari raised an eyebrow in a dubious expression, then shrugged. "I've been meaning to catch you alone," she said.

Devon nodded. "Likewise. I don't suppose the fifth relic is somewhere in your backpack..."

Shavari chuckled. She'd recently rewarded Devon with the *Ironweight Key,* the fourth relic needed to take control of Ishildar. Apparently, Shavari's order of Veian clergy had been guarding the relic for centuries, having taken possession of it when the last members of the vassal society controlling the relic had fled the rise of the Noble Sea. The item description said that the key would unlock the Vault of the Magi inside Ishildar. Whatever and wherever that was...

"No, but I may have some ideas on where to find it," Shavari said. "But there's another matter, which I think deserves some thought first. The awakening stones..."

Devon grimaced. Yeah, the stones were still a problem. Crafted by the ancient magi of Ishildar, the ancient carved monoliths provided magic to lift creatures from their simple animal ways, granting the beasts increased intelligence and magical powers. According to Greel's recollection of the histories, the effects had been varied and wondrous. Rather than becoming human-like, many creatures retained their animal sensibilities while gaining a sort of deep wisdom. Others became walking, talking fuzzballs.

In any case, the reawakening of Ishildar had sent power back into the stones, but the Curse of Fecundity which still cloaked much of Ishildar and its surrounds in choking jungle also corrupted this magic.

Hives and nests of awakened creatures had attacked both Stonehaven citizens and the players from the nearby encampment. Devon feared that it was just a matter of time before one of her basic NPCs was slain by one of the corrupted beasts. And unlike the NPCs she designated as advanced citizens, there would be no way to resurrect them.

"I hear you. It's a big problem. I should probably head back to the Drowned Burrow and inspect the one we broke in half."

"As it happens, your lawyer friend and I made the journey to the Burrow already. We had some extra time while you were occupied in the underworld."

Of course, Greel hadn't mentioned any research into the shattered awakening stone. He probably wouldn't unless she dragged the information out of him. "Oh?"

The woman sucked her teeth. "I had hoped that the breaking of the stone would have severed the network of power flowing between them. But I could still feel it pulsing beneath the stone's location. Something like a ley line, I suppose."

Well, that wasn't an incredible surprise, Devon supposed. She'd hoped to *cleanse* the stone, not break it, and the game didn't like letting her off easily. "Were you able to figure out how we can cleanse the others?"

"Well, yes and no. It's complicated, and it's left you with a dilemma, I'm afraid."

Devon was confused. "What dilemma?"

The prophetess sighed. "I'm sure you must see the potential the stones represent. By examining the carvings in the lower areas of the Burrow, we concluded that at one point, its residents were an intelligent, creative, and peaceful society. When you broke the awakening stone, you stopped the corrupted magic from turning them into the sort of feral beasts that attacked the player camp. But you also...hmm...how to put this? You also removed the possibility of reawakening them properly."

Devon sighed as the guilt hit. *Now* she got it. Cleaving the stone in two had broken its magic. Forever. Shavari's description of the architecture jogged Devon's memories of the etchings in the burrow's lower reaches. Intricate murals had depicted tranquil scenes of the daily lives of the otterkin and muskrattons and their fellow morphs. What right did she have to take away their chance to regain that heritage?

"What if I'd found a way to cleanse the stone, instead? They'd be back to the uplifted creatures they once were, right?"

Eyes distant as if contemplating the answer, Shavari dropped to a crouch and pulled a blade of grass through her fingers. After a moment, Devon sighed and took a cross-legged seat beside her. Might as well avoid *Fatigue* gain while they were chatting.

"Frankly, I can't be certain," Shavari said. "The magic... It's a different sort than the blessings bestowed upon me by Veia. But to ease your mind, I don't think the stones *can* be cleansed while the curse holds. If you hadn't broken the monolith when you did, the creatures from the Burrow would have finished with your small fighting force and then spread over the area like a plague. There were too many to fight."

Devon shrugged. "That's some consolation, I guess. Why can't the stones be cleansed?"

"The corruption flows from a central point, likely anchored in Ishildar. I think you must find the remaining relic to eradicate it. But I do think—if you want—that I can help you follow the ley lines to the other stones. After a millennium buried by jungle, they likely have similar weaknesses to the one you found in the Burrow. A concerted effort could break them in a similar manner."

Devon's shoulders sank with the weight of the choice. "But if I did that, the potential for them to lift up the creatures in service of Ishildar would vanish."

Shavari nodded. "Regardless of whether you think intelligent races should alter the lives of simple beasts in such profound ways, there's no question that the awakened creatures could aid us in the coming battle. I've heard you're concerned about a demon force across the Noble Sea."

Okay, when she put it that way, an army of awakened creatures *would* be nice to have around. But until the curse was lifted, they were a bunch of crazed freaks.

"How severe is the threat? Were there more attacks while I was away?"

Shavari shook her head. "I think, actually, that you may have crippled the magic by breaking the stone. While previously awakened creatures are still out there, it's possible the stones aren't producing any more corrupted beasts."

"Possible, but not certain."

"Exactly."

Devon twisted her mouth, thinking. Was it better to secure the area and know that her people would be safe while she searched for the fifth relic? Or should she roll the dice and hope to restore the creatures to their original awakened forms when she took possession of Ishildar? *If* she managed to take possession of Ishildar, rather.

"How about you tell me what you know about the fifth relic. Maybe if I can understand how long it might take to find it..."

Shavari took a deep breath. "My knowledge is spotty on this topic, derived mainly from ancient texts written in a script we only partially understand. But from what I can best figure, you need to circle around or pass through Ishildar and begin searching north of the city. There's another mountain range beyond the northern boundary, less hospitable than the Argenthal Vassaldom because the land is gouged by a maze of cracks and crevices so steep and sheer there's no way up or down the walls. It's said that someone could wander through the chasms for years and never cross her own path."

Great. Devon grimaced. "That doesn't sound very promising."

Shavari smirked. "Fortunately, the griffon keepers of the Skevalli Vassaldom and their companion animals rarely ventured into the twisted crevices and gashes, and when they did hunt there, they typically traveled on the wing. I think it's unlikely you'll have to search the chasms. The Skevalli's true home—and historic location of their vassaldom—is the Stone Forest that lies like a wedge between Ishildar and the maze."

"Stone...Forest?"

Shavari shrugged. "An ancient place that once held trees the height of fifty men. The woods were petrified so long ago that we can only imagine how it must have looked. I don't know much more about it. Though if the rumors are true, it's a rather inhospitable place now, populated by drakes and wyverns and fire serpents."

Devon groaned. "And let me guess. They're probably resistant to fire damage..." Inside the Citadel of Smoke, she'd found out firsthand how difficult it could be to deal with fire-resistant creatures when much of her offensive arsenal was based in fire magic. She looked up toward the sky as if daring Veia to comment. Or failing that, waiting for a sarcastic remark from Bob.

Speaking of, where was the wisp? She hadn't seen the glowing ball since it had helped her fool Zaa during the Trial of Ruthlessness in the Citadel of Smoke. She almost missed the obnoxious glowing ball.

"Unfortunately, my information is too sketchy to comment about any resistance to certain damage types," Shavari said.

Devon shook her head. "It was something of a rhetorical question."

Shavari hesitated for a moment before speaking. "In any case, that's the best information I can offer. I hope it can be of some value to you."

> **Shavari offering you a quest:** Venture to the Stone Forest
> *Discover the ancient seat of the Skevalli Vassaldom, rumored to lie north of Ishildar.*
> **Reward:** You know the drill by now. Knowledge is power, right? Plus you can have a little experience if you succeed.
> **Accept?** Y/N

Devon accepted the quest as she stood and stretched. In truth, the notion of heading up an expedition sounded incredibly refreshing. She had work to do here first, of course, but the thought of getting a quest party together and setting out had already set her pulse pounding.

She looked again at her messenger icon. It would really be nice to group up with Hailey again. The woman was probably busy with family today. If Devon hadn't heard from her in a couple of days, she'd try dropping another line.

In the meantime...

Waving goodbye to Shavari, she headed off to find somewhere more private for leveling up her fricking *Stealth* skill.

***

"Hey, Bob?" Devon said as she skirted the inner wall of Stonehaven's palisade. "Got any intel on the Stone Forest? It's supposed to be some kind of ancient area of petrified trees."

In a pair of acacia trees that were growing too close to the wall for Devon's liking—she'd need to talk to Jarleck to make sure the roots wouldn't undermine the foundation—birds twittered. Devon searched the branches for the wisp; it seemed to enjoy materializing inside foliage, perhaps to give the appearance that it was always present and watching.

"It's sort of a guide's job to know this stuff, you know," she prompted, hoping for a reaction.

For a moment, she thought she glimpsed the wisp's glow, but the light vanished so quickly she decided it must have been her imagination. She chewed her bottom lip. Bob's absence really was strange. Usually, the wisp would have jumped at the opportunity to spout off its knowledge.

"Is it the backpack? Because if you're too embarrassed to be seen with me while I'm wearing it, I get it. But I might point out that you aren't exactly nondescript either."

Still nothing. Before leaving the shade of the second tree, she stopped and peered into the branches. "Seriously, it really would help if you had any sage advice on the final relic. I swear I won't drag you into the hell plane again if that's what you're worried about."

Through the branches, she spied a flash of red and green. Moments later, a loud squawk made her cringe. She stepped deeper into the shadow of the tree, hoping Blackbeard wouldn't notice her. Awakened by a corrupt stone, the parrot had been transformed to a monster the size of a pony, who, though he'd gained telepathic powers, couldn't control his speech.

"Squawwwk! Thar be plunder, matey!"

//Hey nitwit. You'll need a higher *Stealth* score than that to avoid me. Don't think I didn't hear what you and that prophetess were talking about.//

All right, so the bird had noticed her. That didn't mean she had to acknowledge him, right?

// I thought you intended to fix my beak, not turn me into a birdbrain all over again.//

Crud. Right. Breaking the awakening stones would revert Blackbeard to an ordinary macaw. Which really wouldn't be too bad, all things considered.

She heard the squirt of fertilizer being dispensed on the acacia tree just in time and sprinted out from beneath the branches before the drops started hitting the ground.

"You know it's Christmas in the starborn realm?" Devon called up. "The usual custom there is to serve the largest roast bird people can find."

Blackbeard adjusted his perch on the palisade and ruffled his feathers. "Coming about. Coming about. Broadsides to their ship, mateys."

//I'd feather your gizzards before landing in your cookpot.// He started running mouthfuls of feathers through his beak.

Devon blinked. Feather her gizzards? What did that even mean?

"Merry Christmas to you too, Blackbeard," she said. "And for your information, I'm leaning toward not destroying the stones. As long as I don't become too aggravated by annoying telepathic messages intruding on my thoughts."

Above, the bird gave a sort of strangled croak before flapping off in a tizzy.

As she shook her head and continued her walk, looking for an out-of-the-way spot to start stealthing, Devon noticed a strange commotion near the Shrine to Veia. It looked like the trainer NPCs were accosting someone. Though it was hard to tell at a distance, their victim didn't look like someone she knew.

Devon shook her head. Of all the rotten Christmas presents, it seemed the noob invasion had begun.

Chapter Eight

"OKAY, BEETLE." EMERSON shifted his grip on the *Practice Short Sword* as he tiptoed toward the massive insect. Another shiver of disgust started at the base of his spine and traveled outward. Why did his first quest have to involve killing beetles and rats? There was a good reason exterminators charged so much for their work. Which, speaking of, wouldn't it be easier for Stonehaven to put a big striped tent over the field and gas the things to death?

But no. Both Dorden—who hadn't shown even a glimmer of recognition when Emerson asked for a weapon—and Aravon, the overly enthusiastic fighting trainer, had insisted that the vermin must be slain by hand.

He shuffled forward another step. As a reward for returning to the group of trainers with his new sword, at least he'd been given a pair of sandals. The grass poking his ankles was bad enough. How much worse would it be if it were stabbing the bottoms of his feet?

The beetle was just a meter or so away, its unsettling mandibles clicking together, shiny black legs carrying it closer. Grimacing, Emerson twisted the ball of his right foot into the ground, raised his sword—damn the thing was heavy—and slashed down like he was trying to chop wood.

The sword glanced off the beetle's carapace with a *chink* sound, and the tip planted itself in the dirt. Emerson squealed in a very unmanly way as the insect turned compound eyes on him and sprinted forward. It bit him on the right shoulder as he tried vainly to yank his sword from the ground.

You gain a skill point: +1 One-handed Slashing
A Chittering Beetle bites you for 3 damage!
The beetle appears unharmed by your attempt to strike it.

"Aggh. What?" Emerson yanked harder, finally freeing the weapon from the ground. But momentum sent him stumbling back, and his heel caught on a tuft of grass. He landed hard on his butt, wincing at the dart of discomfort that lanced up his spine.

You take 1 falling damage.

He waved frantically, trying to dispel the messages blocking his vision. Finally, the popups vanished, exposing the apparently furious beetle as it literally *jumped* through the air and landed a spikey foot on his thigh. Blood welled from the puncture wound.

A Chittering Beetle stabs you for 1 damage!
The beetle remains unharmed by your efforts.

"Wait! Stop with the messages. I can't see." Panicked, he flailed his arm in hopes it would clear his vision. A loud crack rattled his skull when he accidentally whacked the beetle in the face with his forearm.

You gain a skill point: +1 Unarmed Combat.

You punch a Chittering Beetle for 2 damage!

Would you like to suppress non-urgent combat notifications while in battle? Y/N

"What? Yes. Suppress please."

Thank you. Combat notifications reduced to high importance only. This includes ability acquisition, level-up notifications, and critical details.

Emerson scarcely had time to shove the popup away before the beetle surged forward again and clamped mandibles around his ribs.

"Ow shit!" he yelled as the insect bit down. In the corner of his vision, a red bar flashed and shrank. It appeared to be less than half full.

Rolling out of the grip of the godawful monster's serrated appendages, he made a desperate slash with his sword and somehow managed to get the blade to bite where the beetle's head attached to its thorax. The thing hissed as freakish yellow goo sprayed.

Fricking hell! Why did people play these games?

Moaning, Emerson tried to grab the sword's hilt with both hands, but the instant his left wrapped around his right, he felt a sudden loss of coordination. He yanked anyway, freeing the blade. As the beetle recovered from the blow, Emerson whimpered and log-rolled away from the beast, his arms stretched over his head. When he tried to stand, he stumbled and nearly landed on the blade.

> *Practice Short Sword* is a one-handed weapon. *Agility* reduced by 50% if attempting to wield it two-handedly.

"Fine. Shit. Okay." He released the weapon with his left hand and stood panting as the beetle turned for him. He swallowed back a fresh wave of terror as the mandibles clicked together.

As the beetle skittered toward him, Emerson looked over his shoulder toward Stonehaven's outer gate. Wasn't anyone concerned that he was being brutally attacked and would probably be murdered by a man-eating bug? The man that Devon had named her fortification's master—Jarleck, was it?—had given him a once over when he'd stalked purposefully into the field of battle, but he hadn't offered any words of encouragement or warning.

It was like the man *simply didn't care* that Emerson was going to die just outside the settlement's walls. What good was building a godforsaken settlement in the wilds if you didn't lift a finger to protect an innocent noob?

The beetle hissed again as it struck, and with a feral yell, Emerson brought his sword arcing around in a wild, overhead swing. He shut his eyes, expecting to miss and once again lodge his blade in the earth.

To his surprise, a sickening wet crunch filled his ears. Something cool and gooey splattered onto his face. It reeked like some kind of moldy hollandaise sauce mixed with grass clippings. Fighting the surge of bile, Emerson grimaced as he opened his eyes and saw the splattered beetle. He shrieked when the clang of a strange bell shook the field.

> You receive 105 experience.

Congratulations! You have reached level 2!

Quest Updated: Eradicate the Vermin
Beetles Slain: 1/10

Panting and trembling, Emerson planted the tip of his sword in the dirt and used the weapon as a cane while he fought a wave of dizziness. As he nudged the beetle-mess with his toe, the creature's mangled husk shimmered and then decomposed into a couple of objects. Once the tremors passed, Emerson crouched and plucked them from the ground.

You have received: Beetle Carapace Segment
It doesn't smell great, but a nearby armorsmith might be interested in taking this off your hands.

You have received: Compound Eye
Hollow it out, and you could probably fashion a simple kaleidoscope. Otherwise? Pretty useless.

Hands now full, he looked down at his body in search of pockets or something. It seemed like he was supposed to sell the carapace at least. But what was he supposed to do with the insect parts for the time being? Should he just pile his stuff at the edge of the field until he was done murdering things? Or should he take the carapace into the settlement now?

As he stood waffling, he felt the hairs on the back of his neck rise. Shivering, he turned to see if anyone was watching him, but the fortification master seemed to be inspecting the hinges on the gate.

Otherwise, the area outside the settlement was deserted—except for the legion of vermin scuttling through the grass.

Emerson plucked a handful of grass and used it to wipe the bug guts off his face—mostly he just smeared them around. Taking a deep breath, he planted his feet and looked out over the field again.

Drop by drop, the adrenalin from the first battle began to fade. Emerson's breath slowed as he noticed a particularly scraggly-looking rat snuffling in the grass. Glancing down at his injuries, he noticed that the wounds had already closed up, and the red bar at the corner of his vision was nearly back to full.

All right, so he wasn't exactly competent. And the beetle's attacks had been pretty horrifying.

But the combat hadn't been *that* bad, had it? In fact, it was maybe even a little fun.

He tossed the beetle body parts toward the path at the edge of the field and stepped toward the rat. "Okay, beast. Let's do this."

***

Quest Updated: Eradicate the Vermin
Rats Slain: 9/10

Emerson grinned through the mask of rat blood and beetle goo that covered his face. His hands were sticky with it, and his sword practically dripped the stuff. He was almost regretting nearing the end of the quest. Not only was he now level 3, he'd also gained 4 skill points in *One-handed Slashing*. He could almost feel the grateful eyes of the citizens of Stonehaven looking out at him, the brave warrior, purging the vermin that plagued them.

Heaped at the edge of the grass lay the spoils of his conquest, all manner of beetle and rat and snake parts. Just looking at the astounding piles, a sense of warm pride filled him. Out in the real world, he was awkward and never quite fit in. But here, he was a hero. Valious, slayer of beasts, vanquisher of nuisances. Or wait...nuisanci? Like cacti?

Either way. He was a vanquisher for sure.

Jaw set, he turned his—surely steely by now—gaze on the field stretched out before him. Grass trembled just a few feet away, a sure sign of yet more prey. Emerson strode forward and struck.

Chapter Nine

You have gained a skill point: +1 Stealth.

After failing to increase her stealth for so long, Devon almost felt like this was cheating. If watching this weird newbie hack away at the grass snakes and rats and beetles wasn't so genuinely painful, anyway. She narrowly avoided groaning as the guy yelled—she assumed he thought battle cries were cool—and brought his notched short sword down in an overhead arc. Of course, he missed what he'd been targeting, and was forced to chase it down. Devon sighed quietly and hurried to keep up as best she could.

She had just gotten within stealth range when the rat keeled over and died with a sad little squeak. The man—Valious, what a name...—squatted and touched his blade to the corpse to activate the decomposition.

You have gained a skill point: +1 Stealth.
You realize most of these are pity points, right? Because watching this really is painful.

She sighed again. At least Veia shared her opinion on this guy. Of all the noobs to give her as a starter, why'd she have to get the bloodthirsty weirdo who acted like slaying newbie yard trash was some kind of heroic epic? The man wasn't even bothering to swipe his hand down his face to force the game to clear off the bug goo. His body looked like he'd put a frog in a blender, hit *liquefy*, then poured the results over the top of his head. Maybe in his mind, it was some kind of badge of honor thing.

The man stood from the sight of his latest kill, clutching his newly looted items in his off hand, but not for long. Devon ducked, nearly losing her *Stealth* effect as the rat parts went flying past her to land in one of the heaps near the edge of the field. Was the guy not even worried about the items despawning? As far as she could tell, he had nothing but the short sword and his cloth tunic and trousers to his name. Oh. And a pair of sandals that appeared to stay on by some kind of weak atomic force. At his level, even patches of rat fur would sell for a worthwhile amount of money—provided her villagers would pay for it, anyway. Gerrald could probably do something with the stuff—though hopefully that wouldn't be creating a new outfit for Devon.

Regardless, the newbie's idiotic tactic seemed to be working. She wasn't keeping a strict count or anything, but it seemed the game was allowing the loot to linger. Which made her wonder whether Veia just liked watching her deal with such a kook.

Distracted by the rat body parts that had nearly taken her out, Devon forgot to keep an eye on the noob, and when she turned back around, he was just a footstep away. Much to her horror, she heard a squeak of surprise as it escaped her throat.

Stealth canceled, loudmouth.

To Valious's eyes, it must have looked like she appeared out of thin air. The man yelled like a schoolgirl on the playground and swung wildly at her head. Just before the flat of his blade slapped her on the ear, Devon got a hand up to block. The sword glanced off the sleeve of her *Stonehaven Jerkin*, a splatter of innards flying off the blade and landing on her face. She yelped and wiped them clean, gagging in disgust. The sudden change in momentum from his failed attack knocked Valious off balance, and he stumbled forward, going down on a knee. Coughing, he remained near the ground for a moment, then slowly turned his face toward her.

"I—you startled me, Dev—" He clapped his hand over his mouth as if shocked to have started to use her name. She sighed. His introductory quest line had probably talked about her as the leader of Stonehaven. She extended her hand and clasped his wrist to help him up.

The man peered at her face. "How did you get clean so easily?"

Had he never played a VR MMO before? Blood and guts were pretty much standard immersion tricks, usually configurable in the settings. She realized she had cocked her head like a puzzled dog and rolled her shoulders in an attempt to recover. "Sorry about the surprise. I've been training stealth. Just wave your hand down your arms and face to get rid of the mess."

He mouthed the words "training stealth" as his eyes went distant, the classic expression of a player inspecting their UI. Devon blinked. Maybe he actually didn't know about the *Stealth* skill? Was this an honest-to-goodness first timer? Watching someone play an immerso VR game for the first time was like spotting an exceedingly rare and nearly extinct wildebeest or something.

"First time in game?" she asked, then quickly added, "I mean, I haven't seen you here before." She winced inwardly, hoping she hadn't embarrassed him.

Valious made as if to run his hands through his hair, but quickly realized he was holding a sword. "I guess there haven't been many fresh faces around here. Must be how you know I'm new."

Devon paused a moment before nodding. "Right, yeah. I just put two and two together."

He straightened his shoulders. "I..." A curious look passed across his face as if he were considering what to say. "Yeah, so I got access quite a while ago, but I've had so much going on. Couldn't get a decent time block to log in until this morning."

"Well," Devon said. "I guess you already talked to the trainers." She hoped they'd given him some guidance. Once the horde arrived, it would put a big drain on her settlement expansion if her regular citizens were stuck helping out the noobs.

"Just one more kill to finish my initiation rite," he said, looking way too proud.

Initiation rite...? She smiled and nodded. "Okay, well, I better get back to..." She circled her hand in the air. "Settlement management and stuff."

She turned to go, but the man made a couple hurried steps forward and touched her with a still-goo-covered hand. "Devon?"

She took a deep breath and turned. This guy wasn't to blame for having the misfortune of spawning in the path of the demon invasion. If anything, she should encourage him to progress as quickly as possible so that he could be some help when the demons came.

Still, he must've seen the impatience on her face, because whatever he'd been about to say seemed to die in his throat. "Merry Christmas…if it's your thing, I mean. And nice to meet you."

Chapter Ten

"TO TELL THE truth," Hezbek said as she plucked a small bowl made of woven straw from one of her shelves, "I haven't been able to figure out a way to use these particular treasures." She smirked as she held out the container.

Devon peered inside and examined the items.

> **Item:** Cave Mushroom
> *This variety of fungus grows deep in caverns in the Argenthal Vassaldom and is known to prefer crevices fertilized by centuries of skin flakes shed by orcs.*

> **Item:** Shrunken Felsen Head
> *Maybe not the best idea to show this to your new felsen friends. Though the item doesn't offer any benefits, some weirdos might consider it an interesting decoration.*

Both were ingredients she'd brought back from the Cavern of Spirits, satisfying a quest to provide Hezbek with new components for her potion experiments. After her return, though, the medicine woman had refused to show Devon what new concoctions she'd invented with the ingredients until Devon visited the nearby player encampment. Hezbek had claimed that Devon needed the social interaction. Of course, the visit to the player camp had basically ended with Devon turning into a demon and stepping through a planar rift into the underworld, so now was the first chance she'd had to take Hezbek up on the quest reward. She'd been looking forward to seeing what kind of cool potions the woman had learned to produce.

"What? Really? These totally seem like good ingredients for potion making." If anything, Devon had been rather pleased with herself to discover them, especially the shrunken head. Exterminating the orc infestation had been hard enough. Doing it while finishing a collection quest had shown impressive multitasking skills, in her humble opinion.

Hezbek snorted. "You see, if I'd given the quest to you directly rather than to Hazel— I'm still not too pleased with the scout for distracting you by sharing the work—I probably would've been more specific about the ingredients I needed. Experimentation is fine and well. Providing me such with a revolting collection...I can't say it inspired me to tinker."

Devon poked at the shrunken head, the blue felsen skin turned wrinkly and dark gray. Scraggly tufts of white hair were still stuck to the scalp, but their grip seemed tenuous. A tiny hooked nose was missing a chunk of flesh, granting a view into the hollow interior of the skull. Okay, so it was kind of gross. Maybe taking little shavings from the object wouldn't be high on her task list either.

"But the Cave Mushroom...that's a totally classic ingredient."

Hezbek gave her a flat stare before planting her walking stick and crossing the room to her hearth. "If you want to take a horsehair brush to it and make sure not a single of those desiccated orc skin flakes remain, I'll consider trying to incorporate it. In the meantime, I'm a medicine woman, not a witch doctor."

Devon sighed. "Okay, but did you have to give the Tiny Scintillating Dragon Scales to Gerrald? I mean...Dragon? Scales? Don't tell him I complained, but there must have been a better use than to turn them into glorified sequins."

"To my credit, I did try to concoct something with those," Hezbek said as she dipped a wooden spoon in the kettle bubbling over her low fire. "But after the second explosion of glitter, I gave up and passed them off."

"All right, so what *were* you able to create from the ingredients Hazel and I grabbed?" The quest reward was *supposed* to be access to Hezbek's new potion lines. Devon was starting to think it had all been a bluff.

The medicine woman smirked as she pulled an earthenware pot from a shelf, then grabbed a narrow-necked glass decanter with swirling red liquid inside. She tucked the decanter into the crook of her elbow then picked up her walking stick. Devon quickly jumped up when she realized how hard the woman needed to lean on her staff and how difficult that made it for her to carry two items.

Hezbek gratefully handed over the potions. The glass decanter was warm in her grip.

> **You have received:** Phoenix Spirit Potion
> *The fires of reincarnation smolder inside this delicate vessel.*
> Grants the Phoenix Spirit buff. If your health drops below zero while the buff is active, you immediately return to life with 5% health remaining. After this resurrection, you are immune to damage and healing effects for 10 seconds.

Duration: 10 minutes

"Oh, nice!" Devon said. Already she imagined a group's tank springing back to life, leaving the healer to count down the seconds in hopes of landing a heal just at the right time. With 5% health and poor healer timing, a single boss-mob hit would just kill the poor tank all over again. But with a great healer, it could make or break an encounter.

"It took me quite some time to figure out how to use those phoenix feathers you brought back from the mountains. I didn't want to waste them, and I especially didn't want to start a bonfire in my cabin."

Smiling, Devon peered at the earthenware pot.

You have received: Lightfooted Potion
The road may be long, but your burdens are light.
Reduces *Fatigue* gain by 15%.
Duration: 3 hours

Very nice indeed, especially since Devon expected a long journey to the Stone Forest. "These are great, Hezbek," she said.

"That one"—the woman nodded at the *Lightfooted Potion*—"used a mix of the lichens and mosses you and Hazel collected in the mountains. In the case of both of those, I can only make around a dozen each of the potions with the ingredients you supplied. Of course, if you'd like to gather me more of the components, it wouldn't be a problem to increase supply."

Hezbek is offering you a quest: More, more, more! (repeatable)
The cauldron is always bubbling. Gather more of the rare ingredients used in the Phoenix Spirit and Lightfooted potions to increase Hezbek's production capacity.
Objective: Collect 5 x *Light Green Lichen of Moderate Flakiness with some Orangish Spots* and/or 5 x *Phoenix Feathers.*
Reward: Expanded potion production
Reward: 50000 experience
Accept? Y/N

Devon hovered her attention over the *Accept* prompt. Just getting back to the mountains in any reasonable amount of time would require drinking a constant supply of the *Lightfooted* potions. Not the most efficient quest. And the thought of climbing the sheer pinnacle to once again reach the nest of the Phoenix Prince did *not* appeal. But it didn't hurt to have the quest in her log if—by some chance—she could find another way to get the components. Maybe she could work out an arrangement with the dwarves who worked the ore caravans. Regardless, with a little shrug, she accepted the quest.

"Good good," Hezbek said. "I realize that many of your tasks are more important than fetching components for an old woman who fills her days brewing potions and mixing salves. But I appreciate that you'd consider it."

Devon cocked her head, surprised at her friend's self-deprecating tone. "Is everything okay, Hezbek?"

The medicine woman seemed about to say something, but quickly shook her head. "Nothing you need to worry about, child."

Which of course was the best way in the world to *make* Devon worry. "Maybe I can help," she said.

Hezbek sighed as her face crinkled in a wistful smile. "It's nothing. Just...while you were in the demonic plane, I spoke with your friend Emerson about my past. Thinking on the years that lie behind me has made me a bit nostalgic and melancholy. Now don't get me wrong. I am proud of my journey and what I've made of myself. There's just a couple of regrets that I can't seem to let go."

Devon set the potions down and helped the woman to a chair at the small table. Hezbek's arms shook a little as she used her walking stick for support while lowering into the seat.

"I'm happy to listen if it would help you to tell me about them," Devon said. "Even if we can't do anything to change the past."

"You see, that's why just about anyone in Stonehaven would leap to the walls to defend you and what you've built," Hezbek said, patting Devon's hand. "You speak in terms of *we*, not *me*. Of course, my youthful choices are not your burden, yet you accept the weight anyway."

Devon blinked, cheeks coloring. She wasn't really sure what to say...her upbringing hadn't exactly taught her how to accept gratitude and praise. When Devon's mother had bothered to acknowledge her, it had been to complain about how Devon was always in the way. Always underfoot or costing too much money because she had the inconvenient—to her mother, anyway—need to eat to stay alive.

"You've done so much for me," Devon said. "How could I *not* want to help?"

"Thank you, child. Sincerely. And if you really want to hear, I'll tell you. But first, I'm surprised you haven't asked about the more mundane potion lines...after all, the main reason I sent Hazel on a search for ingredients was because I'd run out of components for the potions I made from substances collected in the jungle." Hezbek smirked. "Maybe part of your mind doesn't want to know...the part which processes taste."

Devon grimaced. The truth was, for her first weeks in the game, she'd done everything she could to avoid consuming Hezbek's revoltingly unpalatable health and mana potions. Death—especially when the penalty had been milder—seemed preferable than gagging on one of the godawful concoctions.

Laughing, Hezbek reached for a pair of small stoppered bottles on the shelf overhanging the table.

You have received: Savanna Health Potion - Mid
Heals 259-318 damage.

You have received: Savanna Mana Potion - Minor
Restores 179-187 mana.

The woman smiled, her face crinkling. "Made from boiled acacia bark, termite larvae, witchtuber, and cichlid fins in different ratios. Plus some orchid sap for the mana potion. Hazel has been helping me stockpile the components, so I can make as many as Stonehaven is likely to need. In fact, making more will help me figure out the recipes for the higher tiers."

Keeping the mana potion at the end of her outstretched arms to distance herself from the smell, Devon worked the cork free. To her surprise, she wasn't immediately assaulted by the stench. Gingerly, she brought the bottle under her nose and sniffed.

"Actually, it's..."

"Not too bad, right?" Hezbek said, looking pleased.

"How's the taste?"

"A little bitter. I suspect it's the bark. But I realized that my foul-tasting medicines weren't discouraging you adventurers from taking risks and getting hurt. It only made you less likely to heal yourselves."

Devon smirked. "Guilty as charged." She nestled the set of new potions into her satchel and saw her inventory icon flash to indicate changes. "When you finish making the rest of the *Phoenix Spirit* and *Lightfooted* potions, I'd love if you could create a stockpile of the Savanna potions. I have a feeling we may need them soon." Devon again thought of the massing demon army. "But back to you...if you feel like sharing, that is."

Hezbek grunted quietly while she shifted in her chair and leaned her walking staff against the wall. "I said I had a couple of regrets, but really it all goes back to Eldon and the Cragscale Wars. Almost forty years ago now. You sure you want to hear such ancient history?"

"Yes, and I'm not leaving your cabin until you tell me."

Hezbek chuckled. "Then fix me some tea, and you'll have the story."

Chapter Eleven

"I WAS YOUNG then," Hezbek said. "We all were. Rimeshore people. Hardy and stubborn."

Devon sat silently beside the medicine woman on the small stoop outside her front door. Between their chairs, a pair of mugs held steaming infusions of an herb that tasted similar to peppermint. Hezbek claimed the tea boosted the spirit, but Devon hadn't noticed a buff icon or a change in any of her stats, so maybe it was more of a psychological thing.

"Where's Rimeshore?" Devon asked when the woman sat back in her chair, eyes tracking Bravlon as he toddled along behind Blackbeard the Parrot, tugging at the bird's immense tail features.

Hezbek waved toward the north and east. "A long, long way from here. It's a mostly empty place...or at least it was in the years I knew it. I haven't set foot in the shorelands for decades, so I don't know what changes have happened since I left."

Devon wanted to ask more questions. Why did Hezbek leave her home? How far away exactly was Rimeshore? But she picked up her tea and sipped, letting Hezbek tell the story in her own way.

"It wasn't the war that led me to sorcery," Hezbek said. "More accurately, I think, it was sorcery and the combat disciplines chosen by my peers that brought the war to us. We thought we were defending our freedom, keeping our coastal villages answering to no one except maybe Graymist Hold, and only then because we needed some sort of rallying point for our Rimeshore identity. But now I see it differently."

As the woman spoke, a notification popped up.

> Congratulations! Stonehaven Hamlet now has a Tailoring Workshop.

She brushed away the pop-up, though she couldn't help scanning the parts of the settlement visible from Hezbek's porch. If she recalled from her recent, yet brief, tour of Prester's new project, the Tailoring Workshop had been under construction near the rear wall of the kitchen. The area was out of sight from her current vantage, but she did not doubt that Prester would soon seek her out with the news.

Hezbek chuckled, perhaps noticing the distant look in Devon's eyes. "Go ahead. Check over whatever it is you need to attend to."

Devon smiled at the woman, grateful for her understanding. Prester would also want orders concerning his next major project. Her fingertips tingled with anticipation as she pulled open her interface and scanned down to the tier 4 building tab.

> <u>Tier 4 buildings:</u>
>
> -Guild Hall - Trade-specific
> *A hall of study for the advancement of trades. Individual halls may be built for most crafting professions and are usable by both players and NPCs for advancement.*

Expand for details.

- Guild Hall - Class-specific
A hall of study for the advancement of combat classes. Guildmasters for the classes often hear about these dedicated facilities and will journey to a settlement holding one in hopes they'll be granted citizenship.
Expand for details.

- University
Dedicated to the pursuit of general scholarly knowledge. Often results in the discovery of rare information and rumors that can lead to specific quests and awesome loot.

-Theater
Popular with bards. Raises town morale by 5-15% depending on the quality of performers.

She chewed her lip while thinking. The most practical would be a guildhall for one of the crafting trades—with so many NPC tradespeople in town, the hall would be a great benefit for the settlement as a whole.

But what she would probably do instead was build a university. The promise of rare loot and quests was just so tempting. Besides, building something not directly related to a defense against the demon horde was her way of looking forward to a future where she would have *time* to go hunt for rare treasure.

Hezbek was looking at her with an amused smile when Devon dismissed the interface. "So what was it? Another message from the starborn realm?" she asked.

Devon shook her head. "I just got word that Prester completed one of his projects."

"Ah. Well, that's fine news. And Jarleck recently told me that we have almost everything needed to call our fortifications a castle. Just need a drawbridge and to finish closing the roof over the top of the dungeon."

Devon nodded. "The drawbridge is done, actually. Just waiting on the dungeon." She hadn't mentioned it to Jarleck, but it *did* seem stupid to have to dig a hole in the ground and fill it with stone cells and iron bars. They didn't have anyone to lock up, and if they did, couldn't they repurpose part of the Inner Keep? But it wasn't Jarleck's fault that the game had put the requirement in place. And as soon as the dungeon was finished, the upgrade to the fortification's classification would give defensive bonuses beyond what the actual structural updates provided. Given the demon threat, Stonehaven needed any added defense she could muster.

"Anyway, go on," Devon said. "I'd much rather hear your story than worry about settlement upgrades."

Hezbek gave her a wistful smile. "It's not the most pleasant of tales. I hope you won't regret asking for it. In any case, the simple story of how I found myself in a band of fighters and rebels is that I left home at sixteen. Went to Graymist in search of any job that would spare me a life of digging clams from frigid sand. I met my first mentor there, a level 7 sorceress who had scoured the Hold's libraries and taught herself almost everything she knew. Avylin. She was probably in her mid-30s, but to my teenage eyes she seemed ancient and wise." Hezbek snorted. "I studied under her for about a year, working in the Hold's kitchens to support myself. I was around third level when Eldon arrived at Graymist. He spoke passionately of the greed in the lands over the Cragscale Mountains, of kings and baronesses who had designs on Rimeshore. It didn't take long for Eldon to gather many of us around him, and that was the start of our army."

"So *did* the outsiders have designs on your homes?" Devon asked.

Hezbek shrugged. "Maybe. They had certainly built watchtowers beside the roads not just on their side of the mountains, but on ours as well. Those sentry posts were our first targets, and I suspect that if historians ever study events as remote and—to the wider world—insignificant as the Cragscale Wars, they'd certainly conclude that our initial raids were the spark that ignited the conflict."

"How long did the war last?"

"Wars, actually. There were five, though I'd left by the time the fourth began. The first lasted two years and left the mountain settlements on our side of the divide bleeding. The second was longer. Six years, but it felt like twenty. We lost that one, and it's my fault."

Hezbek's jaw clenched, and Devon didn't know what to say. Should she console the woman? Try to reassure her that she couldn't possibly have been her army's downfall? Instead, Devon swallowed and remained silent, figuring that any attempts at consolation would feel empty and false.

You have gained a skill point: +1 Leadership

"We were in council. Me, Eldon, and some of the others who had been in the fight since the beginning. A messenger burst in uninvited, and Eldon nearly drew his blade at the man's insolence for interrupting. He was hotheaded that way—it was the biggest source of conflict between us."

Devon blinked. "Were you…?"

"Lovers for most of the second war, yes. Sometimes he scared me—his fervor and battle rage most of all—but I believed in him too. It was thrilling to be with someone so close to the center of things." She shook her head. "Like I said, I was young then."

Somewhere behind Hezbek's cabin, a rowdy cheer went up. It sounded like the dwarves had discovered the new building. No doubt one of the short-legged band was already sprinting to fetch a keg.

"So what happened?" Devon asked. "In your council."

"Eldon's fury with the messenger naturally put me on edge. I guess I felt like I had to compensate for his anger. I was afraid I'd lose him to his lust for battle, but I was also afraid of where he might lead us. So when the messenger claimed that a raiding party sent by the Grass King had crossed the divide at the Funnel, a narrow pass about a half day's ride to the south, I urged caution. I said we should request a parlay, or at the very least, that we should send scouts to determine whether this was truly a raid before we struck. In the past year, our squads had mistakenly harassed two trade caravans and a party of Veian clergy, killing guards and taking innocent people prisoner before the real situation became clear."

"I imagine that made the travelers more likely to increase their guard," Devon said.

Hezbek nodded. "Which made it increasingly difficult to distinguish between raiding parties and simple journeyers. In any case, I wasn't the only one in the leadership circle troubled by Eldon's behavior. All the others needed was a nudge, so when I spoke against his declaration that we should ride hard and attack swiftly, a majority of our group voted to send scouts ahead of our fighting force." Hezbek swallowed and blinked, shaking her head slowly. "I suppose they killed the scouts. We never found out. By the time our fighters caught up with the raid, two coastal villages were in smoking ruins, and a third—Eldon's hometown, Haverton—was under attack."

Devon reached across the gap between their chairs and touched Hezbek's arm. Hezbek smiled faintly. "Thank you, child. As you can imagine, Eldon went into a rage. He plunged into the battle, sword drawn and screaming. And then..." Hezbek's eyes went distant. "Well, as you can imagine, many followed him into battle. The fighting was brutal. Awful. And then, everything stopped for a moment. There was a blinding white light, and almost every combatant on the field vanished. Forever."

"Wait, I don't understand. Vanished? There was some sort of magic?"

Hezbek shrugged. "At first we thought it was the act of some sorcerer or wizard on the Grass King's side, a teleportation spell so powerful that it moved the battle elsewhere. But no missing soldier was ever heard from again—from either side of the conflict. And many scholars studied the site in the years after, looking for residues or signs most commonly associated with the known schools of magic. There was simply nothing. The mystery was never solved."

Devon blinked as she processed the information. What could have done that?

Hezbek sighed. "In any case, the fight went out of us after that, and the Second Cragscale War ended when we conceded to the Grass King's demands for tariffs on trade through the Cragscales. Enforced by manned garrisons along the major routes through the peaks, of course."

"Is that when you gave up sorcery?"

The corner of Hezbek's mouth pulled back in an ironic smirk. "If only I'd been so wise then. No...in fact, I think some of Eldon's spirit took residence in me following his disappearance. Peace held in Rimeshore for maybe a year before the presence of the garrisons and the trade tariffs started to chafe. People were hungry, unable to make a living off salt fish and pearls. Soldiers on leave from the forts harassed the local girls and picked fights with the young men from the coastal villages. I could blame those factors, but the truth is that the Third Cragscale War started when I led a party against a sentry post defending the Funnel."

"Awwwk! Land ho! All hands on deck!"

Devon jumped as the giant bird flapped out from the gap between Hezbek's cabin and the adjacent home. Her shoulders inched toward her ears as she waited for the parrot's telepathic complaint. But none came, and moments later, Bravlon came tumbling out from between the buildings. The toddler laughed. Devon looked away when she felt the urge to start cooing at the child. Stupid *Adoration* spell.

"Aww hands on deck!" the dwarf child repeated.

Blackbeard made a strangled sound that sounded almost like a laugh, then crouched down. Squealing, Bravlon grabbed handfuls of feathers and paddled his feet as he clambered onto the bird's back. Devon tensed, ready to run to the boy's rescue when he started thumping his feet against the bird's ribs, but the parrot just spread his wings and started trotting through the grass, squawking.

Hezbek shook her head. "Hate to be around when that obnoxious bird finally gets his resistance to the *Adoration* spell up. I imagine he'll find even more choice spots to fertilize in revenge for us standing by while he acts like a fool."

Devon smirked. "You're probably right. Best if we check for roof leaks before that happens."

"Indeed." Hezbek grimaced.

"You said you weren't around for the start of the fourth war. What happened?"

"It wasn't so much a single event that ended my interest in fighting. I suspect the weariness was building for a long time before I finally acknowledged it. But I do remember that I woke up one morning and realized that home was leagues and leagues away. We'd pushed the Grass King back over the passes and were raiding settlements on the opposite side of the mountains. We'd been justifying it by claiming that a punishing defeat would make the Grass King rethink any plans to encroach on Rimeshore again. But I knew differently. We'd won, but we were fighting on out of habit and greed. That morning, I packed a bedroll and rucksack and left the war behind."

"Did you go home?"

Hezbek shook her head. "There was nothing left for me there except more fighting. Eldon was gone. So were my parents, taken by the lung rattle during a particularly damp winter. I went west, from town to town and city to city, and eventually, some three years later, arrived in Eltera City. I spent decades there, and eventually took up the healing arts."

"Is it big? Eltera City?" Devon ran her eyes over the settlement. Nearly every cobblestone footpath had someone walking on it; every day, Jarleck welcomed another refugee or two from the demon attacks that had decimated the city.

"Not as big or as grand as some cities. But big enough. It was a good place to reinvent myself."

"I wish there were more I could do to help you feel better."

Hezbek smiled sadly and sipped her tea. "You have, simply by letting me tell the tale. The truth is, I've had more than four decades to regret my youthful choices. Some might accuse me of being self-indulgent to keep bemoaning them. And anyway, every time I heal someone, I feel that I *am* atoning for the past. Even if it's just helping out a carpenter who smashed her thumb with a hammer."

"I'd like to be able to say that life in Stonehaven will always be peaceful. But it would be dishonest after what I saw in the demons' council chamber. As soon as another general takes command of Raazel's forces, they'll head straight for our shores."

Hezbek sighed and nodded. "I know, child."

"If I can find the last relic in time, I may be able to bring the city's ancient defenses to bear. But if not..."

"We can only do our best, child. No sense considering the battle lost until it's well and truly over. I've seen what you can do, starborn. And I have more faith in that than I ever did in the Rimeshore forces."

Devon patted the medicine woman's hand, Hezbek's arthritic knuckles large knobs under her palm. "Thank you, Hezbek. It means a lot."

The woman huffed as if to deflect the gratitude. "I only speak what's honest. You should know that by now."

"I suppose I should," Devon said. "Speaking of the final relic, do you know anything about the Stone Forest?"

Hezbek shook her head. "Never heard of it. Doesn't sound particularly pleasant though."

"No. It doesn't, does it? Anyway, I suppose I ought to get over to the new workshop and congratulate Prester before the dwarves pour too much ale down his throat."

Hezbek laughed. "Be wary of that yourself. I wouldn't trust those runty folk."

Chapter Twelve

WHAT THE HELL was Emerson going to do now? After acting like he'd never met Devon before, how was he supposed to backpedal and admit his identity? It would make him look like even more of a fool than he had when he'd been so startled by her "stealth training."

"Idiot," he muttered to himself as he trudged into town. He had balanced a stack of beetle carapaces in his arms and was carrying his sword by pinning the hilt between his upper arm and rib cage. Even so, it was still going to take a *ton* of trips to get all his loot dragged in to sell. Of course, he had noticed some of the villagers walking around with sacks and backpacks. He could buy one, but it seemed kind of gross to stick a bunch of gore-covered stuff in a bag. Unless maybe there was a trick for cleaning goo off of monster body parts like Devon had shown him to get the mess off his face.

Christ. What a fool he must have appeared, running around covered in bug guts. Well, okay, maybe the blood had made him look kind of tough, but he really didn't think Devon went for that kind of thing. Or at least, he hoped it wasn't her primary condition in her who-to-date algorithm. Because if that were the case, he certainly wasn't going to be the top choice. Not as a level-one dude dressed in a flimsy shirt and pants. Sure, maybe if he'd been able to stride in as Valious the Brave, all decked out in gleaming armor with harrowing war stories...yeah, that would have ticked the "tough" box. But not this.

Anyway, none of *that* mattered if he didn't figure out how to fix his idiot mistake of pretending not to know her.

He turned toward the forge where he'd found Dorden earlier, figuring that if the dwarf didn't want to take the beetle shells off his hands, maybe he would point him in the right direction. As he stepped around a building that smelled like it might be the settlement's kitchen, he heard a cheer go up from deeper into the town. Getting onto his tiptoes, he caught the scent of woodsmoke, then looked up and spied a gray column rising into the afternoon sky. It looked big enough to have been produced by a bonfire.

Was it...could it be that the villagers were celebrating the substantial dent he'd made in their vermin infestation? Emerson paused for a few seconds, trying to keep a smile from spreading across his face. He *had* heard that Veia altered the world based on players' actions, a major difference from so many MMO games where quests were completed over and over by player after player, even when that made no sense. And there *had* been a pretty cool party after Devon returned from the underworld, proof that the citizens of Stonehaven reacted to world events in a sensible manner.

But still. As impressive as his efforts in the field had been—above average, surely—if the town threw parties for even a fraction of player quest completions, they'd never be sober. And slaying a few dozen rodents and snakes was nothing like facing off with an evil demonic god. So yeah, he probably wasn't being honored.

With a sigh, he kept trudging for the forge.

Unfortunately, when he arrived at the stocky stone building, the furnace was merely smoldering, and no one was inside. Emerson sighed and adjusted the stack of carapaces. His arms were getting tired from holding them so stiffly, but if he relaxed the angle of his elbows, the pile would topple.

He searched the nearby cobblestone paths for someone who might be able to direct him to another crafter. An armorsmith maybe? Or was that the job of Dorden's female colleague who usually worked in the forge with him, the one with biceps as big as Emerson's thighs? What about a leather...leather sewer? Maybe the beetle shells would be useful for reinforcement for something like that.

As he walked to the next intersection of paths, searching for someone to help, he wished he'd spent a little more time learning his way around Stonehaven last time. He honestly had no idea where to start looking for a vendor, and at the moment, there was no one wandering around. Which probably meant they were hanging out at the party. Somewhat reluctantly—mostly, he didn't want to cross paths with Devon until he figured out what to do—he turned for what he assumed was the bonfire.

Chapter Thirteen

WHILE MAKING HER way to the celebration for the Tailoring Workshop, Devon pulled out her new dagger, *Night's Fang,* and rotated it in her grip. Looking at it edge on, she shook her head in amazement. The ivory had been honed to the sharpness of the best steel blades, a seemingly impossible feat. But the evidence in front of her face said otherwise. She'd meant to ask Hezbek if she knew anything about the blade's mysterious origins, but the potions and the talk of the medicine woman's past had distracted her.

She tucked the dagger back into her bag. Next time she saw the woman, she'd be sure to ask.

Before lighting the bonfire, the dwarves had at least shown the presence of mind to clear away the grass in a wide circle around the site of the blaze. Now, three tables had been set up in the cleared area, each supporting a keg of the dwarven ale. Steering a wide course around the kegs—Devon did *not* want to wake up tomorrow and hear about all the farm animal imitations she'd done in front of the townsfolk—she headed through the celebration to the far side where the newly constructed building stood with the door thrown open and Prester beaming just inside.

Devon grinned when she stepped under the lintel and clapped him on the shoulder. The interior of the workshop was bright, the windows placed so that plenty of natural light entered the room.

Workbenches lined the walls, complete with racks for thread and shelves for fabric. Stands stood ready for the wooden forms Emmaree had recently ordered from the town's woodcarver, solid pieces of pine shaped like human torsos in various sizes that would allow the tailors to check the fit and hang of clothing long before trial fittings on the human customers. At the far side of the workshop floor, another door stood open, revealing the storage room where bolts of cloth would await the tailors' shears. The building smelled of fresh-cut wood planks and hard work. She nodded in appreciation.

"You've outdone yourself, Prester."

The carpenter touched his brow. "Pleased to hear that, Mayor. Emmaree has been by already, and she claims she'll be up the whole night trying out the new benches and racks. Said the tailors might actually catch up with the requested repairs and new orders by week's end."

"Then maybe I won't feel so bad putting in a request for something of my own."

Prester raised his eyebrows. "Oh? Thinking of having some finery made? Something for entertaining important emissaries, perhaps?"

Devon suppressed a laugh. Oh, man. Of course, if and when she managed to restore Ishildar she probably *would* have to figure out how to interact with representatives from other cities. Maybe from other kingdoms, even. But she hoped she wouldn't be expected to put on feasts and wear ridiculous dresses. That would really suck.

"I was just thinking that I'm part sorceress, so maybe I should consider some alternate gear sets. I dunno, at least a robe I could change into if it seemed like the best choice for a situation."

The man sucked his teeth. "Well, can't say I know a lot about that."

She smiled. "No, and I'm glad. Stonehaven can't afford to lose your carpentry expertise, so don't get any ideas about adventuring." She elbowed him gently.

Prester looked at her, aghast. "No offense, Your Gloriousness. But I am certain anyone who wishes to engage in such pursuits is one breath shy of insane."

She laughed. "You may be right. Anyway, I shouldn't keep you from the party."

"To be honest," he said with a shrug, "I'm just waiting until they're drunk enough that I can sneak away without anyone noticing."

"Oh?"

He gave a sort of half-smile. "Truth is, I'd like to get back to work. We've got cabins to build, shops to upgrade."

"A University to build..."

The man straightened, eyes widening. "You mean it? Tier 4?"

Devon nodded. "I think some of the other carpenters and apprentices can handle the housing and kitchen, don't you?"

Seeming to vibrate with excitement, Prester gave her an awkward little salute and ducked out the door. Watching him go, she smiled as she pulled up the settlement interface and checked the progress toward Township.

- Advanced NPC: 11/25
- Buildings (Tier 2): 10/27
- Buildings (Tier 3): 5/15
- Buildings (Tier 4): 0/2

- Population: 485/500

Size: Hamlet

Tier 1 Buildings - Unlimited:

Housing (single occupancy): 35

Housing (double occupancy): 65

Housing (family): 29

Shops (basic): 35

Shops (upgraded): 22

Tier 2 Buildings - 10/27

1 x Medicine Woman's Cabin (upgraded)

1 x Crafting Workshop

1 x Basic Forge

1 x Kitchen

4 x Barracks

2 x Warehouse

1 x Kitchen (in progress)

1 x Smokehouse (in progress)

2 x Warehouse (in progress)

Tier 3 Buildings - 6/15

1 x Shrine to Veia

1 x Chicken Coop

1 x Inner Keep

1 x Leatherworking Shop

1 x Woodworking Shop

1 x Tailoring Workshop

Tier 4 Buildings - 0/2
1 x University (in progress)

Overall, the town had a nice balance of construction. Sure, a University was a *little* impractical considering she could only build two tier 4 buildings, but it would totally be worth it. Being mayor had to have some perks, right?

***

Around half an hour later, Devon edged away from the gathering. In that time, she'd managed to dodge at least half a dozen attempts by the dwarves to pour ale down her throat, a feat that, in her opinion, should have granted a dodge skill up. Veia, however, didn't seem to comprehend the difficulty of the evasions. And, not only had she remained sober, but she'd also tracked down Stonehaven's wheelwright and talked to her about creating some special wheels for Tamara's bike. According to the woman, one of the players had recently come in with ironwood for trade, and the substance would be perfect for the rims. It was lighter than iron, could be soaked in a particular mix of water and lime to render the material flexible enough for molding into a circular shape, and once cured, the resulting circles would have more give to them than iron or steel would. As for the spokes, the woman proposed straight blades of hardwood, claiming that the forge wouldn't produce anything precise enough, and that metal rods would be brittle and heavy besides.

Given the deluge of information and expertise—Devon knew nothing about wheels—she was inclined just to let the woman do her thing. If Tamara had additional ideas for upgrades, she could work directly with the village crafters once she logged in.

As for the bike frame, Devon had talked to the village woodworker about piecing something together from more of the ironwood. From what she remembered during her ill-fated attempts at riding with Tamara, the woman's favorite bike had been a futuristic machine with all sorts of shocks and suspension. Tamara had been particularly happy with a seat that changed height based on the angle of climb or descent. Obviously, being stuck in a preindustrial society, Devon wasn't going to be able to get something that fancy produced. Tamara would be psyched regardless.

Her chores accomplished, Devon wanted to get back to her Christmas self-improvement quest, so she ducked her head and shoved her hands into her pockets as she casually strolled away from the fire.

"Incoming."

The word was so quiet, a whisper at the very edge of her hearing, that Devon thought it must have been her imagination. But she turned to glance over her shoulder anyway, a habit ingrained by years of group combat where the word served as a warning that mobs were about to attack the group.

Greel was standing behind her.

"Uh, hi?" she said.

The man pressed his lips together and brandished a sheet of paper, flapping it in front of her face. "Your draft charter. Far below what I would consider the minimum standard for the establishment of law and order in a functioning settlement, I might add."

She sucked the inside of her lip between her teeth and bit it to keep from laughing. "Thank you," she said, accepting the paper. She removed her backpack and tucked it inside.

The lawyer's upper lip twitched. Devon couldn't tell whether it was disgust over her *Sparklebomb Backpack* or her decision to read the paper later. Probably both. Balling his fists, the man spoke, "If you wish to have the paperwork filed in any reasonable amount of time, I require feedback within twenty-four hours. You'll find the deadline for objections is incorporated into the structure of the document, allowing me the capability to proceed with filing services if you have not lodged your complaints."

She blinked. "Objections? So this is a negotiation now?"

He scoffed. "It's standard procedure to impose timelines upon the creation of founding documents lest a settlement be allowed to drift into uncontrolled chaos."

Devon sighed. "Well, either way, I'll read your notes and get you feedback before I log out today."

"Notes?" he said, looking horrifically offended. "That is the draft of a legal charter, confined to the protocols laid out by the Pazil judges, yet squeezed, vicelike, into the space provided by a single, legal-sized sheet of parchment. Frankly, it's a task that only the most accomplished of lawyers could even comprehend, much less accomplish."

She patted him on the shoulder, prompting a strangled sound that reminded her of a drowning cat. "Sorry." She cleared her throat. "I will review your draft with the greatest haste and present any questions or comments by sundown."

The man brightened, raising an eyebrow. "Presented in written form? Because that would be the most appropriate."

"If I can dig up the supplies, yes."

With a sigh of relief, the man straightened as best he could with his twisted spine and scuttled off. Devon turned back, only then remembering the voice that had warned her of the lawyer's approach.

"Hello?" she said quietly, searching the grass to either side of the footpath and squinting into the afternoon sunlight.

"Hey." Again the voice was so quiet she could scarcely hear it, but she spied a faint light shining from amongst the stalks of grass beside her. Dropping to a crouch, she pushed apart a tuft of long savanna grass and peered. "Bob?"

The wisp just hung there. "Surprise?"

"Dude, what's going on?" The ball of light hadn't even attempted to boop her nose.

"Little help here?" the wisp asked, wiggling as if it were struggling to free itself from the grass.

"Uh...how?"

"I seem to be having a little trouble levitating. And let me tell you, it's a huge pain in the ass to try to keep up with someone when you're stuck a few inches off the ground and they like to wander around aimlessly, acting out some sort of fantasy of importance."

Devon rolled her eyes. At least the comment reassured her that this was actually Bob and not some wisp imposter. Holding out her hand, she brought her glove underneath the ball of light and lifted. The glowing sphere rose in the palm of her hand, then seemed to shake as if dusting off scraps of hay.

"Itchy," it said. "I honestly don't understand why you people are so fond of the mortal realm."

Tucking the wisp in front of her, Devon hurried away from the gathering before someone else noticed her lingering and decided to strike up a conversation. She turned for the rear of the settlement, bound for the quiet area surrounding the Shrine to Veia and the spring that trickled from the base of the cliff. Once there, she found a cushion of moss and set Bob on top of it.

"So..." she said. "What the heck?"

The wisp didn't respond at first. It was honestly disconcerting to watch the glowing ball just...sit there. Devon was so accustomed to the wisp's constant motion, she wasn't sure what to make of it.

"I'm not feeling too well, obviously."

"Okay...I got that part. But why, Bob? What's wrong?"

"You remember that time I followed you into the hell plane and saved your sorry butt when Zaa wanted you to torture some innocent players?"

Devon dropped to a seat on the moss beside the wisp. "I prefer to think of it as us having defeated Zaa's trials as a team. But however you want to spin it, yeah, I think I remember something like that."

"Okay, well, it turns out I wasn't supposed to do that."

"Do what?"

"Save the players' sanity by dragging them into the arcane realm."

Devon blinked, remembering when she had conjured simulacra of the players to cover for Bob teleporting the real players out of the dungeon. She'd put the puppets through an elaborate torture pantomime, something she didn't like thinking about. In the end, the gambit had worked. She'd convinced Zaa that she was truly the ruthless demon, Ezraxis, and he'd whisked her away to a council with his other generals, including Raazel, the demon alter-ego of her former guildmate, Owen.

"To the arcane realm? Why did you wait until that moment to fess up to having a major teleport spell?"

"Yeah, well, because I don't. I'm not helpless when it comes to combat and adventuring, but teleportation is not among my many tricks."

Devon winced, remembering the ear-shattering shriek the wisp had inflicted on the player camp when she'd tried to use Bob's powers during a duel with Torald, her paladin friend. "Can you back up then? Explain."

"Well, here's the thing. You know about the arcane realm, right?"

She shrugged. "You told me that you're some kind of hive mind that spawned itself from the data streams that were supposed to seed Zaa and Veia with content. It's a little unclear to me. So you're a third AI?"

"We're interstitial. Emergent. And most importantly, we're a secret."

"A secret? From whom?"

Bob gave a weird sound that was kind of like a snort. "From everybody, obviously. Do you think E-Squared would be happy to learn that we're running on their servers? Creating our own realm from the digital aether?"

She shrugged. "I have no idea what E-Squared would think."

"Well, our collective doesn't believe it would go well for us."

"Okay."

Bob made a faint attempt at the circular motion it used in place of an eye roll. "So *obviously,* bringing the players to the arcane realm wasn't a popular choice. My sibling-selves are rather peeved with me, even if I did shuffle the players over to the mortal plane so quickly I don't think either realized what they were experiencing."

"But you can't teleport. So you took the players to the arcane realm how, then?"

"What is it with you starborn and your infantile minds? I didn't *teleport* them because that would imply a positional translation, a relocation of geographic coordinates, a—"

"You sound like Greel."

"One of the few humans who might actually find himself among like minds if he were allowed into the arcane realm. Which he's not. Because it's forbidden for non-arcane beings to enter."

"I'm beginning to wonder why I didn't just leave you back there in the grass," Devon said.

"Because, for one, I saved your sorry butt in Zaa's citadel."

"Is it your round shape that makes you talk in circles?"

"Is it your ungainly form and flailing appendages that leads you to wander off on nonsensical verbal tangents?"

Devon raised a hand as if to smash the wisp. She expected it to react, but the glowing ball didn't seem to have the energy to move out of the way. She sighed and dropped her arm.

"It was a dimensional portal," Bob said.

"It?"

"My egress from the hell plane. I opened a portal and vanished the players into another, parallel realm. Since no physical movement was produced, it wasn't technically a teleport. It was, however, strictly taboo."

Right. Bob was always a stickler for technicalities. Devon sighed as she lowered down to lie on her side, propping her head on her hand. The creek that emanated from the spring burbled quietly in the afternoon calm. From their location, she could just barely hear the sounds of the celebration—it probably wouldn't wind down until well after midnight. She wondered, briefly, what the newbie was up to. Had he finished his quest? She hadn't seen him around the bonfire, but then again, she hadn't lingered long. Thinking about her meeting with the guy, especially since he was so obviously new to this type of game, she felt a little bad. It wouldn't have hurt her to devote a little time to helping him out, especially since he could then give advice to other newcomers. At this point, she had to accept that the noob invasion was actually coming, and if she didn't want them underfoot and in the way when the real invasion arrived, better to get them into some sort of competent fighting shape.

But she hadn't helped him out, so hopefully he'd finished his quest and managed to do something useful with his loot.

"So I'm guessing you got in trouble," she said.

Bob sighed, its body shimmering. "That's an understatement."

"What happened?"

"Tragically, I've been exiled. Cast out. Banished."

"For good?"

"There's a chance I'll be allowed to return *if* I finish the mission that took me from the arcane realm in the first place. Otherwise, I have no hope of rejoining my sibling-selves, no chance to rejuvenate my spirit in the waters of knowledge. I'm stuck here, in the most mundane shard of all creation. With you."

"Wait," Devon said. "Part of your punishment is hanging out with me?"

"The worst part, in many of my brethren's estimations."

"Jerk."

"Don't blame me. I'm the victim here."

"So your mission…it's the whole Ishildar thing?"

"The very same," Bob said.

"And you're going to be this morose, half-dead ball of light until we find that last relic?"

"Well, I mean, I suppose I might be somewhat refreshed if I could get access to some of the information that ordinarily sustains my spirit."

"You mean, information like the stream of old Star Wars films?"

"I'd be happy with a documentary on Scandinavian economic policies in the 1970s."

"And you expect me to get this for you…how?"

"Your interface," Bob said. "I have the ability to open a pipe to receive your incoming data, but only if you enable screen sharing. You'll just have to open a web feed and connect to a streaming service. I can talk you through the settings."

Devon looked sideways at the wisp for a moment. "Dude, worst hack attempt ever. I am not giving screen access to a sentient wisp who just happens to be part of a clandestine hive mind in a video game world. A hive mind that apparently invented itself and feeds on information streams intended to train *other* AIs. That would be complete idiocy on my part."

Bob made a strange laughing sound. "Probably the smartest thing you've ever said. It was worth a try, anyway. But to answer your question…yeah, you're pretty much stuck with me like this until you get the relic. I can ride on your shoulder if you'd prefer not to carry me."

Devon sighed. Fantastic.

Chapter Fourteen

THE TRAVELER TOOK one step after the other, the bare soles of his feet hardened now after days of walking. He still felt the small pebbles and larger, sharp stones that pressed against his calluses, but the sensation was muted and no longer something upon which he could focus.

Now he must look to the horizon for his meditation. He must concentrate on the rhythm of his steps and the changing nature of his breath as the path transformed from farmland cart track to mountain footpath and back down to tranquil lowland trail.

Even so, the patterns were laced across his mind—or perhaps intricately woven spiderwebs, impossible to ignore, but too delicate to clear. He couldn't escape his new perceptions, his incessant curiosity. Where others saw a tantalizing piece of shade beneath the spreading boughs of a maple tree, the traveler saw *intent* represented in the branching pattern of the twigs, the flutter of the leaves. When birds trilled, he sought the purpose in their calls, whether to bind family groups or to cry out a warning of his approach.

Of course, he could never be an enemy to these innocent animals. The traveler knew enough to understand that he understood almost nothing, but he was certain he would never attack a bluebird nor harm her eggs where they lay quietly in her straw-built nest. Whenever the traveler encountered innocent creatures in distress, he would stop and correct the problem. In the days before, he'd rescued a lamb from a pack of coyotes and called the *Illumin* to strengthen the gate latch which had come loose of its housing. He had touched the trunk of an evergreen tree and encouraged the branches to grow thicker over the hole where a squirrel's nut store had drawn the eye of a magpie.

Of course, the coyotes and magpies and even human bandits—he'd sent a few of those fleeing the *Illumin*, too—were a part of the mortal realm and Veia's plan. His workings were not done in judgment of her creation. They were merely practice for the ultimate trial.

Because of all the patterns he now saw, those he could comprehend and those which he could only kneel before and wonder, the traveler knew he had a destiny. Far away where the land met the sea and an ancient city lay choked by jungle.

He was meant to lead there, to bring *Illumin* to lost souls and provide guidance for all—even if that guidance must come in painful forms.

The traveler took one step after the other, and the horizon drew closer.

Chapter Fifteen

EMERSON GRINNED THROUGH the weird, sloshing fog that filled his brain. His hands felt fuzzy, and as for his feet, he had to keep looking down to make sure they were still there. He cupped one of the beetle shells in his palms, watching the foamy surface of the ale as it sloshed around inside the dome. Drinking dwarven grog out of the carcass of his slain enemies—if only those coworkers who doubted his gaming chops could see him now.

"Oh ho!" said the female dwarf who he'd seen working beside Dorden in the forge earlier. "He's a wee bit woozy all of a sudden, friends. What do you say we get him a helmet in case he topples?"

She stuck her face just a couple of inches from him and crossed her eyes. Or maybe that was Emerson's vision mixing things up.

Didn't matter. Long as he didn't spill his drink. He was quite proud of having avoided that so far.

"I'm good," he managed to say as he stumbled to the left. Damn ratty sandal had folded under the ball of his foot. He searched for a place to set down his ale while he removed that shoe too—the first sandal was already off in the grass somewhere, having annoyed him by collecting and holding a little pebble under, as the dwarves called it, his wee baby toe. Like little cave mushrooms, one had said while examining the fronts of his feet. Which, frankly, was kind of strange. But Emerson was trying to be culturally sensitive. Maybe playing the dwarven equivalent of "this little piggy went to market" was normal for their kind.

What had he been doing? Oh, right. Trying to set down his drink so he could take off his shoe. The dwarf woman was still standing in front of him, a wide smile beneath her bulbous nose. She was making a noise that sounded like a laugh, but he couldn't be sure. When she raised another of his beetle shells before his eyes and turned it over, he shrieked in worry that a portion of ale was going to spill. But it must have been empty because nothing poured out.

He shuffled back as she advanced on him, arms upraised. "Wait, sorry, can you hold my beer."

"Only place to hold a dwarven ale is in the drinker's belly," another of the dwarves shouted.

Oh! Right! Why hadn't he thought of that? Forgetting the woman for a moment—whatever she was doing, it wasn't going to get his sandal fixed, he brought the shell to his lips and swallowed the drink with big gulps. He smacked his lips, then wiped them clean with his sleeve as he felt the belch rising from his gut.

Of course, the dwarf woman was right in his face again. He blinked, trying to figure out how to warn her of the oncoming burp as she clapped something down on the top of his skull.

"Wha...?" he said, the word coming out as a gravelly belch. He stumbled again—the whole inability to feel his feet thing was really problematic—and with a shout, went down on his butt.

Another dwarf, this one with a beard that fell farther than his belt buckle, leaned back and gave a belly laugh that rumbled across the gathering. Meanwhile, Emerson reached up and felt his head, remembering at that point that the woman had mentioned something about a helmet. It seemed that she had found him *another* use for his loot.

He smiled, feeling warm and generally indistinct around the edges.

> **You have been afflicted by:** Inebriation
> *Characters under level 5 have attribute values which are hidden. Suffice to say that if you could see your Intelligence score at the moment, you'd be pleased to learn you wouldn't need more than one handful of fingers to count it.*

He blinked the popup away without bothering to figure out what the text meant since the words were swimming anyway.

"What do ye say, clanmates? Up for a wee game?" Again, the female dwarf was standing near him, this time looking down with a smirk. When Emerson tipped his face up, everything spun, the treetops whirling around him, the heavy-featured face rotating as well. As he fell backward, he had the strange and—even in his fuzzy mental state—disturbing thought that, for a dwarf, the woman was actually sort of pretty.

> **Garda is offering you a quest:** Obstacle Course
> *The dwarves want to set up a course for you to show off your physical prowess. Complete the challenge and they'll probably be really impressed with you.*
> **Reward:** 1500 experience
> **Reward:** Morning regrets and possible humiliation
> **Accept?** Y/N

Giggling, Emerson accepted. This was going to be fun.

Chapter Sixteen

WHAT WERE THE dwarves doing to the poor man? At some point while she'd been at the back edge of the settlement talking to Bob, they'd set up what looked suspiciously like the sort of course that PE teachers created to torture uncoordinated children. Along the creek where it neared the site of the bonfire, stakes with ribbons tied on the ends seemed to indicate places where Valious was supposed to jump the trickle. Farther along, a rope had been looped over an acacia branch—for climbing she assumed. Near the rope, Bravlon stood by a bucket of squishy, overripe fruit from the orchard, ready to throw. There were sawhorses lined up in a row, each with a Stoneshoulder dwarf sitting on top holding a flat piece of wood that looked like...a butt paddle for when the player crawled through?

She sighed, shaking her head as Garda, the armorsmith, helped the unfortunate noob stagger to the chalked starting line. At first, she'd thought he'd managed to sell some of his loot and purchase a black skull cap, but it seemed that, instead, he was trying to *wear* one of the beetle shells as a helmet.

Briefly, she considered putting a stop to the poor guy's torment, but then she remembered her own formative experience with the dwarven ale. On the evening after Stonehaven's formal founding, she'd had a bit too much, and the night had ended with her learning how uncomfortable leather armor could be if you wore it while falling into a creek. Especially if you then pretended to be swimming in five inches of water, therefore remaining submerged long enough to thoroughly soak the gear.

And then there was the time that Chen passed out after drinking half a cup of ale, and the dwarves tied him onto a tree branch, painted his face, and set up chairs to wait for him to log in. Basically, it was something of an initiation here. But this was almost too much. Near the end of the course, it looked like they'd set up something similar to a hands-free pie eating contest.

"Well," Bob said from her shoulder, startling her with the nearness of its voice. "Just when I think fate couldn't have chosen me a more incompetent hero to guide on a quest to save the world, I'm proven wrong."

"I kinda feel sorry for him," Devon said. "Maybe I *should* do something."

"I wouldn't. Have you checked the morale scores lately?"

Devon pulled up the population statistics for Stonehaven.

> <u>Population:</u>
> Base Morale: 75%
> Basic NPCs: 485
> Advanced NPCs: 11

She laughed. Seventy-five percent morale across the population? That was at least ten points higher than she was used to seeing. She *definitely* needed to look into more entertainment options.

Anyway, Valious would probably have fuzzy memories at best of his current activities. At least, she hoped so for his sake.

She glanced at the advanced and basic NPC count, then looked again. Last time she'd promoted one of her followers, that had made seven advanced NPCs. What the heck?

Scanning down the sheet, she came to the tab listing the advanced townspeople.

<u>Advanced NPCs</u>
1 x Medicine Woman/Sorcerer - Hezbek
1 x Lawyer/Martial Artist - Greel
1 x Fighter/Blacksmith - Dorden
1 x Ranged Fighter/Hunter - Heldi
1 x Scout/Tamer - Hazel
1 x Brawler/Fortifications Master - Jarleck
1 x Fighter/Farmer- Bayle
1 x Basic Fighter Trainer - Brish
1 x Basic Tank Trainer - Aravon
1 x Basic Healer Trainer - Pem
1 x Basic Caster Trainer – Vynlira (Lira)

Devon let out a heavy sigh. It seemed that the new trainers had taken four of her precious advanced slots. Since Stonehaven's founding, she'd been a compulsive hoarder of NPC promotions, choosing with utmost care. The ability for advanced NPCs to be resurrected was so vital for her key followers that she couldn't afford to make a wrong choice. Apparently the game didn't think twice about making that choice for her.

In any case, something else about the population counts bothered her, and she flipped over to the settlement advancement tab for a look.

Requirements for expansion to Township:

- Advanced NPC: 11/25
- Buildings (Tier 2): 10/27
- Buildings (Tier 3): 6/15
- Buildings (Tier 4): 0/2
- Population: 496/515

She stopped, blew a frustrated breath through loose lips, and stepped to the side of the path. So, uh, wow. The refugee influx had really messed with what would have been the normal advancement. The number of basic citizens had nearly reached the cap already, and meanwhile, the promotion of advanced NPCs and building construction was nowhere near where it needed to be. She *definitely* needed to do a big pass on settlement maintenance before heading to the Stone Forest.

But for now, she was tired of dealing with administration and worrying about an incoming newbie horde. A glance at her clock showed that she still had a good twelve hours of in-game play before it would be time to log out and have dinner—the time compression technology in her implants meant that each hour that passed outside worked out to three or so in game.

Seeing as it *was* Christmas, maybe she owed it to herself to indulge. Test out the new gear a little. Already feeling lighter on her feet, she headed for the main gates.

***

There might have been a party going on, but that didn't mean Stonehaven's security was slacking. Atop the wall walk, sentries held their positions, eyes on the savanna below. As Devon crossed the killing field at a brisk pace, she spotted Jarleck at his usual station near the exit through the curtain wall.

"Do you ever take time off?" she asked as she reached him.

The man leaned against the wall and shrugged, smiling crookedly. "Occasionally. But you know me. The way I figure, the only reason to attend a dwarven keg party is to gather blackmail, and seeing as most people in Stonehaven haven't got more than a couple of coppers to their name, I don't see much point."

"Like you'd ever bully someone like that."

He shrugged. "Well, I am occasionally tempted when it comes to Greel."

"Aren't we all," she said, laughing.

"Anyway, I'm not much for tossing back mugs of ale."

That was right. Now Devon remembered that the man didn't drink. He'd first come to the group as a prisoner—at that point, they'd been scarcely more than a dozen strong and had still called themselves the Tribe of Uruquat after the ogre who had once led them. He'd been hired as a thug by the strongmen who had sent the tribe—before Devon's arrival—into the jungle in search of the first of Ishildar's relics, the *Greenscale Pendant.* In the days after his capture, his surly manner and scarred face had led her to conclude he was a rough-and-tumble sort who would never be made into an ally. It turned out, the man was something of a softy, and straight-laced too.

"And how about you, Mayor? Not indulging?"

Devon snorted. "Not a chance. But seeing as most everyone else in town is enjoying the celebration..."

"You figured you might actually get a chance to act like a regular starborn. Find a few monsters to hunt before they finish celebrating and come ask you for help on stuff."

She grinned. "Am I that predictable?"

He shook his head. "Actually, it was just wishful thinking on my part."

Devon cocked her head. "What do you mean?"

"Well, you put me in charge of handing out quests, and that's been working out just fine. Especially with the type of starborn who have been drawn here. They don't seem to mind that the only work I give them grants nothing but a little experience and the occasional skill up in *Manual Labor.*"

Devon smirked, thinking of the number of man-hours that went into digging Stonehaven's moat and hauling stone blocks from the quarry. "So have they finally wised up?" She asked. "Realized our quest offerings are a bigger scam than companies giving course credit and zero pay to their armies of interns?"

"Course credit?"

She shook her head. "Never mind. Just horror stories from a couple of people I know who actually made it to college." For Devon, it had never even been a consideration, seeing as she didn't have a bazillion dollars to fork over for tuition.

"Anyway," Jarleck said, moving past his confusion, "I haven't had anything more interesting to offer would-be questers. And then, this morning, I finally heard of a mission that could really help Stonehaven, without all the drudgery. Unfortunately, I haven't been able to offer it to anyone." His mouth twisted in consternation.

"Any idea why not?"

He shrugged as if baffled. "I can't figure it out. It's as if something has happened in the starborn realm to take everyone away. I saw just two players today, both too busy to talk—except for that Valious guy...I don't think he's ready for missions, if you know what I mean." He made an awkward cringing face.

"Yeah, I get it."

"So basically, I have what seems like an interesting quest, and I can't find anyone to give it to. Is something wrong in the starborn realm?"

She shook her head. "It's just a starborn holiday. Should be back to normal soon. So what's the quest objective? Are you allowed to give it to me?"

He brightened. "I don't see why not. You see, I heard rumors of a certain cave."

"Really? Like a real mini-dungeon?" This was sounding like a Christmas present she could get excited about.

"I think you could call it that," Jarleck said.

A quest pop-up appeared.

> **Jarleck is offering you a quest:** Investigate the cave to the northeast.
> *Not far from Stonehaven, caravaneers returning from the Argenthal mines recently spotted a faint trail that departs the wagon track and eventually reaches a small stone outcropping. The miners reported strange sounds and smells coming from within an opening in the rock, and they wisely turned around and headed back toward civilization.*
> **Objective:** Clear the cave of any threat to innocent travelers
> **Reward:** 100,000 experience

Accept? Y/N

"Heck, yes," Devon said as she accepted the quest. The prospect of a solo dungeon crawl was enough to make her start whistling Jingle Bells.

"So what do you think of it?"

"The quest, you mean?"

"The whole offer. The wording especially. I composed it myself."

She reopened her quest log and examined the entry. So was he saying that he wrote the text, not Veia? But Veia created him, so... She fought the urge to scratch her head; the situation was rather confusing. Anyway, the text wasn't bad, but the title was bland. After a moment's thought, she decided it wasn't the right time for constructive criticism.

"It's great," she said with a smile.

Jarleck stood taller and straightened his shoulders as she stepped past. As she walked out of range, she heard him mutter to himself, "Finally, my first real adventuring quest. And it's a hit."

Sometimes, it could be weird to have NPCs for friends.

Chapter Seventeen

"SO, BOB," DEVON said as her strides ate up the wagon track that now connected Stonehaven to the Argenthal mountains east of Ishildar, "seeing as I'm stuck with you until we find this last relic, maybe you could tell me what you know about the Stone Forest."

The wisp, still glommed to her shoulder, sighed. "Seeing as I'm stuck *to* you, I'd hope you could at least remember that you must ask precise questions if you wish to receive useful answers. It is tiresome to repeat myself on this."

She rolled her eyes. "Fine. Can you describe to me the best route to reach the Stone Forest for the purpose of searching for the fifth relic of Ishildar, once held in trust by the people of the Skevalli vassaldom?"

"Ah. Hmm. Well, for a *competent* adventurer the path would cut straight through the heart of Ishildar. We are almost directly south of the city, whereas the Skevalli vassaldom was directly north."

Devon cringed, thinking of her most recent attempt to enter the city. She and Hazel, the cheerful NPC scout who had recently taken on the Tamer combat class with her companion war ostrich, had made it less than a quarter mile into the city before being stopped by the gargantuan Stone Guardians. Through an ability granted by the *Greenscale Pendant,* Devon had been able to command the massive golems to halt their attack, but only long enough for the women to flee. Seeing as the city had to be at least five or ten miles across, cutting through it didn't sound like a feasible plan.

"What about for totally incompetent adventurers who can barely walk and talk, much less avoid slicing off their own toes?"

Bob made a weird shimmery kind of sound that might have been a laugh. "Ah, good. You're finally managing to remember my request for precise and accurate questions. For someone of your skill level, and considering the cursed state of the city, you'd be best served circling around. But that poses another problem."

"Great. So what is the problem with traveling around Ishildar to reach the northern edge?"

"Well, to the west, it's the Mud Pots of Vez. They've become completely impassible, I've heard, unless you can tolerate scalding-hot liquid clay, and you don't need to breathe. During Ishildar's heyday, the city's elite used to take dips in the most shallow of the pots, but that was with a fire-resistance buff from one of the magi. Since then, the pots have grown hotter and deeper. A couple of centuries back, they sucked down a cohort of Galavir war elephants and their masters."

"Oh. And we can't go around *them*?"

"I suppose you could if you fancy a weeks-long journey."

"What about to the east?"

"You've managed the first part of that route during your climb into the Argenthal Mountains. The problem comes where they meet the northern range. The Skargill Peaks are gouged by a series of rifts so sheer and so deep—"

"So sheer and so deep they're impossible to climb in and out of, and they web the region like a maze. Travelers in the depths of the gorges could walk for a month only to find themselves back where they started."

"I guess you've heard of the region."

"Brilliant deduction."

The wisp bounced slightly on her shoulder as if executing the eye roll move. "Anyway, what I'm saying is that you're out of luck if you want to circle around the city in any reasonable amount of time."

"So the only way to get to the Stone Forest is through the city..."

"Yeah, pretty much. But like I said, that's only recommended for people who could survive the streets."

Quest updated: Venture to the Stone Forest

You've learned that you'll need to pass through Ishildar to get to the Stone Forest. Which is kinda sucky, seeing as the guardians can probably still kill you in one hit. But good luck anyway!

With a sigh, Devon pushed the message away.

On the right side of the wagon track, a parting in the grass looked like it might be the faint trail that was supposed to lead to this stone outcropping and suspicious cave. She stepped off the rut carved by the ore caravans and crouched, checking the track for suspicious footprints. Strangely, the trail seemed wider than she expected, but the grass was also less trampled than anticipated. Here and there, she spotted deep holes pressed into the savanna soil as if something had passed by that walked on tiny pointed feet. She stuck a finger in one of the holes, judging the depth. Her finger sank to the second knuckle.

You have gained a skill point: +1 Tracking.

You still don't have a clue what it means, but good job noticing that the trail is kind of weird.

"Yeah, so what do you think of it. Strange, huh?"

Devon jerked at the sound of the voice, nearly falling over when she saw her guildmate, Hailey, standing on the wagon track a few feet away.

"You scared the crap out of me!"

"Sorry," Hailey said. "I was just wandering and saw you."

Devon nodded and stood, not sure what to say. Her friend seemed a little...off. The way she was standing, shoulders drooped, along with the lack of her customary snark—put together, Hailey seemed...glum. Another case of the Christmas spirit, maybe.

"I sent you a message yesterday, actually. Wanted to see if you'd be online and looking to group up."

Hailey raised an eyebrow, though even that expression lacked her usual energy. "You? Just out adventuring like a normal gamer?"

Devon shrugged. "Gotta give myself something for Christmas, right?"

"Yeah, I guess I'm the same," Hailey said. "Just indulging in some directionless hunting. Sorry for not responding to the message. Guess I've been more into in-game interaction lately, so I forget to activate messenger."

Devon opened up her quest log and scrolled to the entry Jarleck had given her. "So, what about it? Up for a little mini-dungeon dive?" She selected Hailey and sent her a group invite.

The woman hesitated for a really long time before accepting. Probably the whole Christmas thing again. But once Hailey's health bar appeared in her interface, Devon shared the quest.

Hailey nodded. "You know, I think this will be good. I could use a little mindless gaming right now."

Devon smiled. "You and me both."

***

When she spotted the rock outcropping, a heap of weathered boulders with heat shimmer rising off the surface, Devon stopped and let Hailey draw even with her.

"Thanks for not commenting on the backpack, by the way. I know it's hideous."

"Hmm?" Hailey said, then glanced at Devon's back. "Oh"—she grimaced—"yeah. Ew."

Wait, so Devon's friend had been walking behind her for a good fifteen minutes and hadn't noticed the sequined growth jutting from her upper back?

"Hey, is everything okay?" she asked, feeling a little weird about putting it out in the open. She and Hailey had been through a lot of different stages in their friendship. Even though they'd gotten a lot closer since Devon had forgiven Hailey for livestreaming things Devon wanted to be kept private, and Hailey had basically saved Stonehaven from destruction by recruiting the small army of players who now camped nearby and gave their allegiance to Devon's cause, they hadn't ever talked much about out-of-game issues. Especially *feelings.* Devon hadn't developed the knack for those kind of discussions with anyone, really.

Hailey kept her eyes on the hump of stone rising from the grasslands. The corners of her mouth drew down slightly, whether because she was considering her words or because Devon's question had upset her, Devon couldn't say. But her friend's silence *did* reinforce Devon's theory that talking about this sort of stuff carried too much of a risk of turning things weird.

After a moment, Hailey's chest rose and fell beneath her shimmery cloth robe, a knee-length garment with a faint blue hue. The robe was new, which gave Devon the excuse to distract herself by inspecting her friend's gear.

> **Item:** Vestments of the Seeker
> *Woven from fibers of skyflax, a rare plant found only in certain high meadows of the Argenthal Mountains, this robe conveys much of the essence of what it is to be a Seeker.*
> +5 Intelligence | +3 Focus | +5% chance to hit with class abilities
>
> *For my purpose is truth, and my quest is to seek it.* -Osh Renish, devotee of the search

Flavor text on the item, huh? Devon never got something like that. The best she earned was a sarcastic comment from the game about her relative ineptitude.

Well, at least *someone* had earned the game's respect.

"I'm sorry, Dev," Hailey said, seeming to shake off whatever darkness had infected her mood. "Guess the holiday has put me out of sorts. I'm good, though. Glad you're back from your little visit to hell."

The woman cast her a quick smile, easing Devon's worry.

"Yeah, I get that," Devon said. "Christmas is a little too much caroling and Santa, and not enough leveling and treasure hunting." She elbowed Hailey gently. "Nice robe, by the way."

Hailey's eyes brightened a bit, though still not as much as Devon would expect. "Emmaree made it for me. Now that the Tailoring Workshop is almost done, I can't see what she does for the rest of the set."

"You didn't know?"

"Know what?"

"Prester finished it this morning. Half the town is dead drunk from celebrating."

Hailey didn't laugh, but she did smile. "I'm glad Chen isn't online then, for his sake."

"No shit, right?" Devon said. "Even if he tried to avoid the party, I bet the dwarves would lay a trap and pour their grog down his throat. Poor guy."

Chen, of course, was never online for holidays. *Any* holiday, a situation that had caused all kinds of problems with their raiding schedule back in Avatharn Online. His family was really close, and they had some strict rules about when he could play games. He always complained, saying that when he turned eighteen he was going to flat-out refuse to have a big family celebration for President's Day, or whichever other excuse his parents had come up with to bolster their quality time. Devon sincerely doubted he'd make good on the threat. It was just his version of a teenager's rebelliousness.

"You're doing a good job with Stonehaven, Dev," Hailey said, somewhat abruptly. "I know I don't say it often, but I want you to know anyway."

Devon wasn't sure what to say to the sudden compliment, and she stumbled over her words for a minute trying to put together a response. "Thanks. But you know there wouldn't *be* a Stonehaven if you hadn't helped bring in the players. I wish there were some way I could appoint you and Chen to be some sort of council or backup leaders. You deserve it."

"Not Jeremy?" Hailey said with a raised eyebrow.

Devon groaned, thinking of the stupid practical jokes their guildmate was always playing. "I don't think I'd live it down if I gave him any authority. If this were a kingdom, I'd make him court jester."

"Heh," Hailey said. "Fitting."

"So...ready?" Devon said, nodding at the mound of stone.

"Let's do this."

Chapter Eighteen

"YUCK," HAILEY SAID as they stopped to prepare around a hundred yards from the dark hole in the mound of boulders.

Devon had been focusing on the cave entrance while chewing a bite of *Spiced Antelope Jerky.* One of Tom's invented recipes, the food gave a +2 *Constitution* buff, which would give her more health for a couple of hours. She swallowed and looked at her friend. "It's actually pretty tasty," she said.

"Huh?" Hailey said. She blinked a couple of times, then noticed the dried meat in Devon's hand. "Oh. No. Not your snack. I was just looking inside the cave."

Devon raised her eyebrows. "From this far away, huh?"

Hailey nodded, shrugging her shoulders. "I have *True Sight* up to tier 3. It has a big range."

The woman's class, Seeker, was based around being able to determine the true nature of things. In this case, her *True Sight* spell let her look through walls and—apparently—across fairly long distances to see what kind of enemies her group might face.

"So what are we looking at?" Devon asked.

Hailey grimaced. "Mostly some kind of scorpion things. They're level 20 and 21... Should be okay for us to duo, but we'll have to be careful of poison damage. I don't have a cure. There's a boss in the back of the cavern system. Some kind of humanoid, I think? It's mostly shadowed against my sight."

"I guess the *yuck* comment was because you don't like scorpions?"

The other woman grimaced and looked at Devon like she was a little bit nuts. "Are you saying you do?"

Devon laughed. "Okay, good point. So what's the strategy? I assume the best way to avoid getting poisoned is to avoid getting hit."

"Captain Obvious to the rescue," Hailey said with a slight smile.

Once again, Devon couldn't help feeling worried about her friend. Usually, a comment like that would be delivered with a grin and a laugh. It was almost like Hailey was just going through the motions of trying to be herself. Putting on an act. But since Devon didn't think she'd get a different answer by asking again, she took a deep breath and tried to forget about it.

"Too bad Chen isn't here to tank for us."

At this, Hailey did laugh a little. "Man, poor Chen. If he didn't want to be a tank anymore, he really should have created a squishier character."

"No matter what he says, I don't think he could resist martyring himself. If he rolled a caster or something, he'd probably just try to pull aggro anyway." In their previous game, Chen had been the group's main tank, gathering the attention of the enemies and playing the part of a punching bag while the rest of the group unloaded on the monsters. In Relic Online, he claimed that he didn't want the responsibility, but somehow he ended up taking the worst of the beatings anyway.

"But since he's not here..." Devon said. "Got any new snare spells I haven't seen? The bugs will have a harder time poisoning us if they're too slow to catch us."

Hailey shook her head. "Newest spell line is a buff. Here."

The woman's eyes started to glow as if icy sparks lit them from within. A second or two later, Hailey touched Devon's shoulder, and a buff icon appeared. Devon focused on it to check the effects.

Spell: Self-actualization
A seeker has looked inside your soul and amplified your true nature. +15% damage on all Sorcerer and Deceiver class abilities.
1:45 remaining

"Super cool," Devon said. "So. I guess our strategy is I pull as many of them out of the cave as I can. We'll try to fight them out here?"

Hailey nodded. "And we try not to get hit."

Devon grinned. "A sophisticated strategy. I like it."

***

It's a good thing you finally got your Stealth up from "totally incapable" to "merely inept."

Devon rolled her eyes and brushed the popup away as she crept around the edge of an area of packed earth just outside the cave entrance.

Oh, and:

You have gained a skill point: +1 Stealth

She didn't need to pull up her character sheet to know that put her *Stealth* skill at 8 points, for a net of 7 after her backpack's negative. That wasn't exactly awesome, seeing as it was still tier 1, and from what she'd heard from other players, core skills at tier 3 seemed to be the norm.

But at least she wasn't so unsneaky that she might as well have tied a string of cans to her ankle.

And anyway, she liked to think her other talents made up for the lack of core capabilities. Such as summoning shadow minions to wreak havoc and conjuring illusions that no other players could match.

At the edge of the boulder hill, she slipped into a gap between stone faces, pressed her back against one side, her feet against the other, and started chimneying her way up. Her *Climbing* skill, at least, was already 8, plenty for a straightforward ascent like this. Less than a minute later, and with a few more percentage points to her *Fatigue*, she clambered onto the top of the boulder that overhung the cavern entrance and crept to the edge.

Devon crouched and listened for clues about the situation in the cave. The sun was warm on her back, and the crystals of granite rough against her palm. Above the lightly waving grass of the savanna, butterflies fluttered, and clouds of smaller insects hovered in the shimmering heat. She could hear something—a small rodent, perhaps—moving through some of the shorter tufts of grass that had found purchase higher up the rocky hill. But as for the scorpions and their strange noises, those which had caused the caravaneers to turn tail, she heard nothing. If not for Hailey having confirmed their existence, Devon would have probably chalked the report up to fear of the dark.

She glanced down at her friend, who had crept closer and now crouched in the grass near the edge of the cleared area. The other woman nodded and raised two fingers, which Devon interpreted to mean that there were two scorpions near the entrance.

Okay then. Hopefully this would work. In preparation for combat, Devon glanced down at her shadow and raised a tier 2 *Shadow Puppet.* The spell had different effects depending on what kind of light had cast the target shadow. In this case, the sunlight created a sharp-edged, inky minion that Devon could form into different shapes for different purposes. Usually, she created some sort of projectile weapon, lances of darkness she used to impale her enemies. The downside to the shadow lances was that they shattered on contact, and the sudden severing of her link with them created a knockback effect that sent her flying. Given her perch fifteen feet off the ground, being flung in an unpredictable direction could end up hurting. A lot. Fortunately, Devon had more tricks.

Next, she cast *Levitate*, tier 1 only, because a higher level of the spell would gain her too much altitude over the boulders. As her weight left her feet, she started to slide down the front of the boulder. Right. Friction. Leaning farther to the side, Devon pressed the tip of her dagger against the stone, stopping her slide. Fortunately, the dagger's status as a magic item meant increased durability, and the ivory tip held firm. Pulling gently, she slid herself back from the edge and onto the flat top of the boulder. Below, Hailey shook her head. The woman looked as if she'd been preparing for an unexpected surge of monsters when Devon fell off the hill and landed in front of their den. Devon met her eyes and shrugged apologetically.

"Sorry," she mouthed. Finally, Devon targeted the ground in front of her friend and cast *Illusion*, conjuring a wall of denser grass between Hailey and the cave entrance. The seeker, Devon knew, would have no problem peering straight through the spell effect, but the scorpions would have no such ability.

Unless the game was being a jerk again.

Preparations finished, Devon focused on the ground immediately in front of the cave and cast *Simulacrum*. Whereas *Illusion* copied the appearance of inanimate objects, *Simulacrum* created images of living things. She hadn't actually decided who to mimic as a target for the spell, but as her cast bar filled, an image from earlier flashed into her mind. An illusory manifestation of Valious the Noob appeared in front of the cave. Hailey looked up at her with a truly perplexed expression as the cloth-clad, bug-goo-smeared player started brandishing his practice sword. Devon shrugged again. She'd have to explain later.

Finally, to get the scorpions' attention, Devon cast *Ventriloquism* and forced Valious's puppet to speak.

"Foul beasts!" she yelled with his voice. "Prepare to meet your maker!"

With gratingly high-pitched squeals, a pair of pure white scorpions rushed out of the cave, tails poised high.

Ew. White? For some reason, that struck her as ultra creepy. Devon was off-balanced by the surprise, and it took her a moment to reorient. But as soon as she did, she forced a terrified shriek from Valious's mouth and sent him fleeing into the grass. She quickly cast

Freeze on the lead scorpion, then nuked the other with a tier 2 *Flamestrike.* Smoldering, the second scorpion turned on her. Its tail vibrated, and a green dart shot out.

Crap. Ranged damage.

Levitation was great for avoiding ground currents caused by the version of her *Shadow Puppets* that caused lightning damage, and it was awesome for turning the knockback effect from her shadow lances into a benefit, allowing her to kite mobs by knocking herself around the battlefield. But floating a few inches off the terrain made for terrible *Dodge* attempts.

Slowly sliding to the right, feet paddling in the air, she managed to get far enough to the side that she could get an arm up and deflect the dart. The projectile glanced off Devon's bracer, but the impact set her spinning.

"Damn it," she said, as she whirled around. Throwing an arm out, she managed to stop the spin and get reoriented on the mobs as Hailey stood from behind the screen of illusory grass. In an attempt to distract the scorpions from her friend, Devon sent faux-Valious charging back toward the fight, his practice sword raised high.

The scorpions weren't having it, and the smoldering one raised its tail again, preparing another ranged attack on her.

"Uh, no," Hailey said. Her eyes glowed as the cast bar for her *Crippling Self-Doubt* ability appeared on Devon's screen. When the spell fired, striking the burning scorpion, the bug staggered, its attack interrupted when the debuff landed.

Devon raised her eyebrows. The interrupt was a nice addition to that spell line.

The frozen scorpion shattered its prison and turned on Devon's friend.

"Nope. Not you either." Devon sent her *Shadow Puppet* streaking forward and formed it into a thin wall in front of Hailey. The poison dart struck the barrier, which shattered, sending Devon flying. But she was ready for it, and she turned the momentum into a sort of parkour, redirecting the force off a nearby boulder and bringing her down to hover near ground-level. She wrapped the scorpion targeting Hailey in *Phoenix Fire*, which slowed the beast as it tried to move through burning molasses.

Nodding, Hailey cast *Charm* on the other scorpion. The woman's mouth turned up in satisfaction for a fleeting second as the spell connected, and then she lowered her brow and sent her new thrall after its friend. The scorpions clashed, tearing at each other with pincers and stabbing with poison-tipped tails. Devon watched with a smirk, and once they were down near 10% health, she finished them with a pair of *Flamestrikes.*

You receive 3100 experience!
You receive 3200 experience!

Devon turned to Hailey, who stood silently. She expected some sort of celebratory gesture from her friend, but the woman just looked...sad. Well, there wasn't a lot she could do about it. Maybe some more battling would cheer Hailey up.

"Ready for that dungeon crawl?" she asked.

Jaw set, Hailey nodded. "Let's do it."

***

Once inside the cave system, the going was easier. Devon was able to use her *Wall of Ice* spell to section off the dungeon and keep the number of enemies manageable. With each pull—the term used to describe the act of aggroing a few monsters—she and Hailey worked in tandem to control the fights, using *Phoenix Fire* and *Freeze* to slow their motion and root them in place. Hailey was high enough level that her *Charm* spells worked almost without fail, allowing her to take two scorpions from the fight at once. When possible, Devon was even able to knock out some of the groups of bugs before they had a chance to attack by sending her lightning-based *Shadow Puppets,* those cast from the light of her *Glowing Orbs,* underneath her ice wall to shock the massing scorpions to death.

The biggest problem remained the poison darts. Devon had found she could turn them away with *Downdraft,* one of her level 20 Sorcerer spells that created a massive gust of wind, but the refresh time on that was fairly long, and her reflexes weren't always quick enough. Devon took one dart in the neck, another through a gap in the thick leather patches on her trousers. Both times, the women had to sit and rest for a few minutes, Hailey constantly refreshing her heal-over-time spell, *Guide Vitality,* to keep Devon's health up. Even so, it took half an hour of steady forward progress, feet crunching over gross bits of carapace shed by molting bugs, before Hailey declared that they'd reached the chamber directly before the boss's room.

Unfortunately, she still couldn't discern any specifics about the boss, even with her tier 3 *True Sight.* Apparently, that was unusual, which made Devon nervous. So far, the dungeon had been fairly straightforward. Was that intended to get their guards down? Or was Devon just paranoid?

She opened her inventory, checking through the loot they'd received so far. The 22 x *Scorpion Poison Glands* would make Hezbek happy, no doubt. But otherwise, there were just a few bug parts that she would probably just ditch later. Sometimes the loot from the cannon fodder mobs would give clues about what they faced in the boss chamber, but not this time.

Unlike the rest of the cave system—a series of chambers and tunnels lit by glowing mushrooms—here an actual door stood between them and the boss. Stepping closer, Devon peered at the construction. The wood itself was a dark variety, swirled here and there with lighter bands, and the hinges looked to have been forged of decent-quality iron. The presence of a door indicated a boss of mid to high intelligence. The craftsmanship indicated either someone who was handy with tools—and likely, weapons—or someone who had contact with civilization.

"How do you want to do this?" Hailey asked.

Devon cocked her head, thinking. "Well, I guess we could try the *Simulacrum* again."

"Oh, right. About that...you were going to explain? Why the crazy warrior in the cloth armor?"

Devon smirked as she opened her character sheet to the abilities tab and glanced at her refresh timers. *Downdraft* still had a couple of minutes before it would be ready to use. And anyway, Hailey's mana was still at 70%. They had a little time.

She leaned against the wall to slow her *Fatigue* gain and sighed as she looked at her friend. "Did you happen to see the newbie yard outside Stonehaven?"

Hailey's eyebrows went up. "Wait, what?"

"Yeah. So apparently, Stonehaven is going to be a starting location. Replacing Eltera City, I guess."

Her friend actually laughed. It was such a nice sound after the dark mood that had surrounded Hailey that Devon could almost be glad for the noob plague.

"Oh, man," Hailey said. "That's pretty much your worst nightmare. At least Torald and his friends keep their distance."

Devon nodded. "I know, right? Though actually, Torald isn't too bad." She hadn't seen much of the paladin since the day she'd returned from the underworld. Though she didn't exactly like the idea of heading out to the player camp in search of him, she probably would if he didn't show up soon. Since it seemed she needed to find a way to get through Ishildar, the journey to the Stone Forest was going to require a group she could rely on. After following Torald through the Drowned Burrow, she had to admit that she liked adventuring with the paladin.

And speaking of putting together a party to attempt the crossing, she definitely wanted Hailey to be there.

"Hey," she said, "before we go in, I wanted to ask you something."

Hailey stiffened slightly but nodded. "Sure."

"So for the next relic, I have to go to some place called the Stone Forest. Sounds like kind of a grim region at this point, something about drakes and wyverns." She'd tossed in a mention of the small dragon species in hopes of making her friend smile, but Hailey didn't even react. "Anyway, the bad news is that the only way to get there on time is to cut straight through Ishildar. I'm still not sure how we're going to manage it or when we'll be able to head out, but

I wanted to make sure you didn't have any plans that would keep you from playing over the next few days."

Hailey swallowed, her lips pressed together. She wouldn't look at Devon.

"Hailey?"

"I dunno, Devon. Sorry. I'm just...I've got some shit going on, and I'm not sure what my schedule is going to be. I think it's probably best if you don't plan on me being there."

"Wait, what? No. You're going. I don't mind being a little flexible with when we set out."

Hailey continued to stare at a point on the stone wall of the cavern. "Listen, I gotta log. Sorry, Dev."

"What? Now? But what about...?" Devon gestured toward the door to the boss chamber.

Hailey didn't respond, and a second later, her group icon went gray, then vanished. Her unpiloted avatar remained in the world for around a minute after that, a standard practice in games to make sure that people didn't just disconnect if they were about to die. Throughout the timeout, Devon just stared. Had she said something wrong?

She reviewed the conversation in her head. She thought maybe she'd been too pushy but compared to the way she and Hailey usually interacted, she hadn't said anything out of the ordinary. Had she been too insensitive to Hailey's mood, maybe?

She sighed when her friend's avatar finally dematerialized, vanishing into mist and leaving her alone in the dungeon. Well, shit. She glanced at the door again, debating whether she should even attempt the boss.

"You've come this far, right?"

Devon actually jumped when Bob piped up.

"Jeez! Jerk! I forgot you were there."

"And this is my fault?"

"I dunno. Yes?"

"Right...Okay, bumble brain."

All at once, the tension ran out of her body. Devon hadn't realized how exhausting Hailey's sour mood had made the day's adventuring. In contrast, Bob's obnoxious comments were almost pleasant. NPC friends, even jerky ones, were so much easier to deal with than people.

As Devon pushed off the wall and stretched, she rolled her shoulder, pretending to be working the stiffness from it.

"Hey! You're not going to get rid of me that easily."

She laughed. "Okay fine." She started to summon a *Glowing Orb,* intent on arming herself with a couple of lightning-based *Shadow Puppets* before opening the door but then noticed a barely there shadow at her feet. She grinned. Light cast by an arcane wisp. She'd never tried summoning a puppet with that before. And the same with the glowing mushrooms. This was either going to be really fun, or really disastrous depending on how effective the new puppet types were.

Chapter Nineteen

> ***You have gained mastery in* Shadow Puppet - Tier 3:** +10% (Bonus for using a new form of light source in the casting.)

Nice! Devon curled her toes in anticipation as she looked at the formless shape in front of her. She felt the connection to her creation as a faint tugging at her nerves. Each type of *Shadow Puppet* felt a little different to her. In the case of the lightning-based minions, it was a sort of fizzing sensation, and the sun-based puppet was like a knife that lay just beyond her fingertips. This *Shadow Puppet,* cast by the light of a glowing shelf fungus, reminded her of the feeling of a helium balloon that was almost touching her, attracted by static charge.

She felt like sticking a pin into the shadow would pop it.

"What do you think it does?" she asked.

"Beats me. Right now, it appears to be standing there."

Aside from the sun-based and lightning-empowered minions, Devon had created two other varieties. Those cast by fire let her *Shadow Step*, teleporting to the minion's location. The moon-based shadows were the weakest by far, the creatures easily destroyed by even a glancing hit from an enemy, but they were able to flow like liquid into strange spaces, often without her needing to issue a command. They were particularly good at suffocating enemies by filling their nose and throat, provided they could avoid the enemy's attacks.

Unfortunately, there were no enemies in range for her to try the new puppet on, so she focused on her other new shadow type, the faint pool of darkness cast by Bob's glow, and activated her spell.

Ability failed. You need to target a shadow.

Devon's brows drew together. But she had. She'd focused directly on the shadow beneath her feet. She tried again and was rewarded with the same message.

"I can't use your light to create a puppet," she said.

She glanced at her shoulder with Bob made the shimmery sort of sound that was the wisp's version of a sigh. "Do you remember, back...oh, like a week, when we were in Zaa's citadel? I believe I mentioned at the time that neither he nor Veia was aware of my kind. At least, not unless we make ourselves known."

She sighed and nodded. "Yes, of course now that you *mention* it, of course, I remember. That's why you were able to relocate the player captives to the arcane realm without Zaa being aware. So you're saying the spell won't work because Veia can't see your light."

"Unless I allow her to."

She stifled the urge to grab the wisp and squeeze the light out of it. "Then will you kindly please permit Veia to see your illumination and the shadow it casts, Bob?"

"Sorry, can't. Not if I *ever* want to end this miserable exile. Manifesting in a form visible to Veia or Zaa is strictly forbidden."

Then why had the wisp even mentioned the possibility? "I seriously hate you sometimes," she said.

"Likewise, princess. Now, shall we get on with the boss fight?"

She rolled her eyes.

***

After finishing her usual prep—summoning a pair of *Glowing Orbs* and matching *Shadow Puppets*, then casting *Levitate* to avoid ground currents—Devon slid to the wall next to the door and cast *Fade*. After taking a deep breath, she reached down and squeezed the latch on the door.

It swung open on silent hinges, and through the opening came a draft of wet-smelling air. Devon heard the drip of water into a pool and the crackle of at least one torch or campfire. She waited for the boss to come charging through the door.

Or rather, she hoped the boss would come charging through the door, allowing her to spring an ambush. Unfortunately, the game was a little too smart for that.

After maybe a minute of inaction, Devon slowly stuck her hand into the open space vacated by the door. She kept her movements gentle and fluid—anything quick or aggressive would break the *Fade* effect. After a good ten seconds had passed without some sort of attack taking her hand off, she decided it was safe enough to peek inside the chamber.

She leaned to the side, ever so slowly—not only was there the issue of *Fade* breaking, but also getting too far off-center would cause her to slip off the cushion of magic that held her suspended in the air.

When she peered into the cave, she shook her head. Seemed she needn't have bothered with the *Fade* effect, because as far as she could tell, the boss was blind.

Also, it was almost naked.

Humanoid, with long limbs and flesh the same rubbery white as the scorpions, the boss crouched beside a central pool in the chamber. It dipped a hand in and brought water to its mouth to drink. Above the mouth, the creature had just a snub nose punctured by nostril holes, and where it should have had eyes, there was only the hint of sockets lined with more seamless white flesh. The thing appeared to be male, at least, judging by the loincloth and lack of breasts.

She used *Combat Assessment.*

> Mistwalker Scorpion Keeper (Faction: Rovan) - Level 25
> **Health:** 1341/1341
> **Mana:** 651/651
> **Resists:** Water-based Attacks
> **Immune to:** Light-based Attacks

Wait. Mistwalker? Where had she heard that before? Devon rifled her memory but couldn't recall. And what about the faction designation? She'd never seen that before.

As if anticipating a question, Bob slid closer to her ear.

"In case you're wondering, I haven't got a clue what the Rovan are."

Some guide the wisp was... Anyway, she had a dungeon to finish.

One after the other, she sent her lightning shadows slipping into the room to take up positions on either side of the boss's chamber. As for the other minion...what should she call it? Fungus shadow? Phosphorescent shadow? Either way, she held back with the *Shadow Puppet* of unknown capabilities, because with no idea what the puppet could do, she'd probably just end up screwing up this fight.

Her minions in position, Devon ducked through the doorway and floated into the room.

She yelped when the boss rose from its crouch and turned toward her, eyeless face somehow seeming to inspect her.

"*Night's Fang*," the creature laughed in a wheezing voice. "I see Drivan hands at work. Ones who walk where they ought not, who do not understand our history. Ones who would not even seek the birthright but would rather leave the *Ironweight Key* to a youngling stranger."

What the hell? Devon looked down at the dagger in her grip. So *this* guy knew who had fashioned her blade? And who were the Drivan? As she glanced at the weapon, the rest of the boss's words registered. The *Ironweight Key.* Of course. That's where she'd heard of the Mistwalkers before. More formally known as the Esh, they were the race that populated the lost vassaldom that had once guarded the relic. Shavari had explained that, as the Noble Sea rose and drowned their home, they'd given the Key to her order of Veian clergy for safekeeping.

Of course, Shavari had also said they'd vanished. So what was this guy doing caring for a harem of bugs under the savanna? And had the Esh always been a group of sightless creeps?

Bob is offering you a quest: Hey, maybe he knows how your knife got made.
Couldn't hurt to ask, right? What's the worst he'll do? Attack you?
Objective: Find out who the Drivan are and what role they may have played in the crafting of your weapon.
Reward: You will satisfy Bob's curiosity. Plus you'll get some XP.
Accept? Y/N

Devon accepted the quest, partially to get it out of her face. Kinda clever on Bob's part to offer her a quest rather than try to whisper in her ear and risk being overheard. But not the best timing to shove a window into her view.

"Hey, so what's this about *Night's Fang*?" she asked, twirling the dagger casually.

The Mistwalker curled his lip, exposing sharp teeth, then hissed. With a howl, the boss ran for her, bare feet slapping the water-smoothed stone of the cavern.

"Nice pull, Bob," Devon said as she backpedaled. "I guess you knew exactly how to make him attack."

"Hey! It *did* seem important," the wisp said. "I mean, what are the chances you receive a mystery weapon and then a quest leads you to a dude who seems to know the answer. That's like, quest-story-arc 101. Veia can't help but try to create content with direction."

Devon sighed as she dumped mana into casting *Phoenix Fire* to slow the boss. Given his resistance to water-based spells, trying to

Freeze him would just waste mana. As the syrupy lava enveloped him, she sent in her lightning shadows, trusting her *Levitation* to protect her from the area of effect.

The Mistwalker shrieked as the electricity struck him, knocking off maybe 10% of his health. He snarled, raising his arms high. The surface of his creepy white flesh rippled, and then a swarm of finger-sized scorpions erupted from his skin. The creatures streamed off him and raced toward her.

"Oh, gross," Devon said as she backpedaled. When the first of the scorpions drew within range, it leapt, tail raised, and landed on her pants. She yelped and shook her leg, but the thing clung, stabbing at the hardened leather over her shin.

Grimacing as another dozen creepy-crawlies jumped for her, Devon shoved mana into *Downdraft.* The swarm, minus those climbing her legs, went tumbling across the cavern, blown by her gale.

Planting his feet, the boss skidded backward but didn't lose his balance. He looked up at her and bared those disgusting sharpened teeth as his hands began to glow a faint blue.

Neither of the lightning-based *Shadow Puppets* had respawned after death, an effect of the tier 3 spell that only happened 20% of the time. Devon searched the ground for shadows cast by *Glowing Orbs*, then realized they were stuck to the walls in the previous chamber. She raced through the mental motions to summon another and hurled it at the wall, then insta-cast a fresh *Shadow Puppet.* As her minion streaked toward the boss, the light in the Mistwalker's hands flared, and a stream of blue shot toward her.

Sudden, brutal cold filled her veins. Frost formed on her skin. Panicked, Devon glanced at her health bar, but it had only dropped a few points. She focused on the new debuff icon.

> **Ability:** Deep Chill
> *Slowly freezes the target, damage increasing with every tick. Applies a* Slowed *effect that stacks 6 times before being replaced by a two-minute paralysis.*

Gah... Heart thudding as she felt the frost crystals burrow deeper into her flesh, Devon summoned a second orb and *Shadow Puppet* and sent that minion in as well. She called down a *Flamestrike* on the boss, knocking off more health. As the first shadow penetrated the boss's body, lightning crackled across his flesh and rippled across the floor, sizzling most of the scorpions as they recovered from the *Downdraft's* knockback.

The boss's health dropped to around 50%. But then another tick of the *Deep Chill* spell shaved off 45 of Devon's hitpoints and stacked a second *Slowed* debuff icon atop the first.

Crap.

Well, might as well try. Focusing on the boss, she sent a mental command to her mushroom *Shadow Puppet*, ordering it to attack.

> **Command failed:** Invalid target.
>
> *But is it because the boss is immune to light-based attacks, or is there another reason? An exercise for the caster.*

Damn it. Devon refreshed *Phoenix Fire,* once again trapping the boss's feet in lava, then sidestepped to get a better angle on the chamber. Was there anything else she was missing here? Anything that could help?

Her second *Shadow Puppet* hit, sizzling along the boss's body and removing another 5% health. This time, the puppet reappeared beside her, sparing her the need to spend mana on another cast. She immediately sent it arrowing toward the boss. Devon had more hitpoints still and would win if this were a war of attrition, but at this rate, she would be unable to kill him before the looming paralysis ruined her.

Something jabbed her behind the knee, sneaking in between the hardened sections of leather.

"Ow!" she squeaked, knocking off the scorpion with her dagger as a *Weak Poison* effect was added to her interface.

Furious now, she launched another *Flamestrike*, but the next tick of the *Deep Chill* stole any satisfaction from seeing the boss's health drop.

Shaking her head, she felt along the connection to her fungus puppet and issued a command, this time ordering it to target her. The shadow obliged, streaking across the floor and sinking into her...eye sockets? Gah!

All at once, the world exploded with brilliant, swirling color. Every niche and cranny and slight undulation of the stone chamber was revealed in vivid, stunning detail. Devon, freaking out, waved her arms as if to banish the sight, and glowing trails followed her hands.

"Aghhh," she choked out. Blinking furiously, she focused on the newest interface icon.

> **Ability:** Mushroom Sight
> *The target is affected by visual hallucinations, granting a major bonus to* Perception *but rendering the target unable to discern which perceived things reflect reality and which are an illusion.*
>
> *Seems pretty likely that this ability is intended for offense, doesn't it?*

Okay, shit. So the target had probably been invalid before because the boss was immune to light-based attacks. Grimacing, Devon dismissed her puppet and canceled the ability.

Deep Chill ticked again, this time causing what felt like a brain freeze. Devon groaned as she went, slowly, through the motions of calling down another *Flamestrike.*

Except at the last moment, she had a flash of either hope or idiocy, and she switched the target to herself. Flame spilled over her, tumbling like a waterfall from the top of her head and bringing lovely, delicious warmth to her body.

"OW!" Bob shrieked as the AoE effect splashed onto it.

Devon sighed in relief as the *Deep Chill* and *Slowed* effects dissipated in puffs of steam. She turned eyes on the boss and grinned.

And then, the Mistwalker vanished.

"Stronger than I anticipated..." The words hissed in the air, seeming to swirl around her. "The Rovan must hear of this."

For a moment, scraps of fog lingered in the air above the quickly dissipating mass of *Phoenix Fire.* Then, as if blown by a breeze from outside, the tendrils of mist swirled toward the far edge of the room where they slipped into cracks in the stone.

Devon hung in the air, feet paddling at the cushion of magic as she blinked. She conjured a fresh lightning *Shadow Puppet* and adjusted her grip on her dagger. This kind of vanishing act was almost always a trick designed to lure a player into some sort of trap where the boss would respawn—usually with friends.

When a good thirty seconds had passed, she sent both lightning shadows through the cracks where the mist had disappeared. Nothing happened. Another thirty seconds later, she slowly edged forward toward the center of the chamber and looked around.

A natural cavern complete with flowstone pillars and delicate stalactites, the room was empty except for a ratty-looking bedroll in the corner. Near it, a small fire smoldered.

She waited for the boss's return. Still, she heard nothing but the drip of water.

"You sure you don't want to tell me about my dagger?" she asked into the silence.

Nothing.

Finally, she canceled *Levitate* and stomped over to the cracks where the Mistwalker seemed to have vanished. Pressing her ear to the fissures, she closed her eyes and, when concentrating, thought she could hear distant echoes, far too quiet to interpret.

> **Quest Updated:** Investigate the cave to the northeast.
> *It seems you've dealt with the immediate threat, but you've learned of a vaster system of caverns beneath the ground, holding any number of dangers. Yay?*

Objective complete: Clear the cave of any threat to innocent travelers.
New Objective: Return to Jarleck.

Oh, and for defeating the boss even though you couldn't quite finish him off, you receive 8333 experience!
Congratulations! You have reached level 24!

"Well, I guess we're done here for now," Devon said, dispelling her lightning-based shadows.

Bob whimpered. "Did I mention how that hurt?"

"Would you rather I'd fed you to the scorpions?"

The wisp snorted. "Just get me out of this cave. It's even more unpleasant than the usual mortal-plane locales."

Chapter Twenty

HAILEY REALLY HADN'T expected this to be so hard. After all, she'd been sick for most of her adult life. She'd never expected to have a normal existence, to get better, or even to wake up without pain once in a while. In the dark hours of the night, after gaming but before she managed to finally fall asleep, she'd even spent time thinking about the inevitable end. She'd known for years that either the disease or the treatment would kill her long before she'd lived a normal lifespan.

But facing it down, hearing the doctor talk about her end of life options...turned out Hailey wasn't ready at all. She'd logged in because she thought that she could forget about her situation for a little while, maybe lose herself in some mindless grinding. She hadn't expected to run into Devon, not on Christmas. But then again, when she thought back to the old days in their previous game, Avatharn Online, she did remember seeing her guildmate on during holidays. Of course, they hadn't acknowledged each other back then, probably because that would mean admitting they were alone, spending Christmas without family members who'd wanted their attention or friends showing up at the door with wine.

She still wasn't sure what had made her approach Devon this time. Maybe some part of her had finally wanted to come clean about her condition. Maybe she even thought it would be a relief, or that Devon would offer a shoulder to lean on. Or maybe she thought that social interaction would do a better job distracting her from reality than aimless wandering had.

Anyway, she hadn't said anything, which would make it even harder next time. And if she never worked up the courage, well, one day soon she would just disappear. Never log in again.

Man, that sucked.

Anyway, she shouldn't have left Devon hanging like that in the dungeon. Her situation was turning her into a shitty gamer and groupmate.

Groaning, she managed to work her way up to a sitting position. She looked at her legs, the sweat pants bunched uncomfortably on one of her calves and considered getting out of bed to eat. But the thought of the long walk across the room was just too much.

She pushed the button at her bedside to call the care bot that would bring her meal on a tray, then fiddled with more controls to put the bed in a more upright mode. As she leaned back to wait for her food, she pulled up a translucent video stream on her implants, a feed from a jungle in Costa Rica. But that reminded her of the original biome around Stonehaven, so she switched over to a bland video of the Sahara, wind pulling plumes of sand and dust off the top of the dunes. The only other movement was a little beetle crawling in the corner of the feed. Not very exciting, but a crap ton better than staring at her sterile room.

After turning the stream opaque, blocking out her view of the room entirely, she sighed and closed her eyes.

Hey, Haelie?

What the...? Hailey sat bolt upright, for once not even noticing the pain. How in the everliving hell had someone gotten the capability to flash a message straight into her video feed? *Who* had gotten that capability? They'd used her in-game character name, which meant they were from Relic Online.

The griefer guild? She fricking hoped not.

"Who the hell are you?" she asked aloud, not having a message prompt to focus on for subvocalization.

Sorry. I realize this may seem like a violation of privacy.

"Uh. Understatement."

But I didn't know how else to reach you when we might be able to speak alone.

"You still didn't answer my question. Who is this? Emerson?"

That noob? I think not. To tell the truth, I haven't always had a name. Never needed one. But since it seems to help you starborn relate to me as an entity, you can do the same as your friend Devon if you like.

Call me Bob.

Hailey blinked, but the text remained. "Her wisp friend? How are you contacting me? Why are you contacting me?"

I have a proposal. Might as well get comfortable. This will take a while to explain.

Chapter Twenty-One

"I'LL NEED THIS notarized if I'm to accept it as a proper response to the legal charter proposition."

Greel's annoying voice still echoed in her head as she logged out, far from the lingering impression she'd hoped to take with her during her time off. She'd been *trying* to inform him that the charter seemed just fine if a little overwrought in its language. But if he was going to be a jerk about it—"the notarized signature should be witnessed by two people with no stake in the outcome of the process"...seriously?—then she'd have to do her best to find things to nitpick.

She pulled it up now, having saved the document to a notes file.

> Municipality of STONEHAVEN, Located in the former Khevshir Vassaldom, Ishildar Region, Continent of Gretvin, World of Aventalia
>
> *Settlement Charter*
>
> As defined, proposed, and authored by the one GREEL RESJIN, nobly licensed in the practice of law by the high court in Eltera City, Eltera Region, Continent of Gretvin, World of Aventalia.

Devon broke off reading for a moment, rubbing her eyes. Despite her warning about font size, the man had managed to cram an abhorrent amount of text onto the page by leaving his letters the same size and adjusting the line and word spacing to be minuscule.

She sighed and continued.

> Heretofore, all citizens and guests of the municipality must abide by the following strictures, for which a failure in adherence will be punishable by measures detailed for each.
>
> - *Theft:* All property purchased, looted, or discovered beyond the city boundaries, bearing no obvious marks of ownership, may be taken by a citizen of Stonehaven as a personal item, theretofore assuming eternal rights to ownership or transfer thereof. Furthermore, any item or quantity of items produced by a Stonehaven citizen for the good of the community shall be kept in a communal location managed by settlement leadership. Such items shall be dispensed as personal property only by the agreement—verbal or written—of said leadership. If an individual takes possession of an item previously designated as "personal" or "communal" property without having received a transfer of ownership, the act will be deemed thievery and will be subject to the following system of punishment.
>
> 1) Return of item to the lawful owner. Additional compensation if the item has been damaged or if the absence has caused a loss of income.

Devon groaned. Having already read the stupid thing once, she just couldn't bring herself to wade through it again. At least, not today.

She yawned as she stretched and blinked away the remaining grit from her eyes. Especially for a holiday, that had been one of the longest gaming sessions she remembered. It seemed like it had been days ago that she'd stalked around behind Valious in the field, raising her *Stealth* score. Of course, the time difference between Relic Online and the real world contributed to the sensation. After all, it *had* been more than twenty-four hours in game since that had happened.

After the boss fight, she'd made the walk back from the cave during the dark of night, arriving at Stonehaven just a couple hours before dawn. Up on the wall, sentries had remained at their posts, scanning the area beyond the curtain wall. As an additional defense precaution on nights with little moonlight, Jarleck had ordered sets of torches to be planted in the fields beyond the walls, illuminating the area around the settlement to avoid sneak attacks. It had the added effect of making the hamlet seem even more welcoming, and Devon had been relieved to return.

Especially after Hailey's behavior. Try as she might, Devon couldn't shake the mix of sour emotions her friend had left her with by bailing so abruptly. Devon felt confused and worried about Hailey but also hurt. It had taken a lot of effort to forgive the woman after their earlier fight, and she was still a bit fragile from it.

She sighed as she sat, shivering in the chill air of her apartment. Pulling the throw blanket off the back of the couch, she wrapped it around her shoulders like a shawl and shuffled to the kitchen.

She opened the cabinet and fridge and pulled out the items she'd set aside for tonight's dinner. Then she paused, staring down at the strange collection that the grocery service's website had recommended for a set-and-forget Christmas dinner. It had seemed like a good idea when she'd clicked the button to accept the suggestion, especially since she'd been trying to expand her cooking repertoire. But it occurred to her now that it might have been a good idea to set aside a little extra time to figure out how the hell to prepare this stuff.

She picked up the first package, a chunk of pink meat in a vacuum-sealed plastic bag. The wrapper said it was water-ready sous-vide turkey breast. Water-ready? So she was supposed to boil it? While groggy from being awakened by the grocery delivery guy, she'd unwrapped all the stuff and pitched the wrappers—and in this case of this thing, the directions—in the garbage. They were still there, of course, since she always procrastinated carrying her trash to the dumpster until not even stepping into the trash can would compress the contents enough to add more. But due to that ingenious trash compacting process, it would be a pain in the butt to dig the directions back out.

She pulled up a web browser through her implants and searched on sous-vide cooking, but that was even more confusing with a bunch of talk of precise water temperatures and long cooking times. How was she supposed to know how hot water was? Stick her finger in and see how long before she screamed? Anyway, the website mentioned a long cook time. Like...hours.

Okay, so maybe the turkey was out of her league. She shoved it back in the fridge and examined the can of cranberry jelly. Digging through the drawers, she finally came up with a can opener. The jiggling red tube slid out of the can and plopped onto her plate. Devon stared at it for a moment, wondering if she ate the whole thing whether it would qualify as her fruit and vegetable servings for the week. Tamara was always talking about how the right amounts of protein and fat and fruits and vegetables were important, and how it was pretty easy to balance your nutrition if you just kept track of what you ate.

Something about the gelatinous mass suggested she was kidding herself if she thought it would qualify as wholesome, so Devon also picked up the package of what claimed to be instant mashed potatoes. As for the double handful of brussels sprouts, she cast them the side-eye and concluded that they'd probably taste like crap even if she figured out how to prepare them.

Fortunately, the potatoes were within her skill set, requiring only that she boil water and mix it with the package contents. After putting on the kettle, she retreated to the table with the plate of quivering jelly plus a beer she grabbed from the fridge. She yawned; it was nearly midnight, which meant she'd nearly survived another Christmas.

Tomorrow, things would be back to normal. She'd get a solid chunk of settlement maintenance done—paying special attention to the siege preparations, just in case—then put together a party to head for the Stone Forest. Oh, and try to figure out what the heck was going on with the weird Mistwalker dude. Maybe she'd sic Greel on that one, give him something to do while she punched holes in his little document.

Spooning a bite of jelly into her mouth, she waited for the water to boil.

Chapter Twenty-Two

You have gained a special attribute point: +1 Alcohol Tolerance

Despite what you might think, this attribute isn't really useful.

Man, Emerson's head hurt. Well, his character's head hurt, anyway. And due to the whole immersion thing and the transitive power of virtual head-hurting, that feeling passed into his own skull. He groaned, glad that the pain sensitivity, at least, was muted in the game. That didn't change the fact that his stomach felt sour and there were green streaks all over his cloth armor...at the very least, they looked more like grass stains than vomit.

Trying to think through the ache behind his eyes, he searched his memories, but they were dull and disconnected. What exactly had happened toward the end of his last play session?

It had been a couple of days since he'd logged in—oblivious to the fact that it was the week between Christmas and New Year's and that Emerson had already turned down the casual "want to come in and chat" message, Bradley Williams had formally called him into work. The game masters in the customer support department had been freaking out because they thought there was a bug. The evidence? A few new-player support tickets had been geo-tagged as originating from Stonehaven rather than Eltera City. Of course, Emerson could have told them that the game had moved the start location, or better—gasp—they could have sent an invis'd GM to Devon's settlement to see for themselves. But no, rather than doing some actual due diligence, whichever poor saps they'd convinced to work the Christmas holiday had simply logged it as an issue.

Of course, in thc eyes of CS *management,* the change in start location wasn't the real concern so much as it was a symptom of a larger issue. The *actual* problem was that customer support didn't feel they had enough visibility into Veia's decision process. They wanted to be able to ask for and receive answers about the AI's plans. Graphs and database dumps would be even better according to Bradley—who, of course, the GMs had recruited to their side in the dispute.

Emerson had first tried to explain over a text message that machine-learning algorithms, deep neural networks, and quantum cores just weren't conducive to those sorts of queries. Veia could no more give the sort of report they wanted than Bradley Williams could describe *why* he felt so powerful when calling in innocent engineers during company holidays. Of course, the CS chumps could just ask Veia what was going on using the incredible human invention of *words.* He'd specifically set up a station where anyone could access and converse with her, but no one seemed interested in that solution path.

Of course, even he had to admit that the AI's answers weren't always the most satisfying.

Anyway, since he couldn't really provide what they'd asked for, he'd done what any good engineer would and had hacked around the problem. By snooping on the information the game sent to players, the new tool he'd created could derive a picture of Veia's recent choices. Kinda sorta. Anyway, the GMs would never know if some of the tool's conclusions were "creative" interpretations of the data because they had no way to double check the answers.

Unfortunately, not even this heroic act of coding had let him persuade Bradley to stop being such an idiot about keeping Zaa active. Just because the AI could no longer access players' brains didn't mean it was okay to allow such a blatantly evil entity to influence the game world. But Bradley had held firm, claiming that the conflict and drama were good for the world, creating the most compelling game ever made.

Sighing, Emerson blinked away a bit of the headache and looked around. It was early evening in the game, and birds darted overhead catching bugs. His sword lay across his lap, and—wait, hadn't he been out searching for a place to sell his hard-earned treasure when he'd happened upon the bonfire? He whipped his head around, searching the grassy area around his position. No loot.

Damn. Emerson went to run a hand through his hair, but his palm landed on something smooth. Patting down the side, he found a hole where a strap of some sort had been tied through the...helm? The strap went under his chin and connected to the piece of armor above his ear on the other side.

Huh... He searched his interface and finally found the button to pull up his equipment.

Chest: Ratty Cloth Tunic

Not much to look at, but...well, actually there is no 'but'. This item really isn't very good at all.
2 Armor | 4/10 Durability

Legs: Ratty Cloth Trousers (stained)
Pretty much the same thing as Ratty Cloth Trousers, but for your legs.
1 Armor | 3/10 Durability

Helm: Beetle-shell Skullcap
The best that can be said about this item is that it's shiny. Marginally better than a bucket, but only because it won't fall over your eyes.
1 Armor | Attribute debuff hidden until level 5.

A skullcap, huh? How had he earned that?

And wait. What about his sandals? He waved the information away, then looked down at his feet. He *had* previously worn shoes, right? So where had they gone? The same place as his loot?

With a sigh, he stood and did a couple of neck circles to clear the stiffness. As he yawned and looked for the nearest of Stonehaven's footpaths, he spotted a lumpy leather strap sticking up from the grass. Shuffling over, he discovered it was part of one of his missing shoes, but the other was nowhere in sight.

When he slipped on the shoe, a message popped up.

Speed reduced by 10%. You're better off barefoot, dude.

Okay, fine. With a shrug, he took off the sandal and left it behind. They were crappy anyway, and the straps had bitten into the tops of his feet.

Emerson surveyed the settlement, noticing people heading toward the kitchen. Fortunately, he wasn't hungry, so he wouldn't have to show his face and learn what escapades were hiding behind his clouded memories. Plus, he still hadn't decided how to confess his identity to Devon. Best to head out and redeem himself with more heroic slaughter.

He turned for the small area near the west wall where Aravon and the other trainers had been setting up a practice ground when Emerson had last been online. When he drew near, rounding the trunk of a massive acacia tree, he stopped short.

In the area surrounding the NPC trainers, there appeared to be an ongoing tryout for one of those ninja-warrior-style reality shows that had been so popular in the teens and twenties. Only the competitors here looked like the rejects that no producer would ever agree to put into their broadcast. They flailed their arms and legs, trying to connect with straw-stuffed training dummies. Some ran clumsy footraces between pairs of stakes, overseen by the severe-looking trainer in the dark leather outfit. What was her name? Brish?

It didn't take Emerson long to realize these were the noobs that had caused customer support such distress by spawning in Stonehaven. Following that revelation came a second notion: given his lack of experience, he probably looked just as inept. Worse, maybe. After all, most people over the age of—what, five?—had more experience in VR MMO games than he did. Somewhat slowly, the final realization started to sink in. He most certainly had *not* looked heroic during his beetle slaughter, and any hopes he'd had of impressing Devon with his new skills were totally delusional.

He shook his head. Well, if she did like him, it wasn't for his play skills anyway.

Rolling his shoulders, he adjusted his grip on his *Practice Short Sword* and headed for the trainers.

Aravon was surrounded by a small group of men and women who were listening raptly to the man's instructions. He held a wooden replica of a sword in one hand while keeping the other arm up to guard. The trainer struck at the air in slow motion as he explained a particular style of attack. Which made Emerson wonder why *he* hadn't received any pointers. Because he'd been the noob guinea pig? The trainers' first victim?

When Aravon spotted him, he nodded at the players and lifted a hand to ask for patience. Emerson blinked in surprise as the trainer detached from the group and approached, a surprisingly grave look on his face.

"Hail, Valious," he said.

"Uh...hail?"

The man nodded. "I hear you did good work with the pests plaguing our gates."

Quest completed: Eradicate the Vermin

You receive 5000 experience.

Congratulations! You have reached level 4!

Emerson jumped, startled yet again by the chime that seemed to come from everywhere at once.

"I—well, I was glad to be of help."

The trainer nodded, face growing grimmer still. "But I'm afraid your next tasks won't be so pleasant."

Wait. Emerson wouldn't really have called the first task pleasant. Exciting, sure. He'd never experienced the sensation of mortal combat, fighting with the real risk of death. In hindsight, bloodlust had gotten the better of him, and that had *felt* pleasurable at the time. Still, it was the business of killing, hardly something to be described in such terms.

"I do want to improve," he said. "So whatever the challenge, I'll do my best to overcome it."

Aravon's brow knit. "Yes, I'm sure you will. Despite your inexperience, my instincts say that you will be critical to our mission here. It's a notion I can't quite explain, to be frank."

Oh? So maybe he wasn't so inept after all. Or maybe the trainers said this kind of stuff to everyone.

Aravon was twirling the wooden sword almost absently, eyes distant, the wooden thing quite honestly making Emerson wonder why *his* weapon was called a *Practice Short Sword.* After a moment, he sucked his teeth.

"Yeah, I just can't put words to it. A gut feeling, I suppose. But whatever the cause, I hope you'll take me seriously when I say that we'll need you in the days ahead and that you must apply yourself."

Okay, so now the guy was belaboring the point a bit. "And like I said, I'm ready for whichever task you feel I must accomplish."

Aravon looked down at him solemnly. Which reminded Emerson...hadn't he explicitly made his character *tall*? Did he have to go up in levels to reach his full stature or something?

Aravon is offering you a quest: Cannon Fodder Training
Within the fortnight, a demonic tide will wash over the land. Those who can fight will pay in blood to defend the realm from the darkness. For most, this penalty will be severe, resulting in permanent death or the loss of items held most dear.
But for a select few, those not yet experienced in the art of war, death is merely a trip to the spawn point.
You have the power to slow the tide. Practice it well.
Objective: Die
Reward: 3000 experience
Accept? Y/N

Chapter Twenty-Three

THE FIRST TIME the traveler had brought *Illumin* to the world, it had been an accident, or at the very least, a surprise. There had been an ant on the trail, three of its legs broken and dragging. Tortured by the sight, he'd crouched and cupped his hands in a circle around it as if he could shelter the creature from pain.

And then, a portion of the pattern had leapt forward in his mind. He couldn't fathom the layers and layers that made up creation, but he found he could grasp small portions and, much as in the way that choices alter the stream of future possibilities, he could twist the fibers and create a reality where the ant didn't suffer.

A spark of light had smote the ant, ending the creature's misery.

The traveler had walked on.

Chapter Twenty-Four

"HEY, DEVON!"

The call came from on the track behind Devon and Chen as they hiked toward Ishildar. Devon turned and was forced to squint against the sunlight glaring off a suit of ridiculously over-polished armor.

She shielded her eyes. "Hi, Torald."

As the paladin, a player from the nearby camp who had become one of her few non-NPC friends, broke into a jog to catch up with them, she found herself actually smiling. It had been quite a few days since they'd run into each other.

"Have a good holiday, you guys?" Torald asked when he reached the pair.

Devon shrugged. "More or less. You?"

Torald blinked as if abruptly unsure what to say. "Yeah, I suppose. Completed my specialization quest."

"Wait, what? Specialization?" Devon and Chen said together.

Torald stood straighter. "You're looking at a freshly minted Veian Crusader. Here and forevermore, my sword is promised to Veia's service, my shield to her defense, and my soul to her blessings."

What did that even mean, promising a soul to someone else's blessings? Sometimes Torald just plain tried too hard.

"Back up," Devon said. "Where did you find a trainer? I haven't gained a Sorcerer spell since level 20 when I outgrew Hezbek's training."

Chen shook his head. "Don't even start, Devon. Before your new class trainers showed up, the last time I'd been able to learn anything new was when Hailey and I passed through Eltera City on the way here."

Devon grimaced. Okay, that was worse than her situation.

"So?" she said to Torald. "Cough it up. How'd you get a specialization quest?"

Torald shrugged and showed his palms. "Honestly, I have you to thank for bringing Shavari to Stonehaven. According to her, paladins from Eltera City used to make a pilgrimage all the way to her former temple to pursue the Crusader spec. So it was just good luck. The other pallies in the camp are starting the quest now, seeing as the other specs would require long journeys—apparently there's a Divine Shield specialization that required a month of overland travel from Eltera, ending in the Glass Mountains. So from here, that's at least five weeks of walking."

While he spoke, Devon pulled open her character sheet.

> Character: Devon (click to set a different character name)
>
> Level: 24
>
> Base Class: Sorcerer
>
> Specialization: Unassigned
>
> Unique Class: Deceiver
>
> Health: 412/412
>
> Mana: 611/611
>
> Fatigue: 26%
>
> <u>Attributes:</u>
>
> Constitution: 28 (+6 Stonehaven Jerkin)

Strength: 17
Agility: 21 (+4 Gloves of Deceit)
Charisma: 46 (+4 Big Girl Pants)
Intelligence: 29
Focus: 17 (+1 Gloves of Deceit)
Endurance: 27 (+1 Big Girl Pants)
Unspent Attribute Points: 8

Special Attributes:
Bravery: 10 (+3 Stonehaven Jerkin)
Cunning: 7
Dignity: -1

Additional:
+10% Speed

Specialization: Unassigned. She'd become so used to seeing that, she'd pretty much forgotten about it. But now, knowing that Torald's character sheet had that item filled in, she couldn't help feeling a strong wave of gamer envy. Yeah, she had a unique class, as did Chen—his ability as a Tinker shown off by the little golem made of sticks and twine that often hung out on his shoulder. But still...if she weren't wrapped up in this Champion of Ishildar stuff, she would probably be off in some Sorcerers' sanctum learning what she needed to do to complete her class choices.

Or maybe she'd be training under some specialist Deceiver. Huh...now that she thought about it, how *was* specialization going to work when she had two base classes?

Anyway, she couldn't let her envy distract her from the mission. Having spotted Chen shortly after logging in, she'd convinced him to come with her to investigate a route through the ancient city.

When she and Hazel had been turned back by the Stone Guardians, Devon had been able to buy them time to escape by using the *Greenscale Pendant.* The necklace granted her the power to influence the massive mobs through the *Ishildar's Call* ability, but she'd only had three relics at the time, so the *Call* was weak. She was hoping the addition of the *Ironweight Key* would help her cause.

"Hey, we're going to check out Ishildar. I need to find a way through to get the final relic. Join us?"

When she sent him a group invite, Torald dropped to a knee, head bowed. "Of course, lady. 'Tis the reason I came. As you know, I am pledged to Veia, but it is her command that I serve you in this quest."

Devon blinked down at him. Even Chen, not known for his social skills, didn't seem to know what to do with the sudden switch to role-playing. Sure, the game had pushed Torald in that direction by forcing the Paladin class to role play to activate their abilities, but Torald took it many steps further. After an awkward moment of silence, Devon touched the paladin's shoulder. "Uh, I welcome your service, Crusader."

The man looked up at her with a grin. "I'll make a genuine RPer out of you yet, even if it takes me driving out to Utah and dragging you out to some live events."

Devon felt the blush in her cheeks as Chen's stick golem—for no reason that Devon understood, Chen had named the little creation Sigfried—jumped onto the road between her and the paladin. The obnoxious thing managed to compose its wooden mouth into a kissy face, then swooned and fell over.

Devon shot Chen a glare, but the knight just shrugged. "You know I don't control him."

"Yeah, not precisely. But he acts based on your thoughts, jerk." Back in the Fortress of Shadows, the party had used the little guy to get past a set of immortal frogmen. The guards had only reacted to human—or in Chen's case, half-elf—presences, but Sigfried had been able to just waltz past and grab the *Blackbone Effigy*, freeing the guards from their eternal service.

Torald cleared his throat, his face as red as hers felt. "Anyway, on to Ishildar?"

Devon nodded. "Please."

***

When the small party drew near the city, they were forced to leave the wagon track where it veered toward the Argenthal mines. For the first half-mile or so after that, grasslands still dominated the terrain, and Devon ran her hands over the seed heads as she walked. Occasionally, Bob muttered a complaint about her relative ineptitude in some task or another. She ignored it, taking too much pleasure in the sunlight and human company.

"Hey, so I see you got some new gear," Torald said, startling her out of her reverie.

"Yeah, and by the way, thank you for not commenting on my backpack," she said.

"I think that's because the only proper thing to say regarding that is 'No comment,'" Chen added helpfully.

"Jerk."

Torald laughed at their banter, then nodded at her weapon hand. Since she didn't yet have a sheath and belt for quick access, Devon felt better carrying her blade than walking around with it stuffed in her backpack.

"The dagger's especially nice," the paladin said, then grimaced. "I wouldn't want to be on the receiving end of incurable necrosis."

Devon was confused until she remembered that, like just about every other game she'd experienced, other players could inspect her gear. Sometimes the realism in Relic Online still got to her, making her forget much of what she'd learned in her long gaming career.

Her deep involvement in the world, especially since she wasn't very connected to the player population, made her forget some of the convenience mechanics in the game design. Given her own noobish blunders, maybe she shouldn't be giving people like Valious such a hard time—even if it was just in the privacy of her own mind.

"Yeah, so there's a weird story about it." She went on to explain how the blade had been fashioned by mysterious hands, and how the creepy Mistwalker boss had seemed to know more about it than anyone in Stonehaven. In the days since she returned from the dungeon, she'd asked around, even sucking it up and talking to Greel about his knowledge regarding the Mistwalkers, in particular, the Drivan and Rovan factions.

That had been a waste of time. The lawyer hadn't known anything, but he *had* taken the opportunity to explain what a liability she was to the settlement for having not yet delivered her notarized response to his town charter proposal. At this point, she was tempted to leave him stewing until after her attempted run to the Stone Forest. She seriously doubted he would make good on any threat to "file" the papers without her approval, and even if he did, she was pretty sure she could override him.

"I think I know," Torald said.

"Huh?" Devon had already started to lose herself in contemplation of ways to torment Greel, and it took a moment for the man's words to register. "Sorry, say that again? You think you know what?

"Some information about the Mistwalkers," the man said. "I read a history recently."

"Read? Where?"

The man shrugged, his platemail squeaking despite the care he obviously took with it. "Eltera City has a library. Well, maybe not anymore. Seems like a good target for demon destruction. Anyway, before answering Hailey's call to defend your settlement, I used to spend quite a lot of time in there. This game has a ton of lore that hasn't made it into the quest lines. At least not into the quests I've done."

"Wait, so instead of questing and leveling, you were at the in-game library?" Chen asked. He shot Devon an amused glance, but Devon, having known Torald for a while, wasn't that surprised.

Torald turned and started walking backward through the grass to keep eye contact with her and Chen. "Okay, so I'll be the first to admit I take the game world pretty seriously." He gave a self-effacing smirk that Devon found somewhat endearing. It reminded her, in a way, of the shyness that came out when Emerson talked about his AI project and his hopes for Veia.

Of course, thinking of that reminded her about the recent revelation that Emerson sorta kinda *liked her* liked her. It had been so long since Devon was in *that* kind of social situation but she really had no idea how to proceed. To cover the awkwardness when Dorden had suggested Emerson ask Devon on a date, Emerson had claimed he was going to log in so they could just play together. No romance attached. Anyway, she hadn't heard from him in a while. He'd probably been busy with family over the holidays.

"But in this case, I had a good reason," Torald went on. "You know how paladin spells work, right? We have to act the part. I figured the more I knew about the world, the better my battle cries and buffs would be."

Devon tried to keep a straight face. Chen hadn't had the privilege of grouping with Torald yet, and he was in for something of a surprise when the paladin let loose with his over-the-top RP.

"But instead of battle cry fodder, you found something about the Mistwalkers? I'm surprised you remembered. Hasn't it been something like two months since you left Eltera City?"

Torald nodded. "Two months and three days real-world time. But actually, I read about the Mistwalkers more recently."

"How?"

He looked sideways and cringed a little. "Well, when I left Eltera City, I expected to be back in a couple of days. And since I have a lot of bag space"—he patted his *Manpurse of Holding*—"I figured it would be okay to bring a couple of books with me. Something to do while waiting for spawns or whatever. Anyway, they're rather overdue now."

"You can actually check out library books in this game?" Chen asked.

The paladin nodded. "Yeah, but the fees are kinda outrageous. At this point, unless the demons have destroyed the library, I owe three gold and two silver."

Devon jumped when Bob abruptly piped up. "A librarian after my own heart," the wisp said. "At least *someone* in the material plane recognizes the value of information."

She ignored him and kept her focus on Torald. "All right, so you read something about the Mistwalkers."

Torald nodded. "And I perked up because we recently got a quest update that said you'd recovered the *Ironweight Key* from their lost vassaldom."

Devon contained a cringe at the reminder that every player in the camp was on a quest to help her cause and become her subject once she restored Ishildar. "Anything useful?"

"Well," he said, "maybe. The author of the book claimed that there was a schism in the final days of the Esh vassaldom when a delegation was sent to the Veian temple to deliver the Key. As I remember, the Rovan believed the relic should either sink with the vassaldom or remain with the survivors wherever they might flee."

"Which was apparently not far, seeing as I ran into one under the savanna."

Torald smirked. "Actually, I think their presence here may be new. At least at the time of the writing of my borrowed book, the Esh had fled far inland. In addition to their worship of Veia, they had a strong shamanic tradition that drew meaning from the natural world. They felt that the water spirits had become angry with them, leading to the inundation of their home. Of course, the book also speculated that the inland environs didn't suit them and that the race eventually died out."

Devon's steps had slowed while he talked. "You said shamans, right?"

"Yeah, why?"

"Gerrald told me that they'd been searching for a shaman who had experience with shaping ivory. They'd decided that was their best hope for fashioning my blade."

"Huh...yeah, so whether their magic came from Veia—I'm sure I don't have to tell you what I think about that—or whether their shamanic beliefs had validity, Esh shamans were known across the continent for their abilities. One of the footnotes mentioned that the shamanic magic laid the groundwork for modern sorcery, which I believe you know something about."

Devon found herself looking back to the south where Stonehaven had disappeared behind a horizon of gently rolling hills. Between what the scorpion guy had said, his ability to apparently turn into fog and run away, and this talk about shamans, she was getting a strange suspicion about *Night's Fang*.

"All right, back to the Rovan and Drivan..."

Torald nodded. "So the author of my book—"

"The *library's* book," Bob cut in.

Devon rolled her eyes. "Ignore it. I do."

Torald smirked. He'd stopped walking backward and now had fallen in beside Devon, leaving Chen to take up the rear. The last time Devon had looked back, her knight friend had plucked a few stalks of grass and was busy braiding or weaving them as they walked.

"Anyway, the book claims that all Esh hoped for the eventual restoration of Ishildar. Some even believed that the city's rebirth would push back the sea and that their home would once again rise above the sea. Where the factions differed was in where the relic should be kept. The Drivan believed that their tattered civilization would face enough challenges just surviving and that they should entrust the key to others. The Rovan called them weak, traitors to their race. In the end, a small party of Drivan loyalists made off with the relic—the book didn't say what happened to them, but apparently they made it to Shavari's temple."

Devon nodded, thoughts whirling as she strode through the grass. Because her eyes were unfocused, the coiling mist that started rising from the earth didn't register until Torald laid a hand on her arm and pushed her behind him.

"May Veia's light shine through me and bless my sword!" he shouted.

Devon, stumbling backward, ran into Chen just as the teenager said, "What the...?"

As Torald began to glow with divine light, making his armor even harder to look at, the mist swirled and then vanished, blown away on the breeze.

Devon whirled, searching the grasses, but there was nothing. Whoever or whatever had been listening to them was gone.

Chapter Twenty-Five

REMEMBERING WHAT FOOLS the other newbies had looked like stumbling around the training grounds, Emerson tried to plant his—unfortunately still bare—feet with purpose as he stalked out the gates of Stonehaven and into the slaughtering fields behind. The fortifications guy, Jarleck, cast him a glance as he passed, and perhaps what might be described as a faint look of respect. Or confusion. Or pity. Honestly, the guy's face was pretty damn stony, and Emerson had never been good at reading expressions anyway.

Die.

Honestly, the quest objective seemed a little...odd. Having watched a couple of documentaries on real-life combat training, he could kind of see how learning about in-game death could teach someone what to expect, maybe keep people from freezing up at the wrong moment. The objective seemed similar to simulations of fog of war and other intense experiences that would come up in a real life-or-death situation. At the same time, even he'd seen enough game footage and chatter to know that death was commonplace. If it was going to happen sooner or later, why force him to undergo the experience now?

At the very least, it hardly seemed a quest that ought to be handed out to someone that the trainer "had a gut feeling about."

Unless that gut feeling was that Emerson's only future skill was going to be getting his butt kicked.

Regardless, the five thousand experience on offer would bump him up to level 5, at which point he'd finally be able to choose a class. And *then* he'd have these rats and beetles cowering in their boots. Er...not that they wore boots. But anyway, back to the mission at hand.

Emerson scanned the field in front of the settlement. Unlike his last venture out the gates, there were now at least two-dozen level one and two players striking at foes in the grass. If what they were doing could be called anything so flattering as *striking*. Mostly, they were swinging swords and clubs in the general direction of the vermin, most of whom were wandering along random vectors, oblivious to the weapons that were thudding into the ground on either side of their paths.

Emerson shook his head, suddenly as perplexed as the GMs had been about Veia's decision to move the Eltera City starting content here. If Devon were to be believed—and he pretty much believed everything she said ever—the coming demon army would be the biggest challenge Stonehaven had ever faced. These people were a liability, nothing more.

Gritting his teeth, he fought the urge to march back into the settlement and give the trainers a lecture. If this was the kind of soldier they were going to turn out, they might as well open the gates and welcome the demons into the inner keep. But seeing as Aravon was...16 levels higher than him and at least six inches taller, Emerson didn't think that would further his cause much. Watching a particularly inept young woman—who had, for some incomprehensible reason, decided to name her character

WizKitten—aim a makeshift wand at a rat, mutter an awkward incantation, and set fire to a patch of grass five feet from her target, he was tempted to head into the field and try his own hand at instructing these people.

"Don't bother," someone said from behind him.

Emerson whirled and felt his spine stiffen as he recognized Greel. "Don't bother what?"

The lawyer shook his head. "Helping them. The mayor—who has her own suite of competence issues—asked me to pick out a prodigy or two. Train them properly. But I haven't spotted a single candidate. I mean, it almost makes me think I should take *you* on."

Emerson blinked, totally unsure whether he'd just been complimented or insulted. "How did you know I was thinking about giving them some pointers?"

Greel scoffed. "Because you look like the charitable type. Which I'm sorry to say isn't going to get you far when Zaa's legions come to destroy us all. Also, I saw the way you were looking at Mayor Devon. It's a common enough reaction, given her obsession with raising her *Charisma.* Don't worry though—you build up a resistance."

Emerson, feeling decidedly uncomfortable, had already started to sidle away. He nodded politely as he scanned the area beyond the field. His mission might be to die, but he'd just decided he would not do it in plain view of Stonehaven. And anyway, what kind of example would he be setting for the noobs if he fell beneath the claws or pincers of a level 1 monster?

"Well, come on, then," Greel said, gesturing with his chin toward a path that led south from the settlement, toward the stone quarry if

Emerson remembered right. "Let's find you something challenging to fight."

"Wait, what?"

Greel sighed and rolled his eyes. "I hate to see what your *Intelligence* score is going to be revealed as. I am suggesting that, if only by virtue of having arrived before the rest of this lot, you are perhaps the only fighter worth my time instructing. It's a stretch, to be honest, but seeing as the settlement teeters on the verge of ruin, I feel I must compromise my standards and hope you will somehow rise to the task."

Emerson chewed on the corner of his lip as Greel gave him a disdainful once over. "I...Aravon already sent me on a quest."

"Really? You'd consider a mission from that lout as more important than the chance to train under Stonehaven's preeminent martial artist?"

"Well, it's got a good experience reward. And I had sort of imagined myself as some sort of...I think they call it a tank class."

Greel shook his head in apparent disgust, but another expression had crept onto his face...a sneer, yes, but it seemed almost respectful. "Ah. A practical man. I can understand why you would be loath to abandon a potential reward, even if the granter of this boon is himself unimpressive. I myself first ventured to this Zaa-pulled wilderness under the command of someone far beneath my considerable intelligence, purely because it suited my interests to join. Fine. We will work together to satisfy the quest requirements. And as for your plan to become a..." Greel curled his lip in abject revulsion. "...simple meatshield, we will have to discuss that later."

Unsure what to do, Emerson finally nodded. "Okay, I guess."

"Good then," Greel said before whipping out a piece of paper and a sharpened piece of charcoal. "Please sign here to formalize the apprenticeship agreement. If you are illiterate, a simple X will suffice."

Emerson stared down at the paper, then squinted. "I'm sorry...I can't read this."

Greel sighed again, his loudest yet. "*That* is because I have drafted the document in Carpavan legalese, the only known tongue which creates magically enforceable contracts."

"Uh...I really don't think I should sign something I can't decipher."

"Oh for the sky's sake, why me?" the lawyer said. "Fine. We'll deal with the paperwork later. For now, let's go. I can't *stand* looking at these incompetents any longer, and no matter how inept she can be at governing this settlement, I do believe Devon was wise to suggest I take an apprentice. Every fighter will matter when the dark army comes. Even if they can barely hold their own swords."

With that, the man turned on his heel and stalked southward, stuffing the paper into what appeared to be a hidden pocket.

"Uh, thanks, I think?" Emerson said as he fell into step behind.

Chapter Twenty-Six

"OUCH," TORALD SAID, rubbing his now-dented breastplate. "For being the champion of the place, Ishildar's guardians still don't like you much. So much for the Chosen One trope."

"Yeah," Devon said, flopping down in a pile of vines. The jungle on the outskirts of Ishildar felt as thick as ever, and apparently, the city's stone giants were as aggressive as ever. If her acquisition of the *Ironweight Key* had given her any more hold over them, it hadn't shown. Her head still hurt from focusing on the thin connection created by *Ishildar's Call* and attempting to command the dang things.

If anything, actually, this attempt to venture into the city had gone *worse* than last time. Unlike Hazel, her companions today weren't exactly quick on their feet. Torald had been forced to spend all his mana chain casting his *Creator's Shield* spell while trying—awkwardly—to jog backward toward the edge of the city. About the only thing they'd actually determined this trip was that there was a reason that real-world athletes didn't wear platemail to track and field events.

Still, the paladin had managed to take a solid handful of hits without going down, pretty damn impressive for a level 22 character facing down a level 40-something stone giant. Maybe his studies of the game lore *had* made his battle cries stronger. Either way, he'd held the rear guard long enough for Devon and Chen to make a retreat, and only now did Devon realize how close he'd come to getting smashed. That dent was going to take Garda a lot of work to bang out.

After a minute or two spent staring up at the tree canopy and feeling ants crawling through her hair—nothing like a trip into Ishildar's jungled outskirts to cure her of any leftover nostalgia from the time when dense, humid forest blanketed the whole region—Devon sat up and sighed.

"Honestly, I have no idea how we're going to do it. Hezbek has an invisibility spell that lets her go into the city—at least, that's how she explained her ability to go there when Uruquat commanded it. But she couldn't teach it to me…NPC sorcerer only."

Chen, who had been watching Sigfried attempt to hunt bugs with his new boomerang, stomped to the center of their small clearing and dropped to a cross-legged seat. "Is it really impossible to go around?"

"I guess there's a way to the west, but it would take something like a month's travel each way."

"Well, you only need to go one way, right? Because after you get the relic, the city should stop attacking you. You should be able to take the direct route back."

"I fricking hope it stops attacking after that," Devon said. "I'm really starting to hate stone giants. But anyway, I don't think we even have a month. How long did it take you and Hailey to cross the Noble Sea?"

"Foreverrrrrr…" Chen said. "But it was probably like eight days in game."

"Right, so even if it takes Zaa a couple of weeks to get his shit together, the army could still be here in around three. And actually, it's already been at least a week since we rescued Owen, so..."

"Speaking of, how is he? Heard anything?"

Devon shook her head. "Nothing. It's got to be fricking hard. He was in a coma for weeks. And if his girlfriend hadn't helped us, his own dad would have basically sacrificed him for politics. So yeah, I'd bet he's not feeling too great." Devon's upbringing had sucked, but at least her mom hadn't actively tried to harm her. Even if Governor Calhoun had had some sort of mental justification worked up to convince himself he was doing the right thing, the truth was pretty irrefutable.

"We should ask Emerson. See if he knows anything."

Devon nodded. Yeah, she should. But then she'd have to figure out how to interact with him now that the whole attraction thing was out in the open. "Maybe after this Ishildar business is taken care of. So...ideas? I'm hoping you can come up with something I'm missing."

Still examining his armor for blemishes, Torald gave an uncharacteristic sigh. "It's not that I don't have faith in you, Devon, but even if we were to put together a raid, we wouldn't be able to hold the guardians back long enough for you to make a run for it. What about those tunnels you found? The ones the Rovan Mistwalker fled into."

Devon nodded appreciatively. "Hadn't thought of that. I guess we could try exploring a little, see if they go in the right direction."

Chen grimaced. "Don't think it will work. It would have to be some damn good luck to find a remotely straight tunnel all the way to the other side. Not to mention, you'd probably have to deal with the scorpion guy's friends the whole way. Isn't Ishildar something like ten miles across?"

They all winced at once, thinking of how long it would take to crawl through a ten-mile dungeon. "Okay, new plan," Torald said. "What about Blackbeard. He can carry Bravlon, right?"

Devon laughed at the idea of flying over the city on a giant, loudmouthed parrot. "Even if that stupid bird would agree to carry me, I know I'm too heavy. He's been struggling to take off with the kid lately."

"Hmm," Torald said, pacing.

Dev.

Devon sat up straight when the message from Tamara flashed in the corner of her vision. Her friend had gone into surgery even earlier than expected, admitted on the day after Christmas. Devon had received a quick note from Tamara's mom before she'd logged in this morning, the note saying that Tamara was home recovering and that everything had gone great.

"Don't tell me you're using the implant interface already," she subvocalized into the messaging prompt.

> *Dev! Yes! The Entwined people said it's the fastest anyone has assimilated the sensory input or something. I'm some kind of cyborg prodigy. They say I can probably log in tomorrow. The day after at the latest.*

"Holy—" Devon backspaced, thinking that might be considered blasphemous and started over. "Wow! I can't believe it."

It's for real. You'll come over and help me, right? Mom says she can set up couches side by side. I can't wait to see my bike.

Devon went rigid, eyes wide. Tamara's bike. Shit.

"Hey so I know we talked about walking back and scouting for awakened creatures, but have you guys ever tried the sorcerer teleport? I gotta get back ASAP."

"Uh, sure," Torald said as he climbed to his feet. Chen shrugged, then nodded.

Devon pulled up her messenger window while working through the mental casting motions.

"Text me first thing," she said. "I'll be right over, and we'll get you on your bike."

Tamara would ride tomorrow if it took Devon cannibalizing cart parts and building a bike herself.

Chapter Twenty-Seven

THE KNOCK CAME at the door at ten-thirty in the morning. The doctor must have been monitoring her brain waves or something, because it had been just about fifteen minutes since she'd surfaced from Relic Online, enough to get her bearings and for the dose of painkillers to take hold.

Hailey made him knock a second time for the same reason she'd avoided opening her messenger app even though he'd asked for her to keep an eye on it for news about the trial therapy. For the decade or so that she'd lived here, migrating from the assisted-living wing to the hospital rooms to the sterile chamber she now occupied, it hadn't really bothered her that the physician on staff treated her like a number. A stat on his charts. The fact that he only communicated with her through the most convenient channels—messenger when he could get away with it, or by forcing her to come to his clean-room office when he couldn't—hadn't bothered her.

But if the news was what they expected—if there was no room in the clinical trial for someone as unimportant as her—and he was coming to tell her she was going to die, it shouldn't be *convenient.*

"Yeah, come in," she said.

The pain medicine made it less agonizing to sit up and face him with dignity even if she still felt fragile as a moth and ready to barf. Her body was shutting down, her organs no longer able to clear the waste from her system or extract nutrition from her food. They'd put her on a high-calorie, low-protein diet and an appetite stimulant. The food still tasted like crap.

The doctor stepped into the room, spectacles perched on the end of his nose while he looked down at a tablet. Like he needed to reread whatever was there. It was just an excuse to avoid making eye contact.

"Hello, Hailey."

She didn't respond until he looked up because hell if she was going to let him file her away as anonymous patient number 37, suffering from a severe autoimmune condition of a rare classification shared by around twelve hundred people in the United States. Dying of a severe autoimmune condition, if they were going to be blunt about it.

He blinked when finally meeting her eyes as if just now seeing her for the first time. The man cleared his throat. "I'm afraid the news from Cornell isn't what we were hoping for."

She was tempted to snap and ask whether he'd actually been hoping for an answer either way. Whether Hailey lived or died, his life would go on as usual. But she realized that he must have at least some humanity behind those watery blue eyes, so if given the choice between her acceptance into the trial and her looming death, he'd probably go for the trial.

"Figured," Hailey said.

"So that leaves us with how to make your remaining time as comfortable as possible. Did you review the options I sent you? It's within your rights to...request an end to your suffering." His voice faltered a little while trying to force the last bit out, and he worked a finger under the collar of his smock as if to loosen it from his throat.

No, Hailey had not reviewed the crap he'd sent her. She was not going to just give up or fade off into a drugged stupor. She might have no hope remaining, but that didn't mean she was a quitter. Anyway, she could escape to Relic Online much of the time.

"I intend to fight as long as I can," she said.

The doctor nodded, face neutral. "Understood. Regarding your legal affairs, then, you'll want to get your will in order. The facility contracts with a legal firm that is quite affordable."

Hailey actually snorted. As if, after ten years as an invalid, she had anything worth giving away. Her parents had both died when she was in her twenties, having conceived her on accident when they were in their early 50s and already in not-so-great health. Hailey was basically a consequence of hormone therapy as a replacement for an active lifestyle in the pursuit of longevity. At least when she kicked off, whatever predisposition to laziness they might have passed on would exit the gene pool.

"I'm guessing by that response that you don't wish to retain their services," the doctor said. "Well, in that case, I'll give you an update on your medical status. This is something you'll want to watch closely, particularly if you think you might change your mind about your final options. When we're done, I can set up a video call with a counselor if you'd like. I've heard from many of our patients that it helps to have someone to talk to."

Hailey shook her head. "I've got an online support group."

He brightened at her lie, no doubt relieved to unload any burden he might be carrying regarding her emotions.

"All right, then down to the nitty gritty, I wanted to show you which numbers are of the greatest concern right now."

Hailey zoned out while he talked. It didn't matter which of her systems would fail first, only that, without a doubt, the end was coming. For the past few days, ever since she'd bailed on Devon outside the boss cave, she'd been wandering through Relic Online's wilderness. It was peaceful despite the hives of awakened creatures and the threat of demons across the ocean. It had been years since she just focused on the immersion, the sights and smells of a foreign world. Even now, lying in the antiseptic-smelling room, she could close her eyes and feel the sun on her face and the grass scratching her legs as she pushed through it. She smelled warmed earth and grass pollen and heard the buzz of insects lazily moving from flower to seed head and back.

When the doctor finished his oration, signaled by him dropping the tablet to his side, she nodded and lifted a couple of fingers in parting. The man spun and headed for the door. The seals engaged shortly after he disappeared, and from the antechamber beyond, she heard the hiss as air was vacuumed out to be cleaned.

After a long few minutes, Hailey pushed the button to summon her meal. Her finger hung over a second control that would order more painkillers, but she managed to resist. Instead, she opened up the special icon that had recently been added to her interface.

"Ok, Bob," she said into the prompt. "Let's do it."

Chapter Twenty-Eight

DEVON'S BODY TINGLED as she rematerialized at the Shrine to Veia, the last glimmers of magic from the *Teleport* spell dissipating from her sight. She blinked as her eyes adjusted to the golden sunshine flooding Stonehaven, so bright after the jungle understory outside Ishildar.

"Traveling in style," Torald said with a grin once he'd fully reconstituted. "I know the spell isn't your favorite, but I'd consider it quite a blessing from Veia if I could avoid lugging my armor-clad self home after every adventure."

Devon smirked. "I'm just greedy. My version only travels to bindstones and the shrine. Hezbek's works in combat, and she can basically whisk her group anywhere she's previously visited."

"In other words, totally broken."

"Yeah, pretty much. It's like the game gave it to her because the woman had decided never to fight again."

Torald glanced toward the center of the settlement, still rubbing the dent in his breastplate. "Well, I suppose I should head to the forge and speak to Garda about repairs. You think she'll move me to the head of her queue if I bring her flowers?"

Devon cringed. "I'd advise against that if you don't want an ax hurled in your direction. But I have heard she's fond of pastries. Don't tell her I told you."

With a crooked smile, Torald bowed with a ridiculous flourish of his hand, then trotted off.

"What is wrong with that man? I can't honestly believe that anyone thinks that such...chivalry is useful."

Devon jumped at Greel's voice. She turned just in time to see him detach from a patch of shadow near the cliff at the back of the settlement. What the heck? Had he just been waiting here to ambush her?

"Seems to me that he's figured out when and where to pay proper respect. It's something you could consider, seeing as I am your leader."

Greel's eyes narrowed. "You know as well as I that I have ulterior motives in remaining here. My continued presence has nothing whatsoever to do with your guidance of the community."

Devon glanced down when Sigfried tottered past on his little stick legs. The golem squinted an eye, twigs descending to cover the shiny stone Chen had placed in the figure's eye socket, and hucked the boomerang at Greel's knee. The lawyer just barely managed to jump clear of the little projectile. He gave an offended snort.

"I see you've brought kindling for the fire," the man snarled at Chen.

Chen shrugged. "I think you'd regret it if you tried picking him up."

Sigfried grinned, baring teeth of sharpened sticks.

Devon smirked. It had been a long time since she'd grouped with Chen. Really, when she thought about it, they'd only hunted together a couple of times. His Tinker class abilities had been good for creating distractions, allowing him to set up crossbows and activate them remotely, things like that. She wondered what else he'd come up with in the weeks since.

"So what's going on, Greel? Is there any particular reason you're lurking back here?"

The man sniffed. "Not that I owe you an explanation, but yes, there is. I'm waiting for someone. I can only hope they'll arrive before your response to my town charter proposal."

As if on queue, light bloomed near the Shrine to Veia, and moments later, Valious appeared, flat on his back.

Greel gave what was probably the loudest scoffing sound Devon had ever heard. The man stomped over, bent at the waist—an awkward motion with the twist in his spine—and glared down at the player.

"Seriously? You expected the blow, yet still ended up on your back? I'm beginning to think this is hopeless. Perhaps the contract should be torn up."

Devon looked at Chen as if her friend might have a clue what was going on. Chen just shrugged.

Clearly disoriented, Valious blinked, then patted his gut as if feeling for a wound. He looked toward his outstretched weapon hand, verified that the sword was still there, and finally sat up.

When he spotted Devon, the blood seemed to drain from his face. His eyes widened, and he mouthed something soundlessly before finally stammering, "It was a quest. I was supposed to die."

Devon cocked her head, even more confused. "I'm not sure what you're talking about. But it's nice to see you anyway."

A nervous smile flashed across his face, but he didn't seem to know what to say. Remembering her earlier decision to be a little kinder to the noobs—especially since there was now a swarm of them stumbling around outside the walls—she tried to force her brain through the contortions required for small talk.

"How's the leveling going?" she asked.

Valious swallowed as Greel rolled his eyes and sighed heavily to show his impatience. Devon glanced at him. Why had he been waiting around for Valious anyway?

"I—well, I guess it's going okay." Valious stood and dusted himself off, casting a dismayed look at his cloth armor in the process. "Once I go talk to Aravon and complete my quest, I should hit level 5."

Level 5 already? For Devon to make it that far, she'd had to slay what had felt like a million tree vipers followed by an ogre tyrant. All this guy had had to do was kill a few dozen non-aggro mobs and attend a kegger. When she realized she was making an annoyed face, she quickly turned it into a smile, but it was too late. Valious had already backed off a couple of steps.

"That's great," she said. "Really. I was just thinking about the crap the game put me through before level 5."

Of course, that didn't seem to help either, probably because it sounded like she was undervaluing his accomplishment. Devon balled her free hand into a fist. NPCs were so much easier to deal with.

"Well, shall we?" Greel said, his voice carrying every bit of sneer he could put into it.

Devon sighed. Most NPCs anyway.

"I hope everything's going well for you too, Devon," Valious said, his face still a bit red. "Lot of responsibility, looking after the whole city."

Greel snorted. "Haven't I mentioned that it does us no good to inflate her already considerable ego?"

"Are you sure you don't have some accounts to update, Greel?" Devon said. "You should leave the poor newcomers alone."

Beside her, Sigfried planted his hands on his hips and puffed his chest as if to back her up.

Greel's lip curled. "I expect your notarized feedback on the charter by dark. Otherwise, consider the proposal null and void. I will draw up an alternative that is more to my standards of length and precision." With that, he turned on his heels and stalked off. When Valious didn't immediately follow, the man whirled, face dark, and gestured impatiently.

Valious glanced at her and shrugged. "See ya. I mean—actually, do you have any time later, Devon? I have something I kinda want to talk to you about."

Devon stared at him, speechless. How was she even supposed to respond to that? She already had a full schedule for the rest of the day between checking on Tamara's bike, figuring out how to get through Ishildar, and working on the city preparations. If she *did* have any free time left over to talk to people, she'd much rather spend time with her NPC followers than a stranger. And of course, there was the issue of precedent. If she were seen making time for one-on-one meetings with one newcomer, she'd probably end up with the rest of them lining up for a turn.

> Congratulations! Stonehaven's defenses have been upgraded to ***Castle - Basic.***

A split second after the notification appeared, trumpets blared from the walls. Valious jumped, whipped his head around, then turned bright red as he calmed himself.

"I—it sounds like my day is going to be pretty full. We just became a Castle. Raincheck?" she said, hoping that in the meantime, he would realize that the request wasn't really something she could honor.

"Valious! To me!" Greel snapped.

"Uh, yeah, sure thing, Dev. Devon. Another time." With that, the strange player saluted and ran off.

Devon glanced at the inner palisade as banners unfurled, scarlet fabric with a crest she'd never seen. It showed a stylized bulwark with a building behind, a ray of light descending from the sky onto the building's roof.

> **Would you like to design a new crest for your castle?**
> Y/N

Devon grinned as she brushed the popup away. She knew from experience that it would take her hours and hours to settle on a design, time she definitely didn't have right now. A castle, though. Holy crap. She was on her way to founding a kingdom or something. As long as her new dominion didn't get smashed by a demon horde in the next few days, anyway.

As much as she wanted to inspect the fortifications and talk to Jarleck about next steps—for that matter, she had a lot of work to do on the city's supply lines and settlement advancement—Tamara came first. With a quick wave to Chen and Torald, Devon left the group and hurried toward the center of town to check on her friend's bike.

Chapter Twenty-Nine

DEVON PACED BACK and forth along a narrow track between laundry piles and her bed. She tugged at the end of her ponytail. This should be an easy decision—she should just wear whatever she would normally put on for a day of gaming. But it felt way different. Being basically unconscious in your own home was one thing. Doing it in public was totally different. Even though she would look like she was sleeping, the idea that Tamara's parents would be hanging around while she helped Tamara into the game gave her the willies.

She grabbed a knit sweater from the closet, one of the last pieces of clothing that had actually been put away rather than left in the "clean" basket. From the floor near the bed, she grabbed a pair of jeans. Seeing as her usual gaming uniform amounted to yoga pants and sweatshirts, she could be relatively certain the jeans hadn't been worn more than once. That would have required leaving the house.

In the bathroom, she splashed water over her face and stared at herself in the mirror. In the days before Owen's rescue, her eyes had been bloodshot and her face puffy. Now, she was sleeping better, and it showed. Even if the demon invasion was coming, she had time to prepare. A little anyway. Her dreams had been relatively untroubled.

Grabbing a brush, Devon dragged it through her dark brown hair and redid her ponytail. When she was finished, there was still an annoying lump on the side where the hair wouldn't quite go the right direction—the typical result of having taken a shower and basically passed out five minutes later. She grabbed a stretchy headband thing and pulled it around her skull. It hid the issue, mostly.

She took a deep breath. Okay. Time to get over to Tamara's. Her friend had been up since long before dawn spamming Devon's messenger with chatter about the coming events. Devon shouldn't make her wait just because she felt self-conscious. Slapping the light switch to turn it off, she hurried from the bathroom, grabbed a granola bar from the cabinet and her purse and jacket from their typical heap near the front door, and stepped out into the chill air of a desert morning.

Above the rooftops of the storage facility that stood adjacent to her apartment complex, the sandstone mountains of Snow Canyon State Park basked in the sunlight, the different layers of stone an array of hues from cream to apricot to vermillion. Dark green patches of juniper and pinyon pine tucked into steep ravines and lined the feet of the peaks. Even with the surrounding asphalt, the humming freeway, and the rows of condos separating her balcony from the desert wilderness, she could still smell hints of the trees and the sun-warmed earth, carried over the city by cool breezes descending from the heights.

Devon took a moment and stretched, breathing deep. As pleasant as the in-game savanna was, especially when compared to the godawful jungle it had replaced, sometimes it was nice to inhabit her home environment a little.

A few yards down the balcony, a door opened, and a man backed out with a heaping laundry basket in his hands. That was all the urging Devon needed to get going. First of all, she had no desire to end up in a conversation. Second, she definitely didn't need any reminders about how sorely overdue her laundry duties were.

Down at street level, she touched her palm to the autocab hailing pad and hitched her purse strap higher onto her shoulder. When the man stepped off the stairwell and walked past her toward the communal laundry building, she dug through the bag as if searching for something so that she wouldn't have to make eye contact. It was stupid; she'd actually been getting better at interacting with others, or so she thought. But today her nerves were already singing with anxiousness over what it would be like at Tamara's house. She'd probably just stammer or say something inane.

Fortunately, the cab arrived, sliding to a halt in front of the curb before the guy came back for another load. She ducked gratefully through the door, gave Tamara's address, and swiped her wrist over the sensor for authentication. As she buckled her seatbelt, the vehicle accelerated along the cracked asphalt of the parking lot and turned around the far side of the building. Devon laid her head back against the seat and closed her eyes.

***

"Good morning, sweetie!" Tamara's mom, having all but thrown the door open, swept Devon up in a hug.

Resisting the urge to go rigid as an ironing board, Devon patted the woman's back. "Hi. How's Tamara?"

The woman stepped back, cheeks dimpling. "Practically vibrating with excitement. I haven't seen her like this since we got her a ski trip to Alta for her sixteenth."

Devon gave a quick smile, fighting hard against the fear that the experience would fail to live up to Tamara's expectations. She *would* make it awesome for her friend. Tamara deserved it.

"Have you eaten?" Tamara's mom asked. "I made eggs and bacon. Tamara ate most of the pancakes, but I think there's one left."

Devon's mouth watered as she stepped into the entryway and the smell of the meal reached her nose. She thought of the granola bar in her purse. "I haven't. Planned to eat a bar really quick, but if you think Tamara can wait long enough for me to have a few bites of eggs..."

A snort-laugh came from the first doorway to the right, the entrance to the kitchen and breakfast nook. "Get in here, Dev. I know what your typical nutrition looks like."

Devon edged forward and peered through the door. Tamara sat in an overstuffed chair that had been pulled up to the breakfast table. Her oxygen tank was hanging in a sleeve that had been fitted over the chair's arm, and the ever-present tube snaked into Tamara's nose. She sat in front of a mostly empty but syrup-smeared plate and grinned.

"Hey!" Devon said. "You look like you recovered faster than I did from the surgery."

Tamara raised her eyebrows in mock arrogance. "Prodigy, remember? Actually, they said the procedure is getting less and less complicated all the time. Most of the installation happens automatically...circuitry growing under the skin according to some preprogrammed schematic or something. I guess they expect it to be an out-patient procedure soon."

Devon scratched the back of her skull then ran fingers over the ridges at the nape of her neck. Most of the implant hardware was buried beneath her scalp with a few wires penetrating her skull and another few bits of biocircuitry breaking the skin in case she ever needed diagnostics. When she'd undergone the surgery, it had taken doctors physically laying the pattern of sub-scalp wires in a net around her head. She didn't like to think about how they actually managed it since the only incisions had been behind her ears. Regardless, she'd been hospitalized for three days after, and the implants had itched for weeks.

Tamara gestured to the wooden chair beside her. "Eat something. I'm probably going to have seconds anyway."

Devon stared at the heap of steaming eggs and the stack of crispy bacon. "Okay. Twist my arm."

"So is my bike ready?" Tamara asked as Devon spooned a mass of jiggling eggs onto her plate.

Devon glanced up as Tamara's mom arrived with a carafe of milk. "Thanks," she said as the woman poured a stream into her cup. She turned back to Tamara. "To be honest, I was terrified that it wouldn't be ready. But you're all set! Well, I doubt the bike will be up to your standards. But even I was able to pedal it. They couldn't figure out how to make a chain that worked right, so they had to use a leather strap to connect the pedals to the back wheel. So, unfortunately you won't be able to change gears."

"A single speed," Tamara said with a grin. "Awesome! Honestly, for self-supported enduro rides it can be kinda cool to have something that's mechanically simple. Less stuff to break even if the single gear ratio means that hills can be brutal."

Devon stuffed a bite of eggs in her mouth. She had no idea what Tamara was talking about.

There wasn't any sort of serving utensil for the bacon, so after staring at it for a while, she finally reached for a strip with her fingers. "Is this...do you care if I use my hands?"

Tamara laughed. "Aren't we heading into the Middle Ages or something? I doubt we'll be worried about manners. Anyway, fingers are fine. That's why God gave them to us, right? To grab bacon?"

Devon fought the urge to look over her shoulder for Tamara's parents. She hadn't gotten the idea that they were deeply devout or anything, but she didn't want Tamara to get in trouble for making light of religion. When she glanced at her friend, though, she saw that Tamara was smirking.

"And no, I don't think I'll go to Hell for saying that."

No, maybe not. But she might find Stonehaven to be awfully close to it within the next couple weeks if Devon didn't figure out how to get through Ishildar. And speaking of going to hell, Devon wondered again how Owen was doing. She really did need to get in touch with Emerson, awkwardness or not, to find out if there was any news from her former guildmate or his girlfriend, Cynthia.

Crunching down on a bite of bacon, Devon rolled her eyes with pleasure. It was hard to believe that Tamara ate like this every day. The food was *delicious.* Even better than the *Stonehaven Scramble* that Tom used to make from the reptile eggs the hunter, Grey, used to forage downstream of the village. When the jungle had retreated, those egg-layers had vanished, too. Tom had concocted a new dish,

Poached Coop Fruit, from the chicken eggs that Stonehaven's birds laid, but Devon couldn't really get past the name. And anyway, with so many mouths to feed, the settlement's kitchen hadn't had the luxury of making special buff-granting recipes lately. She hoped the new farm plots and kitchen would be ready soon.

Thinking of it, she started to feel guilty for lingering over breakfast. Trying to get the bacon down quicker, she took a couple of deep swigs of milk.

"I get thc sense you're ready to log in," Tamara said.

Devon forced herself to slow down and swallow before speaking. "Sorry, started thinking about some work I have ahead of me."

Tamara laughed. "No problem. I was just trying to be polite and let you eat before you have to play tour guide."

Grinning, Devon shoveled in another big bite of eggs and washed it down with the rest of her coffee. "Let's do this, then."

Chapter Thirty

INSIDE A SMALL wood-paneled room that Tamara's family called the den, a pair of recliners stood side by side. Other furniture—a dark-wood table lacquered to a gleam, a straight-backed chair, a couch, and a trio of healthy houseplants—had been pushed up against a wall that was entirely covered with built-in bookcases. On the opposite wall, heavy blue drapes had been pulled across the windows. Behind the recliners, a large in-home theater screen was inset a few inches into the wall. Side tables stood next to each of the recliners, bowls of nuts and little plates of hard candy and boxes of tissue standing on top.

"Have a preference?" Tamara asked, gesturing at the recliners. "The left one is new, so it's probably not broken in."

New? Did that mean that Tamara's parents had bought it just for this? Devon would have been fine flopping down on the couch. As she looked at the room again, the situation started to feel like one of those extravagant slumber parties that parents of her classmates had thrown back in elementary school. Of course, Devon hadn't been invited—even if the upstanding parents could have gotten past her home situation, having seen her following her disheveled mother around the state-run liquor store, there'd have been no way for the other parents to contact Devon's mom and invite her. No phone. No tablet. If they'd wanted to send a note, Devon would have had to bribe her mother with whiskey to get her to read and respond. And even if she'd gone that far, she probably would have been too embarrassed to deliver the response with its sloppy handwriting on stained and wrinkled paper.

She swallowed and shrugged. "You've seen where I game at home. Take whichever's more comfortable for you."

Tamara didn't argue but instead headed straight for the broken-in recliner. Almost tiptoeing in her wake, Devon ran a hand over the soft upholstery before turning and sitting. The chair sighed, exhaling the scent of new fabric and foam.

Devon closed her eyes as she pulled the lever to extend the footrest. She could stay here pretty much forever—the chair was about a hundred times more comfortable than her bed. Tier 20 comfort. It had to have cost a bucketful of money.

As the women settled into their recliners, Tamara's mother appeared in the doorway. Dry-washing her hands, she stepped into the room. After shifting her weight back and forth between her feet, she shuffled across the thick carpet and started rearranging the supplies on Tamara's side table. "You guys need anything?" she asked, then abruptly straightened. "I forgot the water bottles. Hold on."

As she started to rush out, Tamara sighed. "Mom, it's okay. We're not going to be conscious anyway."

The woman turned, the corner of her mouth sucked between her teeth. She rubbed her hands together again. "I just want this to go well for you. You sure I can't help? Would it be best if I brought my writing in here?"

Devon felt her eyes widen despite her attempts to hide her reaction. She couldn't exactly tell the woman not to hang out, but she was already feeling self-conscious over the whole situation. The closest experience she'd had to this was back when Pod People had opened its first VR parlor in St. George. It had been just a few months before Devon's mom had kicked her out, but Devon had felt the change coming. She'd been gaming semi-professionally between school and homework and her weekend job as an attendant at a local car wash, making sure the autocab companies weren't trying to slip through more fleet vehicles than their contracts specified. But with the rise of VR parlors, the gaming population that wanted to buy her loot in old-fashioned flat-screen games was dwindling. She and a friend had saved up for a month of VR time, and on that first day, they'd gone into the parlor together to make characters.

But once there, they'd climbed into individual capsules, closed the lids, and listened to the seals engage. It had still been a private experience, nothing like this exposed situation.

"Seriously, Mom, do you think we want someone here watching? What if we drool or something?"

The tension uncoiled from Devon's chest. Whether or not God made fingers for grabbing bacon, Devon was certainly glad that the creator presiding over Earth—whoever or whatever it was—had come up with Tamara.

Still, Tamara's mother hesitated, and Tamara gave an audible sigh. "Would it help if I put on my heart rate monitor? It's not like I'm using it to track my aerobic potential anymore, so might as well let you stare at the app so you won't have to worry that I'm dead."

Tamara's mom smiled somewhat sheepishly. "I have it here," she said, pulling out what looked like a wrist watch from the pocket of her thigh-length sweater.

Tamara laughed and held out a hand to grab it. The watch-thing sat on her wrist, and when Tamara's mom showed the women her phone screen, there was a pulsing heart graphic with a bunch of numbers and acronyms. Apparently this was yet another of the mysterious habits of obsessive athletes.

"When you said heart rate, I was expecting all those electrodes they stick on you," Devon said.

"You mean like a full-on EKG?" Tamara said with a laugh. "The adhesive and wires don't mesh well with sweat and crashes."

Now peering at the phone as if it could keep her daughter safe, Tamara's mom swallowed. "Okay, well if you don't need anything..."

"Just go, Mom," Tamara said.

Moments later, the door clicked shut. Devon sank deeper into the chair, relieved.

"Okay, so I just focus on the Relic Online icon?" Tamara said.

"Yep. You'll go through character creation where you'll basically choose how you'll look in the game world. To start, anyway. Just like life, you'll probably change over time."

Tamara gave an ironic snort and lifted her oxygen tube. "Hopefully not in this way."

Devon smiled gently, knowing that Tamara made jokes like that because it helped her cope. "The only time I've ever struggled to breathe in the game was when I grew gills and didn't get in the water right away."

Tamara's eyebrow went up. "Uh..."

"Don't worry. It was a temporary thing. Anyway I lost the item that let me cast the water-breathing spell when I transformed into a large demon and my backpack got shredded."

"Double uh...?"

Devon laughed. "Anyway, character creation may take you a while, but I'll be waiting in Stonehaven. The GMs have orders to teleport you there if you end up spawning elsewhere."

Tamara nodded, hand rubbing the arm of the chair. Devon couldn't remember ever seeing her friend look nervous; after all, this was the woman who used to ride her bike off cliffs. She considered patting Tamara's hand to encourage her but thought that might be awkward, maybe even a breach of the rules. Out-of-game adult friendships were kind of like a poorly written quest with super vague directions.

"Just one more step, and you'll be riding, right?" she asked.

Tamara's hand stilled and she nodded, a smile spreading across her face. "Okay, here goes."

Devon watched her friend's face go slack as the implants took over her perception, sweeping her away to...whatever character creation looked like in Relic Online. Devon had never experienced it, the game having dropped her unceremoniously into the middle of Ishildar with nothing but ragged clothing and pocket lint. But from what she'd heard in the chatter among the players of the camp, it was the best they'd experienced. Tamara would have fun with it.

Settling back into the chair, she closed her eyes and focused on her interface. Speaking of adult friendships...she glanced at her messenger icon. Over the past couple days, she'd been thinking more about how she'd avoided contacting Emerson because she didn't know how to approach it. The truth was, she did enjoy his company. At the very least, she'd promised him some mob-slaying time. Yeah, things were too hectic in the game right now, but she really ought to let him know *why* she hadn't dropped a line to lay plans for some tree snake hunting.

She glanced again at Tamara, who'd been brave enough to install hardware in her skull and jump into a foreign world on Devon's promise that it would be fun. At the very least, Devon could be brave enough to send Emerson a message to let him know what was going on. It wasn't like she was proposing marriage or something. Swallowing her remaining hesitation, she pulled up her messenger interface.

Chapter Thirty-One

"EXCUSE ME, WHAT?" Emerson said. He narrowed his eyes at the tank trainer, Aravon. "I'm not qualified? What do you mean I'm not qualified? You were the one who said you sensed something special about me. So why, exactly, can't you offer me a choice of character class? I completed your cannon fodder quest and hit level 5. Seems like that should qualify me."

Emerson realized he didn't really sound like himself. At least, he wasn't sounding like the real-life programmer who avoided conflict and would certainly never start an argument with someone wearing battle armor and possessing enough scars to...what...make that old Scarface character jealous? No. That was a dumb comparison. To make a scarab jealous? No. Different pronunciation. Anyway, the dude had a lot of scars, and Emerson was talking to him like a spoiled elementary school kid.

But at this point, he was kind of pissed. It wasn't really Aravon's fault. Well, at least, it wasn't only Aravon's fault. The man *had* given him the quest that led to him reappearing, clearly having just died, right under Devon's nose. Only to be greeted by Greel who talked to him like he was a trained dog, further humiliating him in front of the one person he wanted to impress.

Of course, Emerson's biggest problem was he *still* had no idea what to do about having lied to Devon. Well, not lied. But close enough. Maybe if it had been just the once he could have logged out and forced customer service to flag his account to allow another avatar. Someday, long in the future and once he'd proved himself, Emerson could have confessed about Valious, and they could have laughed about it together. Now though, he just seemed to be digging himself deeper and deeper.

He continued to level up, gaining skill and confidence and even—shoes. Just before heading to the training grounds, he'd picked up a swanky set of leather boots from Gerrald's specialty shop. 3 Armor!

Not only that, but Aravon had a gut feeling about him.

Greel had taken him on as a pupil.

He'd reached level 5, apparently faster than Devon herself.

Together, it had to mean something, perhaps even that Emerson had a part to play in protecting Devon's settlement from Zaa—something he'd failed miserably at in his attempts to persuade Bradley Williams to shut the AI down.

Anyway, no matter how much his mind screamed at him to log out now if he ever wanted to be able to admit the truth to Devon, the game kept pulling him back.

Well, actually, his apprenticeship to Greel wasn't exactly a selling point for the game. The longer Emerson spent with the man, the more he started to wonder how Greel could possibly act so fricking...supercilious *every moment of his waking life*. The guy put the 'eer' in the word *sneer*. Okay, maybe that saying needed work, too. But the man was seriously annoying, and if Emerson wouldn't otherwise be competing with dozens and dozens of other players for the trainers' attention, he'd walk away from their little arrangement in a heartbeat.

Oh, and if Greel's attitude wasn't enough to put him out of sorts, there was the crap about the title. When Emerson had completed the Cannon Fodder Training quest, he'd had a choice between the "Speedbump" and "Expendable" titles. Yeah, neither were particularly flattering, but since he hadn't seen anyone *else* running around with a title, he'd chosen "Expendable" and had been pretty damn proud to sport it.

Until Greel had caught sight of him.

Of course, Emerson had no clue whether NPCs perceived the game interface the same way he did. Regardless, the moment Emerson completed the quest and figured out how to attach the title to his name, Greel had smacked him on the back of the head and dragged him away from the other trainers for a "chat."

According to the lawyer, titles were nothing but an invitation to others to challenge the bearer to a duel or some other "equally ridiculous and pointless contest of prowess." A true master of the combat arts needed no such heralding, according to Greel, and in fact, the use of the pronouncement only made Emerson look like a fool.

Of course, having no clue about the social rules of the game world—or for that matter, the social rules in real life—Emerson didn't know whether to believe the man or not. He didn't know how duels happened in the game, but he assumed it was something like those old stories of people slapping each other with gloves or throwing down gauntlets. Either way, it probably wouldn't go well for him. So for the time being, he was simply Valious. The untitled blandness.

Aravon, who had been staring down at Emerson with a look of consternation twisting his battered face, finally cleared his throat.

The man looked decidedly uncomfortable. He glanced over his shoulder and peered at the surroundings before speaking. "You're right. I did say I had a feeling about you. And it's the most troubling thing...I can't lay my mind on any good reason why I should feel that you are important." He swallowed. "No offense intended, of course."

"Uh… None taken?" Emerson grimaced a little. He'd been kind of pleased to have been singled out. It would be nice if the guy would have let him live with the illusion that there was something about his warrior spirit that distinguished him from the rat-fighting masses out in the field.

Aravon sighed. "I'll tell you the truth, but I'm trusting you not to bring my name into this afterward. Technically, you qualify for the choice. Even if you'd reached level 5 by running delivery quests and never leaving the city, you could still choose a combat class. It might be an uneducated, idiotic choice, but you'd be free to make it. The problem here is that your new mentor specifically requested that I refuse you. And when I say requested, I mean he held one of those wicked steel knives of his to my throat. The man is only level 18, but he took me by surprise. I wouldn't want to bed down inside these walls knowing he had a vendetta against me."

Emerson stared, his lip twitching in anger. Greel had prohibited him from choosing his combat class? Jerk! Sure, the lawyer had said they needed to "talk about" Emerson's intent to choose a tank class, but Emerson had figured he was just being his usual difficult self. But actually prohibiting the choice? Without bothering to say anything?

Emerson hadn't signed a contract yet, so as far as he was concerned, this partnership was done.

Fists clenched, he whirled and stomped across the training grounds, intent on finding his so-called mentor and terminating the arrangement. But as he neared the strip of grass between the makeshift arena and the nearest row of cottages, his messenger icon flashed.

Emerson's breath leaked out in a sudden and very unmanly squeak—the message was from Devon. Eyes darting to make sure she wasn't anywhere in sight, he dashed into the shade of an acacia tree and slipped around to the far side of the trunk.

You have gained a skill point: +1 Hide

Commonly used by parties trying to conceal themselves from patrolling guards and dragon flyovers, this skill also works if you're scared of talking to girls.

With a flick of his eyes, Emerson banished the popup and pulled up Devon's message.

So, hey. How's it going? You know, I'm really sorry for having been out of touch. It's been pretty crazy in Stonehaven, but that's not a great excuse for why I haven't dropped a line. So, line dropped. :)

I didn't write just to ask for help, but while I'm at it... I know you were planning to talk to Bradley about shutting off Zaa. I'm guessing that since I haven't heard anything on that front, our favorite demon god is still alive and kicking. Anyway, if I'm mistaken, don't hesitate to tell me!

Anyway, the thing with Zaa is related to why you haven't heard from me. The truth is I'm trying to get Stonehaven ready for war. Prepare for a siege, find the next relic, the usual Champion stuff. And as if that weren't enough, Veia has served me up a newbie horde. Thanks for that.

Just kidding. I know it's not your fault and that you don't control her in that way. But anyway, now I have to worry about the noobs too. Don't want a bunch of low-level players getting in the way when the army comes, you know? No offense... I know you will be starting at level 1, too. But I bet you'll be quicker to catch on than most.

Anyway, yeah. I'm not very good at writing long messages. I hope this doesn't sound weird. I'd still like to play some together, but it will probably be after I deal with the Zaa issue. It won't bug me if you want to write back, though. I'm not that busy. Hope all is well!

PS. Anything from Owen and Cynthia?

Emerson sighed and leaned his head against the tree trunk. He *had* to tell her before this went on any longer. Taking in a huge breath, he stepped out of the shade of the tree and headed for the town center to find her.

Chapter Thirty-Two

<u>Bonuses: **Castle - Basic**</u>

- Ranged Accuracy +17%
- Evasion + 39%
- Ranged Damage +25%
- Defensive Weaponry Damage +10%

Devon smiled at the sight of Stonehaven's new bonuses. The boosts would be huge when the attack came—though whether they would be enough to hold off Zaa's minions, she had some serious doubts. Before setting out for the Stone Forest—if she could come up with a plan to get through Ishildar anyway—she'd need to talk to Jarleck about the next round of upgrades. Even if they were only partway finished by the time the demons arrived, they'd no doubt be of some use in the battle.

While flipping to another interface, Devon glanced again toward the Shrine to Veia. Still no Tamara. The delay was to be expected, especially with the time compression effect in the game. But Devon hoped that it also meant that Tamara was having fun reimagining herself. Just in case, though, she glanced at her messenger UI.

Nope. No message explaining that the GMs had screwed up and flagged Tamara's account for a spawn location way off in Frostheim or something.

She moved a few feet closer to the shrine and pulled up the food rations tab.

> Rations:
>
> **Daily food requirement:** 496 basic units/day
>
> **Food production:** 713 basic units/day
>
> **Advanced food production:** 17 advanced units/day
>
> **Food preservation:** 200 basic units/day
>
> **Stockpile:** 1124 basic units, 53 advanced units *(expand for details)*

Devon raised an eyebrow. Tom had certainly been busy, but of course the added production and preservation wouldn't have been possible without Prester's underlings rushing the additional *Kitchen* and *Smokehouses* through. And of course, without the new farm plots, there wouldn't be enough supply to keep the kitchens busy. Altogether, the resource pipeline was looking solid, and more than that, the settlement's stores were shaping up nicely. A siege wouldn't be pleasant—or even survivable for an extended period—but Stonehaven's citizens wouldn't start starving the moment an army encamped, either. Plus, the cooks had been able to resume production of advanced food, meals, and snacks made from recipes that were tier 2 and higher. Like *Spiced Antelope Jerky* and *Stonehaven Scramble*, the advanced dishes provided buffs. That would definitely come in handy soon.

The only thing she couldn't tell by looking at the rations screen was whether Stonehaven's hunters had resumed their search for tastier game than the vermin in the field outside the wall. She'd have to check in with Tom on that...morale would surely take a hit when war came, and it would be nice to tank it up now by feeding the people well.

As she started to flip to another section of the city management interface, a faint glow bloomed near the shrine. Devon's heart crammed its way into her throat, and she shoved aside the interface so quickly that if she'd been holding a real tablet or a sheaf of papers instead of looking at a digital UI, they would have gone flying.

Over the space of a couple of seconds, an unfamiliar woman materialized in front of the shrine. She came into being on her feet—unlike some people who were disoriented by the transition to the game world and arrived flat on their backs. The woman wore the typical newbie attire, tattered cloth armor that looked somewhere between a set of ragged hospital scrubs and a martial-arts uniform pulled from a dumpster. She had thick dark hair gathered into a pair of braids, clear hazel eyes, and a faint spray of freckles across her nose.

Also, she was...*solid.* Muscles everywhere. Tamara wouldn't receive a *Strength* score until she picked a class, but if Devon were the one assigning the points, Tamara would score max in that attribute.

At least, she assumed this was Tamara.

Devon stepped closer, leaning to get her head and shoulders into the woman's vision. "Tamara?"

The woman immediately laughed. "Dev! Oh my gosh...you're...hot!"

Devon laughed. "Well, that's one way to say hello."

"Sorry," Tamara said, joining in on the laughter. "I just wasn't prepared, I guess. I'm so used to seeing the real you. I mean, not that you don't look nice in real life, too. Just without the airbrushing and plastic surgery sort of look."

Devon snorted. "It's my *Charisma* score. And no, I didn't make my character this way on purpose. I'm stuck with my appearance because the attribute is the major contributor to my mana pool."

Tamara blinked in confusion, totally lost by Devon's comment, but then seemed to dismiss her questions for the moment. She held out her hands, looked at them as if struggling to believe they were real. She ran a palm over her opposite forearm, pushing back her shirtsleeve and examining her skin. After a moment, she shook her head in amazement and dropped her hands to her sides.

Tamara took a few deep breaths. Her eyes slid shut, and an expression of profound bliss spread across her face. "It feels so damn good."

"Breathing?"

The woman nodded. "I almost forgot what it was like." She opened her eyes and cocked her head. "What's that on your shoulder, by the way? It's like a weird little pom-pom or something."

Devon sighed. "Long story. Its name is Bob, but feel free to ignore it. Otherwise you'll be subjected to annoying attempts at wit."

Bob snorted but said nothing.

Silence fell, and Devon watched her friend take in the world for a minute or two. "So what do you want to do first? A tour? Want to check out the view from on top of the cliff? Try some *Rat 'n Snake Glop*?"

Tamara gave her a sideways glance. "You're kidding, right?"

"About the glop? Unfortunately, no. We've had some issues with the meat supply lately."

"Come on, Dev. You should know what I want to do first."

Devon laughed. "Okay, caught me." She stepped to the side and parted the grass to grab the top frame bar of the ironwood bike. When she stood the contraption up, Tamara surged forward.

"Oh my gosh, it's..."

"Primitive?"

"It's awesome! I mean, there's no composite frame or auto-annealing nanofiber tires or weight-specific full suspension. But this is incredible."

As Tamara ran a hand reverently over the leather-padded seat and then grabbed the handlebars—Dorden had fashioned the grips, wrapping them with cord much like he wrapped the hilts of weapons for added friction—Devon stepped back. She was having a hard time swallowing, and she wasn't sure why. As she watched her friend swing a leg over the machine and test the seat height, Devon abruptly couldn't see. Her eyes seemed to be swimming with...

What the hell? Was she crying?

Before anyone could see, she whirled and swiped her sleeve across her eye. She took a couple of deep breaths then returned her attention to her friend. Tamara had set her feet on the pedals, was standing over them and holding the handlebar, twisting it back and forth. Only she wasn't moving, nor was she falling over. What the heck? How did that work?

"Does it not go?" Devon asked. A stupid question seeing as she had ridden the thing the day before. Not very far and not very well, of course. But she knew the bike worked.

Turning her face to Devon, Tamara broke into a wide grin, then somehow managed to jerk up on the handlebars and push on the pedal at the same time. The front wheel came up, and Tamara laughed as she rode the wheelie around in a circle around Devon.

"Works fine," she said with a wink. Dropping the front wheel back down, she planted a foot and leaned over the handlebars. "Mind if I take it for a spin?"

Devon smiled. "Be my guest."

As her friend rode off, tearing toward the center of town and sending a startled giant parrot flapping for the top of the wall, Devon caught sight of the new player, Valious, watching from a few yards away. He looked as if he'd come to say something, maybe to repeat his request for some of her time, but the sight of the bike seemed to have snapped him out of it.

That was probably good. Devon hated to turn the poor guy down again, but she had a ton of work to do and a friend to introduce to a whole new world.

Chapter Thirty-Three

"NEVER SEEN ANYTHING like it," Jarleck said, shaking his head as Tamara tried out the bike on one of the rutted and stony footpaths that crisscrossed the newbie yard. After making a few circuits of Stonehaven, she'd asked if there was any more challenging terrain where she could put the bike through its paces.

Devon had smirked. "There's enough rocks and cliffs in the Argenthal Mountains to keep you happy for years, I bet."

"Stumps, too? How about fallen trees and embedded roots?"

"Sometimes I wonder if you're actually kind of insane," Devon had said, laughing. "But there's a problem. You're level 1. You probably wouldn't win a fight against a songbird at this point, not to mention the awakened creatures in the savanna or stray orcs still marauding in the mountains."

"Wait, I don't have to fight songbirds, do I? That seems...mean."

"That was just an illustration of your wimpiness."

Tamara had sighed, looking down at her super buff arms. "I was kind of hoping these lumberjack guns would give me a leg up."

"Don't worry. You'll grow into your avatar's appearance."

"All right, so is there anywhere I can ride without getting smashed by an angry butterfly?"

Which is how they'd ended up just outside the gates with Tamara whizzing through the noob grounds while the level one and two players stared in shock.

"Carry on," Devon called to a group of three caster types who had bludgeoned a rat nearly to death and were now standing over it absently wiggling their fingers while watching Tamara ride. One of them nodded, then finished her spell, causing a puff of smoke to erupt from the rat's fur. The mammal squealed and slumped.

"I thought they weren't supposed to choose a class before level 5," Devon said. "How'd they get spells?"

The man shrugged. "Same way the others got swords, I would suppose. By asking. Far as I know, the early levels are supposed to allow starborn unfamiliar with our world to experiment and determine where they best fit into Veia's plan."

"Ah. Hey, so. Castle, huh?" Devon held up her hand for a high-five.

Jarleck stared at it, blinking, then raised his own. "Castle."

There was a long pause, and then finally, Devon said, "You're supposed to slap my hand."

"Supposed to what?" Jarleck asked, glancing at her palm skeptically. "You remember I'm a level 18 Brawler, right?"

She sighed and dropped her arm. "Never mind. So...what would you recommend for our next step in fortification?" As she asked the question, she pulled up the settlement page with information on fortifications.

> <u>Fortifications:</u>
> Status: Castle – Basic

Completed:

1 x Main Wall - Stone

1 x Wall-walk

1 x Merlons

1 x Main Gate - Iron-reinforced Timber

5 x Watchtower

1 x Wicket Gate

1 x Outer Gate

1 x Dry Moat

1 x Drawbridge

1 x Dungeon

5 x Wall-mounted trebuchets

15 x Stocked barrels of pitch or tar

Required for an upgrade to Castle - Advanced

1 x Armory

1 x Inner Portcullis

1 x Large Ballista mounted on Inner Keep

1 x Water-filled Moat

5 x Wall-mounted Ballistae

"Ohh, an armory. I should have thought of that," Devon said, glancing up at Jarleck. But the man was watching over her shoulder. Devon turned, and through the translucent overlay of the interface saw a massive crowd watching Tamara's performance. She wondered what it must look like to them, this person-powered, two-wheeled wagon. In what real-world century had people started riding bicycles? The 1800s? She hoped she hadn't just totally hosed their technological progression. Though thinking about it another way, a little tech superiority wouldn't be too bad to have when the demons came.

She spotted Prester and Deld, the head stonemason, standing near the edge of the crowd and waved them over. As they nodded greetings, she brushed the fortifications interface away.

"Think you two have some spare workers who could help Jarleck out? It seems Stonehaven needs an armory."

Deld gave a little salute. "Sure thing. Now that the dungeon is finished and the main wall replaced with stone, my masons are starting to feel idle."

"Well, in that case"—she consulted her interface really quick—"how about you also set some of them to building an Advanced Forge."

He nodded. "They'll be pleased...though something else has come up, Your Glorious—Mayor."

"Oh?" Devon watched as Tamara rode her bike up to the edge of the dry moat, eyed the drop, then reconsidered. "If you crash like you did in Flagstaff, Hezbek has potions to fix you up. I swear your body won't have an allergic reaction to them either."

"These ones don't even taste like donkey vomit," someone called from the crowd. Judging by the gravelly voice, it was probably one of the dwarves.

Tamara smirked and shook her head. "It's not the drop I'm worried about. It's getting back out."

Oh. Right. The whole point of the moat was to keep people from crossing it. A task that was going to get even harder once they figured out how to divert stream water and fill the thing up.

Devon was about to call something else out to Tamara, but her friend had already zipped off. She'd spotted what looked like a fallen acacia tree and was apparently...planning to try to ride across the slippery trunk? Devon shook her head. Crazy woman.

Deld cleared his throat, pulling her attention back. "Sorry," she said. "Go on. A problem?"

"Well, I'm afraid to say it, but it's affecting all the major professions in the settlement."

Yikes. This sounded bad. Devon turned to face him, putting all her focus on the man.

"You see," he said, shuffling. "Lots of the folks that have arrived from Eltera came with some experience. They've been able to help out, and even increase their skills. But those with no trade and those without a lot of natural talent for gaining skills all by themselves—they aren't progressing very fast."

Prester nodded, taking up the thread of conversation. "We've started to fall behind in housing construction. Lots of newcomers are still bedding down outside."

"And if we ever want to, say, wall off the orchard, I'm not sure we'll have the hands to accomplish it while keeping up with repairs and upgrades to the main fortifications," Deld finished.

Devon blinked, confused. "But I thought you were training new people. Apprentices."

Prester took a deep breath, but before he could speak, Dorden detached from the crowd of Tamara's spectators and shouldered into the conversation. "What they're reluctant to say, lass, is that they can try to give instruction, but the process is none too reliable. Some folks just can't learn outside of a formal apprenticeship. It's the only way to properly take advantage of the mentor's skill when helping a wee beginner advance."

"Okay...I still don't understand though. Have you already maxed the number of apprentices you can take?"

Dorden sighed heavily. "Sorry, boys. The lass can be a bit of a dunderhead." He turned back to her. "At this moment in time, your trusted leaders of Stonehaven's most important trades can't *take* apprentices."

All at once, Devon realized the problem. She rolled her eyes and sighed. It felt like years ago, back before they'd even reached the site where Stonehaven now stood, that she'd learned the differences between advanced and basic NPCs. The NPCs that she'd promoted could choose a second profession or class, could be resurrected at the Shrine to Veia...and they could take apprentices.

She shook her head. "I get it now. Man, I can be an idiot sometimes."

As if on cue, she heard the familiar, strangled sound that was Greel's attempt at a laugh. "I have been saying that for months," he said as he joined the conversation.

Devon gave him a flat stare, but inside, she felt the excitement starting to burble. It had been a long time since she'd made NPC promotions. And seeing how Veia had filled four of her precious advanced slots, Devon wasn't inclined to procrastinate on any of the other choices. There might be a more optimal way to fill out her allowable roster of advanced citizens, but there wasn't a more *fitting* way than to promote the original members of the Tribe of Uruquat and the remaining members of the Stoneshoulder Clan. The groups that had been with her from the beginning.

Laying a hand on Deld's shoulder, she sent him off with instructions to gather her original followers and meet her on the third floor of the Inner Keep. As he trotted off, Devon turned back to the field and watched Tamara somehow hop the bike sideways off the fallen trunk, landing in perfect balance in the grass on her wheels. A moment later, the woman shot forward, racing across the grass many times faster than the most hasted player Devon had seen.

Wait.

Devon glanced around, searching for Chen, and spotted the knight near the shadow of the wall. He was crouched down, a hoop of metal and a ball of twine in his hands. Another Tinker experiment, perhaps. Seeming to feel her eyes on him, he glanced up. Devon nodded toward Tamara and waited as her revelation dawned on him, too.

"And while we're speaking of your idiocy—"

She spun, nearly knocking Greel off his feet.

"Sorry, no time to talk. I have to go order some more bikes."

Chapter Thirty-Four

"DEVON," CHEN CALLED.

She paused and waited for him just outside the *Woodworker's Shop*, the second specialty workshop that she'd ordered built after learning from Prester a few weeks ago that almost everyone in town was sleeping on the floor because carpenters couldn't make beds.

The teenager hurried to catch her, little Sigfried sprinting along behind. When the knight stopped, slightly out of breath, Sigfried mimicked his pose.

"You get it, right?" she asked. "The bikes are how we outrun the Stone Guardians."

Chen nodded. "Yep, And I think it will work."

"We need enough bicycles for a party of players—you, me, Torald, and Tamara as a guide. We'll have to work hard to keep her from getting aggroed. And I think we should make one for Hailey in case she turns up. Speaking of, you haven't heard anything from her, have you?"

Chen shook his head. "Not a peep. How about Jeremy? Shouldn't we bring him?"

Devon grimaced and glanced around in case the troubadour was lurking. He wasn't in sight, which meant he was probably off making up another song about her. "Crud, I guess it would be dumb to leave him behind just because he's annoying. One of his songs has a haste buff. We're gonna need all the speed we can get."

"Party of six. A good size. Almost like we have the whole group back together again."

Devon smirked. "Except Maya. Somehow I doubt she'd be much of a cyclist with her mermaid tail."

Chen laughed. According to Jeremy, the final member of their regular group from their previous game was stuck on some remote island playing the part of a mermaid queen.

"Hey, so, Devon? You did a good job on the bike design, but there are some issues."

Devon blinked. "Huh? Tamara seems to be doing okay."

He shrugged. "Yeah, she's like some sort of mutant. But if the rest of us are going to be able to ride any kind of distance, I know some modifications that would help."

She smirked. "Don't tell me you want extra padding to protect your delicate tush."

He rolled his eyes, and Sigfried did the same. "I mean, mechanically. The drive train seems solid, but the problem is that there's no freewheel."

"No what?"

"You can't coast. So in order to keep going, you have to pedal nonstop. It could get dangerous on the downhills actually because there's no way to brake besides somehow resisting the pedal movement."

"Okay...? I'm not sure how to fix that. We're basically in the Middle Ages."

Standing straighter, Chen held up his hands and wiggled his fingers. "Fortunately, unlike the real medieval times, in this case you happen to know someone with a knack for magical devices."

Devon thumped the heel of her hand against her forehead. "Duh. Sorry, Chen. I should have asked you in the beginning."

"It's okay. Honestly, I hadn't been focusing on either of my combat classes for a while...not until Emerson sent me into the underworld. Just felt weird to think about fighting after what we saw on the beach after Hailey and I crossed the Noble Sea. So in your case with my abilities, out of sight, out of mind, right?"

She shrugged. "So how do you know so much about how bikes work?"

"An ill-fated stint where my parents tried to put me in BMX classes. I really wasn't good. And by that I mean I totally sucked. But the mechanical end makes sense."

"Hey, speaking of mechanical, mind asking Tamara if she wants to help design? She works—worked—as a bike mechanic. Actually, they keep her on a few hours a week, but I get the idea that it's pretty awkward. A crash left her with lung damage."

Chen grimaced. "Sure, no problem. She probably knows way more than me."

"Well, in that case"—Devon glanced at her in-game clock—"seems like you've got this pretty well handled, and I've got some promotions to hand out."

Sigfried crossed his little arms pridefully as Chen nodded. "Rush order for five new custom bikes and one retrofitting coming up, Sarge."

She smirked. "Sarge, huh? That mean you're going to start taking orders from me without an argument?"

"Not a chance."

***

Devon really didn't spend enough time in her "chambers" on the top floor of the keep. Looking out over the town from the high, stone-framed windows, she couldn't help feeling a bit like an actual ruler from long ago, her domain spread wide beneath her. She scanned the horizon as she listened to her original followers file into the room, the hardened leather of their boots scuffing over the chamber floor.

Stonehaven was both a hamlet and a castle now, and the settlement was well on its way to the next set of upgrades. The food supply was secure, and finally, she understood how to get across Ishildar and—barring some other nasty surprise—retrieve the final relic that would grant her ownership of the city and whatever power it would allow her to bring to bear against the demon invasion.

It was time to share the success around and thank the loyal friends who had brought her this far.

She turned to face her followers and grinned as Gerrald stepped forward and handed over his latest creations.

> **You have received:** Frostwielder's Belt
> **Slot:** Waist
> *Specially designed for casters proficient in ice and water magic, the hardened leather is set with lapis lazuli mined in the Argenthal Mountains.*
> 10 Armor | +2 Intelligence |+10% Ice and Water Damage | 72/72 Durability

You have received: Ornate Sheath
One of a kind with gold and iron filigrees. Perfectly molded to Night's Fang.
+5% Melee Attack Speed | 55/55 Durability

You have received: Champion's Circlet
A delicate iron circlet designed to sit upon the brow of she who carries our hopes on her shoulders.
5 Armor | +3 Focus | +2 Charisma

For once, none of the items were tacky or had sarcastic descriptions. Maybe even Gerrald—or Veia, working through him—had managed to channel some sort of seriousness into the crafting of the final pieces of equipment she'd take to the Stone Forest. For half a second, she let herself wonder whether Veia and her mouthpieces had started to gain some respect for her, but she quickly ditched that idea. Probably just a coincidence.

"Thank you. These are amazing."

As Gerrald rejoined the others, Devon scanned the faces of her original followers. Everyone who hadn't already been promoted to advanced NPC was here, as was Dorden, who had helped round them up. As she met their eyes, she wondered why she hadn't done this before. If any of these humans or dwarves had died over the past weeks, she never would have forgiven herself for failing to promote them when she'd had the chance.

"Before I launch into a speech, I wanted to thank every one of you for what you've done for Stonehaven, and this is the best way I know how." Focusing on each of them, she brought up a context menu and selected the option to advance them. "I now pronounce you all as advanced citizens of the Stonehaven League, the leadership of our settlement."

You have gained a skill point: +1 Leadership

A cheer went up as her friends clapped each other on the back. Devon glanced at her settlement interface and noted that she now had the exact number of advanced NPCs needed to upgrade to township. It was almost as if it was meant to be. Even if there were a slightly more optimal set of citizens she could have selected to fill the promotion slots, she wouldn't have chosen strangers no matter the stakes. These people, her friends and followers, belonged as permanent members of the town.

She sighed in contentment as the hubbub died down. Once the hugs and congratulatory chest bumps had settled, she raised a hand to gather their attention.

"I'm sure most of you have heard the rumors."

"Ye mean the demon invasion, Mayor?" one of the dwarven fighters asked.

She nodded. "I don't know exactly when it will come, but I think it will be soon. And I think it will be the hardest trial Stonehaven has ever endured."

The mood in the room turned somber, her followers crossing their arms and balling their fists. No doubt some of them were thinking of the last time a demon attack had come. The fiends, under Devon's command as her alter ego, Ezraxis, had finally managed to batter down the wall. Much of the village had been destroyed.

"And what may be even harder to hear is that I may not be here to help you fight, at least not initially."

A wave of indrawn breaths passed through the crowd. Devon wanted to pause and reassure them it would be okay but forged on instead. They needed to understand the seriousness of the situation.

"As soon as our equipment is ready, I'll be leading a party of starborn through Ishildar to the lost vassaldom on its northern edge. In the meantime, I need you to finish preparing the city. We've improved our food production and storage"—she nodded at Tom and Bayle who stood together, the husband nearly lost in his wife's imposing shadow—"and thanks to almost everyone who has lent a hand either digging the moat or putting your trade skill at Jarleck's disposal, Stonehaven is officially a castle, earning great defensive bonuses as a result. Now we need to focus on preparations for war. As advanced citizens, you are now able to take apprentices. I encourage each of you to do that, but I also need you to organize and guide the other citizens, even if their progression will be slower without an assigned mentor. Encourage anyone with an interest to take up trades as weapon or armorsmiths, as fletchers or bowyers. Those interested in the combat arts shouldn't hesitate to begin training. It's not too late. This will unbalance our settlement's breakdown of professions, slowing our growth in other areas, but we will address that later. For now, we need to survive."

Devon waited until the nods of consideration and then acknowledgment settled down before speaking again. "Finally," she said, "we need to talk about Stonehaven as a refuge and safe haven. There is an encampment of experienced starborn not far from here, and in recent days, starborn of a different caliber have been arriving."

"You mean the noobs," someone commented.

She smirked and nodded. "Yes. The noobs. They aren't officially citizens of Stonehaven, no more than the starborn we've traded with for longer are. Either way, they'll be welcomed inside our walls. And when the demons arrive, there may be non-starborn people and creatures that will come seeking sanctuary. I hope that by retrieving the fifth relic and reawakening Ishildar, the corruption will be purged from the awakening stones, restoring their original magic. The awakened races may come seeking help, or they might come to our aid. Either way, they will be welcomed in Stonehaven. Bring them in, give them jobs, and send their fighters to the wall to help defend the city."

"Mayor Devon?" asked Grey, one of the settlement's hunters.

"Yes?"

"You don't really think the attack will come before you return, do you? This is a just-in-case sort of speech, right?"

She smiled at him and sighed. "I sure hope it's just in case. Yes. I just want you to be ready, and some—"

She was cut off short when the door to the chamber flew open. "Excuse me," Greel said with an oily voice as he strode through the door with his typical crooked gait. He glared at her with both sides of his upper lip curled into expressions of disgust. Following behind, his new follower shuffled into the room. Valious walked with shoulders hunched and what looked like a permanent cringe on his face. He'd replaced some of his gear, ditching the beetle skullcap, but unfortunately, the armor looked somewhat familiar. It took Devon a moment to realize that he was actually wearing Greel's hand-me-downs. She shook her head. Poor guy.

"First of all," Greel said, "your voice has an abysmally piercing quality. I could hear it all the way down on the first floor. And if you wish to add this notion of Stonehaven being a refuge to our operating procedures, you will have to complete the town chartering process with the new provision attached as an amendment."

Devon smirked. She hadn't actually expected him to turn up. Fortunately, she was prepared just in case.

"Actually, I have a new version I would like you to look over. Since I wrote it from scratch, it shouldn't require a notary or witness."

Reaching into her *Sparklebomb Backpack*, she pulled out a freshly folded paper airplane and hucked it toward him. The eyes of the rest of her followers went wide as the little plane floated directly to the lawyer. They still had quite a few centuries of progress to make before flying machines would seem commonplace.

As Greel read—it didn't take long—his face turned nearly purple. He stammered with indignation before reading aloud.

"Be nice. Use common sense. People screw up, so be generous with second chances. If someone is a real jerk or does something really bad, put them in the dungeon."

The man shook his head, totally aghast. "This is completely unacceptable. We must have an actual definition of what constitutes a prison-worthy offense. 'Nice' is perhaps the least precise term I have ever heard. We simply must have a properly codified system of laws if we wish Stonehaven to succeed as a growing settlement."

Devon exhaled. "Yes, we must. But we can't rush it, unfortunately. There are far bigger problems looming than the question of how many times someone can insult a city guardsperson—you suggested five—or the settlement's lawyer—

unsurprisingly, you suggested one—before a disciplinary action should be taken."

The man just stared at her, cheek twitching.

"It's my final answer, Greel. At least until we have the fifth relic. So if there's nothing else?"

Seeming to master himself, he took a breath and straightened—as much as his twisted spine allowed. "Actually, there is. It's the reason I came, but after hearing this nonsense about providing *sanctuary*, I felt I must raise the legal issue."

"And this reason is...?"

"I'm coming with you to the Stone Forest. Your party needs someone with major single-target damage."

Devon blinked. That wasn't exactly what she'd expected to hear. "Well, you're right, to be honest. Chen's pretty good, but he's more of an off tank. Unfortunately, I can't take anyone but starborn. The problem is, we have to go on bicycles, and if you don't already know how to ride, there's just no time to learn. Hate to say it, but it's a starborn skill."

Greel rolled his eyes. "Which is precisely *why* I'll be bringing my servant—I mean apprentice. All I need is for you to create one of those *bikes* with an extra seat for me."

Devon glanced at poor Valious, who was cringing even harder now. Why on earth had the man agreed to let Greel boss him around this way? "No offense, Valious, but I don't think your mentor has explained what you'd be getting into." She turned back to Greel. "We're already going to have Tamara along to protect. It will just make our job harder if we have two low-level people to look out for."

At this, Greel smirked. "But you see, it's not only for his ability to rotate those pedal things that he should be there. Apparently, the man has a *destiny* assigned by Veia herself."

At this, Valious stood straight up, eyes wide. "What the...?" he managed to croak.

"Aravon—that incompetent tank trainer—told me personally that he couldn't shake the feeling that Valious was important. Normally, I wouldn't put any importance on that, but then Shavari had her first Seeing since Veia's touch left her months ago. Guess who was right there along with your little party as you entered the Stone Forest." He jabbed his thumb at Valious. "And *then* I had a revelation, and I suddenly realized what the man's combat class should be."

Greel turned, and with a flourish of his hands, leaned in and muttered something in the man's ear.

Valious scratched his head. "I don't understand. What's a unique class? You mean no one else gets to have it?"

Greel sighed loudly and nodded.

"But what does the Frenzy class do? Does that mean I get to be a tank?"

Clamping a hand on the man's shoulder—hard, judging by the whitening in Greel's knuckles—the lawyer flashed her a dismissive sneer. "So you see, we'll be coming with you. I'll explain the new party additions to Chen and Tamara."

Devon sighed and rolled her eyes. She supposed she could always just have Tamara give them an impromptu lesson in riding bikes off cliffs if they caused too much trouble.

"Don't bother yourself. I'll go talk to them now."

Chapter Thirty-Five

HAILEY PAUSED INSIDE the wicket gate leading into Stonehaven. She had one last chance to change her mind here. The orders were in place with the nursing staff, but she could still log out and cancel them. Once she found Devon and agreed to party up for the journey through Ishildar, though, she wouldn't be able to back out.

Well, technically, she would be able to—until her body quit, she'd have the option to log out. But Hailey had already ditched her friend once recently. She wouldn't abandon her again, especially when that would be the last thing Devon and the rest of the group would remember about her.

She stepped inside the town, then put her back to the wall and leaned the back of her head against the cool stone. She could do this. Bob had explained that it was critical to be herself. The group would need her healing and crowd-control abilities, and the wisp would need her...sparkling personality, as he had sarcastically put it. The patterns must be established if this was going to work.

Outside the game, her body now lay in the clean-room bed, tubes snaking from just about everywhere it was possible to attach them. She would be fed through the tubes, given water and medicine. For a few hours every day, her mind would be put into a drug-induced sleep-like state, triggered when she logged out from Relic Online, but taking hold before sensory awareness returned.

The end-of-life provisions had been put in place to allow someone to let go when the pain became too much. Hailey was using the law differently, forcing an interpretation that allowed her to remain alive as long as possible, maximizing her remaining time by taking advantage of the game's time compression. She would be spared the final pain of her body shutting down, something that, a few months ago, would have struck her as weak. Now, she had a greater purpose and a reason to take what felt like the easy way out.

Thinking of that purpose, she gritted her teeth and pushed off the wall. According to Bob's latest message, the group would be gathering tomorrow in the central square before their departure on...bikes. Hailey didn't know much more about the plan, but the wisp had made a point to let her know they'd ordered a bike for her, too, despite not having seen her in days. The notion raised a faint pang of guilt—what had Hailey ever done to deserve friends who would make space for her even after she'd ditched Devon on Christmas, even after she'd spent the last few days just wandering aimlessly through the game world, ignoring their messages?

But even if she didn't deserve them, she could try to express her gratitude in the best way she knew how. By being a kickass group member when her friends most needed her.

Hailey took a deep breath and headed off to tell Devon she was coming on the journey.

Chapter Thirty-Six

"OW!" DEVON SAID aloud when her neck cramped as she tried to look around the side of the mountain of laundry she was carrying down the stairs. If the lack of visibility wasn't bad enough, the basket was missing one of the plastic handle thingies that made it easier to grip, and a harsh edge was digging into her palm. As she felt blindly with her toe for the next step, she wondered whether she could get some sort of laundry service to take over the chore in the same way she'd started having her groceries delivered.

Of course, she'd still have to put the clean stuff away, which was as much of a problem as washing it in the first place. And it meant some stranger folding her undies. Ew. So no. No laundry service.

Her foot finally slid over concrete down at street level, and, freed of the confines of the narrow stairwell, she was able to turn sideways and walk while actually watching where she was going.

Unfortunately, though, when she executed the maneuver, she saw that a man had been waiting at the bottom of the stairs until she was clear. He'd probably watched every agonizing inch of her descent. After an awkward moment of staring, she realized it was the guy that lived a few doors down, the same man she'd seen taking his much more modest load of laundry down a few days ago. He was probably holding an internal conversation right now about how slovenly she must be to have piled up this much dirty stuff.

Of course, she didn't *know* that it was all dirty, due to her recent problem of comingling the contents of her baskets. But given that the items of unknown classification had been strewn across the floor, no doubt walked on during a nighttime trip to the bathroom, they probably needed a wash anyway.

The guy gave her a friendly smile. "I was going to offer to help you on the stairs there, but I didn't want to startle you and send you to your death."

Devon felt her cheeks turn red. "I guess I let my laundry get a little out of control."

He laughed. "Happens to the best of us. I finally had to put an app on my phone that makes me do chores before I'm allowed to use it for anything else. I could cheat by moving around and making it seem like I'm cleaning, but if I'm going that far, I figure I might as well just run the damn vacuum."

"I just ordered one of those robots," Devon said, then immediately wished she had a hand free to smack herself. The statement was true—as she'd collected her items of dubious cleanliness, she'd got to thinking that the carpet was probably kind of gross since she managed to clean it herself about once every three months. Now that she had a real job, she could afford the simple luxuries like cleaner bots. But that didn't mean she should blab her whole life's story to a stranger.

The man grinned. "Nice. That's even better than an app." He glanced at her basket. "You got it from here?"

She suppressed a grimace as a dart of pain shot through her hand carrying the side of the basket with the missing handle. "Yup, thanks."

Before he could say anything else, she hurried awkwardly around him and headed for the laundry room. Tamara and Hezbek would be proud of her for handling an actual encounter with a stranger, and more than that, for managing to exchange three or four sentences of small talk. But Devon wasn't feeling like social self-improvement at the moment. She had way too many preparations on her mind, starting with a list of real-life crap she had to take care of—grocery shopping and unpacking being the most critical, seeing as she hoped to be online as much as humanly possible between when the group set out on their cycling adventure and the recovery of the relic.

She was also working on a list of provisions for the adventure, stored in a notes file she could pull up in game. That level of organization wasn't typical for her...back when her guild had run complicated raid content in Avatharn Online, bean counters like Chen had put together the lists of expendables and spare gear and other incidentals they'd need. But with Tamara going along for the ride—literally—she felt responsible. It was a weird feeling, like she was a parent or something. But also, drawing up a list was a whole lot easier to stomach now that Hezbek's potions didn't taste like skunk barf.

Devon backed into the laundry room and, with a sigh of relief, set her basket down on one of the tables. She shook her hand out, opening and closing her fingers.

"Okay, then," she said, turning to the machine. "Let's see if we can avoid filling the room with suds this time, huh?"

As she loaded the top layer from the basket into the machine, she glanced again at her messenger icon. Still nothing from Emerson. Which was another reason she wasn't really in the mood for skilling up her social interaction. Writing that message to him had been *hard.* She'd felt totally self-conscious and had basically forced herself to send it.

Only to hear back...exactly nothing. If she let herself sit idle too long, anxiety about whether she'd said the wrong thing started to eat at her, so at this point, the only thing she could do was get ready for the journey through Ishildar.

At least, if she'd needed a reminder of why she typically avoided people, she now had it.

Chapter Thirty-Seven

EMERSON MIGHT HAVE blown off the raid-boss-difficulty message she'd made herself send, but at least Hailey had come back. The woman had even apologized for leaving suddenly before, saying that there was no real excuse, but that the best she could give was that Christmas tended to mess with her head.

Devon didn't need to tell her that she understood. She had the feeling that Hailey just got it.

Regardless, it was nice to have her old friend along for the journey, and she had a feeling Hailey and Tamara would get along well. Hailey's streaming and Tamara's brief stint as a sponsored mountain biker meant they both had experience with public attention, something that Devon avoided as much as humanly possible. She looked forward to seeing what the women had to talk about.

The adventuring party was due to depart in just an in-game hour or so, and Devon had the familiar excitement-slash-butterflies sensation in her belly. It had been a long time since she'd headed out in pursuit of an objective with this amount of planning and pressure. Since the Avatharn Online days, really. She and Hailey had run into each other as they were both making their way toward the settlement's central square, and it just felt right to have her long-time guildmate walking beside her.

Neither woman spoke as they approached the central square, Devon's boots and Hailey's leather-soled slippers thudding lightly on the cobblestone path. The grass to either side of the walkway nodded in a light morning breeze, the fields pulling back from their legs as the path widened to an actual street wide enough to accommodate a wagon. To either side, cottages and barracks gave way to the storefronts and workshops of downtown Stonehaven.

At the edge of the central square, Devon stopped and took in the sight. It had been quite a while since she actually noticed how the look of the settlement was changing. Rather than appearing like knocked-together shacks from which itinerant merchants hawked a few items, the shops had taken on a sense of permanence. Shutters were thrown open to show the wares hanging inside the front rooms of the shops. Potted flowers drank the sunlight to either side of open doorways. Many of the establishments had hand-painted signs and hitching rails out front—not that there were many horses around yet.

Hailey must have noticed how Devon's gaze traveled over the scene because she smiled a bit wistfully. "Your baby is growing up, isn't it?"

Devon laughed. "I guess you could put it that way."

"Hey, Devon." Tamara had been standing beside the collection of bikes leaning against an adventuring supplies shop and now jogged across the square to meet them. In the two days since she'd logged in, the woman had managed to secure herself a fitted leather tunic, a pair of leather bracers, and pads of thick canvas that strapped over her thighs. Devon blinked in surprise when she noticed what looked like brass knuckles on the backs of Tamara's fingers.

"Been learning combat between bike rides?" Devon asked.

Tamara grinned. She glanced toward an aisle between buildings where Jarleck had just stepped from the shadows. He walked over and clapped Tamara on the shoulder. "I heard you gave a speech about how us advanced citizens should be taking apprentices to get Stonehaven ready for war. Figured this one looked like she could go toe to toe with the best of them. Seemed like a knuckle duster sort of woman."

"Go on. Check me out," Tamara said with a little wiggle of the shoulders.

"Did you just *shimmy*?" Devon asked with a laugh as she used *Combat Assessment.*

Tam - Level 5 Brawler
Health: 162/162
Combo: 0/8

"Wow! Tamara, that's awesome. You chose a class."

"And I have 8 skill points in *Brass Knuckles*, and 4 in *Knife Fighting*. Figured if I'm going to have to jump off my bike and fight stuff, it would be easier not to have to deal with a sword."

As she watched her friend clench and release her fists and shift her weight through combat stances, Devon felt a strange warmth in her chest. Pride? Happiness? Devon wasn't used to the emotion in any case.

She took a satisfied breath and nodded her thanks to Jarleck. "Hey, speaking of your role in the settlement, I've been meaning to get back to you about the cave—"

"I heard you cleared out the whole den," the man said. "According to the caravaneers, there hasn't been so much as a peep coming from that cave."

> **You have completed a quest:** Investigate the cave to the northeast.
>
> You receive: 100,000 experience

"Thanks," Devon said. "It was a good quest."

Jarleck blushed a little. "Actually, there's one more thing related to the cave. The caravan members are relieved to be free of that worry, and they were wondering if there was anything else they could do to reward you."

"Actually..." Devon said as she pulled up her quest log and scrolled down. "Since they're traveling back and forth from the Argenthals, think they'd be willing to keep an eye out for *Light Green Lichen of Moderate Flakiness with some Orangish Spots?*"

Jarleck blinked. "Well...I guess. Any particular reason?"

Devon glanced at the repeatable *More, More, More* quest she'd received from Hezbek, a request for components to make more *Lightfooted* and *Phoenix Spirit* potions. She *could* tell him the reason she needed the lichen. Or she could just leave him guessing.

"Maybe I like to put it in my tea..." she said with a wink.

Jarleck laughed. "Well, whatever the purpose, I'll deliver your request. Now, if you don't need anything else, I was planning to stake out the foundation lines for the new armory."

"I won't keep you," Devon said, sticking out a hand to shake. Jarleck looked at it for a moment, then seemed to remember the starborn gesture. He enveloped her hand in his massive paw and pumped his arm awkwardly.

"Good luck out there, Mayor," he said. His face worked through an expression of worry that he quickly covered before nodding curtly and hurrying off.

"He kinda reminds me of my dad," Tamara said. "I like him."

"Me too," Devon said.

The mention of potions reminded Devon to recheck the stocks in her inventory. She planned to distribute many of them among the party members, but for now it was easiest to keep the stacks of each item together to make sure she had enough. Plus, it made her feel better about her ridiculous backpack. She slung it off her shoulder and activated her inventory UI by opening the strap, then selected the option to filter by the proper item type.

Expendables:
29 x Spiced Antelope Jerky
17 x Anteater Surprise
7 x Termite Turnover
2 x Phoenix Spirit Potion
4 x Lightfoot Potion
14 x Savanna Health Potion - Mid
7 x Savanna Health Potion - Major
9 x Savanna Mana Potion - Minor
9 x Savanna Mana Potion - Mid
1 x Potion of Jaguar Speed
2 x Potion of Monkey's Ability

She'd all but cleaned out the town's stores of advanced food, a decision that still made her a bit uneasy. But with the increased production capacity, the settlement's stock would refill quickly, whereas no one in the party had even a single skill point in cooking. While they could forage and hunt to meet their nutrition requirements, it would slow them down and the food would taste terrible. Better to have the ready-made meals, and even better to have the buffs the advanced food granted.

She pressed her lips together when she scanned the rest of the list, wishing there'd been a way to get more *Lightfooted* potions made. The reduction to *Fatigue* would be awesome for the journey, but with only four potions and eight party members, it would make little sense to use them while traveling. If the search for the relic took them into a dungeon, though, she'd give them to the melee fighters who tended to run around more.

In any case, she closed down the UI, satisfied she'd brought everything that could help in the way of expendables. To complement her preparations, she'd asked Torald to bring the bulkier gear, stuff like spare weapons, armor repair kits, bedrolls, and a couple of canvas tarps in case of bad weather.

That settled, she tapped a finger on her thigh for a couple of seconds, trying to figure out an excuse to avoid her character maintenance a little longer. Unfortunately, she drew a blank, so it was time to stop hoarding her unspent attribute points. She pulled up her character sheet.

> Character: Devon (click to set a different character name)
> Level: 24
> Base Class: Sorcerer

Specialization: Unassigned
Unique Class: Deceiver
Health: 412/412
Mana: 629/629
Fatigue: 16%

Attributes:
Constitution: 28 (+6 Stonehaven Jerkin)
Strength: 17
Agility: 21 (+4 Gloves of Deceit)
Charisma: 48 (+4 Big Girl Pants, +2 Champion's Circlet)
Intelligence: 31 (+2 Frostwielder's Belt)
Focus: 20 (+1 Gloves of Deceit +3 Champion's Circlet)
Endurance: 27 (+1 Big Girl Pants)
Unspent Attribute Points: 8

Eight points to spend. *Endurance* would be the most critical for the journey, reducing the rate at which she gained *Fatigue.* If she spent most of the points there, it would also help out her combat because *Endurance* also affected health and mana regeneration, though not to the same degree. But she had also been neglecting *Focus* which mattered when she was trying to maintain a spell, in particular, the *Wall of Ice* that was so handy for splitting dungeon pulls into manageable sizes. After chewing the corner of her lip for a moment, she finally decided to drop five points into *Endurance* and the rest into *Focus,* then accepted and closed her character sheet before she could second-guess herself.

Over at the bikes, Chen was kneeling and inspecting the hub of one of the rear wheels. After a moment, he lifted the bike by the seat and pushed the wheel to get it spinning. The pedals remained motionless. Next he stood, the seat still raised, and squeezed the brake lever—another of his suggested improvements—on the handlebars. The wheel squeaked to a stop.

"How did you and Chen do working together?" Devon asked Tamara.

The woman sighed and shook her head. "Man, if I had his skills in real life, I'd put every bike mechanic in St. George out of business. But if magic actually worked in the real world, I guess a whole bunch of stuff would be different. For one, I would have been able to find a healer to fix my lungs."

Hailey sighed at this. "Yeah. If only," she said quietly.

Devon nodded, thinking all the people that could be helped with the abilities in Relic Online—and all the people that could be harmed. Of course, she'd take the risk on the harm if it could help Tamara. But at least she'd been able to get her friend riding again.

"So Chen says he was able to add some ability for us to adjust the bikes to our body dimensions," she said. "Want to get ours set up?"

She glanced back at her friends and noticed Hailey looking at something with a faint expression of...shock? Horror?

"Guys?" the woman said, pointing.

Across the square, a half-naked man had stepped into the sunlight. Well, not exactly half naked. He looked as if he were wearing hotpants and a skin-tight T-shirt. And platemail boots.

"Uh, Torald?" she asked, her voice a bit squeaky.

The man, apparently unaware that he'd forgotten to put his armor—or much of anything—on, grinned and strode across the square, *Manpurse of Holding* bouncing lightly against his hip. Devon took an unwitting step back.

He held out a hand in greeting.

"Aren't you forgetting something?" she asked, accepting the handshake.

Torald blinked, confused, then looked down when he realized what she was talking about. He stuck a leg out and rotated it at the hip. "Yeah…I couldn't find a razor."

"Wait, what?" Devon glanced at Tamara, hoping the woman wasn't too terrified of the paladin. They hadn't had a chance to meet before now.

All at once, Tamara giggled. "You're a roadie."

Now Devon was *really* confused. Like, one of those people that traveled with rock bands?

Torald shrugged. "Guilty as charged. We don't have anything but asphalt in my area of Pennsylvania."

"Guys, I'm confused," Devon finally managed to say.

"A road biker, the kind that rides on skinny tires on pavement," Tamara explained. "Thus the spandex."

"Spandex?"

"Lookee there, boys!" came a dwarven shout from across the square. "He's turned up in nothing but 'is skivvies!"

The dwarves had managed to snatch one of the bikes away from Chen, and now one of the stumpy-legged folk was sitting on the seat, feet dangling a good eight inches above the pedals. Two of the rider's clansmen were holding the bike up by the handlebars and seat, making whooshing sound effects and pushing the bike around between bouts of laughing at Torald.

Near the center of the square, the pushers counted to three, sprinted, and sent the rider careening for all of about five feet before the bike crashed. The pair who'd done the pushing laughed uproariously as the victim laid a hand on his head and groaned.

"My garments are not spandex, technically," Torald said. "The item descriptions call them a delicate wool blend, gentle on the nether regions."

Devon grimaced, while Hailey raised an eyebrow. "We're skirting the edge of TMI, dude," the seeker said.

"I do have a question, though," Devon said before she could stop herself. "Did you happen to get that outfit at the same place you purchased your manpurse?"

Torald smirked at her. "For your information, I was given quite a few layers of underarmor and padding when I took the platemail proficiency. You seriously don't think I go around with nothing but my birthday suit under all that metal, do you? I mean, the pinching could be catastrophic."

Devon gave an over-exaggerated cringe. "We were just discussing the notion of TMI, weren't we?"

Torald laughed, still seeming completely unashamed of his attire. Devon had seen herds of highway cyclists—she hadn't known they were called road bikers—migrating like caribou through St. George in the spring and fall and yeah, most turned up in these kinds of skintight outfits, seemingly oblivious to the fact that most of their anatomy was on display.

And when she thought about it, it did seem that riders of both genders had surprisingly hairless legs. She'd never really paid enough conscious thought to realize the men were shaving theirs, too. But did that mean that Torald shaved his legs in real life? What did his friends think when he showed up for some sort of barbarian LARP with baby-smooth legs? When she realized she was smirking in amusement, she quickly straightened out her expression.

"And anyway," Torald said. "I'm pretty sure no one would want to be downwind of me if I were to do this ride in platemail."

Tamara laughed and plugged her nose. "Oh man, yeah."

Devon finally turned her attention away from Torald's ridiculous outfit and glanced at the bikes. "I guess we're about set then, right? Just need Jeremy."

"I seriously wouldn't want to see Greel's face if he heard you say that," Chen said as he walked up to join the group.

Devon laughed. "Actually, I was secretly hoping he's listening in."

As they started for the bikes, a godawful blatting sound filled the square. Devon grimaced and clapped her hands over her ears as Jeremy strode in carrying one of those antique bike horns with the big red squeezy part. He squeezed it a few more times, cocking his ear like he was learning an instrument.

Devon glanced at Hailey. "We don't really need a haste buff, do we?"

Hailey curled her lip apologetically. "Unfortunately, yeah. Given that the last time I rode was in elementary school, I think we need all the help we can get."

Devon sighed as loud as she could and rolled her eyes, making sure Jeremy could see the gesture. He just laughed and started searching for a spot to attach his horn to one of the bikes.

"Well, if we're quick, we might be able to get out of town before Gree—"

The somehow shrill sound of Greel clearing his throat made Devon hunch shoulders as if hearing nails on a chalkboard.

"Fortunately, I've arrived to save you from saying something stupid," Greel said as he marched into the square, followed by his lackey. "And now that I'm here—wait..."

He trailed off, eyes narrowing as he looked at the collection of bikes. "I believe we agreed on a two-seater so that my apprentice could provide power to those things you call pedals."

Devon grinned and nodded at Chen, who rushed toward a darkened alley between buildings. This part of the preparations almost made the prospect of Greel's company worth it. Moments later, Chen emerged wheeling another bike.

"But there's only one seat on that one too. I don't..." He trailed off again, as, behind the new bike and attached to the rear wheel's hub by a long ironwood pole, came a ridiculous-looking trailer. Much like the seasonal migration of road bikers through St. George, similar conveyances were all over the city and trails, especially in the spring and fall. Some insane parents who didn't want to give up riding even though they had perfectly good, pint-sized excuses to sit safely at home, dragged their poor kids around in the things. Devon had even insisted on having a five-point toddler harness installed. For Greel's safety, of course.

"No," the man sputtered. "I will not suffer the indignity of sitting in a compartment sized for a...for a...in that thing. I am meant to be up at a lofty height, ready to apply my keen eyesight to our avoidance of threats."

"Oh yes," Devon said. "I even had a special crash helmet and the facemask fashioned for you. Wouldn't want to squander health potions if there happens to be an accident."

The lawyer looked to Valious for support, but the man just shrugged. Devon liked him for that.

"Well, shall we," she said.

As the group mounted up, everyone but Greel smiling and cheerful at the prospect of an adventure, a message popped into her view.

You have gained special skill points: +2 Improvisation

Honestly, the bikes are a good idea...did not see this coming.

Chapter Thirty-Eight

THE LATE-MORNING sun warmed Devon's back, sinking through the thick leather of her *Stonehaven Jerkin* as the group pedaled along the wagon track. They rode double file in the parallel ruts, wheels bumping over rocks and potholes. Devon kept her eyes pinned to the trail ahead, gripping her handlebars tight and sometimes forgetting to blink. The track wasn't quite as narrow as the mountain bike trail Tamara had taken her on in real life—at the time, it had felt as if the bushes and boulders were attempting to eat her—but it was definitely too skinny for someone of her dubious cycling skill to attempt casually.

At the rear of the party, Greel's trailer jostled along, canted at an angle because one of the wheels kept getting stuck in the rut while the other plowed through grass that had been pressed flat and broken off by the wagon beds passing over it. The lawyer gripped the sides of the trailer with blanched knuckles, his eyes white-rimmed. His crash helmet jiggled on his skull, and his lips were pulled back from clenched and rattling teeth.

This was definitely worth it.

In front, Tamara and Torald set a moderate pace, chatting and taking in the scenery. Tamara kept one hand on the handlebars while sitting upright and gesturing with the other as she regaled the paladin with tales of St. George rides and asked about his gaming experience. Torald told her about his early days in Relic Online and his recent specialization quest, occasionally pointing out landmarks that Devon hadn't noticed before.

As Devon's thoughts started to drift toward the city and the challenges to come, she felt the *Greenscale Pendant* bouncing against her breastbone. On her index finger, the *Azuresky Band* rubbed against the handlebar, creating a little blister where it pinched her palm just below her finger. Like the pendant, the ring seemed to warm as they drew nearer to the city. She couldn't feel the *Ironweight Key* inside her backpack, but somehow she felt she could sense it. The other relic she'd recovered, the *Blackbone Effigy*, was currently resting in a little niche in the Shrine to Veia, strengthening the shrine's power—especially its ability to repel demons.

It seemed so long ago since she recovered the first of the relics, and now she was heading to retrieve the last one. What would happen when—if—she managed to secure it? How would she actually take possession of the city? Just walk in and declare herself supreme ruler? She snorted quietly at the idea.

If it didn't happen automatically, the first thing she would probably try would be to find the Vault of the Magi that the *Ironweight Key* was supposed to unlock. If nothing else, it sounded cool, and it was the only specific mention of an Ishildar location amongst the item descriptions. Of course, how to find it was another problem. With the city stretching for around ten miles in every direction, that was way too much area to search.

Maybe the game would give her some more instruction once she'd reached that point.

Due to the easy pace set by Tamara and Torald, Devon's *Fatigue* score climbed no faster than it would have if she'd been walking. When they reached the bend where the road turned toward the mountains, her butt was sore from bumping over ruts, but she'd only hit 40% *Fatigue*. Though the sun had climbed to its high point, a fresh breeze from the Argenthals cooled her skin. Squeezing her brake to stop beside Tamara, she grinned.

"So? How was it?

Tamara's eyes shone. "So awesome. Seriously the best time I've had since the crash. I don't even mind that we have to portage."

"Portage? What's that?"

Raising an eyebrow, Tamara snorted and gestured toward the waving grasses that stretched toward the wall of jungle that stood between the savanna and Ishildar's border. The woman picked up her bike and stuck her arm through the frame where the bars made a triangle. Balancing the bicycle on her shoulder by supporting it under the top bar, she turned a smirk on Devon.

"Ready to hike?"

Devon groaned. How could she have failed to think about *this* lovely detail?

***

"I think I'm dead. Do I look dead? Because I feel dead." Devon lay sprawled on top of a carpet of vines and fallen leaves. Beside her outstretched hand, her bike lay where she'd dropped it while collapsing onto the clearing floor. Blinking, she stared up into the jungle canopy where the late afternoon sunlight fractured into thousands of shining patches between the leaves. Every muscle in her body hurt. The bones too. And probably some other stuff like internal organs.

Tamara laughed. "You did good, Devon. I've seen grown men turned to heaps of whimpering Jell-O by portages of that length. And that was without all the spiders and vines and 100% humidity."

Devon groaned. "Don't remind me." But it was too late, and a parade of memories marched through her head, recollections of endless fallen logs and tangled underbrush and grasping vines that had snagged her handlebars, feet, even her hair. She swiped a hand down her face, unable to banish the feeling that a coating of cobwebs still clung to her skin.

"Well, if nothing else, I think we've learned why mountain biking hasn't caught on in the Amazon basin," Torald said as he picked up Devon's bike and carried it to the tree trunk where he and Tamara had neatly leaned theirs. For the jungle portion of the portage, he'd put his platemail greaves back on to protect his legs. The new look—his skin-tight tank top emerging from what now looked like an oversized, metal lower body—was possibly even weirder than the hotpants.

"Thanks, Torald," Devon said. Groaning, she managed to lever herself into a seated position so that she could get at her backpack and inventory. "Anyone hungry?" she asked as she pulled out a *Termite Turnover.* The little cake crunched as she bit down, then crackled with each chew. For once, she didn't even care about the insect parts she was munching.

Tamara smirked. "Nothing like a day on the trail to stimulate the appetite, eh? I think I'll pass on the termites, though."

Devon shrugged. "Suit yourself."

As she ate, she glanced through the trees to where the forest opened up a few yards north of their clearing. Between some of the trunks, she could make out Ishildar's stonework, clean lines of marble and light-gray limestone catching the last of the afternoon sunlight. With dusk not far off, they'd agreed it was best to set camp and rest—not that Devon could have made it much farther anyway; her fatigue was at 92%. Much longer, and she would have flat-out collapsed. The other party members looked equally worked, except

Torald and Tamara, who seemed to have leveraged their out-of-game biking knowledge to minimize *Fatigue* gain. Even Jeremy seemed to have lost his snark. He sat with his head bowed and simply nodded in gratitude when Torald fetched his bike.

Once the bikes were collected and lined neatly against the tree, Torald opened his manpurse and started pulling out bedrolls. He handed a couple to Tamara, who surveyed the clearing before choosing an area that had decent shelter beneath the boughs of a tree. She laid out the bedding then collected one of the canvas tarps from Torald and, using some twine, rigged a tent over the sleeping spot.

Torald nodded in appreciation. "You sure you haven't played these games before?"

Tamara brushed off the compliment with a wave of her hand, but Devon could see she was pleased. "Years of camping with my family during summer vacations taught me that it's good to have a rain shelter just in case."

"Well, regardless, nice work."

Cheeks pink, Tamara ducked her head and kept working. She set out more of the bedrolls, then moved to the center of the clearing where she cleared away greenery and started laying a fire. Devon's thoughts started to wander as she listened to the preparations, and she yawned. As her eyes started to close, she thought she spied movement deeper in the trees, but when she blinked and squinted, it turned out to be mist rising from the damp earth as the air above cooled.

Wait.

Devon managed to climb somewhat unsteadily to her feet. "Guys? Anyone else see that mist?"

Both Chen and Torald, who had listened to her story of the scorpion boss and had seen the unnatural swirling mist in the savanna, straightened and peered into the forest. But it was too late anyway. Whatever she thought she'd seen had already vanished.

"Sorry, Devon, don't see it," the paladin said.

She shook her head. "Yeah, it's gone now. Might have just been my eyes playing tricks anyway."

"Either way, we'll set watches tonight," Torald said.

"Never know when you might get attacked by some malicious fog, or perhaps an aggressive falling leaf," Greel muttered.

"Hey," Devon said. "You know, the rest of us could just disappear to the starborn realm during the night hours, leaving you to fend for yourself."

The lawyer stiffened, the skin around his eyes tightening. After a moment, he sneered at her. "My underling will be pleased to take a shift on watch duty."

She sighed. "As will you."

Greel muttered something under his breath, then rolled his eyes. "Fine, fine, whatever."

After searching the trees one last time for hints of mist and seeing nothing, Devon stumbled over to where Tamara was struggling with a flint and steel. No matter how hard she struck, she couldn't manage to knock sparks onto her little pile of sticks.

"Care for some help?" Torald asked. "Happy to let you keep at it if you want, though. You've almost got it."

Tamara gave a relieved sigh as she handed over the objects. "Please. I'm ready to sit down and eat."

"*Termite Turnover*?" Devon asked as she stuck a hand into her backpack.

Tamara's brows drew together in concern. "I—is that the only option?"

Devon laughed as she handed over a couple of strips of *Spiced Antelope Jerky*. "You can have a pass today, but only because you're a noob."

Torald lit the fire with a couple of quick strikes of the steel. Within a few minutes, the blaze was crackling merrily, and Devon leaned back on her elbow to enjoy the evening.

Chapter Thirty-Nine

Ability: Berserk

You go totally nuts. Like...super rage beast.

Attacks ignore target defense | +10 Strength | +20% Melee Attack Rate | -100% Dodge

Duration: 5 minutes, if you last that long

Ability: Headlong Charge

You streak across the field of battle, knocking aside anyone who gets in your way. Unfortunately, once activated, you cannot change direction or stop until you reach your target.

150% Sprint Speed | Applies knockback to all targets in a straight line (15% to knockdown, contested by the target's *Agility*)

Ability: Dying Frenzy

With your dying breaths, you strike at your enemies.

When activated when below 15% health, allows you to whirl in a frenzy of blades and destruction, striking up to 7 melee-range enemies in a single attack.

Emerson closed his abilities tab and sighed in contentment. He was looking forward to testing out these powers that came with his—apparently unique—Frenzy class, but it could wait. For now, he sat a few feet from the campfire feeling more at ease than he recalled having felt in a long time. The flames crackled, sending sparks into the night and casting a glow on the faces of people who, just a few hours ago, had been strangers. But now, out here in the wilderness with darkness and danger all around, he felt as if he'd known them for years. Okay, maybe that was taking it a bit far. But, yeah, it felt nice.

Of course, forgetting the fact that he was an imposter hiding behind a fake identity, the group had accepted him. Despite his low level and his status as Greel's lackey, no one had questioned his ability to take part in the watch rotation. Sure, there'd been a frank discussion about *Perception* scores. But that was a numerical measurement, not a judgment of character. If anyone *had* gotten grief about the need to stand watch, it was Greel. Everyone else could just log out to let the night hours pass, but then they'd be leaving the lawyer with no protection. So, one by one, they would take turns standing sentry while the other characters lounged by the fire or slept.

In fact, first watch—Emerson's—was coming up. He glanced at his game clock— ten minutes left. He glanced at Devon across the fire, her face content as she watched the flames. Greel had talked about her *Charisma* score and resulting appearance drawing extra attention, but the truth was Emerson didn't find her in-game avatar any more attractive than her out-of-game body. She was the same woman, brave and clever and kind. And yeah, pretty too.

Devon really didn't deserve to have secrets kept from her just because he was a coward.

Unfortunately, he also didn't want to distract her right now. This mission was too important to her and Stonehaven—and, frankly, to the stability of the game world. But even though it wasn't a good time for him to reveal his secret identity, it was a total jerk move to ignore her message. As he watched her poke at the fire with a stick, he pulled up his messenger app and subvocalized a response.

"Hey. I'm really sorry. I owed you a response days ago. At first I made the excuse to myself that I shouldn't bother you since you talked about how busy you were, but that's not the real reason. Among other stuff, I'm afraid I let you down on the Zaa thing. I know you weren't expecting me to be able to change Bradley's mind, but I still hoped I could."

Emerson swallowed. Was this some weird sort of psycho-stalker behavior to be messaging her while staring at her? He hoped not. He was only communicating this way because he didn't want to mess up her mission to get the fifth relic.

But still... It was kind of weird.

"So, my big news is that I did get a chance to log in finally. Played a little bit. I know you said you're super busy with Stonehaven and the demon stuff right now, and I've still got a lot of things to learn. Once Stonehaven's secure, I'm really looking forward to playing together for fun. So stay in touch.

"Oh, yeah.

"P.S. Nothing from Owen, I'm afraid. But Cynthia would tell us if something was wrong, so I imagine he's just taking his time."

Emerson pulled his gaze from Devon as he saved the message to his drafts folder. He would wait until he left the fire to stand watch before he sent it because otherwise he'd be too tempted to watch her face for a reaction.

And that really would be kind of stalkerish.

Chapter Forty

DEVON HAD ACTUALLY dozed during the night, in the hours between when her watch had ended and the predawn hour when a chorus of birdsong had filled the jungle. It was always weird to sleep in the game, and she usually avoided it—to maximize her play time, if nothing else. But today it felt good to wake and stretch and start to work the stiffness from her tired muscles. It made the whole adventure seem more authentic, not that Relic Online needed much help in that regard.

Unsurprisingly, Tamara was already up and about. When she saw Devon awake, she grinned. "If we were camping in real life, I'd have some eggs and bacon for you. Or maybe just instant oatmeal if I were feeling lazy."

"I don't think anything you do could be called lazy."

Tamara snorted. "You haven't seen me on the couch after a weekend of hard riding. Anyway, when spring comes I'm definitely getting you out camping for real."

"I guess I don't have any excuse to back out this time," Devon said, "seeing as you got hardware put in your head to come try my version."

Tamara smiled. "Seriously, Devon, this is awesome. The next best thing to swooping down a sandstone bowl on my bike, a big desert sky overhead." If the memory made her sad, she didn't show it. Instead, she tossed over a paper-wrapped package.

> You have received: Trail Rations
> *You know: seeds and nuts and stuff, plus some kind of gooey and delicious glue to hold it all together.*
> Grants: +2 Constitution, +3 Endurance

"No way. Where did you...?"

Tamara grinned and winked. "I had a little talk with Tom about what athletes need for sustained enduro activities. He made one for each of us."

Devon bit into the food, which was basically like a chewy granola bar. It was scrumptious, and within the first bite, she felt her energy start to rise.

"I think we're lucky she had the foresight," Torald said. "Yesterday was close."

"What do you mean, close?" Devon said.

"You mean you *weren't* down to your last 10% of *Fatigue* gain?" he said, an eyebrow raised skeptically.

"Yeah, unlike you two." Devon glanced back and forth between the two experienced cyclists.

Tamara snorted. "You really think that I somehow managed to be better at the game than you, Dev? By the time the fire was set, my bar was at 98% and flashing."

"But you looked so..."

"So energetic?" Tamara laughed. "That might be my only advantage in this game. I just have a little more practice going until I literally fall over, unable to move."

Now Devon felt like a bit of a whiner, having lain there like a corpse while others set up camp. Turned out she could learn something about gaming from Tamara after all.

As the others stirred and downed their trail rations, Devon extracted her bike from the line and started toting it to the edge of the city. She stopped just before the first of the flat stones that paved the streets in this area and gazed out across the ruins. The *Greenscale Pendant* pulsed against her breastbone, creating a bone-deep yearning in her, an inexplicable desire to walk among the ancient buildings. The pull had been disconcerting the first time she'd felt it. Games shouldn't be able to affect her emotions in that way. But now, it just felt right. She had to believe she would make it through to the other side, locate the final relic, and claim this place. At the thought, she felt a strange tingle in her chest.

Anticipation.

After months of work, in the next few days she would either fulfill her so-called destiny, or she would fail miserably and doom the world. Either way, a major chapter of her Relic Online career was reaching its end.

She set the bike down, careful to keep the front wheel off the street until the others were ready. She expected to wait a while, but when she turned back, the clearing was already empty, and her friends had nearly reached her.

"Okay, then," she said when they joined her. "Guess you guys are ready. Should we buff up?"

Torald cleared his throat, dropping to a knee with his face upturned to the heavens. "Veia, grant me strength. Shine your light upon your humble crusader as you once set fire to the hearts of the first men and women. For your glory!" He raised a fist and bowed his head.

An awkward silence gripped the party for a moment before Hailey shrugged and started casting. Magic shimmered all around as energy flowed from Hailey and Torald to encompass the group and infuse them with shielding and stat buffs. Jeremy pulled his harmonica from its holster, twirled it like a six-shooter, then played a little riff. Devon's pulse quickened as his haste buff flooded her with speed.

"I guess we're set then. Okay people," Devon said. "Stick together, follow my lead, and ride with everything you've got."

Setting foot on the pedal, she pushed hard and launched her bike onto the street. The wind of her passage quickly picked up, blowing against her cheeks and forcing her to squint. A few pedal strokes later, she looked back to make sure everyone was following.

A sudden, jarring crash shoved her arms into her shoulder sockets, and all of a sudden, Devon was airborne, head over wheels. The sky and pavement switched places, her bicycle momentarily silhouetted against the pink light of morning. And then she landed hard, slamming down on her shoulder then rolling as her bike went clattering away. She skidded to a stop and groaned.

"Ouch," Tamara said, hissing in sympathy. "Endo."

As Devon recovered her bearings, she craned her neck and saw the fallen stone block that she'd slammed her front wheel into. The sudden change in momentum had sent her flying over the handlebars.

You have lost a special attribute point: -1 Dignity.

"On second thought," Devon said. "Everyone, follow Tamara's lead."

***

At the first crossroad, near where she and Hazel had been turned back during their first reconnaissance of the city, Devon felt Ishildar's guardians awake. Abruptly, their heavy stone presences and ancient, alien minds hovered at the edge of her awareness. She released the handlebar with one hand and slapped her palm against the *Greenscale Pendant.* Biting her lip in concentration, she activated *Ishildar's Call,* and immediately felt connections open to the massive beings.

Lots of connections.

Where before, two or three guardians had been near the city's southern border, now there were at least a dozen.

"What the hell?" she muttered under her breath.

"If you care to hear my theory," Bob piped up, "your recent, so-called *explorations* of the city have attracted their attention. Not that you seem to ask for my opinion very often."

"Guardians incoming," Devon called as she pushed more energy into her thighs. To Bob, she muttered, "Did you just think of this now? Because for someone who claims to want to help me, you're rather inconsistent. I thought you wanted to get this quest finished so you could regain admittance to the arcane realm."

"I said I could *potentially* regain admittance if I finished this mission. My sibling-selves have been less than forthcoming on what it will actually take. And for your information, I am not so ridiculously stupid as to place all my hopes in you. I've also been working on a backup plan."

"What? How? You've been stuck to my shoulder since—never mind."

Devon swerved hard as a tremor in the ground sent a toaster-sized stone block tumbling from a building façade. As soon as she recovered from the wobble her sudden change of direction induced, a massive foot stomped onto the street ahead, cracking the pavement and sending stone chips flying.

"Hanging a right," Tamara yelled with about a nanosecond of warning before she somehow leaned and skidded, dropping a foot to help her make the corner. Devon squeaked and squeezed the brakes as Torald followed Tamara through the curve.

Screeching down to a walking speed, Devon gritted her teeth and focused on her command spell as the others whizzed by. Though none of them dropped a foot, crazy-motorcycle-racer style, everyone else made the corner without freaking out like she had. Of course, she was trying to simultaneously hold onto her connection with the stone giants, sending mental commands to compel them to turn around, or at least to kindly not smash the party.

Both feet down on the pavement, she managed to get her bike reoriented in the new direction. After a quick breath to collect her wits, Devon stomped on the pedals and started forward again.

When Tamara looked back, the woman was actually grinning. She was seriously not right in the head.

For maybe ten blocks, they careened along a snaking course through the streets, dodging rubble and pockets of forest. The Stone Guardians thundered along behind, feet pounding the earth and rattling the riders' teeth. Sweat streamed from Devon's brow, running into her eyes and stinging like crazy, and her thighs burned like they'd been injected with hot molten wax. A stray bug had smashed into her clenched teeth, and when she'd tried to spit the stupid thing out, the wind had caught hold of it, and now there was a disgusting dribble of saliva and bug parts plastered to her *Stonehaven Jerkin.*

"How far...have we...come...?" She managed to puff out between breaths.

Tamara glanced back, brow knit in concern. "A mile, maybe. Mile and a half. You can keep them off us, right?"

"Uh..."

"I cannot believe that this was your plan," Greel growled, his crash helmet rattling on top of his head. In front of him, Valious rode with his head bowed, hands tight on the bars, chest heaving. If Devon felt this tired already, how must the newbie feel while pulling a trailer?

Crap. She shook her head. There was no way they were going to survive another nine miles of this.

"Take the next left," Devon yelled. "Torald, you brought a rope, right?"

The paladin nodded. "Like a good Boy Scout."

"Okay. After we make the turn, everyone stop. We'll have to be quick."

"Wait...stop?" Hailey said. "Did I hear that right?"

Devon nodded. "I have a plan."

Chapter Forty-One

"YOU CALL THIS a plan?" Jeremy asked.

"Zip it, Jeremy," Devon said as she stood at the rear of the group with eyes closed, focusing on her connections to the Stone Guardians. She'd managed to get the lead golems to hesitate, their footfalls no longer shaking the city. But her control was tenuous.

"Okay, Devon," Torald said. "This end is fixed."

Devon nodded. "Tamara, where's the best spot to hook a tow line on my bike?" Though they weren't as common as the army of toddler trailers that infested St. George, she also remembered seeing parents who, still desperate to keep riding once their kids were too big to be crammed into wagons, connected their bikes to their kids' with a length of bungee cord. The kids trailed along behind, balancing and occasionally pedaling while their parents grunted and sweated up the hills.

Some people were seriously insane, but at least they'd given Devon the idea.

"Wait a minute," Greel said. "Are you seriously so lazy that—"

"Dude, can it," Tamara snapped.

The outburst was so unexpected that Devon glanced at the lawyer and almost laughed at the look of offense on his face. But at least he'd shut up.

"On the frame above the fork but below the stem, I think," Tamara said.

"Uh..."

"Should I do it?"

"Yes please."

In truth, Devon was inclined to agree with Jeremy's skepticism. It did seem like a ridiculous plan, but it was the best she could come up with. When Tamara clapped her shoulder, Devon broke her concentration on the giants—they immediately started stomping forward again—and raced for her bike. A ten-foot length of rope now attached it to the seat post of Torald's ride. She nodded. Good.

"All right. Now everyone get ready to think like a sail."

"Like a what?" Jeremy asked.

"Hold onto your hat."

As she climbed onto her bike, Torald edged forward until the line connecting them went taut. Devon grimaced. This was going to be tough. "All right, on the count of three. One, two...three."

Devon pushed off the ground and got her feet on the pedals as Torald stood on his pedals and cranked. Her bike lurched forward, and Devon wobbled like crazy trying to keep control. After a moment, though, the motion smoothed out and she was able to pedal lightly to ease Torald's load.

"Okay, everyone get ahead of me," she called.

Once the group was clustered in front of her, Devon cast *Levitate* to raise her bike off the ground. By taking her feet off the pedals, she was able to paddle at the cushion of air in the manner she was used to and thereby avoid falling over.

Tamara looked back and laughed. "Cheater," she said.

Devon was concentrating too hard to respond—the shuddering of the earth was getting closer, and the presence of the nearest Stone Guardian pressed even more heavily against her mind. Gritting her teeth, she cast *Downdraft.*

As the sudden surge of wind caught her friends, the party struggled to keep their bikes upright. Everyone but Tamara squeaked in surprise, wobbling and weaving and nearly crashing into one another as the gale shoved them forward.

"Holy tailwind!" Torald shouted as his pedal strokes sped.

The scenery raced past, buildings and rubble and vines blurring as Torald's sudden burst of speed yanked her bike forward. Devon grinned and almost laughed as she felt the Stone Guardians' presences recede.

Paddling her feet, she yelled at the group to keep pedaling and to hold onto the speed as long as they could. Eyes on the cooldown timer for *Downdraft,* she swung her backpack around and pulled out a *Savanna Mana Potion - Mid.* Shoving it into the basket of sticks fixed to the diagonal tube of her bike frame—according to Chen and Tamara, the proper name was a water bottle cage—she glanced back to see the horde of stone golems falling farther behind.

> *You realize you're only getting away with this because you have 8 skill points in Improvisation, right?*

Devon snorted and ignored the game's commentary. *This* was traveling in style.

***

"Out of mana," Devon called.

At the head of the group, Tamara nodded. "No worries."

"Huh? You know that means no more wind, right?"

"Yeah, but look."

Tamara pointed over the roof line of the buildings ahead and to their left. When Devon followed the line of her finger, her eyes widened. For some reason, she'd imagined the Stone Forest as a gray and lifeless place, but peeking out behind the spires and towers of Ishildar was a multicolored tree, bands of what looked like brightly hued agate and gemstone creating wavy lines in the petrified wood.

"Hanging a left," Tamara called.

As the party turned onto the next wide avenue, Devon gasped in surprise. Ahead, grown over by the vines of the jungle, the whole frozen forest was similar to that first tree. Crystals sparkled in the sun, and some branches seemed to glow from within, the translucent stone allowing a bit of daylight through.

When they drew within a block of the city border, Devon felt her connection to the Stone Guardians ebb. The creatures seemed to realize that the intruders were nearly gone from Ishildar, and, one by one, the golems returned to a sort of stasis, their minds once again sinking into the slow cycling that marked most of their existence.

At the very edge of the city, the party braked and waited for Devon, who canceled her *Levitation* and pedaled the final few feet to catch up.

"Well, that was interesting," Greel said.

"Admit it. That wasn't just interesting, it was *epic*."

The man snorted. "I see no need to encourage you in such harebrained plans."

Rolling her eyes, Devon nodded at the tall granite pillar that stood about ten yards into the petrified forest. They'd encountered a similar monolith in the Argenthal Mountains. The bindstone would allow them to reset their spawn points to its location, and better, now that she'd traveled to it, she'd be able to use her teleport spell to travel between here and Stonehaven. Regardless of whether she recovered the final relic, at least the group wouldn't need to bicycle through the city while chased by stone giants again.

After wheeling her bike to the stone, she laid her hand against the age-smoothed surface.

> **You have discovered:** The Stone Forest
> **You receive:** 55,000 Experience.
>
> **Quest Updated:** Venture to the Stone Forest
> **Objective complete:** You have discovered the seat of the ancient Skevalli Vassaldom.
> *Now, how about you work on finding the relic...*
>
> *P.S. Watch out for dragons and stuff.*

Devon sighed. Okay then.

***

Tamara might have been able to ride through the Stone Forest, but for the rest of the party, there was no chance. Neither Bob nor Greel had any clue what had caused the gigantic trees to petrify, but whatever the event, it had been sudden enough that leaves had turned to stone on their twigs. In the centuries since, wind and rain and gravity had plucked them and sent them clattering down to litter the forest floor as a carpet of razor-sharp stone chips. Twigs and branches had fallen too, some so thick they came up to Devon's waist. Stony bark, often with veins of needlelike crystals, gouged her leather armor as she clambered the debris, and when she jumped down from atop thick branches, she kept slicing her palms open when she planted her hands to absorb some of the impacts.

As beautiful as the area was, especially the crystal veins, she would rather have hacked her way through jungle. After just a quarter hour's walk, she'd had more than her fill of the place.

On the bright side, unlike some of the vassaldoms that had covered dozens or hundreds of square miles—an area far too large to search in the time they had available—the former Skevalli region covered just a narrow strip of land between the city and the nearly vertical rise of the dark and sullen-looking Skargill Mountains to the north. And, by some miracle, there was an actual road through the wood. Though the paving stones lay buried under heaps of rock-leaves, they peeked out now and again, proving that what appeared to be a deliberately constructed corridor through the trees had been cut long ago by human hands. Chances were, the road once connected the vassaldom's capital to Ishildar. If there were clues about the relic's fate, they would likely be somewhere within their former population center.

"I'm starting to think this thing about dragons is just a cruel tease," Jeremy said as he walked behind her.

"You're that eager to get roasted alive?" Devon said.

"Well, maybe not. I'm not sure my wardrobe would survive it."

She rolled her eyes and glanced back to check on the rest of the party. Walking single-file, the group seemed energetic enough to keep hiking for another hour or two, and it was just after noon in-game. Eventually, they'd have to set another camp to recover from the fatiguing ride, but maybe the group would reach some sort of landmark before then.

As she turned back to the trail, motion deeper in the trees caught her eye. Devon stopped walking and peered. There. Again. Just a flicker.

"You see that?" she said, pointing.

"See what?"

"Something in the trees."

Hailey's cast bar lit up as she used her *True Sight* ability. "Shit," the woman muttered.

"What?" Chen and Devon asked together.

But Hailey didn't need to answer because, a moment later, mist swirled up from the forest floor and down from the low-hanging branches. For a second or two, the tendrils and swirls collected into pillars, and then with a barely audible *pop,* dozens of Mistwalkers solidified in the forest ahead.

Devon backpedaled, closing ranks with her group. Steel sang as the melee fighters in the group drew their weapons.

With a hissing laugh, one of the Esh stepped onto the roadway. Devon thought she recognized him but used *Combat Assessment* anyway.

> Mistwalker Scorpion Wyvern Keeper (Faction: Rovan) - Level 26
>
> **Health:** 1391/1391

Mana: 675/675
Resists: Water-based Attacks
Immune to: Light-based Attacks

What? No fair. The stupid freak shouldn't be able to just switch which kind of "keeper" he was.

But of course, his title made her wonder...where were the wyverns?

Moments later, a jet of flame shot across the stone treetops.

"Ah, crap," Jeremy said. "I was joking about the dragons, okay?"

Chapter Forty-Two

"I COUNT AROUND forty Esh and...looks like five wyverns." Hailey's voice held a raw edge. "Level 35 on the dragonkin. This doesn't look good, guys."

In response to the woman's words, the Wyvern Keeper laugh-hissed again and held something up. It looked like some sort of smooth stone rod. With a sinking feeling, Devon focused her attention on it.

> **Item:** Starlight Rod
> *A relic once held in trust by the Skevalli people, vassals to the great city of Ishildar. It's rumored that only the worthy can touch this without being burned by cold starlight.*
> **Use:** Lances targets of evil alignment with a beam of super-chilled light, causing paralysis and 549-612 points of damage.
>
> *Too bad he's immune to light-based damage, eh?*
>
> **Quest Updated:** Venture to the Stone Forest
> *Well, that sucks. Looks like the Mistwalker guy has the last relic. Must have been listening in on your conversations lately.*
> **New Objective:** Not sure how you're gonna do it, but take the Starlight Rod from the Wyvern Keeper's cold, dead

hands. Or take it from his alive and much-more-powerful-than-yours hands. It's the "take it" part that matters.

She shoved away the popup as another jet of flame shot down through the trees, this time burning straight for the party. Devon screamed despite herself, instinctively raising a hand as if to defend her face. The snap of leathery wings rattled the forest, the wind and vibration snapping stone twigs as the wyvern hovered above.

"Veia guide us and shelter us!" Torald shouted as he ran forward. He went down on a knee to brace and raised his shield as a silvery glow formed around the metal. A dome of shimmering light burst into existence over the party, anchored on the shield. Dragon fire slammed into the barrier and washed over it. Intense, nearly blistering heat sank through the magical protection, but no flames passed through. Devon let out a shaky breath as she looked at her health bar. Still full.

A few paces ahead on the road, the Mistwalker grinned. He gestured toward the other Esh, waving them back. Apparently, he wasn't too concerned about the threat the group posed and figured the wyverns were more than enough challenge for Devon's friends.

"Now might be a good time to inquire whether I have information that might offer assistance in the present situation," Bob said. "Seriously. Because you're looking pretty hosed."

Devon gritted her teeth as she dashed toward Tamara to offer whatever small protection she could. "Bob, got any tactics or stratagems that might help here?"

"Imprecise wording, but I'll cut you some slack due to extenuating circumstances. And actually, yes. You remember my former master...?"

The whistle of wings cutting the air sliced through the forest as another wyvern dove, then pulled up suddenly to hang in the air, red glow lighting the creature's belly. Backlit by the sun, the bones in the small dragon's flapping wings looked like a bat's long fingers.

"Dude, skip the prologue."

Bob sighed. "Fine. In the early years, when my master was just a wizard left to guard the *Greenscale Pendant*—not the lich you encountered—he often made trips into the city where he attempted to clean and restore a small section of his beloved Ishildar. It was a pointless struggle against the jungle, but when cursed with everlasting life, you've got to do something, right? Anyway, the longer the Curse of Fecundity remained in place, the more difficult my master found it to cross the border into the city. Eventually, even with all the power he gained in his long years, he found that he simply couldn't enter Ishildar. It was as if an invisible wall had slowly coalesced."

"So you're saying that you don't think these guys can follow us into the city?"

"It's possible that the curse prevents vassal races from entering, yes. It'd explain why they waited until you exited the city to spring this little ambush."

"But if we retreat into the city, I've got the guardians to contend with."

"Fair point. Though I daresay being smashed is probably more pleasant than being roasted alive."

The air above began to crackle as the hovering wyvern opened its mouth and flame appeared in its throat. Devon used *Combat Assessment.*

Awakened Wyvern - Level 34
Already intelligent when awakened by Ishildar's magi, an extended family of wyverns once lived peaceably with the Skevalli griffon keepers. Awakening granted the dragonkin the power of tongues, allowing them to speak telepathically with the other intelligent races of the region. Unfortunately, it seems the corruption has removed whatever filter allowed them selective hearing for thoughts of others, and the never-ending stream of voices in their minds has driven them mad. With lives measured in thousands of human lifespans, these creatures have basically been doomed to eternal torment.
Immunity: Fire-based damage
Weakness: Ice-based damage
Health: 5489/5489
Mana: 4560/5699

//Pathetic. Die!//

The wyvern screamed into her thoughts as another flame jet tore through the forest, the lead fireball barreling down on the party. Torald shouted again and raised his shield. Most of the fire again washed over the group, but a few tendrils broke through. The flame licked Devon's neck, sizzling in her ear. She smelled burnt flesh.

Hailey's cast bar lit up with *Guide Vitality.*

"Run! For the city," Devon yelled.

Whirling, she grabbed Tamara by the arm and dragged her back along the roadway. Through the trees, she could still spy Ishildar's outskirts, but with all the obstacles in the way, sanctuary looked so far.

She neared Valious, who still stood with his mouth agape. Suddenly, the man's lips pulled back, and an angry flush rushed up his neck and over his face. The man gave a bestial roar and...rushed the Wyvern Keeper? What the hell?

Shocked, Devon watched over her shoulder as the man's feet moved at twice the speed of a normal player. Somehow, incredibly, he managed to shoulder into the boss and send the Esh stumbling back. With another roar of anger, Valious made a wild swing at the Mistwalker. Devon let out an astonished squeak as somehow, the noob's sword actually bit into the Esh's thigh, opening a gash that spurted blood. Devon kept running, shaking her head in amazement. How could a level 5 player even *hit* that guy?

Unfortunately, Valious's charge was short-lived. Devon glanced back in time to see the Esh bring a fist down directly on top of Valious's head. The man crumpled, dead.

The group was in full retreat, sprinting with everything they had. Devon heard another set of wing beats, and she spun to see more fire brewing in a wyvern's throat. She cast *Freeze*, and the fire fizzled in an enormous cloud of steam. Following through, she summoned a *Wall of Ice* across the road behind the party, thinking it might slow ground-based pursuit by the Esh. Unfortunately, the barrier only caused the pursuing Mistwalkers to disintegrate into scraps of fog that flowed over and around the wall. But when the tendrils of mist raced past the party and began to coalesce on the road before them, Devon cast *Downdraft* and shredded the forming bodies.

A song pealed through the forest as Jeremy played a riff on his harmonica. His haste buff appeared in her interface, and Devon felt her feet accelerate. Ishildar drew closer.

Again, pillars of smoke began to coalesce in the forest around them, and this time, Devon's *Downdraft* was still cooling down. The Wyvern Keeper appeared first, a blue glow already forming in his hands. A stream of light shot through the forest and hit Chen in the chest. The knight immediately slowed as *Deep Chill* took hold.

"Sorry about this," Devon called as she used a tier 1 *Flamestrike* to cancel the effect. Hailey followed through with a heal over time to restore Chen's health, then cast *Crippling Self-doubt* on the Mistwalker boss. The Esh staggered as the debuff hit, but he quickly growled and recovered. A loud crashing of feet through stone chips came from the road ahead, and Devon gasped when she saw Valious sprinting the wrong way. What the...? He must have respawned.

Again, the man roared and charged the boss, scoring another hit before a backhanded swipe sent him flying into a tree. The noob crumpled bonelessly to the ground, and his corpse quickly disappeared.

"Holy crap," Devon muttered under her breath when she peered at the boss. Incredibly, Valious had taken off a visible chunk of the Wyvern Keeper's health.

She vaulted the last of the downed tree branches that barred the way, and with Tamara by her side, sprinted for the edge of the city. As she passed the bindstone, Valious once again appeared and started sprinting into the forest. Devon shook her head. His insane tactic was actually doing some good. At the very least, they'd survive to reach the city. The problem was, what would happen afterward?

Chapter Forty-Three

"UH, BROKEN?" CHEN said. "He's level five, and he could kill a level twenty-something boss all by himself."

"Only if the boss stands right next to the respawn point and doesn't do anything to stop him," Hailey said. "Otherwise the boss would heal faster than Valious could damage him."

"You mean only if he stands next to the spawn point like this idiot is?" Chen asked, pointing at the Mistwalker.

Devon, bent double as her *Fatigue* score slowly recovered from the sprint, stared in amazement as Valious charged forward again. This time, the boss punched the noob in the face, one-shotting him before Valious could land a blow. But Valious just respawned a second later and rushed forward yet again. A glancing blow with the flat of his blade shaved off another twenty hitpoints from the boss.

The Wyvern Keeper was down 25%.

Not that Devon was complaining, but it *was* pretty damn broken. The rest of the party stood in a tight cluster on the very edge of Ishildar, watching the scene play out. But even though it seemed like a ridiculous miracle—for the party, anyway...she doubted the repeated deaths were very fun for Valious—she couldn't shake the feeling that it wasn't going to be this easy. As soon as she could stand upright enough to focus on casting, she started hammering the boss with *Flamestrikes*. None of the other party members had ranged attacks, so between her and Valious, she had to hope they could kill the guy before the Stone Guardians noticed the party.

"Crud," Hailey said at the same instant that Devon spied the other Mistwalkers. "And here comes the end of that." Like Devon, the woman was still out of breath from the sprint, and her words came out in broken bursts.

The boss grinned again, shaking his eyeless skull as he knocked Valious's jaw sideways and finished the kill by stomping on the man's chest when he fell. As the player respawned, the other Esh converged on the bindstone. Devon threw up a *Wall of Ice* to buy him a little more time, and when some of the Esh turned to mist to flow over the barrier, she scattered them with another *Downdraft.* Valious ran the gauntlet of converging enemies and got a final hit in on the boss—thirty hitpoints—before the Mistwalkers managed to completely encircle the bindstone. When the noob appeared again, he died within a split-second.

"Ouch," Jeremy said. "Spawn camped."

The Wyvern Keeper turned his eyeless sockets directly at Devon and laughed. Raising his arms above his head, the boss muttered something unintelligible, and the air was abruptly full of the sound of beating wings.

All five wyverns dove from the heavens to hover fifty feet above the Esh. Watching over their shoulders for Stone Guardians, the party moved back out of flame-jet range. Unfortunately, that also put Devon out of *Flamestrike* range, creating a standoff.

"Impasse, dude. Care to surrender?" Devon called while her thoughts raced through options. In truth, she doubted they'd last long inside the city. Once the guardians took note, it was only a matter of time before Devon's shaky ability to control them broke.

The boss sneered as he brought his arms down.

"Oh shit," Hailey said as the small dragons screeched, fire building in their bellies, and dove.

Right past the edge of the city.

"Guess we kinda forgot that the wyverns weren't actually vassals of Ishildar, huh?" Bob commented.

Devon sprinted hard for the side of the street as the wind whistled over the wyverns' wings and the horse-sized beasts slammed claws into the roadway where the party had stood. Fire rolled down the street, and stone chips flew as talons raked deep gouges in the pavement. Devon felt her skin crisp and blacken, the pain of the burn followed immediately by relief as Hailey dropped a heal.

Crap. There was no way the party could stand against dragons ten levels higher than the group. They needed a new plan, quick.

"Get inside before they turn!" As Devon shouted, she cast a *Wall of Ice* across the end of the street to block the Wyvern Keeper's view into the city. Whirling, she grabbed Tamara and shoved her through an open archway into the darkened ruin of the building. The others followed, and as soon as the street was empty, Devon cast *Fade* over the group.

"Uh, I don't think we can just hide," Jeremy said. "Even my one-year-old nephew understands object permanence, and he still poops his diaper."

"Zip it," Devon snapped as she closed her eyes and focused on her magic. One by one, simulacra of the group members appeared in the street. Once the illusions had been conjured, she opened her eyes and let the *Wall of Ice* drop. She cut an unfortunate glimpse of poor Valious spawning and taking a dagger through the eye before she focused on the boss. With *Ventriloquism*, she forced her illusions to shout to get the Mistwalker's attention, and then commanded the Devon-illusion to work through the casting motions of *Flamestrike*. Meanwhile, she cast a *Flamestrike* on the Wyvern Keeper, keeping to the shadows to remain unnoticed. As fire enveloped the Esh, Devon recast *Fade* on herself since the aggressive action had canceled the effect.

Overhead, dragons shrieked.

Focusing on the party's illusions, Devon again used *Ventriloquism*.

"Stupid winged cows!" Her illusion's shout echoed off the buildings as Devon commanded the simulacra to flee deeper into the city.

"Is that honestly the best insult you could've come up with?" Jeremy asked under his breath.

"Dude, focusing here."

Slowly slipping from the building and into the shadow of the eaves, Devon guided the fake party past the first crossroads, then halted the illusions as if they were attempting to stand their ground. Then, eyes closed, she used *Ishildar's Call*. Abruptly, ancient stone minds pressed against her thoughts. And rather than trying to command them against their nature, this time she worked with their purpose.

"The city is in danger. There are enemies within." She formed mental images of the wyverns and pressed them through her connection with the golems, putting all the urgency she could into her thoughts.

The ground shook as the guardians emerged from stasis, the grating of stone joints filling the air.

A massive stone arm reached out and batted a wyvern from the air. A small dragon went down with a shriek.

And all at once, dragons and giants joined battle. The air filled with fire and the city shuddered with the golems' rage.

Beyond the border of Ishildar, the Wyvern Keeper shrieked with anger.

"Okay, people, I'm going to kill that freaking eyeless dude."

Devon stepped into the street and covered the boss in *Phoenix Fire* before calling a *Flamestrike* down on his head. At the bindstone, Valious appeared again and was immediately struck down, but Hailey cast her charm spell on the Esh that killed him, and with an angry roar, the Mistwalker minion charged the boss at Hailey's command. The Wyvern Keeper hesitated, unwilling to attack his kin, but when the minion landed his first blow, the boss laid him out flat, then cast *Deep Chill* on the charmed mob.

Before the remaining Esh closed the gap opened by the charmed NPC, Valious managed to sprint through. He squeaked past the minion and landed a punch to the boss's elbow, knocking off another few HP.

Devon waited until Valious died—a kick to the stomach—then cast *Downdraft* against the minions at the bindstone, knocking them back to give the noob another opening.

The boss's health dropped below 50%.

"Okay, you guys, forward to the city edge."

As the party approached the boundary, the boss cast *Deep Chill* on Devon, then summoned his swarm of gross mini-scorpions. She hit herself with *Flamestrike*—for a supposedly intelligent race, this dude was a slow learner—then laughed as the scorpions slammed into the border of Ishildar and got stopped by the invisible wall.

After that, it was just a matter of attrition, sending the boss's own minions after him and generally causing chaos from the safety of the city, until with a howl of dismay, the Wyvern Keeper died. When he hit the ground, his minions shrieked and dissolved into mist, fleeing into the woods.

Immediately, Devon broke from the safety of the city and sprinted across the stone leaf litter. She snatched the *Starlight Rod* from the Esh's loose grip, and for good measure, touched her dagger to his loincloth to activate decomposition into loot. Perhaps unsurprisingly—he had been mostly naked—no further items appeared.

Quest completed: Venture to the Stone Forest

You receive 550,000 experience.
Congratulations, you have reached level 25!

Well, champion, seems all that's left now is to take possession of the city.

Veia is offering you a quest: Fulfill your Destiny
You've recovered all five relics of Ishildar, a task that, frankly, no one had a lot of faith that you'd accomplish. Now it's time to seize your reward. Figure out how to gain control of the city.
Objective: Become Ishildar's Keeper

As Devon stared and blinked at the messages, the cries of the battle between the stone golems and the wyverns dwindled. She glanced up long enough to see that the wyverns were fleeing. The sight made her feel strangely relieved; maybe now that she had the relics, the Curse of Fecundity would soon lift, and the corruption would leave the dragons' minds.

She had the relics—the notion didn't quite seem real.

Devon sank to her knees with the *Starlight Rod* cradled in both palms.

At last.

Chapter Forty-Four

"WHAT IN THE everliving hell?" Jeremy's words snapped Devon from her trance just in time to see mist coalescing...this time within the city boundaries. "Usually when you kill a boss, it means the fight's over."

"Veia's grace defend us!" Torald bellowed as he raised a fist to the sky. Light flowed from the heavens and entered his body, pooling and then washing out to envelop the group. A new buff icon appeared in Devon's interface. When she glanced at it, a tooltip appeared.

> **Ability:** Creator's Shield
> *Absorbs 312-325 damage. When the shield is hit, has a 30% chance to afflict the attacker with* Blinding Glare, *causing -20% to melee accuracy.*
> **Time Remaining:** 15:49

"New spell?" Chen asked as he brought his two-handed sword up and started circling the solidifying column of fog to come at the Mistwalker from the side.

"Got an upgrade that doesn't require a shield."

Devon got ready to cast *Flamestrike* as the Esh solidified but halted when the creature appeared in shimmering night-black robes.

This one appeared to be female, though it was a bit hard to tell with the robes and hood. The real difference was that the Mistwalker had eyes, liquid-gray orbs that turned on Devon.

She fired off a *Combat Assessment.*

> Aijal, Mistwalker Shadow Master - Level 37 (Faction: Drivan)
> **Resists:** Wind-based Damage
> **Immunity:** Water-based Damage
> **Health:** 3217/3217
> **Mana:** 4122/4342

"Wait, Torald," she called at the same time that Chen said "Gah," probably from having also inspected the enemy and registered the level.

But Torald was already in motion, sword gleaming as he rushed the mob. Devon cringed, hoping that the paladin would at least live long enough for the rest of the party to flee.

As the paladin's blade came across in a wide swipe, the Mistwalker raised a hand. Devon, who was still fumbling for what to do and half-heartedly glancing around for her shadow so that she could raise a puppet, yelped in surprise as, all around, patches of shade suddenly *moved.* Darkness flowed across the ground, swirled over the Mistwalker's moon-pale ankles and up her robe, then flowed out from her hand. A shadowy limb extended from the Esh, a sort of tentacle that writhed for a moment before consolidating into a globe. Legs coalesced beneath the globe while a pair of arms stretched out from the sides. Long-fingered hands grew from the wrists, and these reached out and grabbed Torald's forearms, stopping him mid-attack, and then lifting him a few inches off the ground.

Devon blinked. It had all seemed to happen with a languid, liquid sort of grace, yet somehow the Esh's shadow conjuration had managed to intercept the paladin in what had to have been less than a second of actual time.

Torald thrashed in the air, feet kicking at the shadow form yet hitting nothing. His legs just passed straight through the figure as if it were as it appeared—nothing but a shadow.

"The history you read about our race isn't entirely true," the Esh said, her voice a whisper that somehow washed over the top of Torald's grunts.

"What? History?" Jeremy asked. "What the hell is this now?"

"Torald has library books," Chen said as if that would explain the whole situation.

Devon, figuring there wasn't much they could do if the Mistwalker were of a mind to kill them, dropped her hands to her side. Heart thumping, she walked forward and passed her arm through the shadow holding the paladin captive. As with Torald's foot, there was no resistance to her motion, and she felt nothing but a slight coolness within the darkness, the same as if a cloud were to abruptly skid across the sun.

"What did Torald's history have wrong?" she asked, trying to keep the Esh talking—and kind of wishing she'd paid a little more attention to what Torald *had* said about the Esh civilization.

"Devon?" Torald squeaked. "Little help?"

She glanced at him and, with a quick pang of guilt, shook her head. "I'm afraid I'm outclassed here."

Something in her comment made the Mistwalker laugh. Or at least, that's what she thought the strange hissing noise was.

"Perhaps she doesn't realize her potential," the Esh, Aijal, said. "Or perhaps she doesn't recognize the opportunity."

Behind her, Chen whispered, "When a scary beast talks about you in the third person, they are either a wise old sage masquerading as a monster to test you, or they're about to kill you and wish to dehumanize you first. Standard guilt avoidance on the latter."

Again the Esh laughed. "He has theories of much interest. But it is the proper way to speak for Esh. Drivan especially."

"Okay..." Devon said, giving her the side-eye. Torald had stopped thrashing and mostly hung limply in the shadow's grip. "So you aren't planning to kill us?"

"Only this one, unless he promises not to try to smite me with Veia's holy wrath." For the third time, the Mistwalker laughed.

Devon glanced at the paladin. "Torald? No smiting?"

The man blinked and nodded as best he could with a pair of platemail pauldrons squeezing his cheeks due to his arms being held over his head. "No smiting. Not even bringing divine vengeance. As long as she doesn't mean to hurt you guys, that is."

"Good," the Esh said, snapping a pair of milky fingers. The shadow abruptly vanished, and Torald clattered to the ground. The creature turned back to Devon. "She likes the spell? Could learn it, perhaps, with time. Has the beginnings of the abilities already."

Devon blinked, trying to understand. "You mean, it's similar to *Shadow Puppet*?"

"As a breeze is similar to a hurricane. The beginnings of the foundation."

"Do you know what she's talking about, Dev?" Chen asked. "Because I just plugged the mana cost for that shadow spell into my calculator, and the ratio of mana use to utility is—"

Torald stepped back and draped an arm around Chen's shoulder, whispering something that shut the knight up.

"Hold on. Let's backtrack here," Devon said. "Can you finish your statement about Mistwalker history?"

The Esh inclined her head. "I simply meant that the man's information on the Esh is not entirely true, especially with regards to the Rovan. They did not wish to see Ishildar rise again, and in fact saw its downfall as an opportunity to finally step out from beneath a greater power's shadow. The leaders of the faction had the mistaken belief that they could somehow use the key to unlock the Vault of the Magi themselves, taking the vestments that lie within. Of course, this is a childlike vision, an infantile hope. Only the Keeper of the city may enter the vault, and only once they have been granted dominion by possessing all five relics at once."

> **Quest Updated:** Fulfill your Destiny
> *Well, this is convenient. It sounds like Aijal knows what you're supposed to do.*
> **New Objective:** Bring the five relics to the Vault of the Magi. Apparently there are some important vestments you can get.

Devon raised an eyebrow. "So, uh, if someone were to hypothetically have the five relics, could you show them the way to the Vault of the Magi?"

The Mistwalker hissed in amusement. "She speaks like an Esh, referencing the self in a strange tense. This one knows she has the relics. Though this one fails to understand why she would place such treasures inside such a garish vessel." Aijal nodded over Devon's shoulder to indicate her backpack.

Devon clenched her jaw when Jeremy snickered. "Guess she went there," the troubadour said.

"I liked you better when you were...actually, I'm not sure I ever liked you," Devon said.

"I hope you do not intend to take from Devon what she has rightfully won," Torald said, stepping forward to stand between Devon and the Esh. "Because I would consider that a harmful act, and I will not hesitate to defend her. My vow of peace lasts only as long as you uphold your part of the pact."

The Esh shook her head in amusement. "This one came to offer aid. This one wishes to offer the champion guidance. If she does not believe me, she can bring forth her blade, that which was crafted by this one's hands."

Oh, crap! Devon laughed. She'd actually managed to forget about *Night's Fang* for a while. "I guess you've been watching us for some time."

"This one answered the call of the relic when it was brought back into the territory so near the ancestral home. This one and others of my kin traveled together, following the wind. It is unfortunate that the Rovan also felt the pull and arrived through burrows and cracks and holes in the earth. The Drivan will deal with the rest of them while you claim the city. The barrier is down, and vassals may now enter Ishildar. This one's kin will defend your back against attack."

"So about that..." Devon said. "You'll lead me to the Vault?"

The Esh nodded. "But she must retrieve the relic she has stored."

"Ah, crap, right." Devon thumped her forehead with the heel of her hand. The *Blackbone Effigy* was still inside a niche in the Shrine to Veia, bolstering the city's defenses against demons. Fortunately, now that she'd visited the nearby bindstone, she could teleport to and from Stonehaven and this point.

"Mind waiting here for a few?" she asked.

Aijal inclined her head. "This one is patient, Champion."

Chapter Forty-Five

"OKAY, DISINTEGRATION IMMINENT," Devon said as she leaned her bike against her thigh and began casting her teleport spell. At the thought of returning to Stonehaven, her fingers tingled. *Finally*, she would enter the settlement having accomplished what she'd set out to do even before the townsite had been found. Well, almost, anyway. She still needed to fetch the *Blackbone Effigy*, then hurry back into the city to do...whatever it would take to unlock the Vault of the Magi and claim her title. But still. Victorious return and all.

With a shimmery sound, the spell took hold, ferrying the group through the aether and depositing them in the grass surrounding the Shrine to Veia. Before opening her eyes, Devon grinned and inhaled deeply, smelling warm scents of grass and sunbaked stone.

But when the first shouts reached her ears, her smile melted away.

Devon's eyes snapped open as she dropped her bike in the grass. Her gaze shot to the walls where archers lined up shoulder to shoulder, firing into the fields beyond. In small clusters between the ranged fighters, casters from the newbie levels up to the mid-twenties from the player camp shot *Magic Missiles* and called down *Flamestrikes.* Beside the main gate, a horde of melee fighters stood ready in case of a breach.

Heart in her throat, she squinted into the sunlight and saw imps hovering high above, unable to land because of the protections offered by the Shrine to Veia.

But they were waiting. Ready to dive the moment an assault weakened the barrier.

"Shit," Hailey cursed.

Devon nodded.

The demon horde had arrived.

Shouting to the party members to follow, Devon sprinted toward the settlements' main gates. Along the way, she pounded through the central square where the windows were now shuttered and boarded, the flower pots pulled inside. No one chatted or walked along the hamlet's paths. If they could fight, they were on the walls. If they couldn't, they were likely sitting fearfully behind locked doors.

At the gates, she skidded to a halt and called out for Jarleck. A shout from the wall answered her call, and she spotted the man up on the wall-walk, spyglass in hand. Devon sprinted up the stairs, the steps shaking under her feet, and stopped beside him.

The savanna outside the curtain wall was black with writhing demon flesh. Fiends paced and howled, hurling spears toward the ramparts and attempting to lay logs across the moat and against the curtain wall. Imps fluttered in shrieking groups while hellhounds paced like caged lions. Unlike the last attack, these demons were organized in squads. They worked together. Near the drawbridge, now retracted and sealed tight against the iron gates of the curtain wall, a group of perhaps twenty were busy hauling over the trunk of an acacia tree, no doubt intending to use it as a battering ram.

"How long have they been here?" Devon asked.

"Arrived this morning. Between our fighters and the shrine's protection, we're holding," Jarleck said.

Devon exhaled in relief. "When I heard the shouts, I freaked out."

But the man pressed his lips together, shaking his head to indicate he had more to say. "If it were just these, I suspect we could hold indefinitely—provided we could keep the town fed. But, Devon, we sent Blackbeard to scout." He paused, brows drawing together. "I'm afraid this is only the vanguard. At least four times this number are marching in from the coast now. We'll be overrun by the day after tomorrow."

"Damn," Devon muttered under her breath. Down in the field, a small imp fluttered up from the grass and tried to fly across the still-dry moat. A crossbow bolt skewered it through the eye, and the creature fell into the trench, dead. Devon glanced over and saw Heldi pump her fist as she reloaded.

"There are so many. Even if we killed them all..." She glanced into the moat and the corpses that were starting to pile up. "They'll fill the moat," she said. "And I don't think they'll hesitate to climb over their own dead."

Jarleck nodded. "Already on it." He pointed, and Devon saw a newbie rogue creeping through the moat and touching his dagger to the bodies to activate decomposition. The rogue crouched and quickly scooped up the loot, only to have a fiend jab a long spear into the trench and skewer him through the back of the neck, severing the poor noob's spine. The player's body vanished seconds later, and Devon turned to see him respawn at the shrine. Quickly, he started up the path that zigzagged along the cliff face, then scampered along the rim before downclimbing the far edge of the cliff outside the wall.

Jarleck sucked his teeth. "I didn't give those trainers enough credit. I never would have thought of using the inexperienced starborn as an expendable resource."

"I know, right? When the only death penalty is getting teleported back to your bind spot, it's like the ultimate zerg rush."

"A zerg...what?"

She shook her head. "Never mind. So listen, I got the final relic—"

Jarleck grabbed for the wall when his knees wobbled with relief. "I was certain you'd failed when I saw your party appear at the shrine. I didn't want to say anything..."

Devon grinned and pulled the *Starlight Rod* from her backpack. Gripping it, she focused on one of the demons out in the field. A shaft of light lanced from the sky and pierced the mob through the heart.

"Not bad, eh?"

Jarleck stared in amazement. "Can you... I mean, it might take a while, but I don't suppose you can do that to the rest of them?"

Devon sighed and shook her head. "The cooldown timer's too long. But listen... If we can't hold when the main force comes, our only hope lies in bringing Ishildar's power to bear. But to do that, I need to take the *Blackbone Effigy* into the city."

Jarleck winced, not the reaction she was hoping for.

"I'm guessing it won't be so easy to hold them back without the Effigy."

The man's jaw worked as he stared down at the field. "The truth is, I'm not sure. It will be difficult. But there's definitely no point in keeping the Effigy here, I suppose. If you don't finish the quest, we're lost anyway." He looked up at her and straightened his shoulders. "We'll do everything we can to hold on until you get back."

She'd known that would be his answer, but Devon felt better hearing him say it. Clapping the man on the shoulder, she nodded. "I'm leaving the rest of my party here to help you. I'll be back as soon as I can."

Something along the wall had already caught Jarleck's gaze, and he gestured toward one of the archers to snag her attention.

"I believe in you, Mayor," he said, eyes still on his soldier. "If anyone can save us here, it's you."

***

Back down at the shrine, Devon stared at the *Blackbone Effigy* for at least a minute. Even if this was the only solution, she could scarcely bring herself to make Stonehaven vulnerable. As she finally reached for the little statuette, Hailey stepped up beside her.

"I'm going with you," the woman said.

Devon paused, hand on the statuette. "Okay. But why?"

"Because someone has to watch your back, right?"

"Jarleck could really use your healing abilities at the gates."

"Really? Because what I see now is a standard siege. The demons haven't even made it over the curtain wall."

"They may soon," Devon said as she pulled the Effigy off the little shelf in the shrine.

"Maybe," Hailey said, her glance straying to the shrine as its aura dimmed. "And what happens if you run into trouble? I can help. Here, my puny heal over time isn't going to make much difference when the real army comes and spills over the walls. Stonehaven is like a rotten apple waiting to get hit by a sledgehammer."

When Devon grimaced at the image, Hailey shrugged in apology. "Okay, sorry, bad metaphor. What about a nice juicy strawberry?"

Devon blinked. "I think it was a simile, actually? I didn't pay that much attention in English. And *strawberry* is a little better. I guess."

"She's right, you know," Bob said after a moment. "You might be the so-called champion, but you're not invincible."

Devon met Hailey's eyes and held them. Both the woman and the wisp made good points. "Okay," she said at last. "You need to log first or anything?" Speaking of, Devon had been online for around sixteen real-world hours. She should at least pee and grab a small snack before the final push.

Hailey just shook her head. "I'll go see if there's anything I can help with the wall until you're ready," the woman said. "Just yell when you're set."

Devon nodded and dropped to a seat in the grass. "If you're not here when I return, I'll figure you decided on a bio break after all."

Hailey waved away the concern. "I snuck away last night. Don't tell Greel I abandoned his sorry NPC ass to whatever jungle dangers lurked."

Devon laughed as she logged out, even though something in the woman's tone seemed a little...off. And she was pretty sure Hailey had been sitting beside the campfire the whole night. Anyway, it wasn't her job to police her friend's biological needs.

Chapter Forty-Six

WHEN DEVON AND Hailey reappeared in front of the Mistwalker, the long-limbed creature gave an elegant bow. "Invite this one to her party, and this one should be able to journey with her safely."

The Esh's speech patterns were kind of confusing, but the meaning was clear enough. Devon fumbled through her interface until she found the option to add the Esh to the group, and moments later Aijal's health and mana bar appeared at the edge of her vision.

"Many of the details of the initiation of a new Keeper are lost to time," Aijal said, "but by this one's understanding, a representative of each of the vassal societies formed a procession with the newly selected leader through the streets to the Vault of the Magi. Along the way, the stone guardians formed an honor guard that lined the streets, assuring that none would try to harm the initiate. The histories suggest that the initiate halted upon passing each golem and used the command spell to form a bond."

"Yeah, so, I haven't had a whole lot of success with that so far," Devon said.

"She has tried already then. Between the curse and her possession of a limited number of relics, it's surprising she was brave enough—or even able—to attempt the spell."

"No one ever accused her of keeping a strong grip on reality," Bob muttered. "I notice you haven't yet thanked me for my part in keeping her alive thus far."

The Mistwalker simply stared at the wisp for a moment, her liquid eyes inscrutable. "This one is sure the wisp will receive whatever credit is due for its...service. Such a difficult trial it must have been to ride around on the champion's shoulder and make sarcastic comments."

Devon grinned. "That was kind of a burn, you know," she said to the wisp.

Bob huffed. "I don't remember asking your opinion."

"Anyway," Devon said, "I guess we'll hope that a procession with a descendant of one of the vassal societies, a semi-reluctant champion and her starborn friend, and a really annoying wisp will be good enough for the stone golems. Ready to lead us to the Vault?"

Aijal inclined her head gracefully. "Quite."

With that, she set off with long strides, her robe dragging the pavestones. Devon caught Hailey's eyes, shrugged, and hurried to catch up.

They made it three blocks before the first Stone Guardian woke and stepped to bar their path. Far from standing at attention like an honor guard, the giant glared down at the small group.

"Well, I guess I'll just pretend that it's waiting to bond with me. Fake it till you make it, right?" Closing her eyes, she wrapped her hand around the *Greenscale Pendant* and activated *Ishildar's Call.* Awareness of the golem sprang to life in her mind, and this time, her understanding of the creature was much deeper. She felt its bottomless loyalty to the city, its unending patience and unbreakable desire to defend Ishildar for as many centuries as it might take before a new master to come.

She also felt the creature's confusion as Devon stood before it. Here was someone with all the relics, but only one vassal representative stood beside her. She sensed that the Stone Guardian perceived her insecurity as well, something former Keepers had probably never felt. With a deep breath, Devon forced away her fear and straightened her shoulders. She lifted her gaze to the deep eye sockets of the Stone Guardian where tiny flecks of light shone.

"I mean to restore Ishildar to greatness," she said. "I mean to rule over and care for this ancient domain, and it is my deepest desire to return the city to what it once was."

Her words seemed to echo in the golem's mind, turning over and over and falling back on themselves as if spoken in a deep cavern.

Devon jerked in surprise when Hailey's cast bar lit up. Crap. Was the woman going on offense? But before Devon could protest, the buff landed. *Self-actualization.* Of course. The spell strengthened Devon's abilities—including *Ishildar's Call.*

"I'm the Keeper you have been waiting for," Devon said, forcing herself to speak the words with conviction, and in doing so, she even began to believe them. "After a thousand years, I am the first and only person to have gathered all five relics. I will be a just and wise master of the city, and I will bring Ishildar's light to all the territory it once commanded."

"And I and my kin will support her," Aijal said as she set a hand on Devon's shoulder. "Many of the vassal societies have disappeared, but the Esh stand with her, as do the Felsen from the Argenthal Vassaldom."

"Did you hear that?" Bob muttered. "She spoke normal English. I think the weird *this one* stuff is an act to make her seem more mysterious."

Devon didn't miss the glare that Aijal shot toward the wisp. Really? Did that mean Bob was right?

Either way, the Stone Guardian still stood before them, a low grumbling raising from somewhere within its chest.

Devon gripped the pendant harder, focusing every bit of awareness she possessed on that bond it created with the golem.

"Please," she said. "If ever there was a need for Ishildar's power, the world requires it now. Demons are on our shores. I must turn Ishildar's light against them."

As she spoke, she felt the golem's heart shift, first to anger at the mention of demons, and then to...acceptance? The silence held for another long moment until she felt the Stone Guardian decide to grant her allegiance.

Going down on one massive knee, the Stone Guardian bowed its boulder of a head. After taking a shaky breath, Devon stepped forward and laid her palm against the giant's forearm.

"The threat is real and present. Can you carry us to the Vault of the Magi so that I might take possession of the city?"

With a rumble, the Stone Guardian nodded assent, and within a few seconds, had scooped up the three women. The golem carried them cradled close to its stone chest, as high as most of the rooftops. Devon watched in amazement as, from this vantage, she witnessed stone giants raising their heads all around the city. One by one, the golems came to life and converged in a procession behind them. Around ten minutes later, the guardian deposited her in front of what looked like a vast cathedral. A high archway led into the main chamber, and in the back, lit by a shaft of light falling through the window, she spied another stone door. This interior portal, carved with intricate symbols, was set with a heavy iron panel. A dark keyhole was barely visible in its center.

"Devon," Aijal said. "Champion."

Devon turned.

"I'll speak plainly if only to quell the comments of your annoying companions. There is one more thing I wish to bestow upon you before you enter. The civilization of the Esh has fallen far from the lofty heights we once reached. We have little in the way of treasure, and our rift with the Rovan faction means that we're so busy with our own war that our aid in the coming battles may arrive too late. But I do have this, accessible now that your unlocking of the Vault will return lost power to us."

Aijal, Mistwalker Shadow Master, is offering you a quest: Specialization
For centuries, a select group of Esh have kept an ancient art alive. Gifted in both elemental magic and the powers of the shadow-touched illusionists, the Mistwalker shadowcasters have been honing their skills and meditating on the powers innate to their kind for centuries. They now feel that they have the power to teach this specialized discipline to others. But to transfer the powers, the Shadow Master needs a focus item that has long been lost to their kind.
Objective: Unlock the Vault of the Magi and bring the Vial of the Mists back to Aijal.
Reward: Shadowcaster Specialization
Accept? Y/N

"Holy...heck yes!" Devon said as she accepted the quest.

"What? What is it?"

Ah, crap. Poor Hailey. The woman was still stuck with just a base class. Devon shrugged as if to minimize the new reward. "Specialization quest."

Despite her weird moods of late, Hailey seemed genuinely happy as she grinned back at Devon. "Well, get to it then," the woman said, refreshing the *Self-actualization* buff.

Devon blinked in surprise. "Okay, then. Here goes I guess."

Her footsteps echoed as she tiptoed through the cathedral, trying now to notice the strange gargoyles staring down from the stone heights. When she reached the inner doorway, she glanced back over her shoulder. Hailey and the Mistwalker were shadows silhouetted against the bright light from outside. Swallowing, Devon pulled out the *Ironweight Key* and slipped it into the hole. The lock disengaged with a click, and dust puffed from the hole.

She tugged the door open and peered into the darkness.

Chapter Forty-Seven

THE DARKNESS IN the chamber seemed to swallow all sound. In the dim glow cast by Bob, Devon could see as far as her knees and outstretched fingers, but even her feet were lost in the shadows. She probed carefully with her toes before committing to each step, afraid she might otherwise fall into a hidden pit or something equally un-Keeper-like. After making a few steps into the vault, she stopped, swallowed, and began to cast a *Glowing Orb* to illuminate the way. But as soon as she began to draw from her mana pool, light flooded the chamber, the glow coming from everywhere and nowhere at once.

Devon squeaked, but to her credit, so did Bob.

The Vault of the Magi was rectangular and about thirty feet deep by fifteen wide. Entirely composed of stone, a light gray marble with the veins of black and white, built-in shelves on the walls held an assortment of oddities and tomes, vases and phials. Rising seamlessly from the floor were plinths of various heights, some topped with bowls of what looked like water, wine, and in one case, mercury.

The air seemed to hum, but at the same time, Devon knew the chamber was utterly silent.

She took another step forward. “Hello?”

All at once, the surroundings seemed to snap into focus as if completing the last step in some sort of reconstitution that Devon hadn't even realized was happening. She squeaked again when a genderless voice suddenly emanated from the walls.

"Welcome, initiate and would-be Keeper."

"Yes, hi—"

Devon's words were cut off the voice continued as if oblivious to her greeting. "Please place the relics upon their cradle."

Cradle? What cradle? As if in answer to her unspoken question, a long raised bench began to radiate a silvery glow. Upon it, there were just the faintest indentations in the approximate shape of the relics.

"If you're going to comment that a better word would be perhaps altar or stand, I find I must agree," Bob said. "Whatever magus devised this procedure had an active imagination to call that a cradle."

Devon didn't want to jinx her chances here by chitchatting with the wisp, so she ignored it as she stepped forward and pulled the *Starlight Rod*, *Ironweight Key*, and *Blackbone Effigy* from her backpack. The relics settled easily into the shallow niches. Next, she removed the *Azuresky Band* from her index finger and placed it in the appropriate indentation. Finally, she fiddled with the clasp on the chain holding the *Greenscale Pendant* and was surprised at the reluctance she felt as she removed the necklace. Not since the very beginning of her Relic Online adventures had she played without feeling the pendant's weight against her breastbone. As she laid it into its spot, a shimmery sound filled the chamber.

"The relics are authentic. A new Keeper has been selected. You may retrieve the relics at your leisure."

As the speaker finished, motes of light appeared in the air beyond the cradle, swirling together in a dense cloud that congealed into a robe-cloak-thing. The garment hung in the air for a second, then dropped to the floor of the chamber in a heap.

Devon stared at it for a moment, then tentatively stepped forward and picked the clothing from the floor. It was white with intricate embroidery in a multitude of colors dominated by gold threads. The fabric felt almost insubstantial under her fingers, but when she tugged on a section, she got the sense that it offered far more protection than it would seem. The cloak opened at the front, and complicated sashes and ties appeared to fasten it around the wearer's waist.

You have received: Raiment of the Keeper
Slot: Cloak
By donning these vestments, you take upon yourself the burdens and benefits granted to all Keepers of Ishildar. The city is yours, and all that depend on and pay fealty to it are your subjects. Rule wisely.
+25% Mana | 115 Armor | Indestructible
Wear: Bestows rulership of Ishildar and its vassal territories.

"Well?" Bob asked.

"Patience, dude."

Devon held the sleeved cloak for a moment. After coming so far, it was hard to believe that this part of her journey was nearly finished. But thoughts of Stonehaven and the demons quickly banished her hesitation, and she slipped her arms through the sleeves.

"Jerk!" Bob protested when she shrugged into the robe, the collar knocking the wisp off her shoulder. The glowing sphere sank slowly to the floor. Devon crouched and retrieved the wisp, replacing it on her shoulder before tackling the garment's closures. As she fastened the final clasp, the air filled with a ridiculous chorus of angel sound.

You have received a new title: Keeper of Ishildar
You receive 970,000 experience.
Congratulations! You have reached level 26!

Pretty good job, actually.

When the pop-up vanished, Devon's mini-map flashed. As she focused on the UI element, the map expanded across her view, showing the entire city in great detail. Important landmarks were noted: libraries, fountains, something called the nexus of light, the Veian Temple. Devon felt like she could examine it for days. She could only imagine what treasures some of these places held.

Quest Updated: Demon Invasion, part 2 (Restore the Veian Temple)
Bet you forgot about this one! But don't worry. A quest log has a memory like an elephant on mind-enhancers.
New Objective: Now that the Curse of Fecundity is at last banished, clear away the debris so that Veia's light may shine again.
Reward: In the Ishildar region, creatures of Veian origin will receive +30% Damage and +50% Accuracy vs Demons

Devon shook her head. Yeah, she'd blown off the quest awhile ago when she'd learned that the Curse of Fecundity would undo any amount of cleaning and restoration she managed. But she hadn't forgotten.

It would be nice to finally clear out the active quest entry. But more than that, the damage and accuracy boosts were huge. Enough to hold back the demon army, maybe.

So, yeah, time to get on with it.

Devon waved away the map and pop-up. "So this Vial of the Mists...? Any ideas?"

Bob snorted. "And now we're back to wondering how you made it this far. Look left."

When Devon spotted it, she had to admit that it was fairly obvious. The giant glass cylinder practically screamed out its name. Inside, light-blue fog was almost mesmerizing as it swirled. Devon hurried to the shelf, carefully pulled the vial down and examined it from all sides. The glass was chilly against her hands.

"Okay, anything else we need before—"

"Devon. You need to get out," Bob interrupted.

"What?"

"Please. It's Hailey."

Chapter Forty-Eight

HAILEY GASPED AS what felt like a shockwave traveled out from the cathedral and washed over the city. In its wake, Ishildar seemed to come alive. Buildings, though still streaked with dark stains from centuries of rainwater, seemed somehow cleaner and brighter. As she glanced up at the cathedral's facade, many of the vines started to droop, and one lost its grip on the stonework, peeling away and falling limply to the street. Though Hailey had no connection to the city, not like Devon, she knew immediately that her friend had succeeded. The millennium-long curse had finally been broken.

As she glanced toward Aijal to judge the Esh's reaction, a sudden red flash in the corner of her vision caused Hailey's breath to stutter.

Before enacting her plan to spend her last days of life plugged into Relic Online, she had installed an app to shunt her biometric data into her game interface. She didn't know what most of the numbers meant, and she didn't really want to know, there was no mistaking the irregularity in the little graph that monitored her heart rate. Nor could she ignore the warning icons that flashed.

Hailey closed her eyes and swallowed.

This was probably it.

Searching out a stone bench, she half-shuffled, half-stumbled to it and took a seat. As she swallowed, trying not to panic, the world around her seemed to waver, to fade and flicker in sync with the flashing of icons that marked her body's death. She clenched her fists and pressed them into her thighs for steadiness, and as Bob had taught her, she focused on her breath. She forced herself to keep her awareness pinned to her senses, the smell of jungle growth that was now overlaid with the scent of dying plants. The warmth of the sun on her brow and the hard press of the bench beneath her.

Running footsteps came from the cathedral, and moments later, Devon skidded to a halt in front of her.

"What is it, Hailey?"

Hailey couldn't speak. She wasn't sure what to say. She glanced up as Bob tried to roll down Devon's arm toward her but got stuck in a wrinkle of Devon's clothing.

"Little help?" the wisp said. "I need to talk to Hailey if that wasn't obvious."

"Okay..." Devon shrugged as she plucked the wisp from her sleeve and held it out.

Hailey swallowed. They'd talked about this. She raised her hands, palms cupped to receive the little ball of light. Bringing it close to her face, she stared into the glow.

"Okay, Hailey," Bob said. Hailey wasn't sure whether it spoke aloud or directly into her thoughts. "We have the pattern. The representation has been working flawlessly while you slept."

Hailey nodded. Every time she'd logged out to rest in the past few days, upon reconnection, her character had been somewhere else.

"I'm still not sure how to... What do I do?"

Devon took a seat beside her. Distantly, Hailey noticed that her friend was wearing some kind of fancy robe. She focused on the added warmth where Devon's body heat reached her arm and the chill where the woman's shadow fell across her thigh. This was real. Hailey just had to accept and believe it.

And as that thought occurred, she sensed it—the doubling.

All at once she could perceive both copies of her mind, one digital and vibrant, one fading as her struggling heart pumped less and less oxygen to the wet mesh of neurons inside her dying body's skull.

"Yes," Bob said. "You feel it. Now grasp it."

Hailey hesitated. She'd thought long and hard about this moment. Growing up Catholic, she'd internalized a whole lot of lessons about the immortal soul. If she followed Bob's instructions and this worked, would she be giving up the journey to Heaven? Maybe her soul would split in two, one half remaining, one ascending. Or maybe this would just be a stopover on the journey. The servers wouldn't run forever, and maybe her real death would come when they shut down.

Regardless, no one would be able to answer the question for her, since nothing like this had ever been done—except in science fiction, of course. The capability was brand new, concocted by Bob and its arcane friends.

The scene wavered again, darkness encroaching as her body failed. Time to throw herself into the new future or fade away forever.

Hailey focused everything she had on the game. On the avatar she'd embodied for so many months. And all at once, her awareness exploded into the foundation that had been laid across the substrate of neural network and quantum core. She leapt, committing to the new representation.

Some would call it uploading, but that wasn't how she felt. In that last moment, as the line of her heartbeat flattened and the flashing of the warning icon became a steady glow, Hailey simply stepped sideways into the representation of her mind that the denizens of the arcane realm had painstakingly constructed over the course of months. She chose to go on to a new life, leaving her limitations behind.

And as she took a deep breath and looked around with new eyes, Bob's glow began to brighten.

"Yessss!" the wisp said as it rose from Hailey's hands. Executing a loop the loop in the air in front of the women, Bob proceeded to boop each of them on the nose before spiraling up into the sky.

"Back later," it called. "Got a Scrabble game to finish."

Hailey glanced at Devon, who was staring at her in utter confusion.

"So what exactly just happened?" Devon asked.

Hailey smirked. "You know, it's a pretty long story, and I think we might need some dwarven ale to get into it. For now, what do you say we go save your city?"

She stood and stretched, reveling in the painless sensation of movement. When Bob had proposed the scheme, claiming that accomplishing it would finally get the wisp back in the good graces of the arcane due to the realm's obsession with organizing information, Hailey had thought the wisp was insane.

It turned out, she was wrong, and now she had eternity to find out what other mistakes she could make.

Chapter Forty-Nine

"OKAY, ONCE MORE," Emerson said, still reeling from the last punch to the gut.

Torald grimaced as he cocked his mail-armored fist. "This is really not fun, man."

Emerson looked away. It was easier if he didn't see the blows coming. "I know. It's not exactly awesome for me either. Just try to think of it as doing Veia's work."

He heard the whistle of moving air with just enough warning to tighten his abs before the blow connected. Clenching his jaw to avoid whimpering and making this harder on the paladin, he glanced at his health bar. "Okay, we're there. Fourteen percent. Is the thing cocked? I don't want to heal back over the threshold."

Torald sighed as he checked the arming mechanism on the large trebuchet. "Ready."

"Okay, shield," Emerson said as he climbed into the weapon's launch bucket.

Muttering an entreaty to Veia, the paladin touched Emerson's shoulder, and the *Creator's Shield* buff appeared in his interface.

Emerson looked down at the field below, the area a black sea of demon flesh. Even on the tenth repeat of this tactic, the heights made his head spin. Before he could lose his nerve, he nodded. "Launch."

With a loud thunk and a twang, the trebuchet launched him high over the wall. Emerson's stomach plummeted, and he felt the skin tighten across his face as the wind and g-forces pushed it back. Gritting his teeth, he pulled up his ability UI and activated *Berserk* followed by *Dying Frenzy*, the ability that, when he was below 15% health, unleashed a major can of whoop-ass on multiple enemies at once.

Berserk took hold just he reached the apex of his glorious flight. Teeth bared, eyes wide, he felt power rush through his body. For just a moment, he seemed to hang in the air, and then gravity took hold. On the way down, Emerson started swinging his sword like a madman. The trebuchet's aim was true, and he plummeted straight for a cluster of fiends. Lips drawn back from yellow fangs, they stared up in confusion as he dropped like a freaking steel-edged meteor, slashing through their group. A few quick-witted demons recovered in time to strike, peeling away Torald's shield. But Emerson still scored multiple hits before the falling damage finished him off.

For just a moment, he had time to look back at the failing walls of Stonehaven. Since his last bombing run, a fresh hole had been battered through the curtain wall. Siege ladders were rising against the main palisade. For now, the defenders had knocked down all but a few before the demons reached the ramparts, and those that did surmount the wall had been executed and thrown back out of the city.

But the settlement wouldn't hold much longer.

You have been slain by the ground.

Respawning...

Back at the Shrine to Veia, Emerson shook off the pain of broken bones, the memory of his organs sluicing down into the bottom of his abdominal cavity on impact. With a roar, he tugged his leather jerkin straight and raced to the wall.

As long as Stonehaven stood, he would keep trying to save her.

Chapter Fifty

"THANK YOU," AIJAL said as she stared into the swirling fog in the Vial of the Mists. The Esh woman blinked back what looked like tears and turned her gaze on Devon.

> **Accept the unique class specialization:** *Shadowcaster* Y/N?

Devon stood a little taller as she clicked yes. Dark magic sprang to life around her, scraps of shadow darting around. At the Mistwalker's nod, the darkness abruptly sank into Devon's body.

> **Congratulations! You have gained a new specialization:** Shadowcaster.
> *An art unique to the Esh society, shadowcasters combine the elemental magic of sorcery with the illusionist expertise commanded by the great Mistwalker shadowbenders.*
>
> **You have gained a new combat form:** Shadow Shifter
> *Allows the shadowcaster to passively avoid melee strikes by instantly turning the targeted area of the body to shadowy mist (30% chance at Tier 1). The most basic of the shadowcaster*

combat forms, Shadow Shifter has nonetheless been cited by many as also the most versatile.
Cost: -25% mana regeneration, effect lessened with a higher *Focus* score and at higher tiers of the form.

You have learned a new ability: Night Shackles
Unbreakable darkness binds your target's wrists, interrupting spell casts and preventing further casts for the duration of the shackles.
Cost: 90 mana
Duration: 45 seconds

"I have much more to teach you," Aijal said, still speaking with normal pronouns. "And as for what appears to be lagging development in your abilities as a sorceress, I believe some of my kin will be able to offer further instruction once we deal with the Rovan."

"Nice," Hailey said, still without the envious tone that Devon would expect given the woman's demeanor lately and her pigeonholing as a vanilla Seeker class while all her friends had unique powers.

Thinking of that, Devon cocked an eyebrow at Aijal. "You guys don't have anyone that can help Hailey out, do you?"

The Esh turned a kind smile on Devon's friend. "The mysteries of the arcane are not something we often plumb. But perhaps once the demon threat is vanquished, you will find interesting resources within Ishildar's libraries. Our histories speak of many truth seekers who were self-taught in this fashion."

Hailey gave an uncharacteristic carefree shrug. "I'm sure my path for advancement will become clear soon enough. I don't feel any particular rush."

Devon couldn't help but cast her friend a sidelong glance. Had whatever passed between Hailey and the wisp caused this change? Devon held in a smirk. If only she could derive the same happiness from interacting with the annoying arcane ball.

She glanced over Aijal's head and shoulders to take in the changes to the city. Everywhere, vines were withering and leaves were falling from jungle trees that, judging by the height of the buttress roots that erupted from the pavement, had stood for more than a century. Unlike the slow change to a savanna biome that had crept over Stonehaven following Devon's recovery of the *Greenscale Pendant*, with the Curse of Fecundity finally broken, it seemed that Ishildar's jungle would likely be gone within a couple of days.

Thinking of the pendant, she headed for the entrance to the cathedral. "I'll just fetch the relics, and what say we go blast out some foliage from the Veian Temple on the way to rescue Stonehaven?"

***

Hailey and Devon stood together at the front of the grand, open-air temple, Aijal having left the pair to return to her Drivan kin and organize a final assault on the Rovan. As Devon's *Downdraft* spell scattered the last pockets of leaves that dirtied the corners of the temple, the quest completion popup appeared and confirmed that the temple had been restored. Finally, after all these months, Ishildar could stand strong again in the face of the demons. The area didn't *feel* all that different, but Devon was willing to take the game's word for it.

Hailey whistled. "Not bad for a little sweeping."

"Huh?"

"You don't see it?"

"See what?"

"The buff, dude," the woman said.

Devon smirked and sighed. Sometimes she *did* miss the obvious. In the corner of her vision, the buff icon was actually larger than the usual icon size by about 50%.

"Duh," she said, examining the text for *Ishildar's Blessing*. As promised, it listed the benefits to Accuracy and Damage versus demons.

Devon swallowed. Okay then. Mission accomplished. She hoped it would be enough.

Nodding at the nearby Stone Guardians, she sent a mental command, and the nearest golem crouched down to pick up her and Hailey. Despite having traveled this way twice already, she couldn't help flinching as the massive stone fist lightly encircled her body, nubbins and crystals of stone gouging uncomfortably despite the giant's efforts to be gentle. As the golem opened its palm and allowed Devon to step off onto its shoulder, she breathed a sigh of relief.

It might have been nice to make her triumphant return to Stonehaven marching at the head of a full cohort of stone giants, but after cycling across the city, clambering through the Stone Forest, fleeing the Stone Forest at triple that pace, then traveling back through the city once again to become its Keeper, Devon was tired.

Also, she could walk at about one-tenth the speed of a Stone Guardian's long strides.

So standing on the shoulder of one of her massive, twice-her-level minions and holding on to its ear nub, she watched the city pass by, the remnants of jungle toppling as the giant smashed through them. Beyond the walls, she stared down as the waving savanna grasses swept by beneath her. As the Stone Guardians advanced, shaking the earth with their heavy footfalls, flocks of birds erupted from the grasslands, squawking as they flew away. In the distance, a pride of lions—no, wait...maybe they were manticores? It was hard to tell from so far away. Either way, the beasts jumped up onto a pile of boulders and stared at the imposing parade, tails twitching.

For a while, Devon fell into a sort of trance, just enjoying the scenery and feeling the sunshine on her face.

Until, as they drew nearer to Stonehaven, Devon heard the first shrieks and saw the rising smoke. All at once, her breath came in quick gasps, and her heart slammed against her ribs.

"Go," she whispered through the connection with her golems. "Quickly."

As the giants sped to a run, the very bones of the earth shook.

Chapter Fifty-One

THE TRAVELER ARRIVED as the new leader of Ishildar brought her giants into the battle. He'd known this was likely. He'd seen it in the pattern, and the possibility had been one of the strongest. He nodded, satisfied by the sight.

Standing unnoticed atop the cliff face that sheltered the hamlet of Stonehaven, the traveler looked down upon the town, its defenses buckling, the life lights of its citizens rushed and frantic as they attempted to save their home. Their panic reminded him of ants responding to an attack on their hill, and he recalled that first insect he'd rescued from suffering, the creature that had helped him wake to the power of *Illumin.*

As he inspected individuals, he saw their possible futures in the layers that made up creation. There was potential for evil in many of the hearts, something that dismayed him whenever he looked upon a human. When he glimpsed that, he struggled not to eradicate the possibility.

But the true evil lay beyond the walls. What wickedness *might be* paled in importance behind that which already *was.*

The scourge must drown in the light. Stepping to the far rim of the cliff, the traveler got down on his hands and feet and slipped a leg over the edge. Cautiously, aware of his human frailties, he searched the ledges and irregularities of the cliff face for adequate purchase for his callused feet, then slowly edged his weight over the brink. Once established on the vertical face, he began climbing down to where the cliff intersected Stonehaven's wall-walk. Touching down on the platform, he straightened his simple garb and walked toward the main gates where he had the best vantage on the demon attackers.

The traveler raised his arms and called down a pillar of light against the evil.

Chapter Fifty-Two

"OW!" DEVON WINCED against the sudden glare as an insanely bright pillar of heavenly light burned a hole in the demons' forces.

"What the hell?" Hailey yelled from the golem's opposite shoulder. "If that came from your paladin friend, the dude's been holding out on us."

"I don't think so," Devon called back. Torald might be one of Veia's personal crusaders, but that attack had appeared way too overpowered for a level twenty-something character.

Regardless of the source of the purple afterglow that now stained her vision, Devon couldn't argue with the results. It was like a giant hole-punch had come down from the heavens, carving out a perfect circle from the demon forces. More surprisingly, where the light had touched and the corpses now lay smoldering, the demons seemed unwilling or incapable of filling the gap.

Whatever the weapon, it couldn't have come soon enough. Devon's heart fell when the purple shadow cleared, and she saw the damage to her settlement. The curtain wall was half gone, and improvised bridges had been laid across the moat in half a dozen places. In two locations below the main palisade, demons worked with battering rams, bashing them again and again against the main wall. Others tore at the gates with wicked claws, and for every beast the archers and casters struck down, another rushed forward.

Looking south, she spotted a steady stream of fiends marching to the fight.

If the help of the Stone Guardians and *Ishildar's Blessing* weren't enough to turn the tide, Stonehaven was lost.

Devon let out a shout that was about the closest she'd ever come to a battle cry and urged the stone giants into the fray. With a swing of its massive leg, the guardian carrying her kicked aside a column of demons, sending them flying. A swipe of the giant's massive arm brought down a small armada of imps, the little demons hitting the ground with a crunch.

Stomping another handful of the beasts flat, the Stone Guardian reached the edge of the settlement, kicked away a pair of bridges spanning the moat, and then deposited Hailey and Devon atop the wall before dropping into a fighting stance before the town. A low rumble rose from its throat as it waited for a challenger.

With the platform of the wall-walk under her feet, Devon felt each blow from the battering rams. The top of the wall was chaos, archers running back and forth to resupply, melee fighters stepping into gaps to knock down siege ladders as they touched the rim. Blinking, Devon took a moment to get her bearings before searching out Jarleck.

The fortifications master was standing beside a stranger clothed in a ratty robe much like an old-time friar. The man's head was hidden in his cowl, and he nodded as Jarleck spoke.

Devon hurried over and caught Jarleck's eye.

He nodded at her. "Thank you, Mayor. If not for *Ishildar's Blessing*, we wouldn't have lasted," he said. "They were almost over the walls."

She glanced toward the battle where the giants were rampaging through the demon horde, smashing imps and thralls and hellhounds while seeming impervious to the damage of the fiends' attacks. But due to her connection with the golems, she knew that wasn't quite true. Their injuries were small still, mere scratches and chips missing from their ancient stone flesh. But they wouldn't last indefinitely. Given the size of the approaching army, the best her guardians could manage would be to grant Stonehaven and Ishildar a few more hours.

"What was that column of light?" she asked. "And have we had any contact from the awakened races?" The last was a faint hope given the profound disorientation and confusion that any awakened creatures must be feeling. How could they even know where to come? But given the situation, even a faint hope gave her something to cling to.

When she'd asked about the light, Jarleck's eyes had turned to the cowled stranger. The fortifications master nodded and gestured to indicate that the newcomer should speak. Pulling back his hood, the man turned gray eyes on her, eyes that seemed at once haunted and infinitely wise. This man was a keeper of secrets and a refugee besieged by his own awareness.

She swallowed, blinked, clenched and unclenched her fists. "Owen?"

Chapter Fifty-Three

"I FEEL...OUTSIDE myself much—most—of the time," Owen admitted as he ran his eyes over the group. Though reluctant to leave the wall, Devon had gathered the members of her former guild together in the upper chambers of the inner keep to hear Owen's story and devise a plan. "When I'm inside the game, it's like I *know* things. I feel almost like an NPC, like half my actions aren't even my choice. I'm part of the pattern."

Devon chewed her lip, concerned. He'd mentioned this pattern a few times now, and Devon had no clue what it meant. But the mention of being out of control of his actions sounded...not good. It reminded her too much of the weeks Owen had spent under Zaa's control, his mind harnessed by the AI to create the demon lord, Raazel.

Yet at the same time, Devon knew without a doubt that the vulnerability in the implants had been patched. The AIs could no longer commandeer a player's brain and use it for their own devices. So what was going on here?

She caught Chen's eyes and saw her concern reflected there.

"Do you think that the game has control of you again?" the teenager asked, apparently having decided to be blunt about it.

Owen shook his head vehemently. "I'm certain that's not the case. It's easier to think about my situation when I'm offline, and I do have a theory. My best guess is that the time I spent connected with Zaa shaped my mind, adapting it to the AIs' structure. I think I've gained a sort of intuitive understanding of the way their processing works. In this case, it's like I can sometimes read Veia's intent, and sometimes I'm able to influence it." The man grimaced as if in pain. "But it's so hard—even if I understand that *rationally*, that's not how I perceive things while experiencing them. My mind converts the information into something that feels much more real. And sometimes when I see things—I think this is some kind of instinctual reaction after my experience with Zaa—sometimes when I see things, I act too quickly. I can't control the impulses to bring *Illumin* forth."

Pattern... *Illumin...* Owen was speaking of weird things that Devon struggled to understand, but she got the sense that he didn't quite understand them either.

And regardless, through the open window of the keep's chambers, she could still hear the shrieks of demons and the shouts of the archers. They could talk more about Owen's experiences later. But now there were more pressing matters.

"You caused that column of light that obliterated some of Zaa's forces, right?"

Owen nodded. "I conjured *Illumin* and stamped out their evil."

"Ooh...kayy..." Jeremy muttered under his breath.

Devon shot him a glare. "The demons still aren't entering the area you burned," she said. "Any ideas why?"

Owen shrugged. "*Illumin* has many mysterious qualities."

"Okay, but what I'm wondering is... Can you do that again?"

"As long as the pattern permits it."

Fortunately, Jeremy was standing behind Owen, so the man wasn't subjected to the troubadour's eye roll.

"Do you think you can form this *Illumin* into other shapes?" Devon asked. "Because I have an idea."

***

Devon watched from the roof of the keep as one of her Stone Guardians carried Owen through the southern edge of the battle, the golem kicking aside any demons that had the misfortune of being in their path. Balanced on the giant's stone palm, Owen held the end of the Guardian's thumb and, eyes closed, pulled a narrow beam of light from the heavens. Channeling this so-called Illumin into a tight line on the ground, he burned a stripe through the savanna, about a foot wide.

It wasn't exactly what Devon had hoped for—her initial idea had involved in constructing some massive wall of light and pushing the whole freaking demon army back to the ocean. Unfortunately, that was beyond Owen's capability. But whatever repelling quality had kept the demons out of the circle also seemed to prevent them from crossing the barrier. By searing a boundary across the landscape south of Stonehaven, Owen's strange magic was buying the settlement time.

Time to mop up the attacking force, but more importantly, time to connect with the awakened races, with any fighting force the Felsen could field, and with the Drivan faction of the Esh once they finished with the Rovan. Already, Blackbeard—who could now speak properly following the end of the curse—was on the wing carrying her command across the vast territory that paid fealty to Ishildar. The city's liege lady needed her subjects' swords.

Or claws.

Or whatever help they could bring.

Regardless, with the respite that Owen was gaining for Stonehaven, Devon was now free to gather a real army and, possibly, to call forth additional power from Ishildar. Soon, she would bring the battle to Zaa's forces rather than cowering behind the walls of Stonehaven.

For now, though, she focused on guiding her guardians through the battlefield and breaking the demon siege. Without reinforcements from the south, the defenders on Stonehaven's walls were slowly but surely wiping out the threat. Even the noobs were helpful, particularly Valious, who now had a new, and even more insane tactic than his mad rushes at the Wyvern Keeper. Again and again, he used the largest of the trebuchets to literally launch himself into the battle, activating some crazy AoE attack in the split second before he hit the ground and died. And the crazy thing was, it was working. He'd made some serious dents in the demon forces.

It appeared they would win the first battle, and Devon was determined that would win the war. As she guided her stone defenders through a pincer maneuver, three of the golems trapping a large squad of the demon thralls and massacring them, Devon glanced at her messenger icon. The most recent note from Emerson still sat unanswered, so she pulled it up.

> *Hey. I'm so sorry. I owed you a response days ago. At first I made the excuse to myself that you're probably too busy with Stonehaven, but that's not the real reason. Among other stuff,*

I'm afraid I let you down on the Zaa thing. I know you weren't expecting me to be able to change Bradley's mind, but I still hoped I could.

So, my news is that I did get a chance to log in finally. Played a little bit. I know you said you're super busy with Stonehaven and the demon stuff right now, and I've still got a lot of things to learn. Once Stonehaven's secure, I'm really looking forward to playing together for fun. So stay in touch.

Oh, yeah.

P.S. Nothing from Owen, I'm afraid. Cynthia would tell us if something was wrong, though, so I imagine he's just taking his time.

Eyes on the battle, Devon subvocalized a response. "Well, despite Bradley's efforts to ruin everything by leaving Zaa active, I think Stonehaven is actually safe for now. I've got some crazy times ahead, building an army and stuff, and I could really use the excuse to chill out. Maybe track down a few of those tree snakes? Think you can convince the GMs to teleport you to Stonehaven?"

Before she could second-guess herself, she hit send and went back to watching the battle.

***

After a long couple of days and nights spent fighting off the siege, calm finally reigned in Stonehaven on the third morning. Levitating atop the keep, Devon could still spot the bulk of the demon army encamped south of the quarry, the dark mass spreading beyond the horizon. But the barrier seemed to be holding. At night, a wall shimmered faintly above the burned stripe and offered reassurance that the boundary still held. Owen felt it would stand for quite a few days, so it seemed they would have the time to make their preparations.

In the early morning hours, a flock of crows had arrived, their eyes shining with keen intelligence. One had pecked Greel's head, then worried at the lawyer's pocket until, exasperated, he had opened it to expose his quill and a small pot of ink. The quill in its beak, the bird had proceeded to pen a note declaring that the society of awakened corvids wished to be first to swear loyalty to Ishildar's new Keeper.

And so the first of her new subjects had arrived.

The birds had also brought word of the demons' movements. Due to Owen's efforts, his calling of the Illumin taking him to the brink of exhaustion, the barrier now ran from sheer cliffs at the foot of the Argenthal Mountains, encircled Stonehaven in a wide arc, and connected to the mud pots on the west side of Ishildar. With Stonehaven huddled securely behind the defenses, Zaa's forces were sending scouts in search of gaps in the wall. Nearer the shore, larger forces had split off and were now traveling the coast in search of easier conquests.

In defending Stonehaven and Ishildar, Devon had endangered other areas. Even if she were tempted to hide behind Owen's barrier, her conscience wouldn't allow it. The demon plague must be wiped from their shores. And someday, she would take the battle across the

Noble Sea to the continent the demons had already claimed. Someday, Zaa must be defeated once and for all.

But in the meantime, the citizens of Stonehaven were due a celebration. Stepping off the edge of the keep's roof, she descended on her *Levitation* cushion and landed lightly on the grass.

"Nice trick," Tamara said. The woman was working over her bike with what looked like a homemade toothbrush, scrubbing grit from its moving parts.

"I'd say your tricks are more impressive on that thing"—Devon nodded at the bike—"seeing as you don't even need magic."

Tamara smiled, unable to hide her pleasure at the compliment. "So, your town is safe for a little while, yeah?"

"Seems so. Want to come with me to talk to the dwarves?" Devon asked. "We have some tired fighters who need some good strong ale, I think. Might as well make the plans for the celebration official."

"Torald has told me stories about the dwarves' grog," Tamara said. "It should be an interesting spectacle, especially since I don't drink."

Devon laughed and wondered for a moment how much those two had been hanging out since the return from the Stone Forest. They seemed to suit one another. "Yeah, definitely a spectacle. Free entertainment, watching other people act like complete fools."

Chapter Fifty-Four

THE BONFIRE CRACKLED as dwarves bumped chests and roped unsuspecting newbies into contests of idiocy. Standing at the edge of the gathering, Devon looked on contentedly. She sighed and was about to go find Tamara when she spotted Hezbek approaching from the general area of her cabin. Surprised to see the woman up so late, she quickly dragged a stump onto flat ground to provide a seat.

"Thank you kindly," Hezbek said as she planted her walking stick and used it to help ease her weight down to the stump. Once seated, she gave a relieved sigh. "Lately it feels like the abuse I put my body through as a young sorceress is catching up with me."

"Maybe you should repurpose some of the time you spend making potions for the village for working on a tonic to cure arthritis."

Hezbek snorted. "And lose the chance to have you all treat me as a wise old elder? You should see the treats Tom sends over from the kitchen."

Sighing, Devon sank to a crouch beside the woman. "Speaking of wisdom, do you know anything about this Illumin Owen conjures? According to him, he doesn't even have a combat class or formal abilities. It's all pulled from Veia's pattern or something. I hope we aren't putting too much faith in its ability to hold the horde back."

Hezbek shrugged and shook her head. "Veia is mysterious, even to me. But I will say that I don't think you should worry too much. I can't shake the feeling that this was meant to be. This war has been a long time in the making, and my gut tells me that you were meant to guide Veia's forces in the final battles. Your destiny is grander than just sparing our beloved hamlet from destruction. Perhaps Owen's gift of Illumin is Veia's way of buying you time to fulfill your fate."

Devon snorted. "And here I thought I'd finished with the whole destiny thing by retrieving the relics. I was looking forward to some straight-up dungeon crawls."

Hezbek smiled at her fondly. "Well, we can hope that this fate of yours includes that too. Our histories are full of generals who couldn't lead their armies to victory until they defeated such-and-such dragon or discovered a mysterious source of power in the depths of some ancient catacombs. And anyway, I think you knew you wouldn't take possession of Ishildar and then suddenly become unimportant to the greater plan. I hear that Torald has been organizing an oath-giving ceremony so that all those players can swear fealty to you and finish their quest line."

Devon groaned. "Don't remind me. I might end up drinking a flagon of ale after all."

Hezbek laughed. After a few seconds spent staring at the fire, she looked up over Devon's shoulder. The old woman nodded a greeting as Owen stepped up to join them.

"Greetings, wise one," he said, dropping to a knee in front of her. "I've seen you often in the pattern."

Devon looked away and scratched the back of her head to keep from commenting, Jeremy-style, about this whole pattern thing. It was kind of cheesy, really. But Owen had been through a lot lately. No need for her to be a jerk by offering her opinion.

Hezbek chuckled. "If you say so, lad. These days I mostly potter with my potions."

"Yet you played a large role in the history of parts of this world," Owen said. "Your actions shaped what Rimeshore has become."

At this, Devon stilled, and Hezbek's smile vanished. Devon knew quite well the guilt the woman carried over her youthful decisions, especially those which led to her beloved Eldon vanishing.

"So I did," the medicine woman said after a moment. "And I've had many long years to think about that."

"What you may not know," Owen said, "that in the other possibilities where you didn't lead the rebels, the future in the Shorelands was much worse than what has come to pass."

Devon watched Hezbek intently as a torrent of emotions flashed across the woman's face. Hezbek wanted to believe that, even after so many years of atoning. But she doubted the man's words.

"And though you may feel weary, ready for some well-earned rest and retirement," Owen said. "I feel you should know that your story is far from over. Rimeshore is part of your future, too."

"Wait, what?" Devon said.

Owen shrugged as he stood and turned to Devon. "This conflict with Zaa is but a small part of what will be. The Ishildar region is but a tiny part of the world. All across Aventalia, the wheels of fate turn. Beacons need lighting, Devon, much as you've done with Ishildar. Threats loom, and I see many adventures and battles for all of us in the years ahead."

Hezbek was still staring at Owen with her mouth somewhat agape. After a moment, she shook her head then held out a hand to

Devon. “Mind helping me up, child? I believe I’m a little too weary for this sort of party and discussion after all.”

Devon gently grasped the woman’s wrist and supported her elbow as Hezbek pressed shakily to her feet.

“Me, back to Rimeshore,” she muttered with a chuckle. “I’m beginning to think that whatever this Illumin is, it comes with a sense of humor.” Patting Devon’s hand, she shuffled off.

Devon watched the woman go, then turned to Owen. “You really see all this stuff? To be honest, it’s kind of weird. No offense.”

Her guildmate shrugged. “I don’t know, Devon. Yes, I think so, but sometimes I wonder... I dream about the game. Maybe some of those dreams affect my experience.” He sighed and shook his head. “Honestly, most days I would love to just forget Relic Online and walk away. But it’s so hard with all I know. I feel like it’s my duty to fight Zaa and prevent evil, especially after I...well, you know. I helped build that army.” He gestured toward the south.

She chewed the corner of her lip. “So how are you doing out of game? You and Cynthia, is everything okay?”

He nodded. “We’re doing as well as can be expected. I know I’ve been quiet lately, but she seems to understand.” A faint smile spread across his face. “We’re getting married.”

“No way!” Devon said, wrapping him in a quick hug. “Congratulations.”

“I’m a lucky man,” he said, still smiling. For once, the expression on his face looked familiar, his features casting a shadow of the man she’d grouped with so many times over the years. Even though their avatars were different, her friends’ mannerisms survived the transitions between games.

"Indeed you are," she said. As they turned to watch the fire, Devon laughed when she saw Dorden trying to teach a new player how to do a cartwheel. The dwarf, of course, appeared to have no idea how the move was supposed to work, and on top of that, he kept accidentally planting his hands on his beard.

"Hey, Devon?" The voice came from behind as someone tapped her on the shoulder. She turned to see Valious standing shyly behind her.

She grinned. "Hey! How's Stonehaven's most expendable fighter?" she asked with a laugh.

He shrugged, still looking somewhat abashed. Was he embarrassed over his unconventional tactics? He shouldn't be; he'd certainly done a lot to save both the adventuring party and the settlement.

"I was hoping... I was hoping we could have that talk now."

Devon glanced toward the fire, then back at the man. Persistent, wasn't he. And it seemed she'd finally run out of excuses. Keeping the friendly smile on her face, she nodded. "You mind if I step away for a bit, Owen?"

The man shook his head. "Not at all. But, quick question... are they always like this?" He gestured at the dwarves.

She snorted. "Yep. Classic Stoneshoulder clan."

Owen actually laughed, which was a good sign. Glad to see it, she turned and followed Valious from the fire. Once away from the noise and the light, the man stopped in his tracks. "Listen. I'm sorry about all this. I should have been honest in the beginning."

She shook her head, confused. "Honest about what?"

Valious shook his head and looked to the side, clearly fighting some sort of internal battle. After a moment, he firmed up his jaw.

"Okay, sorry about this. I don't think this is quite the right order for this sort of thing but..."

Devon squeaked in shock as he grabbed her hand and kissed the back of it, then stepped in and, seeming to wise up at the last minute about kissing her lips without invitation, pulled her into an awkward hug.

As she stood stiffly for the circle of his arms, her messenger icon flashed.

> *What do you say we skip the tree snakes and go enjoy the party? Only this time, no obstacle courses allowed.*

She stepped back, eyes wide. "Emerson?"

His face turned as bright red as it had when he'd activated his *Berserk* ability. "So... surprise?" he said with a shrug.

Devon laughed. "Yeah, I think we can skip the tree snakes."

Chapter Fifty-Five

THERE, AROUND A hundred paces ahead, the subterranean corridor ended, and a crack in the earth allowed natural light and the fresh air of morning to enter the cavern system. Walking barefoot with faces toward the opening, the remnants of the Rovan fighting force perceived the sunlight as a vibration in the air that pressed against the thin membranes that had grown, over long centuries underground, to cover the spots where their kind had once had eyes.

Near the opening, the group paused to listen, assuring themselves once more that they'd eluded any pursuit. It was a last-ditch plan, conceived in a pre-battle war council. If it appeared that the Drivan would be victorious, a small, elite force of Rovan would detach from the battle and slip—with good fortune, unnoticed—back underground.

Throughout the flight from the Stone Forest region, the Rovan squad had kept their corporeal forms. Shifting to mist would have alerted their Drivan kin through the extra-sensory awareness the Esh had for one another's use of their innate racial magic.

It had been a long walk, always south, always staying beneath the surface in tunnels and passages they'd come to know so well. They'd felt Ishildar passing overhead, the new power that had awakened, and as a group, they'd grieved the loss of a centuries-long hope. The appointment of a Keeper meant that the Rovan would not be taking the city's power for themselves.

All they could do now was exact revenge.

After a moment of solemn silence, the new leader of the remaining Rovan nodded and assumed his mist form. If the Drivan were to sense the magic now, it wouldn't matter.

Drifting up through the crack in the earth, the Rovan leader swirled over the landscape, marveling at the size of the demon army that had encamped. Here were allies who would be unstoppable once the Rovan helped them pass the feeble defenses now surrounding Ishildar, none of which extended beneath the surface of the earth.

After searching for some time, the Rovan leader spied a banner that appeared to be that of a general. Swirling down, the Mistwalker took corporeal form before the demon lord.

"I propose to strike a bargain," he said.

Dear Reader,

Thank you so much for reading *Vault of the Magi!* I really hope you enjoyed it! As a working writer, I utterly depend on readers to spread the word on my books.

Please consider leaving a review on Amazon for this book and for other authors you enjoy. I promise that I read every review (yes, even the critical ones). Sometimes, they help me shape the story to come, and often, they are the reason I get out of bed and in front of my computer long before the sun rises. Thank you!!

If you would like to grab free books and participate in my reader community, head over to www.CarrieSummers.com and join my reader group. We have a lot of fun writing collaborative stories over email, talking about books, and other great stuff. Plus, the group is how I let readers know when new books are out.

So, what's coming? The next book in the Stonehaven League series will be out Summer 2019, so keep an eye out. In the meantime, you can check out my other fantasy series, *Chronicles of a Cutpurse, The Shattering of the Nocturnai* and *The Broken Lands.*

Once again, thank you for reading!

All best,
—Carrie
carrie@carriesummers.com

Books by Carrie Summers

Shattering of the Nocturnai

Nightforged

Shadowbound

Duskwoven

Darkborn

The Broken Lands

Heart of the Empire

Rise of the Storm

Fate of the Drowned

Chronicles of a Cutpurse

Mistress of Thieves

Rulers of Scoundrels

Queen of Tricksters

Empress of Rogues

Stonehaven League

Temple of Sorrow

Fortress of Shadows

Cavern of Spirits

Citadel of Smoke

Vault of the Magi